SIMPSONS COMICS
SHOW STOPPER

MATT GROENING

HARPER DESIGN
An Imprint of HarperCollinsPublishers

SIMPSONS COMICS SHOWSTOPPER

Simpsons Comics #127, #128, #129, #132, #133
Copyright © 2019 by
Bongo Entertainment, Inc. All rights reserved.
No part of this book may be used or reproduced in any manner whatsoever
without written permission except in the case of brief quotations
embodied in critical articles and reviews. For information address
HarperCollins Publishers,
195 Broadway, New York, New York 10007.
FIRST EDITION
ISBN 978-0-06-287877-9
Library of Congress Cataloging-in-Publication Data has been applied for.

19 20 21 22 23   10 9 8 7 6 5 4 3 2 1

Publisher: Matt Groening

Creative Director: Nathan Kane
Managing Editor: Terry Delegeane
Director of Operations: Robert Zaugh
Art Director: Jason Ho
Production Manager: Christopher Ungar
Assistant Editor: Karen Bates
Production: Art Villanueva
Administration: Ruth Waytz
Legal Guardian: Susan A. Grode

Printed in China, 2019

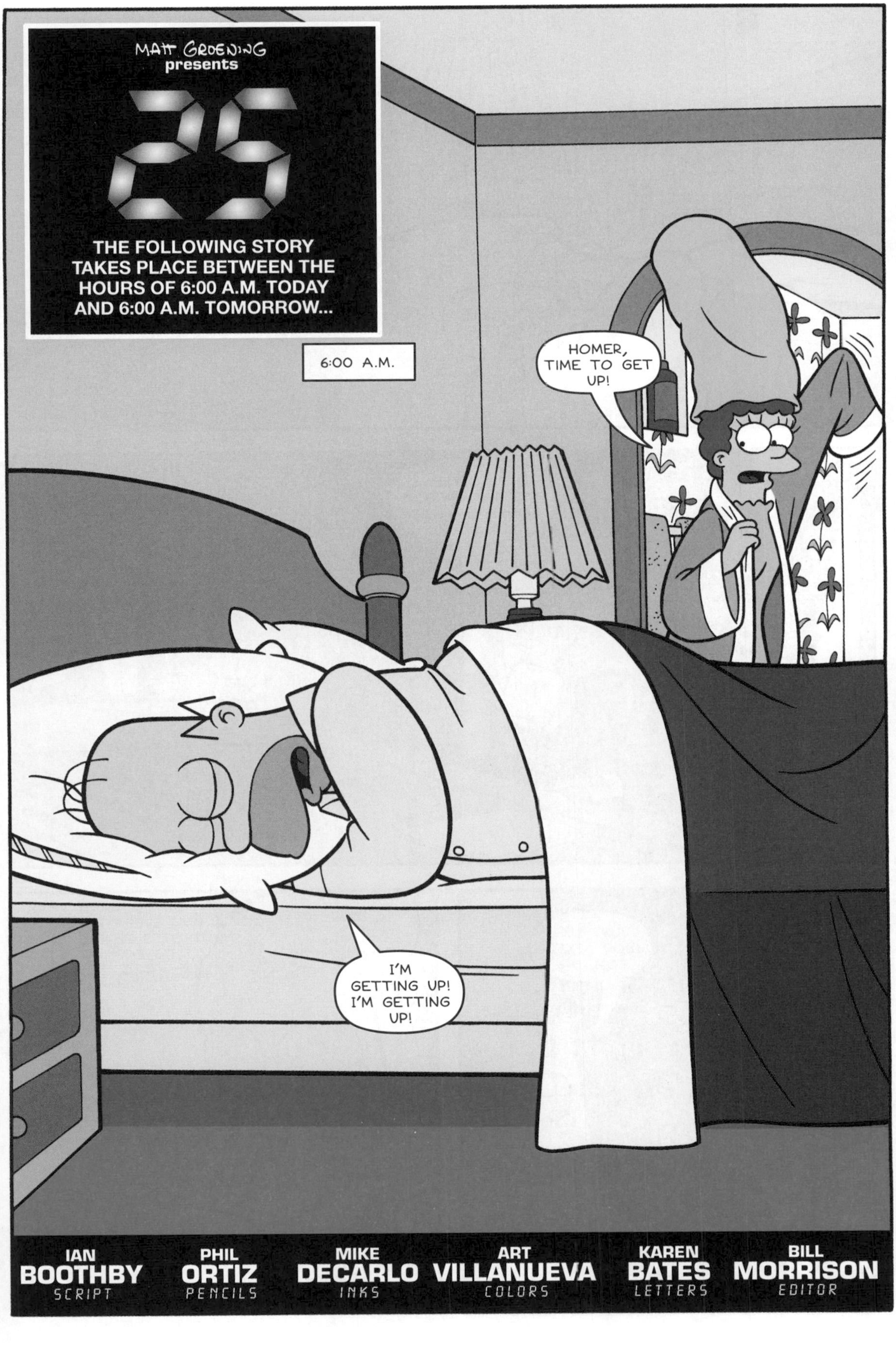
MATT GROENING
presents
25
THE FOLLOWING STORY TAKES PLACE BETWEEN THE HOURS OF 6:00 A.M. TODAY AND 6:00 A.M. TOMORROW...
6:00 A.M.
HOMER, TIME TO GET UP!
I'M GETTING UP! I'M GETTING UP!
IAN BOOTHBY SCRIPT
PHIL ORTIZ PENCILS
MIKE DECARLO INKS
ART VILLANUEVA COLORS
KAREN BATES LETTERS
BILL MORRISON EDITOR

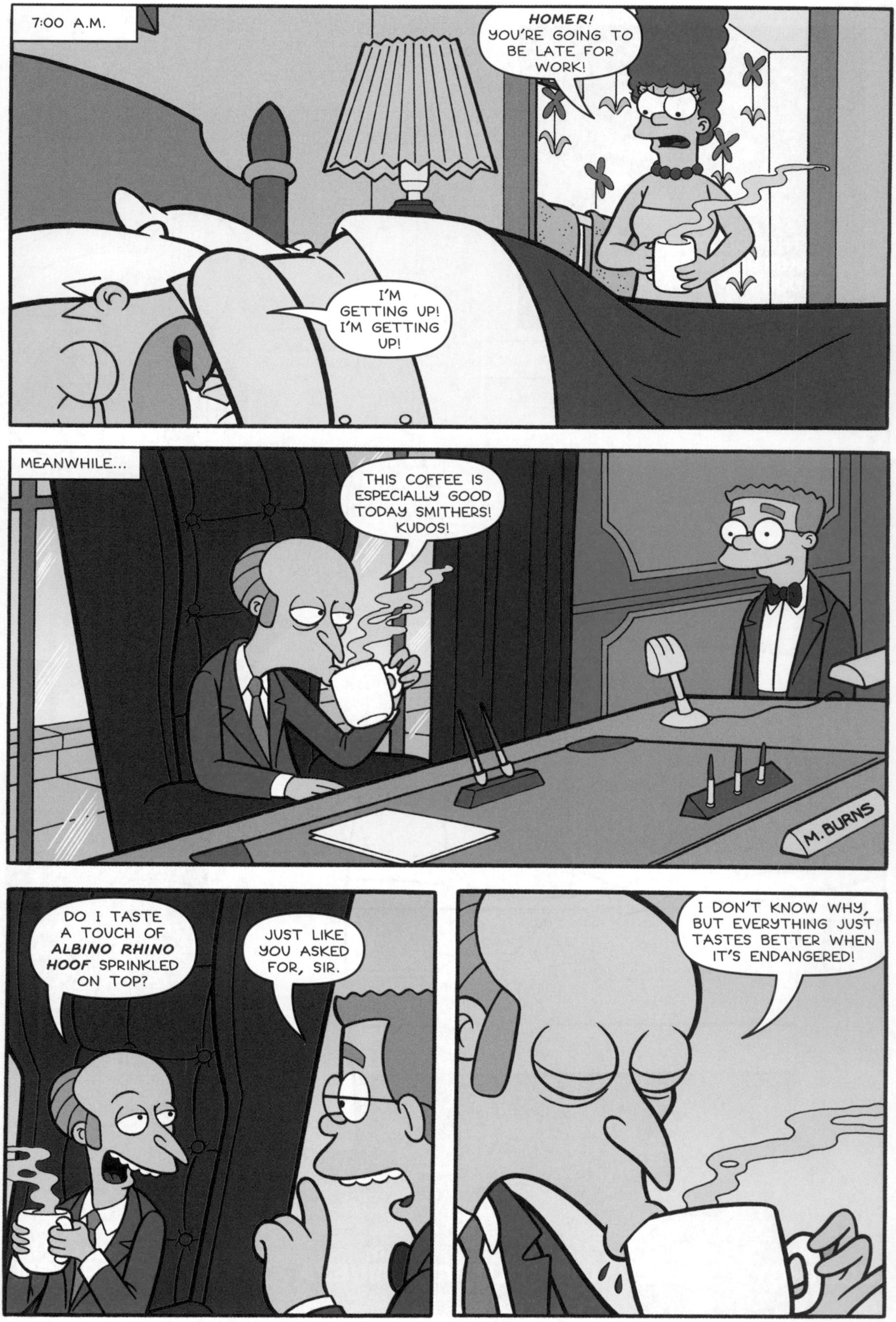
7:00 A.M.
HOMER! YOU'RE GOING TO BE LATE FOR WORK!
I'M GETTING UP! I'M GETTING UP!
MEANWHILE...
THIS COFFEE IS ESPECIALLY GOOD TODAY SMITHERS! KUDOS!
M. BURNS
DO I TASTE A TOUCH OF ALBINO RHINO HOOF SPRINKLED ON TOP?
JUST LIKE YOU ASKED FOR, SIR.
I DON'T KNOW WHY, BUT EVERYTHING JUST TASTES BETTER WHEN IT'S ENDANGERED!

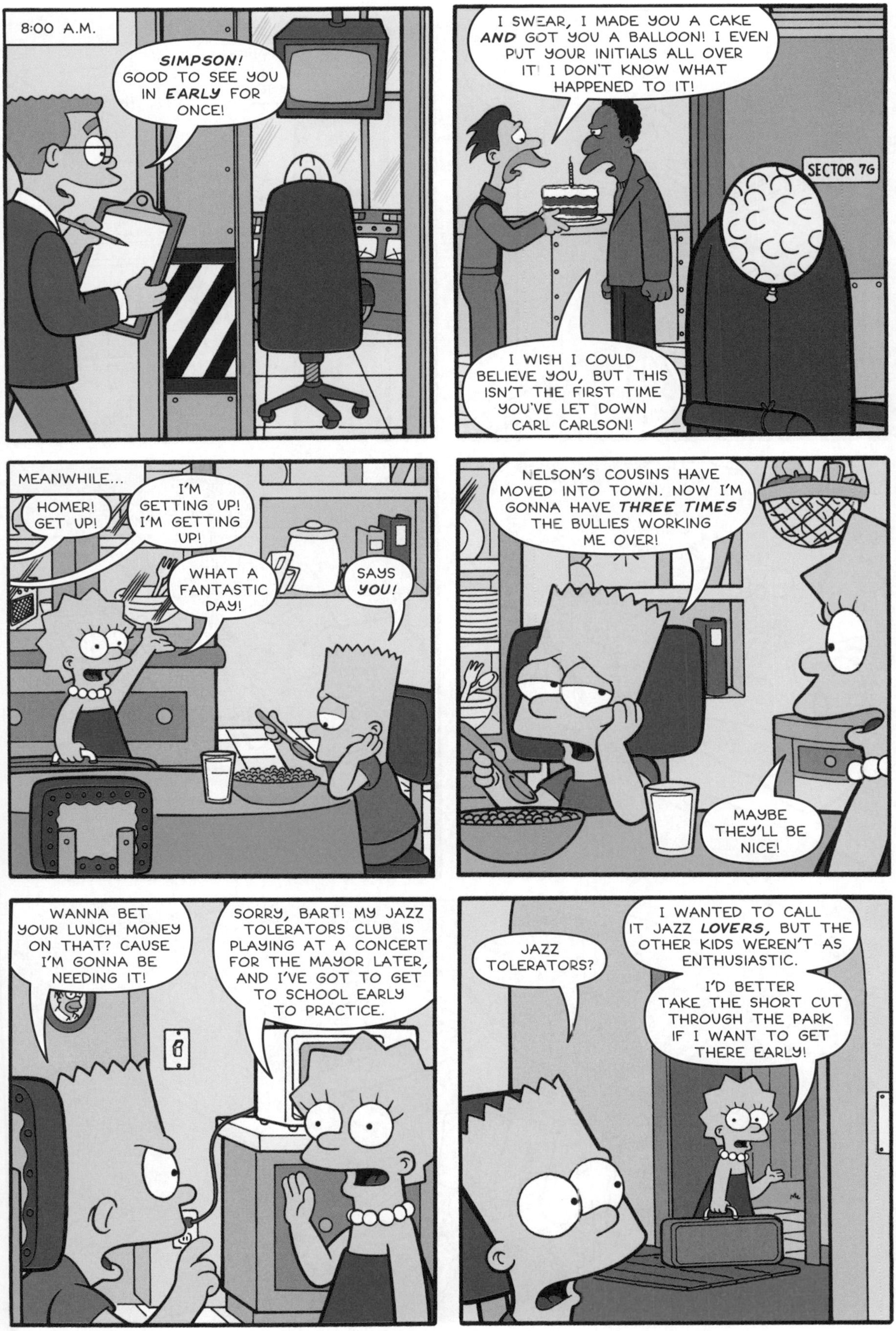
8:00 A.M.
SIMPSON! GOOD TO SEE YOU IN EARLY FOR ONCE!
I SWEAR, I MADE YOU A CAKE AND GOT YOU A BALLOON! I EVEN PUT YOUR INITIALS ALL OVER IT! I DON'T KNOW WHAT HAPPENED TO IT!
SECTOR 7G
I WISH I COULD BELIEVE YOU, BUT THIS ISN'T THE FIRST TIME YOU'VE LET DOWN CARL CARLSON!
MEANWHILE...
HOMER! GET UP!
I'M GETTING UP! I'M GETTING UP!
WHAT A FANTASTIC DAY!
SAYS YOU!
NELSON'S COUSINS HAVE MOVED INTO TOWN. NOW I'M GONNA HAVE THREE TIMES THE BULLIES WORKING ME OVER!
MAYBE THEY'LL BE NICE!
WANNA BET YOUR LUNCH MONEY ON THAT? CAUSE I'M GONNA BE NEEDING IT!
SORRY, BART! MY JAZZ TOLERATORS CLUB IS PLAYING AT A CONCERT FOR THE MAYOR LATER, AND I'VE GOT TO GET TO SCHOOL EARLY TO PRACTICE.
JAZZ TOLERATORS?
I WANTED TO CALL IT JAZZ LOVERS, BUT THE OTHER KIDS WEREN'T AS ENTHUSIASTIC.
I'D BETTER TAKE THE SHORT CUT THROUGH THE PARK IF I WANT TO GET THERE EARLY!

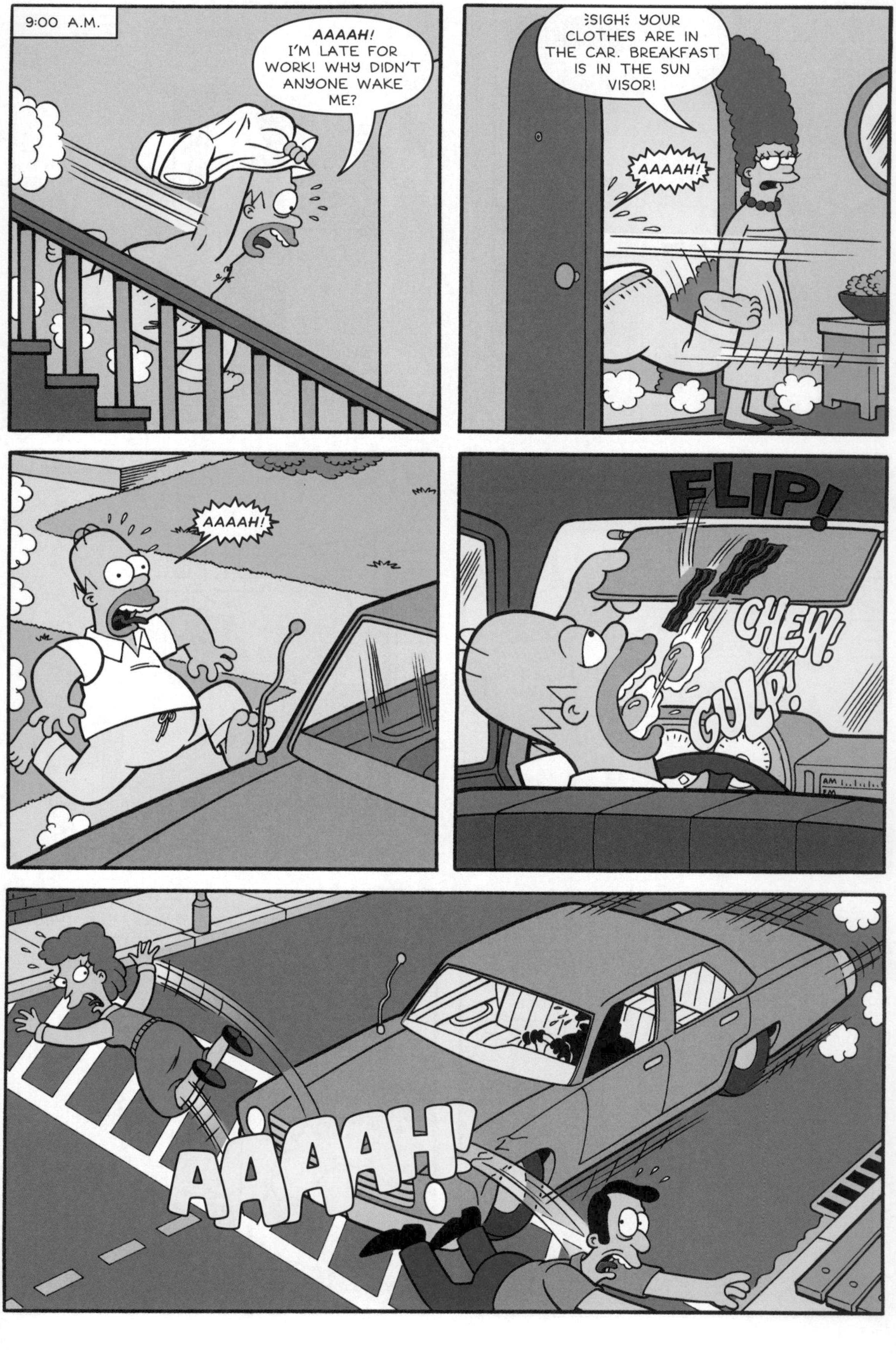
9:00 A.M.
AAAAH! I'M LATE FOR WORK! WHY DIDN'T ANYONE WAKE ME?
:SIGH: YOUR CLOTHES ARE IN THE CAR. BREAKFAST IS IN THE SUN VISOR!
AAAAH!
AAAAH!
FLIP!
CHEW!
GULP!
AM
FM
AAAAH!

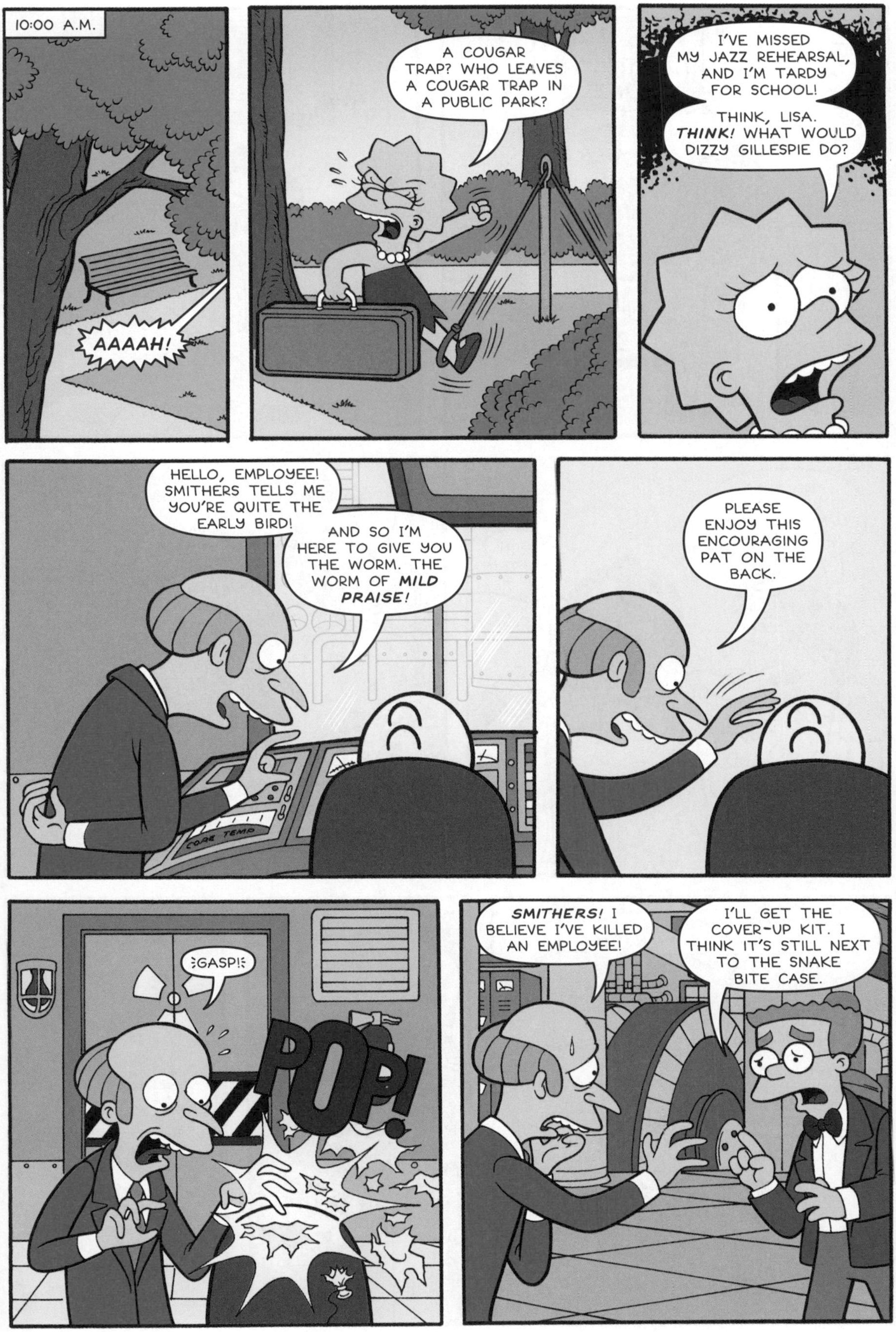
10:00 A.M.
AAAAH!
A COUGAR TRAP? WHO LEAVES A COUGAR TRAP IN A PUBLIC PARK?
I'VE MISSED MY JAZZ REHEARSAL, AND I'M TARDY FOR SCHOOL!
THINK, LISA. *THINK!* WHAT WOULD DIZZY GILLESPIE DO?
HELLO, EMPLOYEE! SMITHERS TELLS ME YOU'RE QUITE THE EARLY BIRD!
AND SO I'M HERE TO GIVE YOU THE WORM. THE WORM OF *MILD PRAISE!*
CORE TEMP
PLEASE ENJOY THIS ENCOURAGING PAT ON THE BACK.
GASP!
POP!
SMITHERS! I BELIEVE I'VE KILLED AN EMPLOYEE!
I'LL GET THE COVER-UP KIT. I THINK IT'S STILL NEXT TO THE SNAKE BITE CASE.

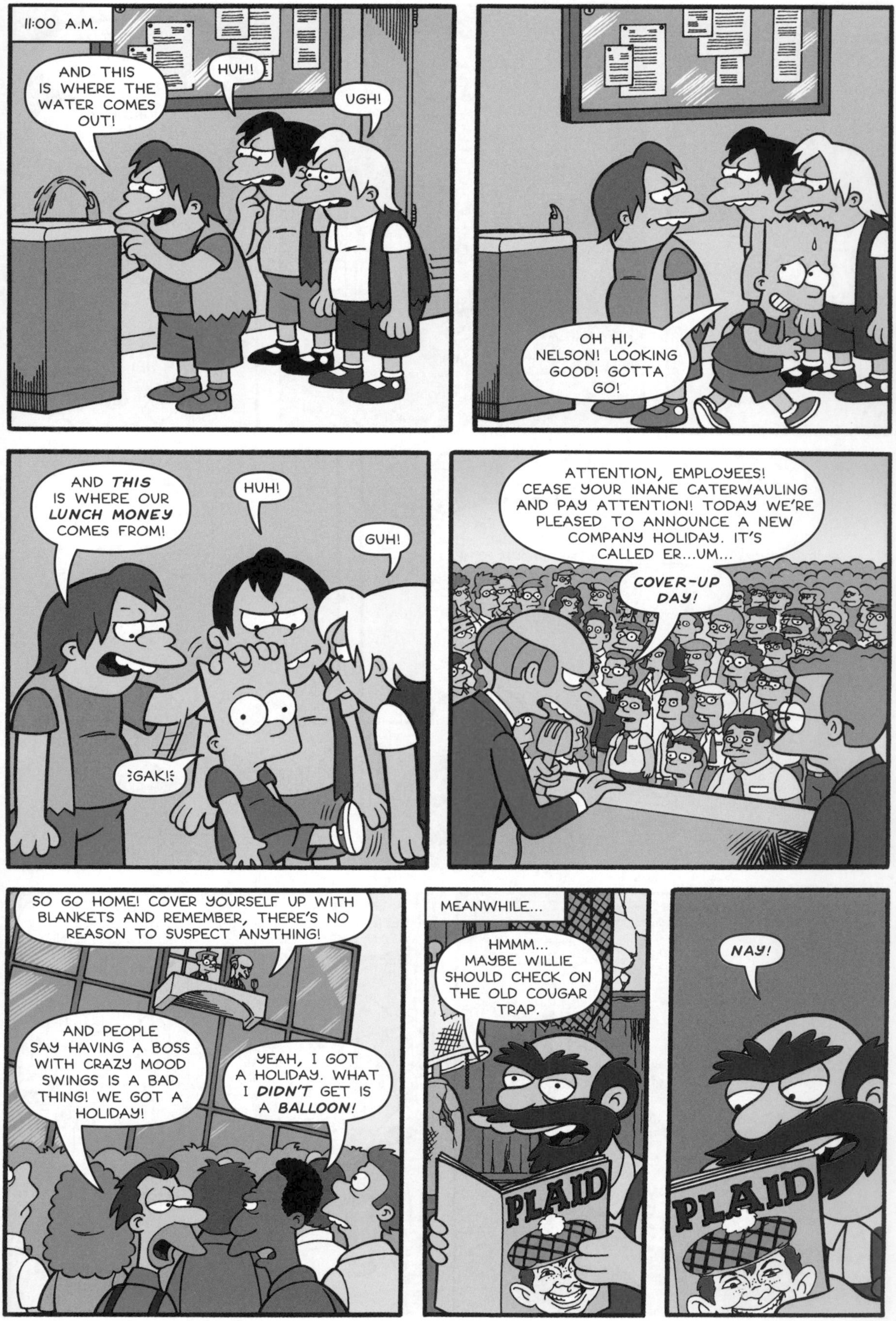
11:00 A.M.
AND THIS IS WHERE THE WATER COMES OUT!
HUH!
UGH!
OH HI, NELSON! LOOKING GOOD! GOTTA GO!
AND *THIS* IS WHERE OUR *LUNCH MONEY* COMES FROM!
HUH!
GUH!
GAK!
ATTENTION, EMPLOYEES! CEASE YOUR INANE CATERWAULING AND PAY ATTENTION! TODAY WE'RE PLEASED TO ANNOUNCE A NEW COMPANY HOLIDAY. IT'S CALLED ER...UM...
COVER-UP DAY!
SO GO HOME! COVER YOURSELF UP WITH BLANKETS AND REMEMBER, THERE'S NO REASON TO SUSPECT ANYTHING!
AND PEOPLE SAY HAVING A BOSS WITH CRAZY MOOD SWINGS IS A BAD THING! WE GOT A HOLIDAY!
YEAH, I GOT A HOLIDAY. WHAT I *DIDN'T* GET IS A *BALLOON!*
MEANWHILE...
HMMM... MAYBE WILLIE SHOULD CHECK ON THE OLD COUGAR TRAP.
PLAID
NAY!
PLAID

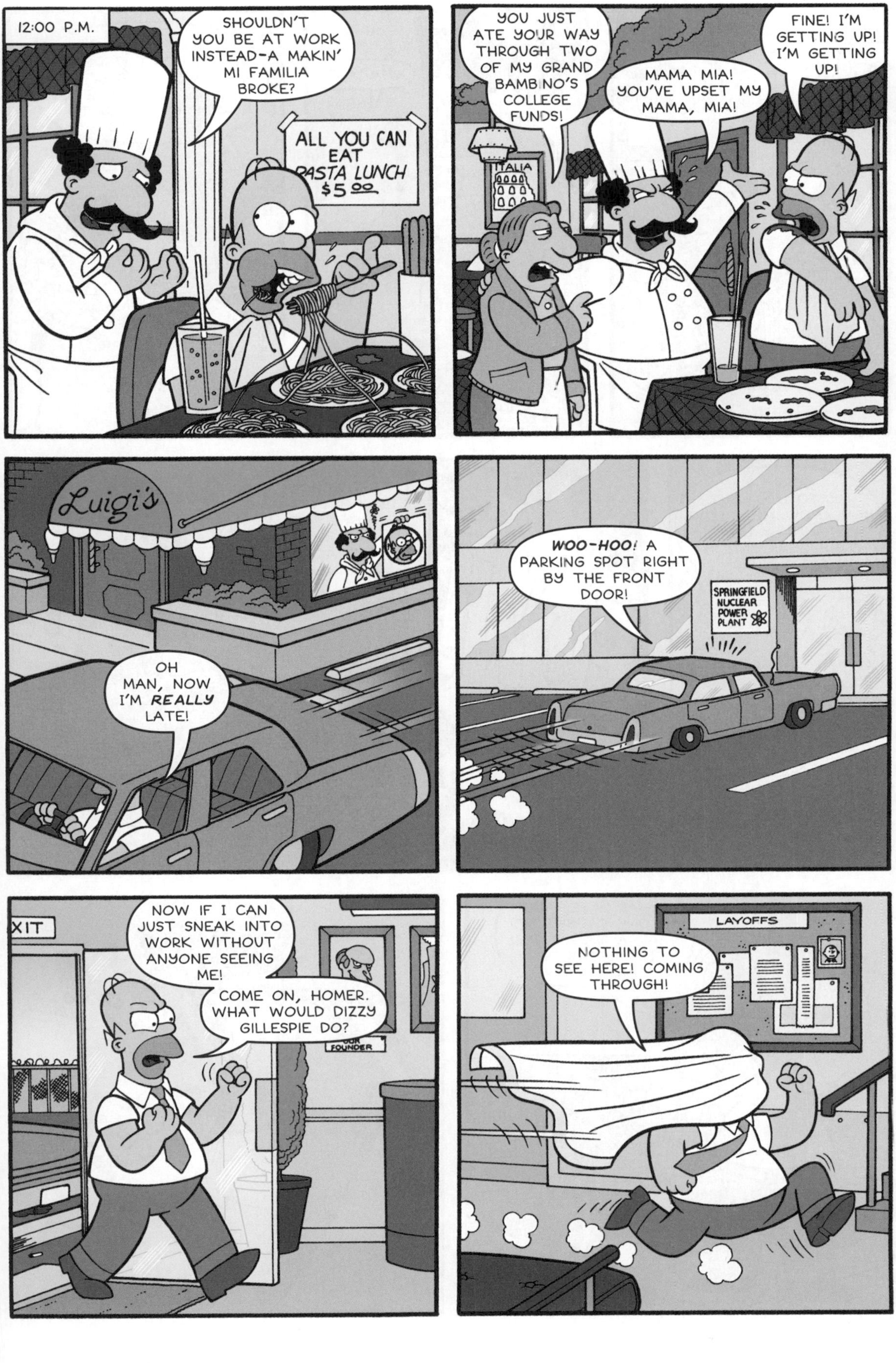
12:00 P.M.
SHOULDN'T YOU BE AT WORK INSTEAD-A MAKIN' MI FAMILIA BROKE?
ALL YOU CAN EAT PASTA LUNCH $5.00
YOU JUST ATE YOUR WAY THROUGH TWO OF MY GRAND BAMBINO'S COLLEGE FUNDS!
MAMA MIA! YOU'VE UPSET MY MAMA, MIA!
FINE! I'M GETTING UP! I'M GETTING UP!
ITALIA
Luigi's
OH MAN, NOW I'M ***REALLY*** LATE!
WOO-HOO! A PARKING SPOT RIGHT BY THE FRONT DOOR!
SPRINGFIELD NUCLEAR POWER PLANT
EXIT
NOW IF I CAN JUST SNEAK INTO WORK WITHOUT ANYONE SEEING ME!
COME ON, HOMER. WHAT WOULD DIZZY GILLESPIE DO?
FOUNDER
LAYOFFS
NOTHING TO SEE HERE! COMING THROUGH!

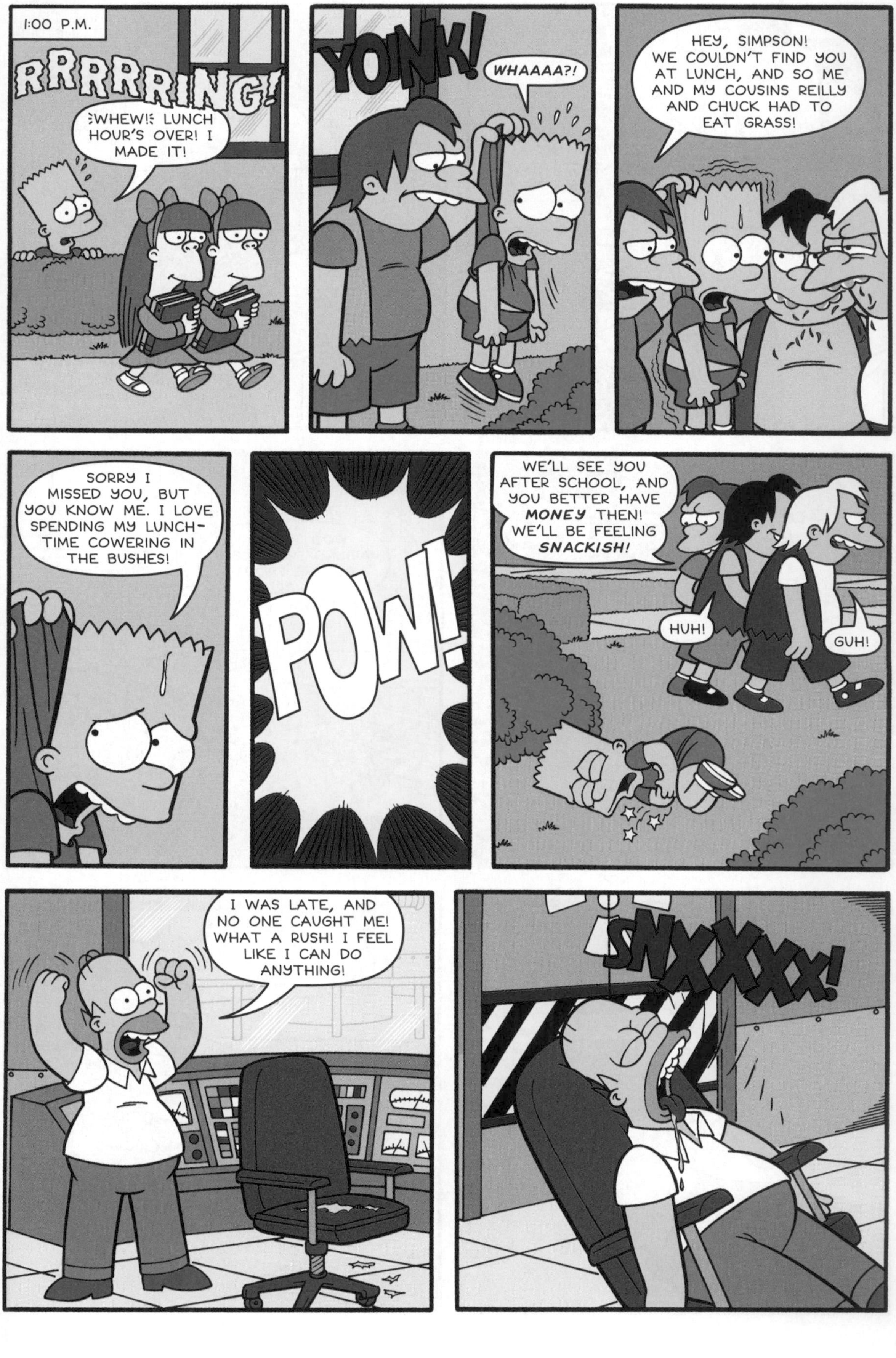
1:00 P.M.
RRRRRRING!
WHEW! LUNCH HOUR'S OVER! I MADE IT!
YOINK!
WHAAAA?!
HEY, SIMPSON! WE COULDN'T FIND YOU AT LUNCH, AND SO ME AND MY COUSINS REILLY AND CHUCK HAD TO EAT GRASS!
SORRY I MISSED YOU, BUT YOU KNOW ME. I LOVE SPENDING MY LUNCH-TIME COWERING IN THE BUSHES!
POW!
WE'LL SEE YOU AFTER SCHOOL, AND YOU BETTER HAVE MONEY THEN! WE'LL BE FEELING SNACKISH!
HUH!
GUH!
I WAS LATE, AND NO ONE CAUGHT ME! WHAT A RUSH! I FEEL LIKE I CAN DO ANYTHING!
SNXXXX!

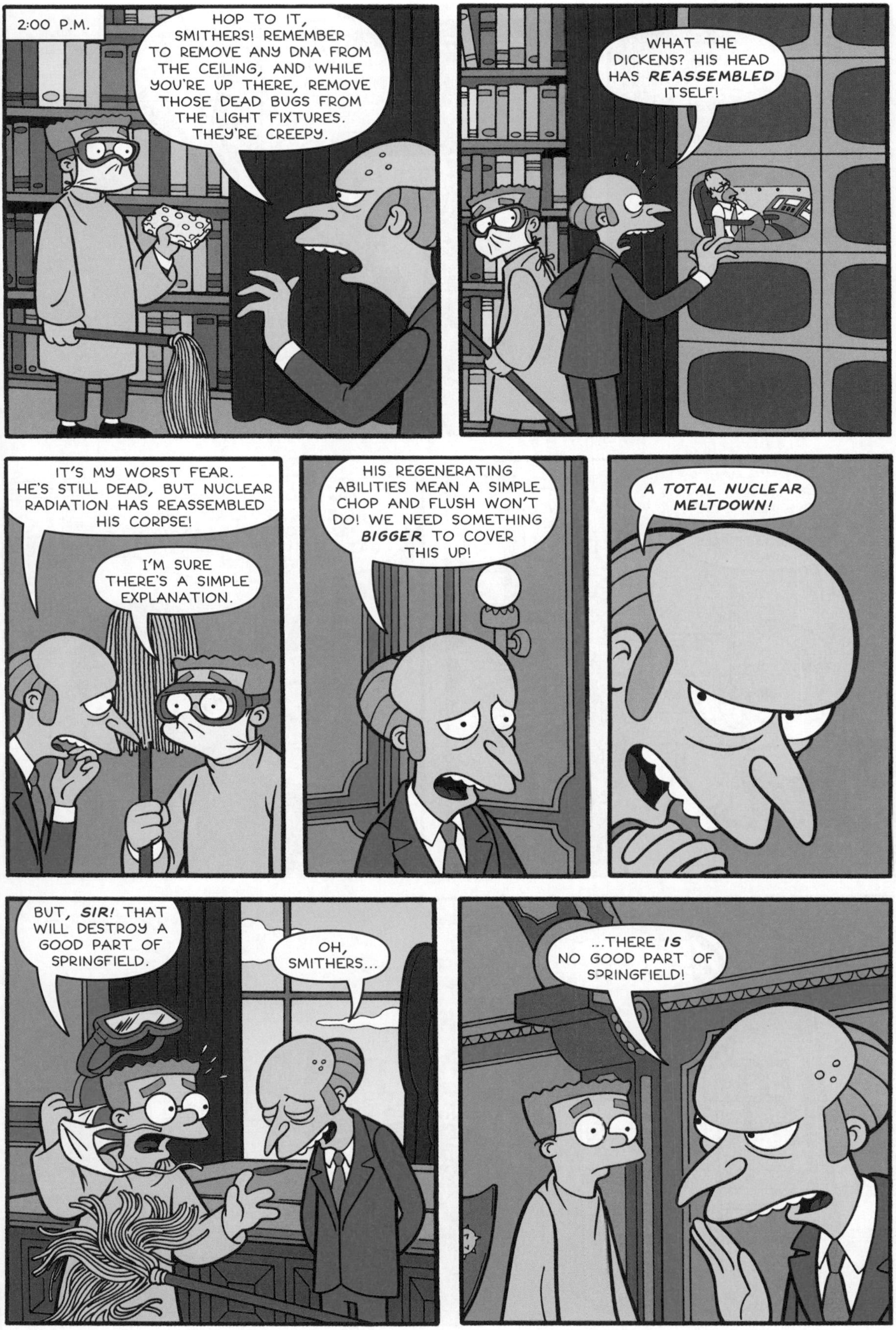
2:00 P.M.
HOP TO IT, SMITHERS! REMEMBER TO REMOVE ANY DNA FROM THE CEILING, AND WHILE YOU'RE UP THERE, REMOVE THOSE DEAD BUGS FROM THE LIGHT FIXTURES. THEY'RE CREEPY.
WHAT THE DICKENS? HIS HEAD HAS REASSEMBLED ITSELF!
IT'S MY WORST FEAR. HE'S STILL DEAD, BUT NUCLEAR RADIATION HAS REASSEMBLED HIS CORPSE!
I'M SURE THERE'S A SIMPLE EXPLANATION.
HIS REGENERATING ABILITIES MEAN A SIMPLE CHOP AND FLUSH WON'T DO! WE NEED SOMETHING BIGGER TO COVER THIS UP!
A TOTAL NUCLEAR MELTDOWN!
BUT, SIR! THAT WILL DESTROY A GOOD PART OF SPRINGFIELD.
OH, SMITHERS...
...THERE IS NO GOOD PART OF SPRINGFIELD!

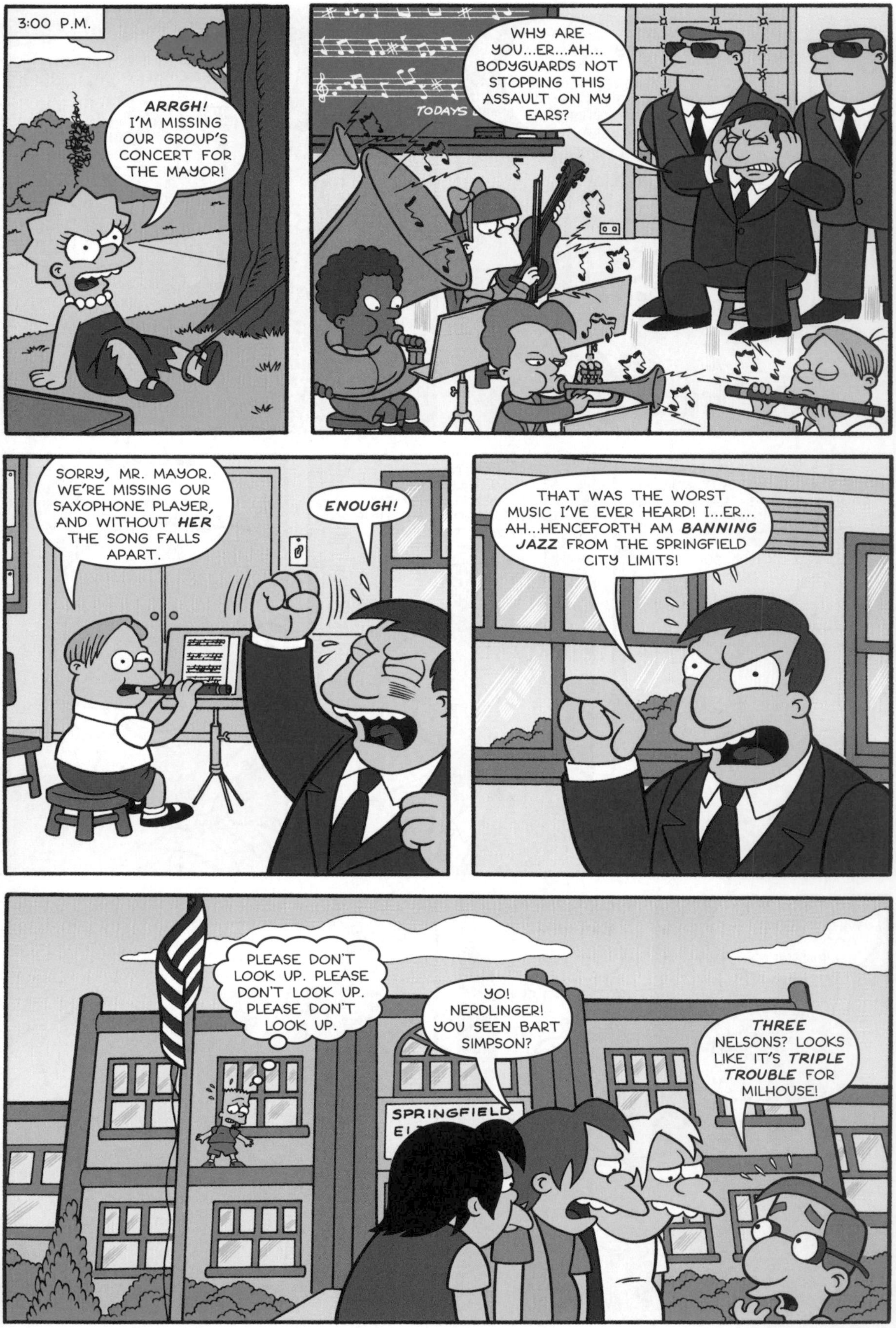
3:00 P.M.
ARRGH! I'M MISSING OUR GROUP'S CONCERT FOR THE MAYOR!
WHY ARE YOU...ER...AH... BODYGUARDS NOT STOPPING THIS ASSAULT ON MY EARS?
SORRY, MR. MAYOR. WE'RE MISSING OUR SAXOPHONE PLAYER, AND WITHOUT HER THE SONG FALLS APART.
ENOUGH!
THAT WAS THE WORST MUSIC I'VE EVER HEARD! I...ER... AH...HENCEFORTH AM BANNING JAZZ FROM THE SPRINGFIELD CITY LIMITS!
PLEASE DON'T LOOK UP. PLEASE DON'T LOOK UP. PLEASE DON'T LOOK UP.
YO! NERDLINGER! YOU SEEN BART SIMPSON?
THREE NELSONS? LOOKS LIKE IT'S TRIPLE TROUBLE FOR MILHOUSE!
SPRINGFIELD

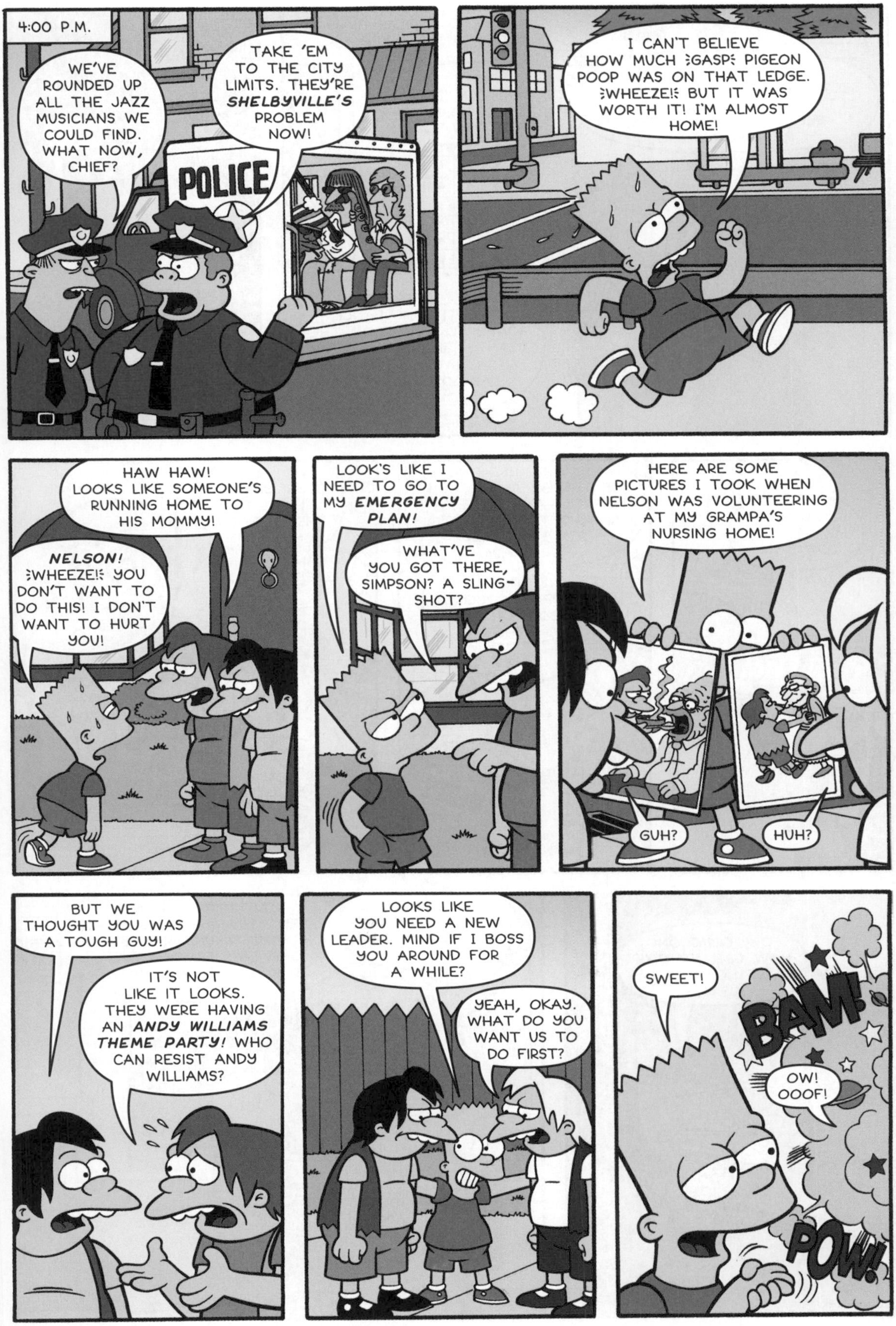
4:00 P.M.
WE'VE ROUNDED UP ALL THE JAZZ MUSICIANS WE COULD FIND. WHAT NOW, CHIEF?
TAKE 'EM TO THE CITY LIMITS. THEY'RE *SHELBYVILLE'S* PROBLEM NOW!
POLICE
I CAN'T BELIEVE HOW MUCH ⦂GASP⦂ PIGEON POOP WAS ON THAT LEDGE. ⦂WHEEZE!⦂ BUT IT WAS WORTH IT! I'M ALMOST HOME!
HAW HAW! LOOKS LIKE SOMEONE'S RUNNING HOME TO HIS MOMMY!
NELSON! ⦂WHEEZE!⦂ YOU DON'T WANT TO DO THIS! I DON'T WANT TO HURT YOU!
LOOK'S LIKE I NEED TO GO TO MY *EMERGENCY PLAN!*
WHAT'VE YOU GOT THERE, SIMPSON? A SLING-SHOT?
HERE ARE SOME PICTURES I TOOK WHEN NELSON WAS VOLUNTEERING AT MY GRAMPA'S NURSING HOME!
GUH?
HUH?
BUT WE THOUGHT YOU WAS A TOUGH GUY!
IT'S NOT LIKE IT LOOKS. THEY WERE HAVING AN *ANDY WILLIAMS THEME PARTY!* WHO CAN RESIST ANDY WILLIAMS?
LOOKS LIKE YOU NEED A NEW LEADER. MIND IF I BOSS YOU AROUND FOR A WHILE?
YEAH, OKAY. WHAT DO YOU WANT US TO DO FIRST?
SWEET!
BAM!
OW! OOOF!
POW!

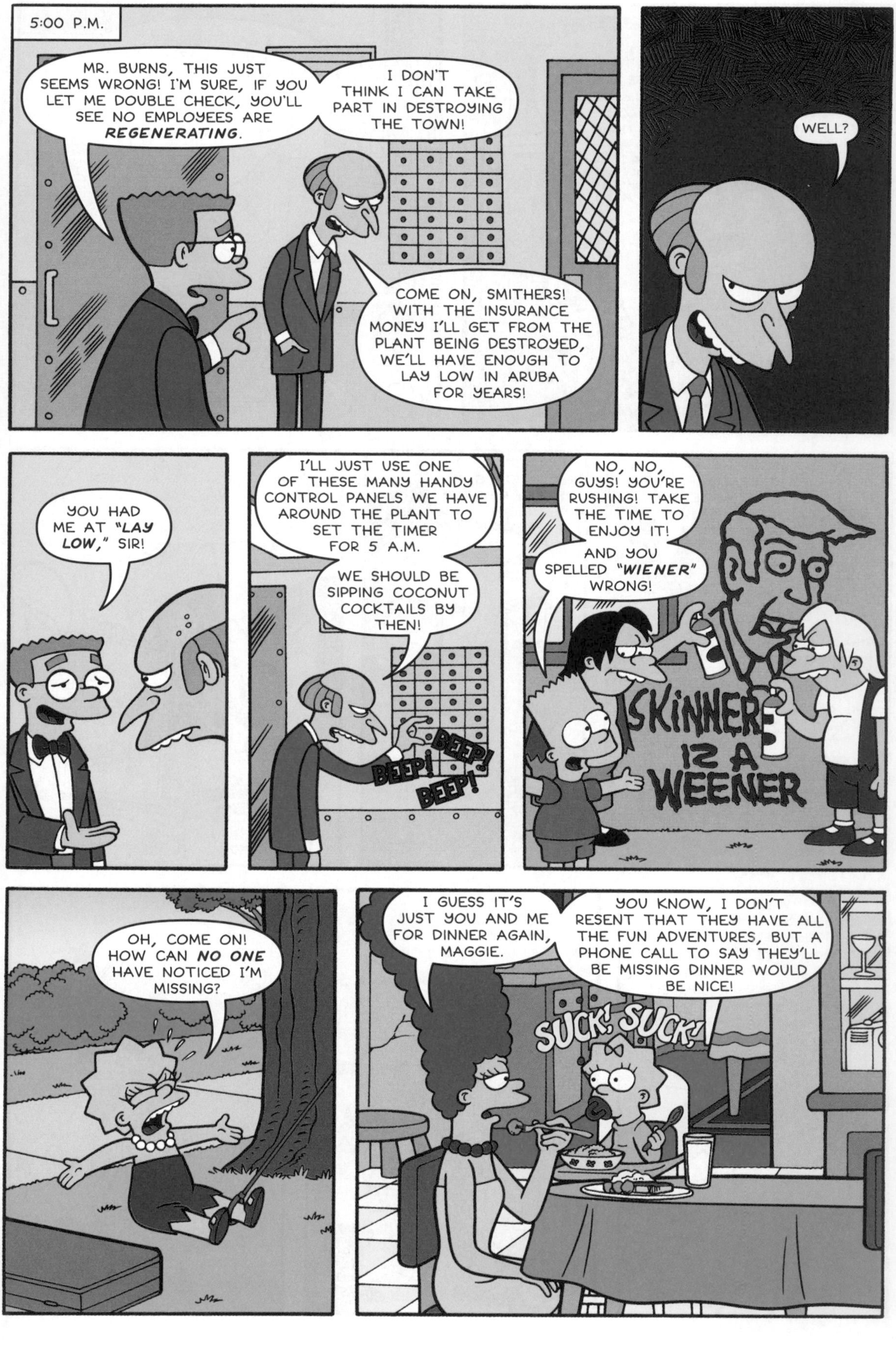

5:00 P.M.
MR. BURNS, THIS JUST SEEMS WRONG! I'M SURE, IF YOU LET ME DOUBLE CHECK, YOU'LL SEE NO EMPLOYEES ARE **REGENERATING**.
I DON'T THINK I CAN TAKE PART IN DESTROYING THE TOWN!
COME ON, SMITHERS! WITH THE INSURANCE MONEY I'LL GET FROM THE PLANT BEING DESTROYED, WE'LL HAVE ENOUGH TO LAY LOW IN ARUBA FOR YEARS!
WELL?
YOU HAD ME AT "***LAY LOW,***" SIR!
I'LL JUST USE ONE OF THESE MANY HANDY CONTROL PANELS WE HAVE AROUND THE PLANT TO SET THE TIMER FOR 5 A.M.
WE SHOULD BE SIPPING COCONUT COCKTAILS BY THEN!
BEEP!
BEEP!
BEEP!
NO, NO, GUYS! YOU'RE RUSHING! TAKE THE TIME TO ENJOY IT!
AND YOU SPELLED "***WIENER***" WRONG!
SKINNER IZ A WEENER
OH, COME ON! HOW CAN ***NO ONE*** HAVE NOTICED I'M MISSING?
I GUESS IT'S JUST YOU AND ME FOR DINNER AGAIN, MAGGIE.
YOU KNOW, I DON'T RESENT THAT THEY HAVE ALL THE FUN ADVENTURES, BUT A PHONE CALL TO SAY THEY'LL BE MISSING DINNER WOULD BE NICE!
SUCK! SUCK!

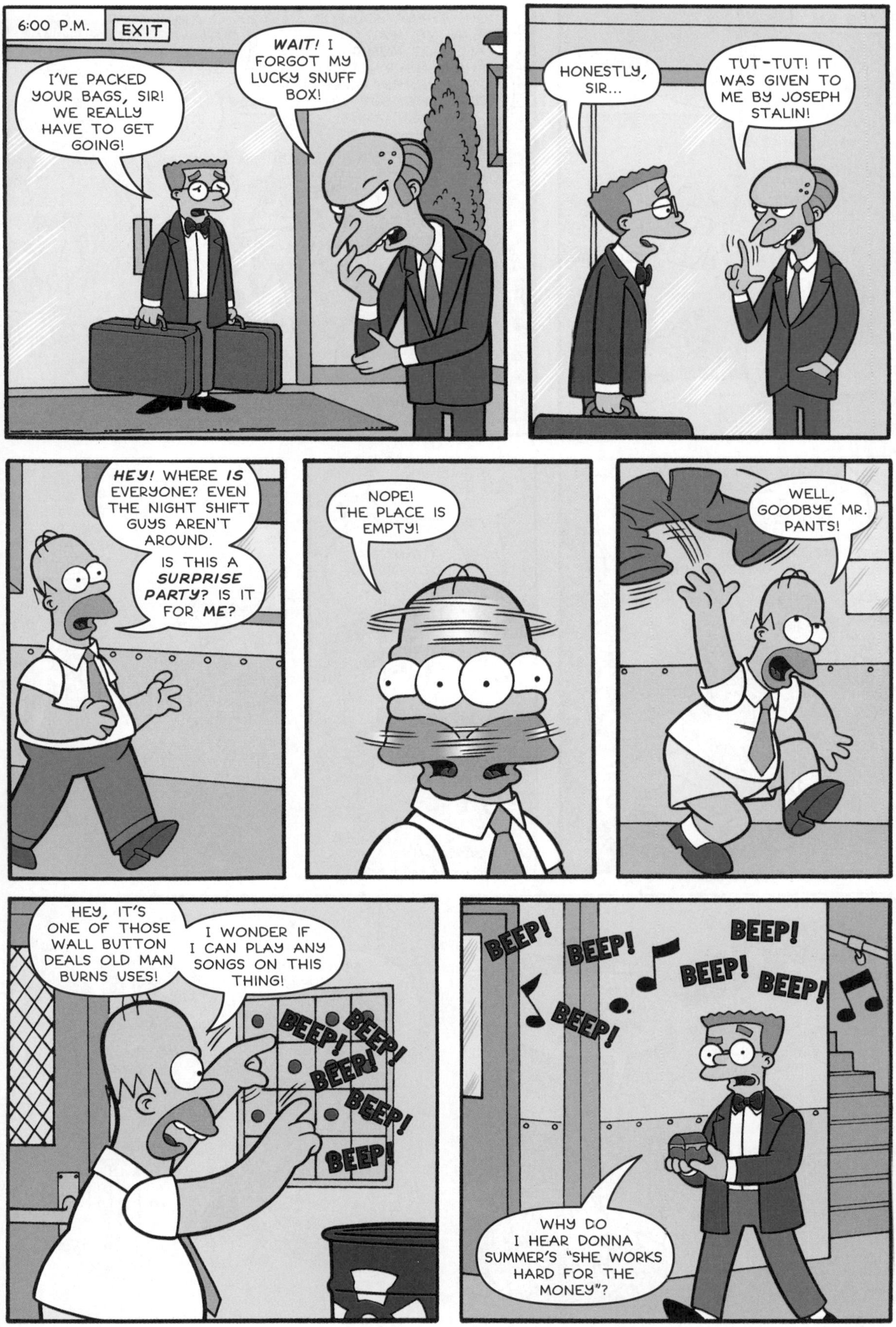
6:00 P.M.
EXIT
I'VE PACKED YOUR BAGS, SIR! WE REALLY HAVE TO GET GOING!
WAIT! I FORGOT MY LUCKY SNUFF BOX!
HONESTLY, SIR...
TUT-TUT! IT WAS GIVEN TO ME BY JOSEPH STALIN!
HEY! WHERE IS EVERYONE? EVEN THE NIGHT SHIFT GUYS AREN'T AROUND.
IS THIS A SURPRISE PARTY? IS IT FOR ME?
NOPE! THE PLACE IS EMPTY!
WELL, GOODBYE MR. PANTS!
HEY, IT'S ONE OF THOSE WALL BUTTON DEALS OLD MAN BURNS USES!
I WONDER IF I CAN PLAY ANY SONGS ON THIS THING!
BEEP! BEEP! BEEP! BEEP! BEEP!
BEEP! BEEP! BEEP! BEEP! BEEP! BEEP!
WHY DO I HEAR DONNA SUMMER'S "SHE WORKS HARD FOR THE MONEY"?

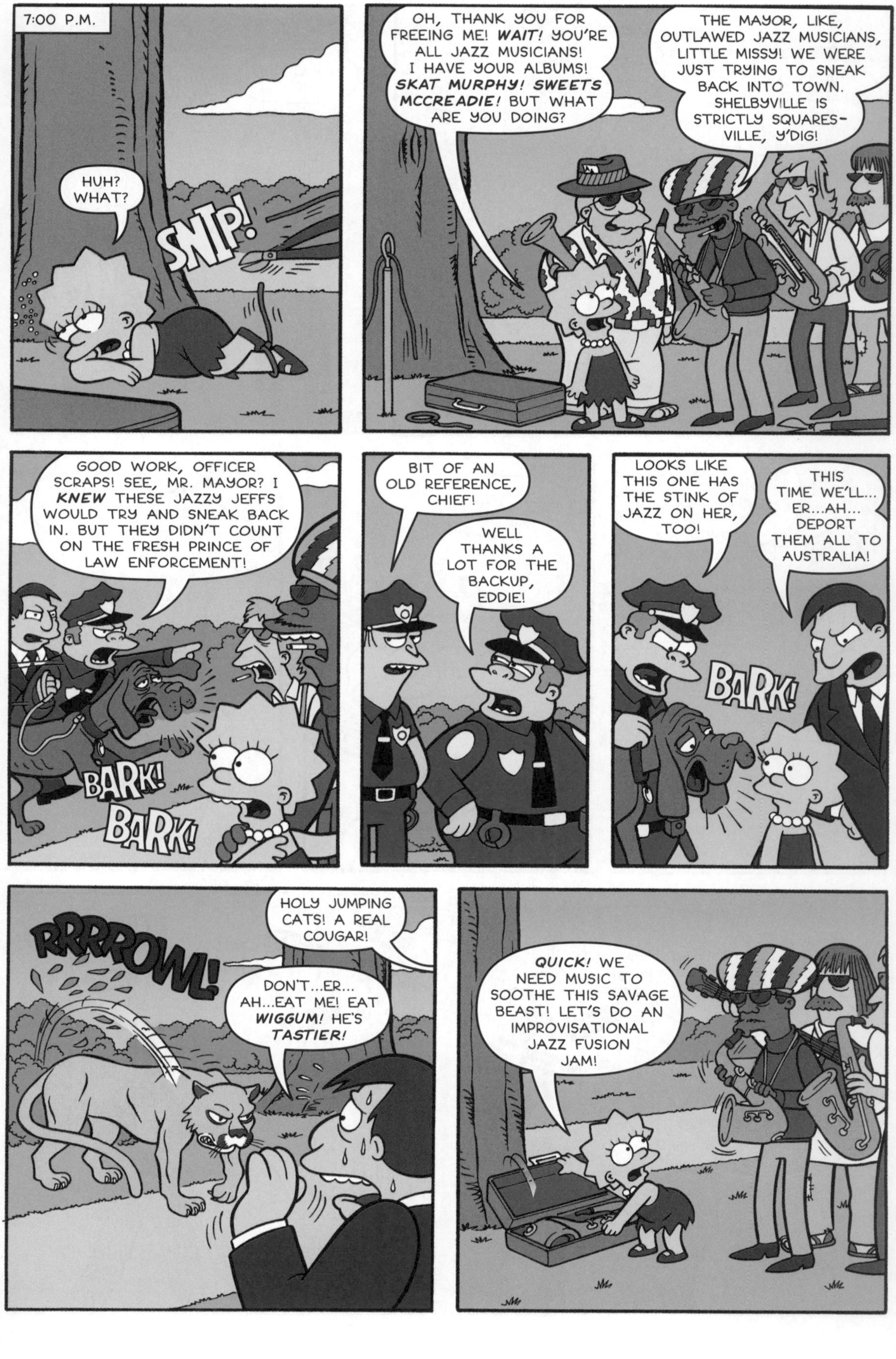
7:00 P.M.
HUH? WHAT?
SNIP!
OH, THANK YOU FOR FREEING ME! WAIT! YOU'RE ALL JAZZ MUSICIANS! I HAVE YOUR ALBUMS! SKAT MURPHY! SWEETS MCCREADIE! BUT WHAT ARE YOU DOING?
THE MAYOR, LIKE, OUTLAWED JAZZ MUSICIANS, LITTLE MISSY! WE WERE JUST TRYING TO SNEAK BACK INTO TOWN. SHELBYVILLE IS STRICTLY SQUARES-VILLE, Y'DIG!
GOOD WORK, OFFICER SCRAPS! SEE, MR. MAYOR? I KNEW THESE JAZZY JEFFS WOULD TRY AND SNEAK BACK IN. BUT THEY DIDN'T COUNT ON THE FRESH PRINCE OF LAW ENFORCEMENT!
BARK!
BARK!
BIT OF AN OLD REFERENCE, CHIEF!
WELL THANKS A LOT FOR THE BACKUP, EDDIE!
LOOKS LIKE THIS ONE HAS THE STINK OF JAZZ ON HER, TOO!
THIS TIME WE'LL... ER...AH... DEPORT THEM ALL TO AUSTRALIA!
BARK!
RRRROWL!
HOLY JUMPING CATS! A REAL COUGAR!
DON'T...ER... AH...EAT ME! EAT WIGGUM! HE'S TASTIER!
QUICK! WE NEED MUSIC TO SOOTHE THIS SAVAGE BEAST! LET'S DO AN IMPROVISATIONAL JAZZ FUSION JAM!

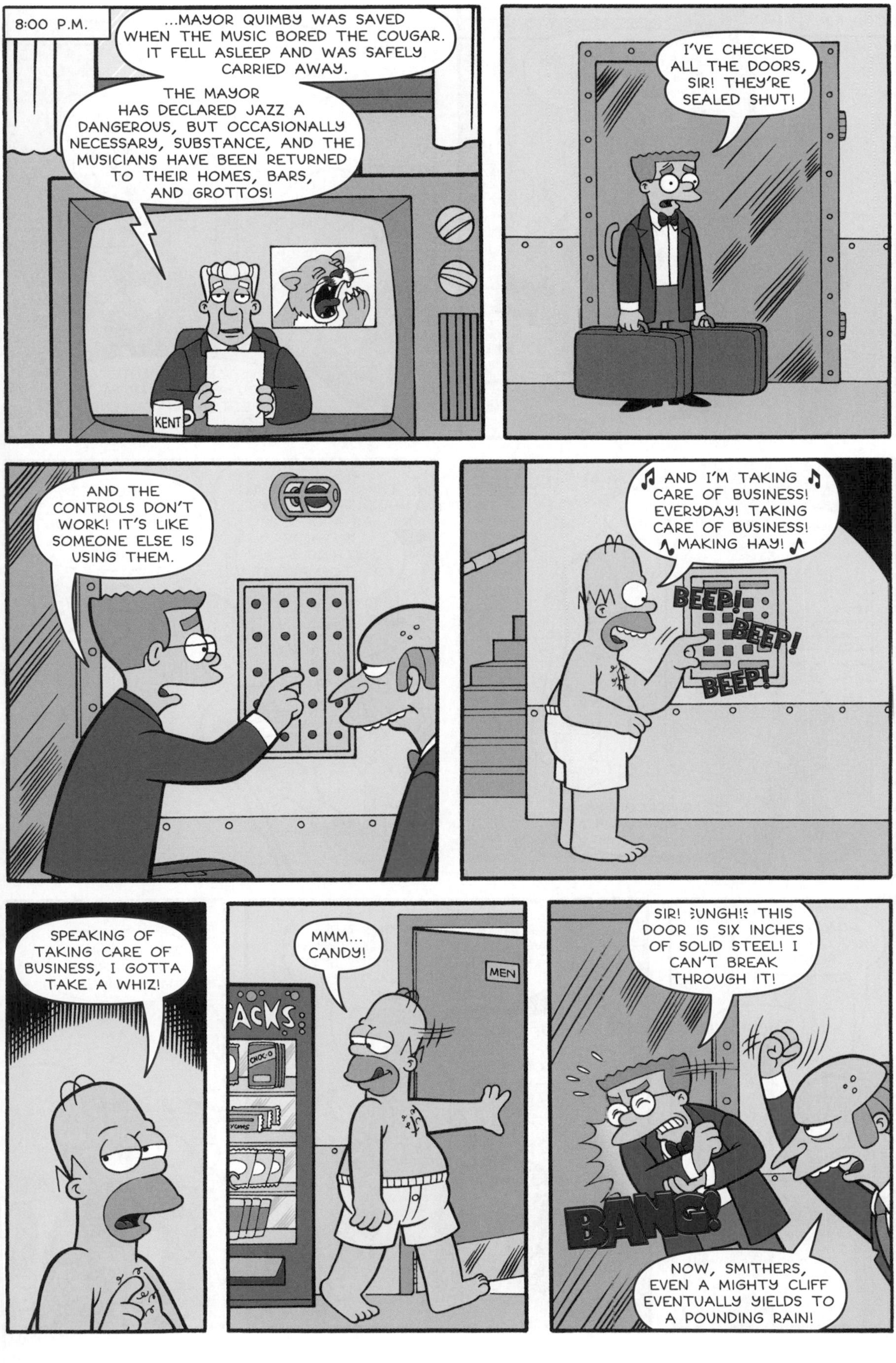
8:00 P.M.
...MAYOR QUIMBY WAS SAVED WHEN THE MUSIC BORED THE COUGAR. IT FELL ASLEEP AND WAS SAFELY CARRIED AWAY.
THE MAYOR HAS DECLARED JAZZ A DANGEROUS, BUT OCCASIONALLY NECESSARY, SUBSTANCE, AND THE MUSICIANS HAVE BEEN RETURNED TO THEIR HOMES, BARS, AND GROTTOS!
KENT
I'VE CHECKED ALL THE DOORS, SIR! THEY'RE SEALED SHUT!
AND THE CONTROLS DON'T WORK! IT'S LIKE SOMEONE ELSE IS USING THEM.
♫ AND I'M TAKING CARE OF BUSINESS! EVERYDAY! TAKING CARE OF BUSINESS! MAKING HAY! ♫
BEEP!
BEEP!
BEEP!
SPEAKING OF TAKING CARE OF BUSINESS, I GOTTA TAKE A WHIZ!
MMM... CANDY!
MEN
CHOC-O
SIR! UNGH! THIS DOOR IS SIX INCHES OF SOLID STEEL! I CAN'T BREAK THROUGH IT!
BANG!
NOW, SMITHERS, EVEN A MIGHTY CLIFF EVENTUALLY YIELDS TO A POUNDING RAIN!

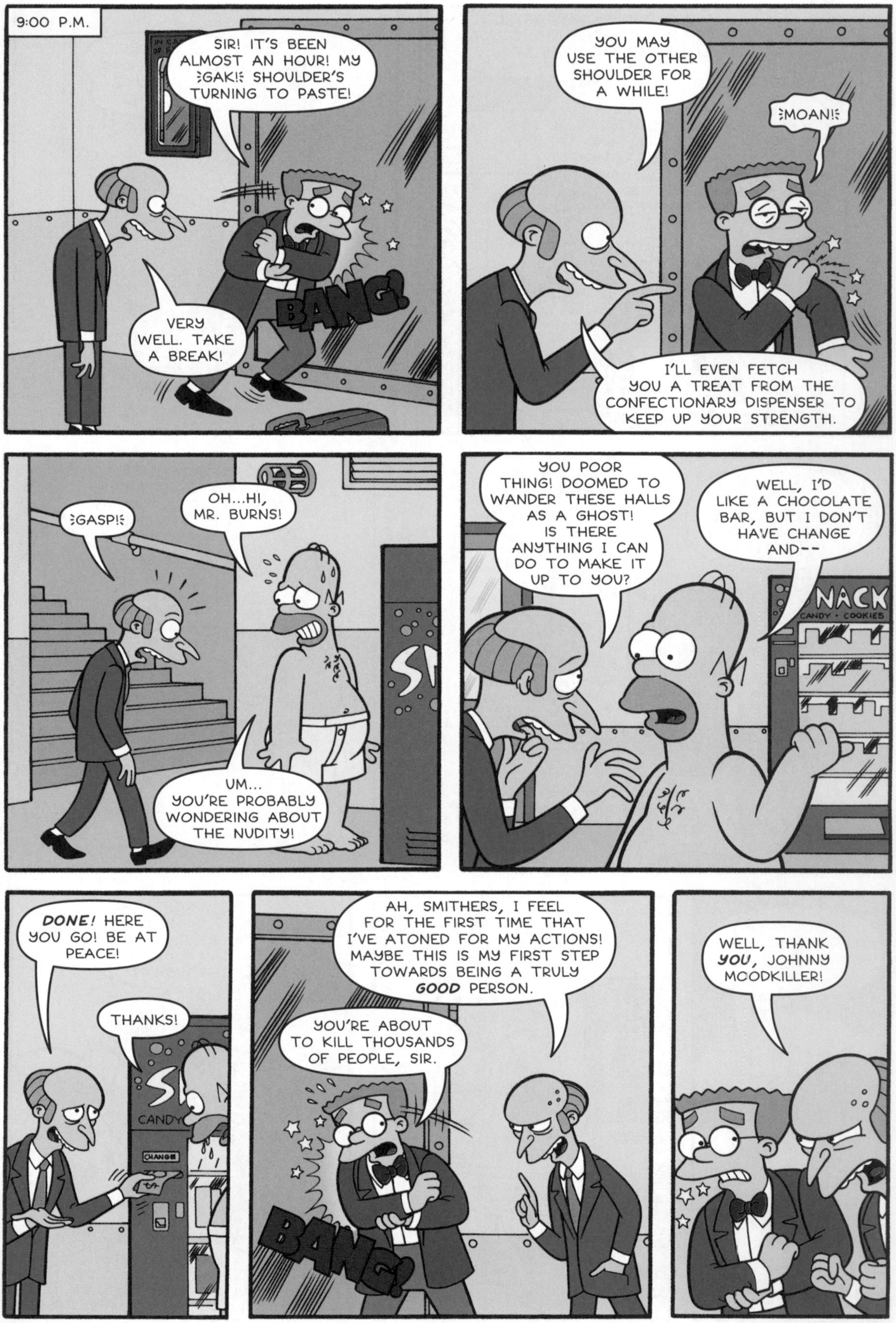
9:00 P.M.
SIR! IT'S BEEN ALMOST AN HOUR! MY GAK! SHOULDER'S TURNING TO PASTE!
VERY WELL. TAKE A BREAK!
BANG!
YOU MAY USE THE OTHER SHOULDER FOR A WHILE!
MOAN!
I'LL EVEN FETCH YOU A TREAT FROM THE CONFECTIONARY DISPENSER TO KEEP UP YOUR STRENGTH.
GASP!
OH...HI, MR. BURNS!
UM... YOU'RE PROBABLY WONDERING ABOUT THE NUDITY!
YOU POOR THING! DOOMED TO WANDER THESE HALLS AS A GHOST! IS THERE ANYTHING I CAN DO TO MAKE IT UP TO YOU?
WELL, I'D LIKE A CHOCOLATE BAR, BUT I DON'T HAVE CHANGE AND--
CANDY • COOKIES
DONE! HERE YOU GO! BE AT PEACE!
THANKS!
CANDY
CHANGE
AH, SMITHERS, I FEEL FOR THE FIRST TIME THAT I'VE ATONED FOR MY ACTIONS! MAYBE THIS IS MY FIRST STEP TOWARDS BEING A TRULY *GOOD* PERSON.
YOU'RE ABOUT TO KILL THOUSANDS OF PEOPLE, SIR.
BANG!
WELL, THANK *YOU*, JOHNNY MOODKILLER!

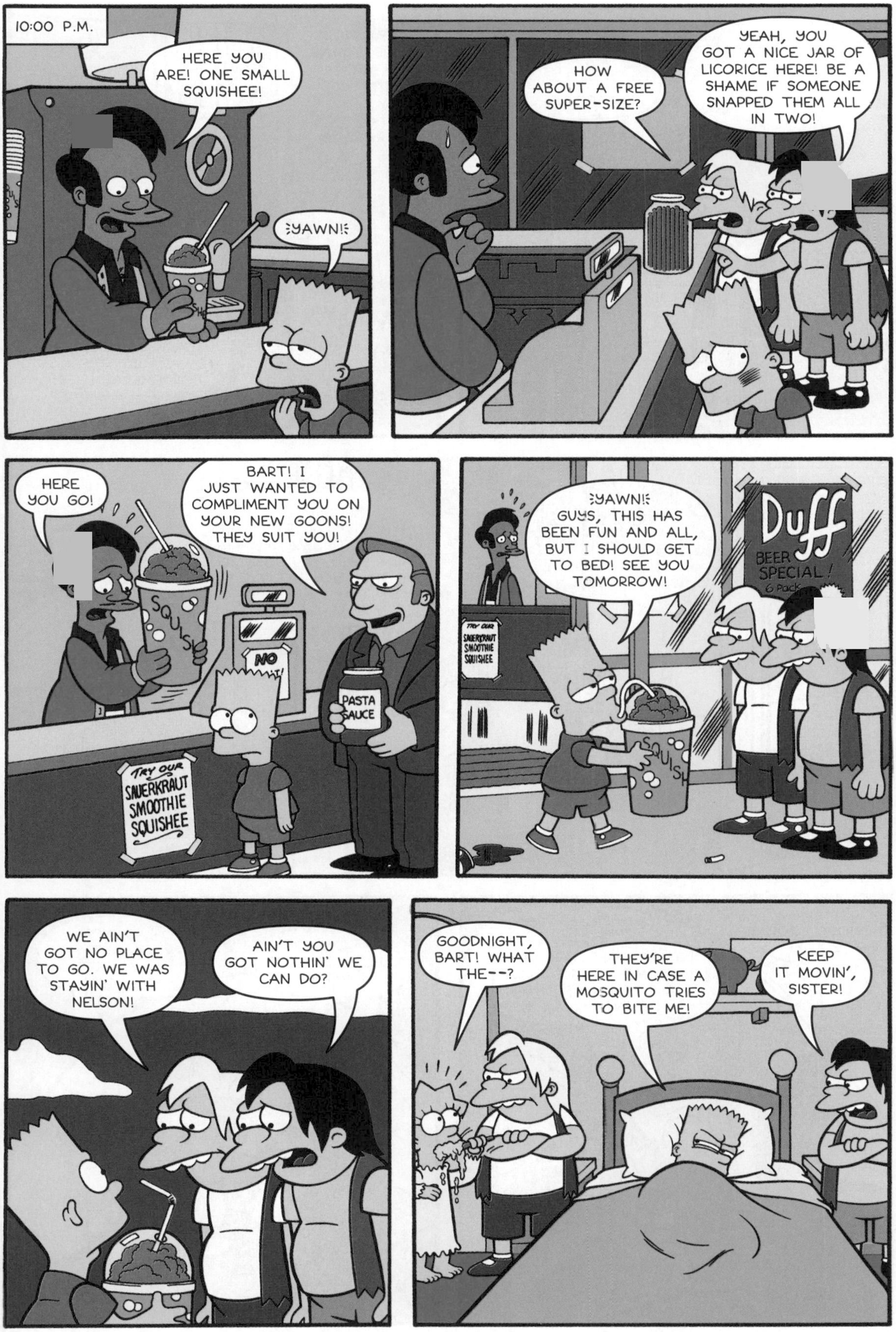
10:00 P.M.
HERE YOU ARE! ONE SMALL SQUISHEE!
YAWN!
HOW ABOUT A FREE SUPER-SIZE?
YEAH, YOU GOT A NICE JAR OF LICORICE HERE! BE A SHAME IF SOMEONE SNAPPED THEM ALL IN TWO!
HERE YOU GO!
BART! I JUST WANTED TO COMPLIMENT YOU ON YOUR NEW GOONS! THEY SUIT YOU!
SQUISH
NO
PASTA SAUCE
TRY OUR SAUERKRAUT SMOOTHIE SQUISHEE
YAWN! GUYS, THIS HAS BEEN FUN AND ALL, BUT I SHOULD GET TO BED! SEE YOU TOMORROW!
Duff BEER SPECIAL! 6 Pack
TRY OUR SAUERKRAUT SMOOTHIE SQUISHEE
SQUISH
WE AIN'T GOT NO PLACE TO GO. WE WAS STAYIN' WITH NELSON!
AIN'T YOU GOT NOTHIN' WE CAN DO?
GOODNIGHT, BART! WHAT THE--?
THEY'RE HERE IN CASE A MOSQUITO TRIES TO BITE ME!
KEEP IT MOVIN', SISTER!

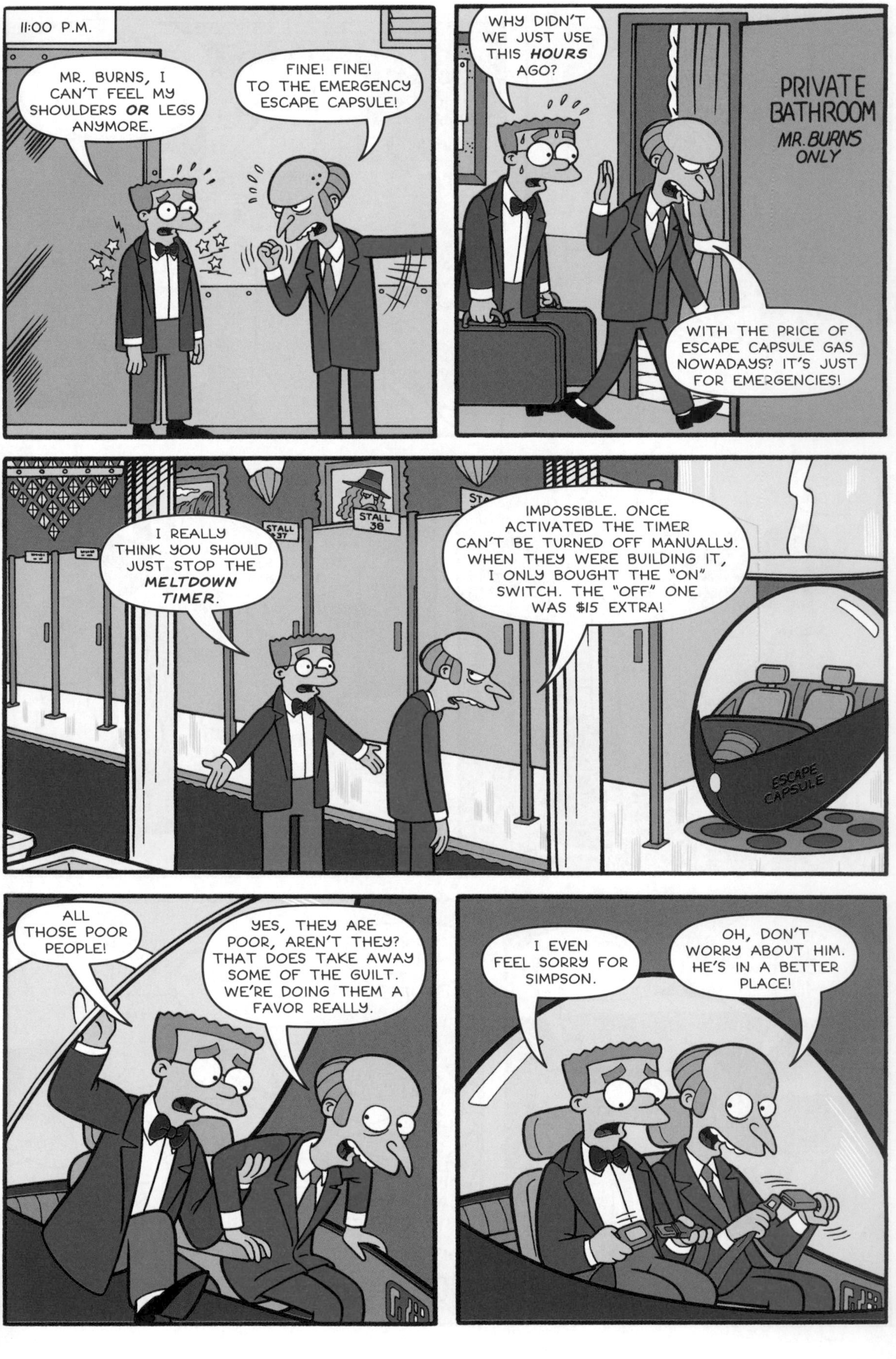
11:00 P.M.
MR. BURNS, I CAN'T FEEL MY SHOULDERS OR LEGS ANYMORE.
FINE! FINE! TO THE EMERGENCY ESCAPE CAPSULE!
WHY DIDN'T WE JUST USE THIS HOURS AGO?
PRIVATE BATHROOM
MR. BURNS ONLY
WITH THE PRICE OF ESCAPE CAPSULE GAS NOWADAYS? IT'S JUST FOR EMERGENCIES!
STALL 37
STALL 38
I REALLY THINK YOU SHOULD JUST STOP THE MELTDOWN TIMER.
IMPOSSIBLE. ONCE ACTIVATED THE TIMER CAN'T BE TURNED OFF MANUALLY. WHEN THEY WERE BUILDING IT, I ONLY BOUGHT THE "ON" SWITCH. THE "OFF" ONE WAS $15 EXTRA!
ESCAPE CAPSULE
ALL THOSE POOR PEOPLE!
YES, THEY ARE POOR, AREN'T THEY? THAT DOES TAKE AWAY SOME OF THE GUILT. WE'RE DOING THEM A FAVOR REALLY.
I EVEN FEEL SORRY FOR SIMPSON.
OH, DON'T WORRY ABOUT HIM. HE'S IN A BETTER PLACE!

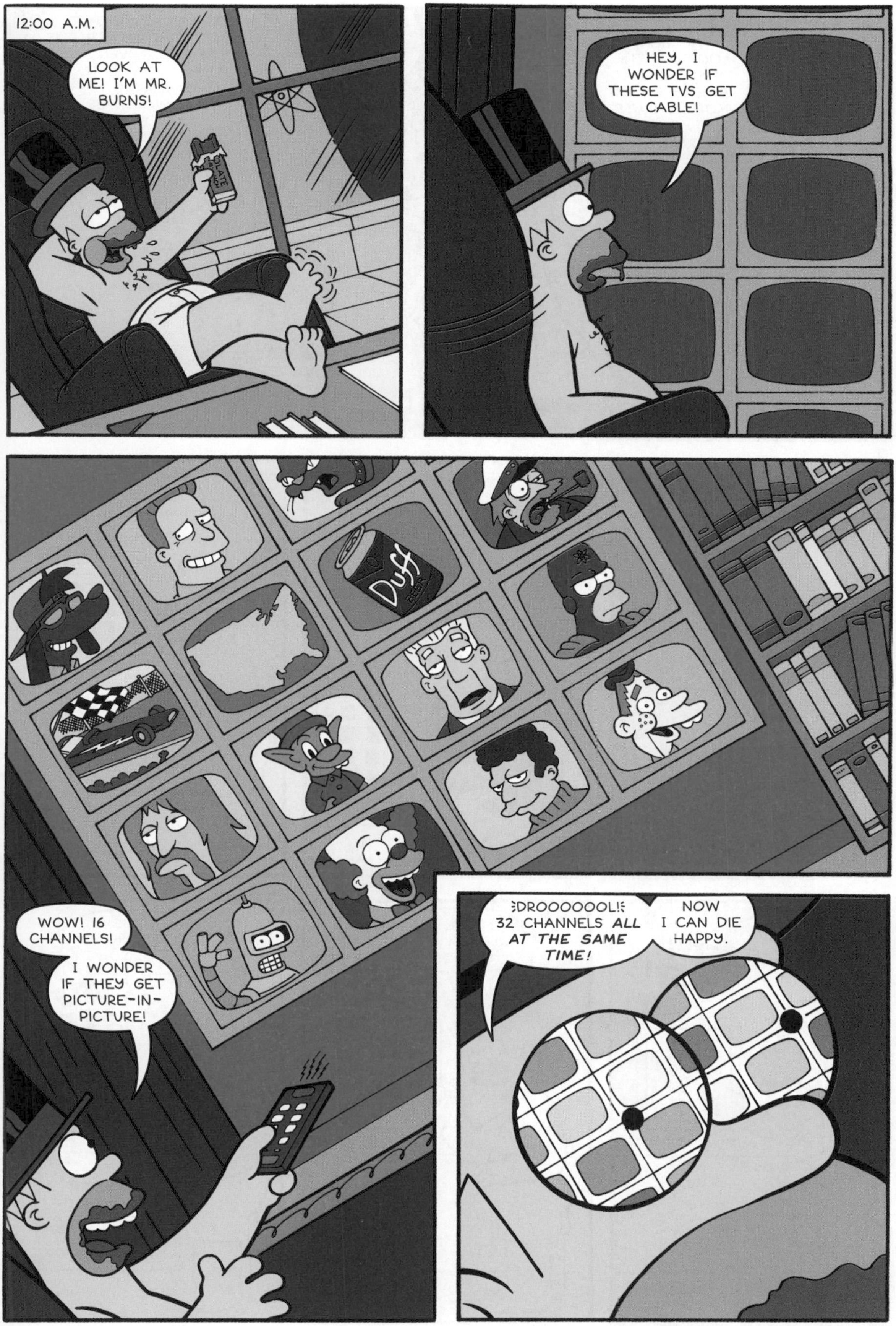
12:00 A.M.
LOOK AT ME! I'M MR. BURNS!
HEY, I WONDER IF THESE TVS GET CABLE!
Duff BEER
WOW! 16 CHANNELS!
I WONDER IF THEY GET PICTURE-IN-PICTURE!
DROOOOOOL!
32 CHANNELS ALL AT THE SAME TIME!
NOW I CAN DIE HAPPY.

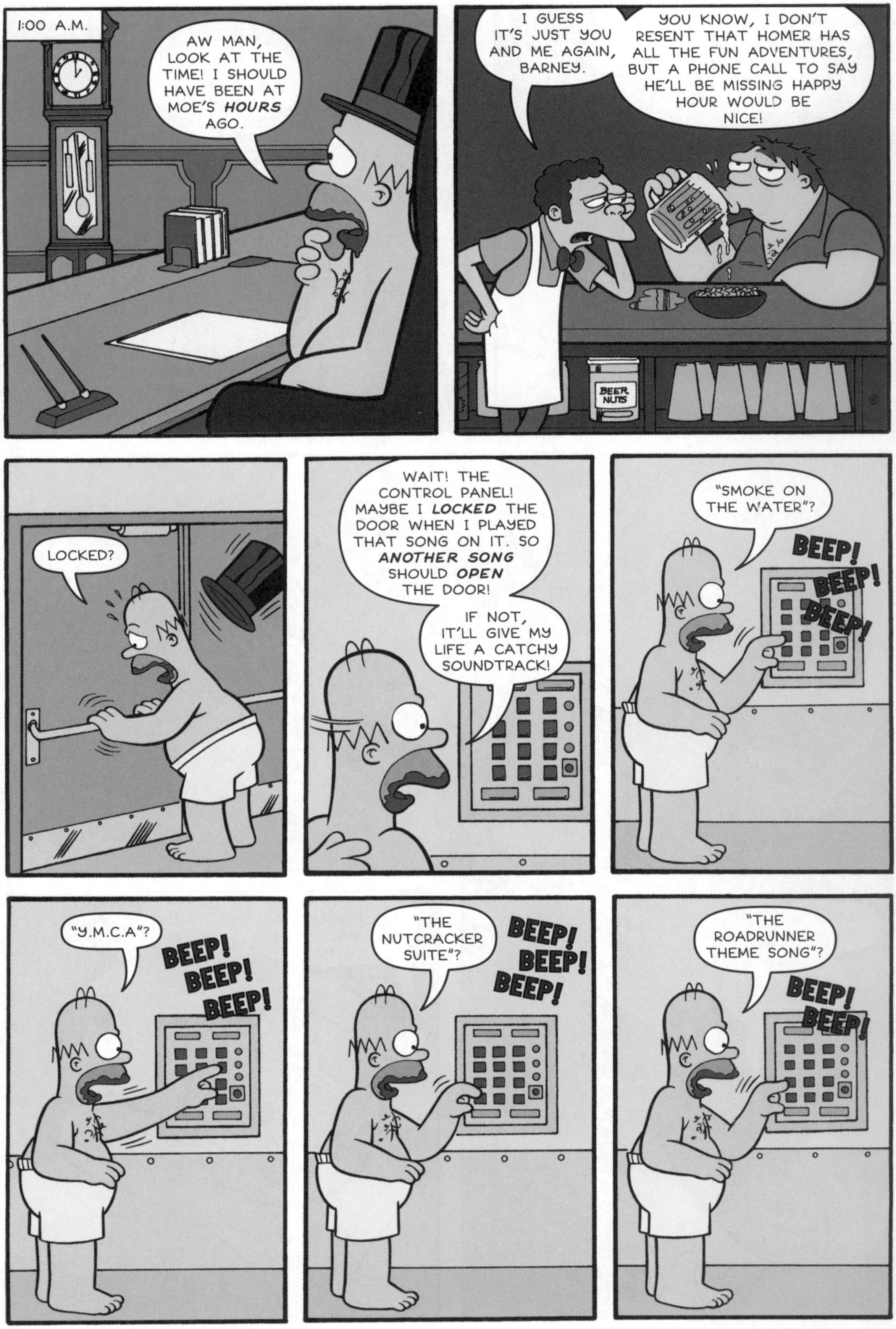
1:00 A.M.
AW MAN, LOOK AT THE TIME! I SHOULD HAVE BEEN AT MOE'S HOURS AGO.
I GUESS IT'S JUST YOU AND ME AGAIN, BARNEY.
YOU KNOW, I DON'T RESENT THAT HOMER HAS ALL THE FUN ADVENTURES, BUT A PHONE CALL TO SAY HE'LL BE MISSING HAPPY HOUR WOULD BE NICE!
BEER NUTS
LOCKED?
WAIT! THE CONTROL PANEL! MAYBE I LOCKED THE DOOR WHEN I PLAYED THAT SONG ON IT. SO ANOTHER SONG SHOULD OPEN THE DOOR!
IF NOT, IT'LL GIVE MY LIFE A CATCHY SOUNDTRACK!
"SMOKE ON THE WATER"?
BEEP! BEEP! BEEP!
"Y.M.C.A"?
BEEP! BEEP! BEEP!
"THE NUTCRACKER SUITE"?
BEEP! BEEP! BEEP!
"THE ROADRUNNER THEME SONG"?
BEEP! BEEP!

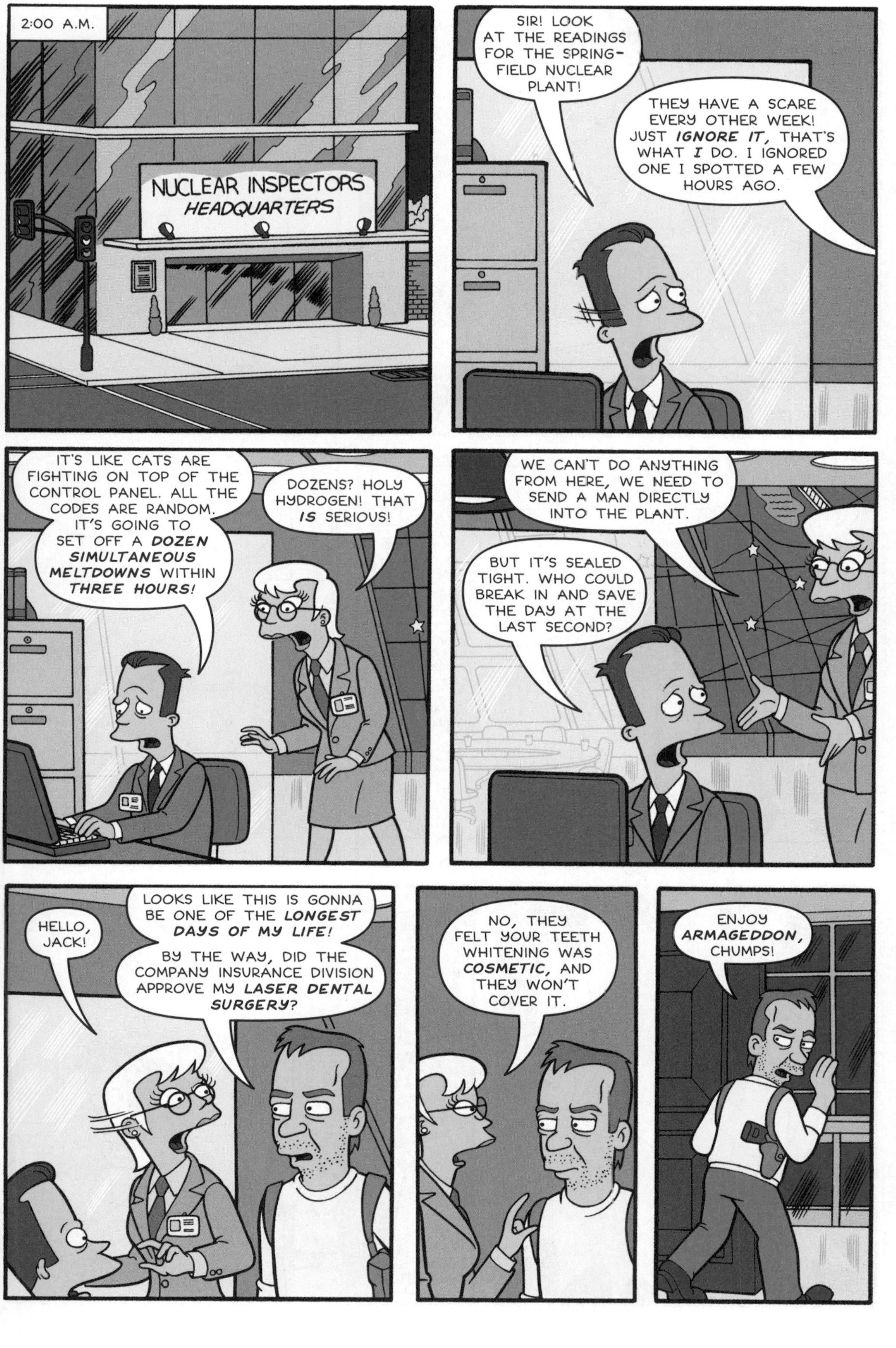
2:00 A.M.
NUCLEAR INSPECTORS HEADQUARTERS
SIR! LOOK AT THE READINGS FOR THE SPRING-FIELD NUCLEAR PLANT!
THEY HAVE A SCARE EVERY OTHER WEEK! JUST IGNORE IT, THAT'S WHAT I DO. I IGNORED ONE I SPOTTED A FEW HOURS AGO.
IT'S LIKE CATS ARE FIGHTING ON TOP OF THE CONTROL PANEL. ALL THE CODES ARE RANDOM. IT'S GOING TO SET OFF A DOZEN SIMULTANEOUS MELTDOWNS WITHIN THREE HOURS!
DOZENS? HOLY HYDROGEN! THAT IS SERIOUS!
WE CAN'T DO ANYTHING FROM HERE, WE NEED TO SEND A MAN DIRECTLY INTO THE PLANT.
BUT IT'S SEALED TIGHT. WHO COULD BREAK IN AND SAVE THE DAY AT THE LAST SECOND?
HELLO, JACK!
LOOKS LIKE THIS IS GONNA BE ONE OF THE LONGEST DAYS OF MY LIFE!
BY THE WAY, DID THE COMPANY INSURANCE DIVISION APPROVE MY LASER DENTAL SURGERY?
NO, THEY FELT YOUR TEETH WHITENING WAS COSMETIC, AND THEY WON'T COVER IT.
ENJOY ARMAGEDDON, CHUMPS!

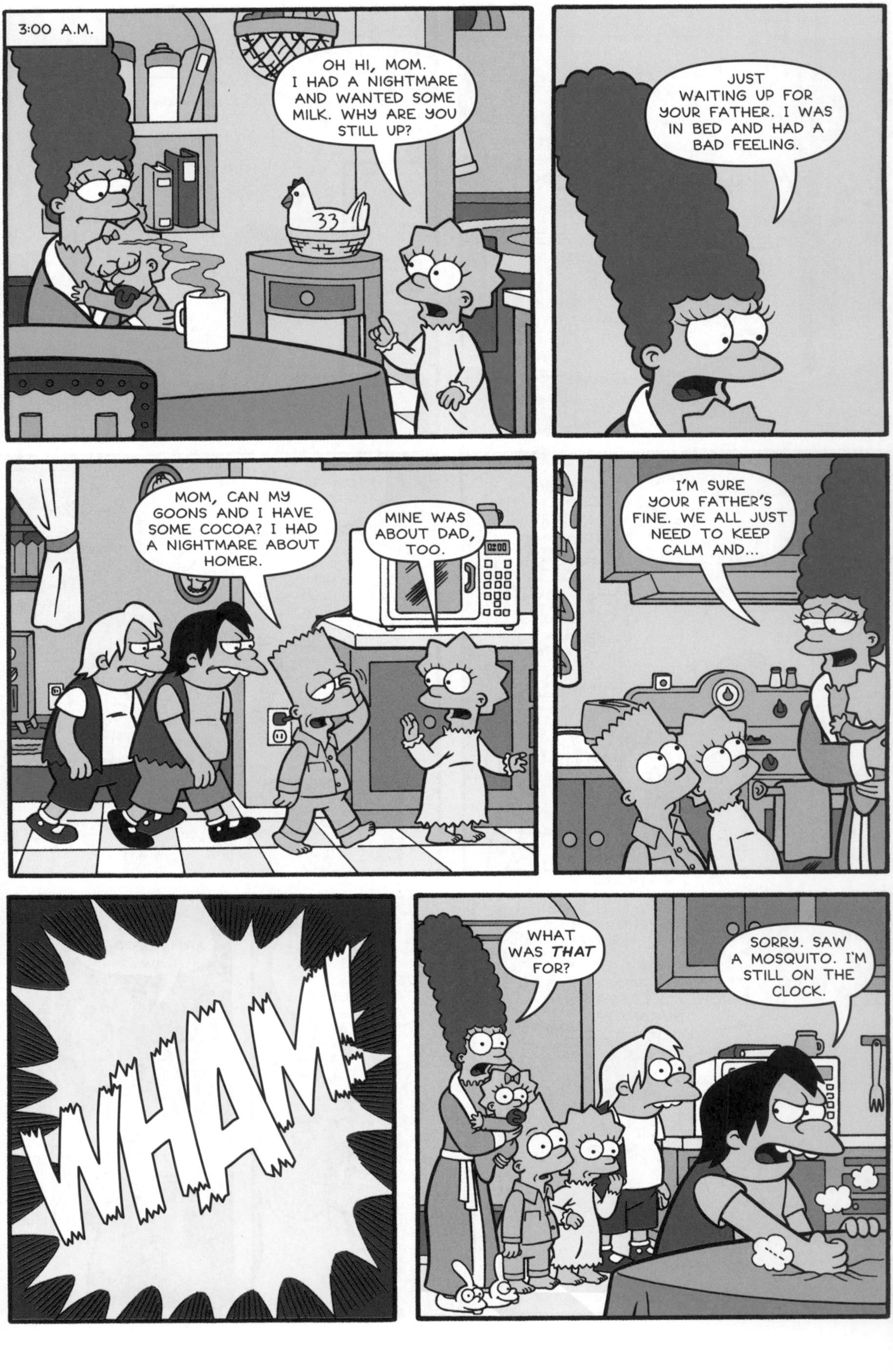
3:00 A.M.
OH HI, MOM. I HAD A NIGHTMARE AND WANTED SOME MILK. WHY ARE YOU STILL UP?
33
JUST WAITING UP FOR YOUR FATHER. I WAS IN BED AND HAD A BAD FEELING.
MOM, CAN MY GOONS AND I HAVE SOME COCOA? I HAD A NIGHTMARE ABOUT HOMER.
MINE WAS ABOUT DAD, TOO.
I'M SURE YOUR FATHER'S FINE. WE ALL JUST NEED TO KEEP CALM AND...
WHAM!
WHAT WAS *THAT* FOR?
SORRY. SAW A MOSQUITO. I'M STILL ON THE CLOCK.

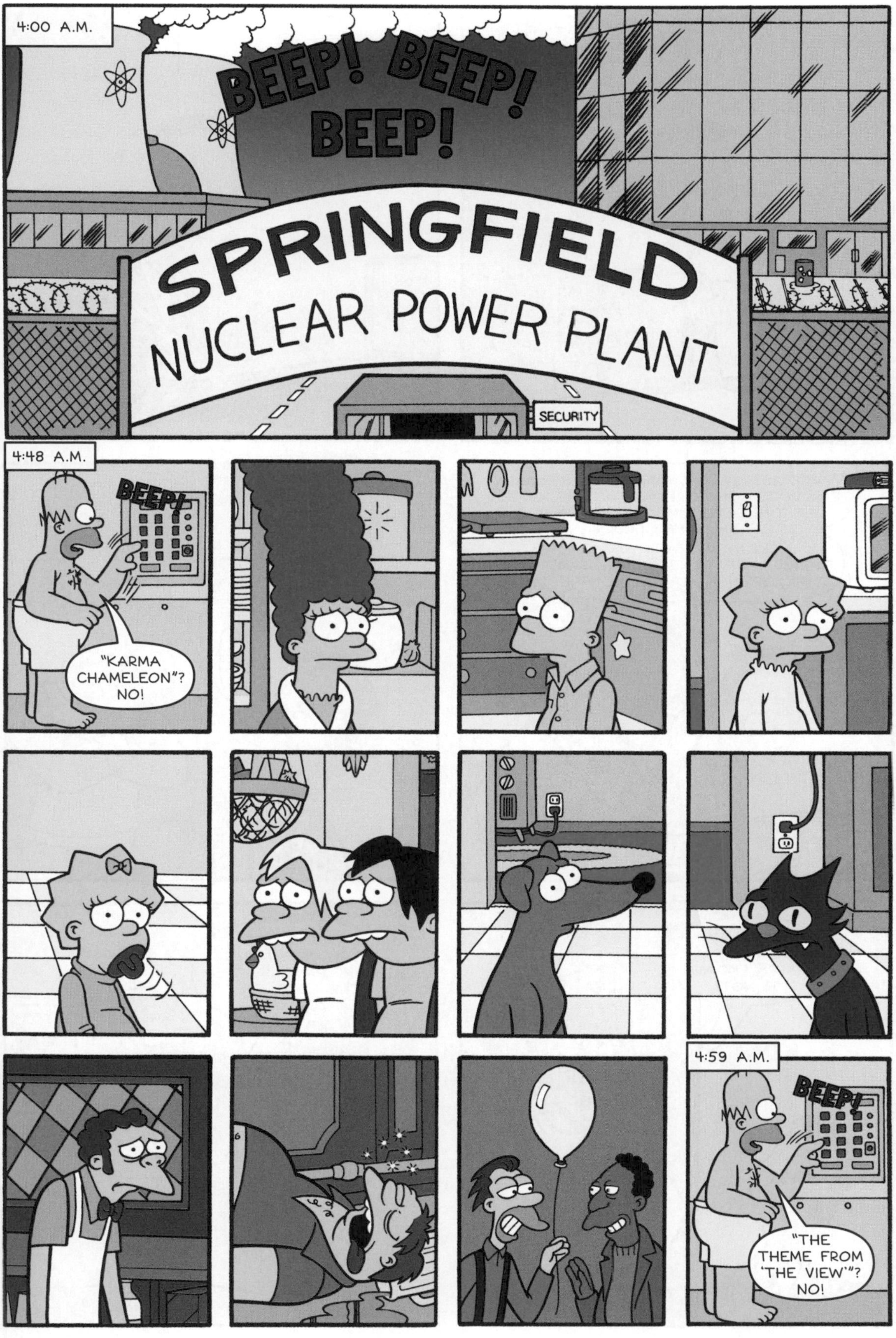
4:00 A.M.
BEEP! BEEP! BEEP!
SPRINGFIELD
NUCLEAR POWER PLANT
SECURITY
4:48 A.M.
BEEP!
"KARMA CHAMELEON"? NO!
4:59 A.M.
BEEP!
"THE THEME FROM 'THE VIEW'"? NO!

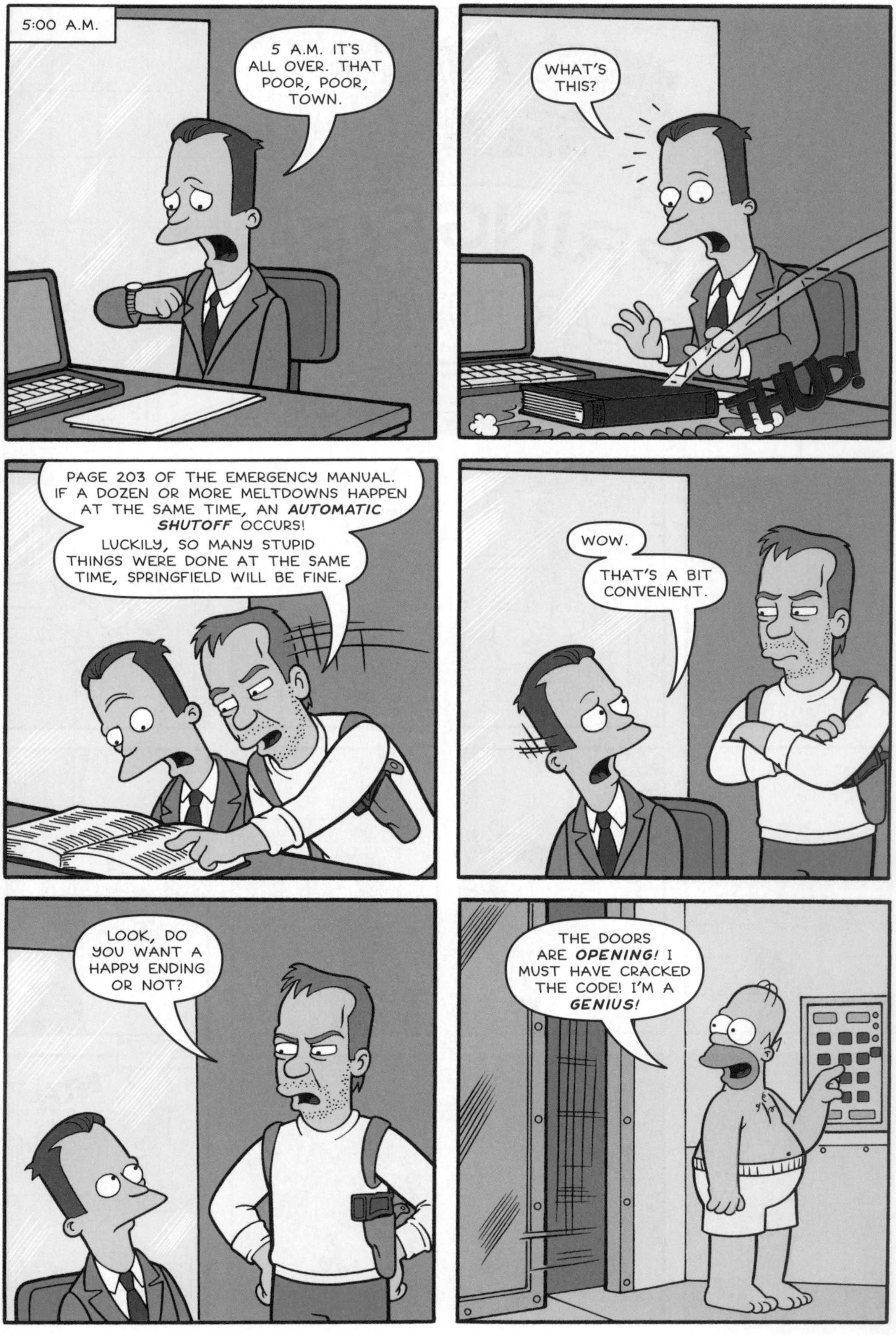
5:00 A.M.
5 A.M. IT'S ALL OVER. THAT POOR, POOR, TOWN.
WHAT'S THIS?
THUD!
PAGE 203 OF THE EMERGENCY MANUAL. IF A DOZEN OR MORE MELTDOWNS HAPPEN AT THE SAME TIME, AN AUTOMATIC SHUTOFF OCCURS!
LUCKILY, SO MANY STUPID THINGS WERE DONE AT THE SAME TIME, SPRINGFIELD WILL BE FINE.
WOW.
THAT'S A BIT CONVENIENT.
LOOK, DO YOU WANT A HAPPY ENDING OR NOT?
THE DOORS ARE OPENING! I MUST HAVE CRACKED THE CODE! I'M A GENIUS!

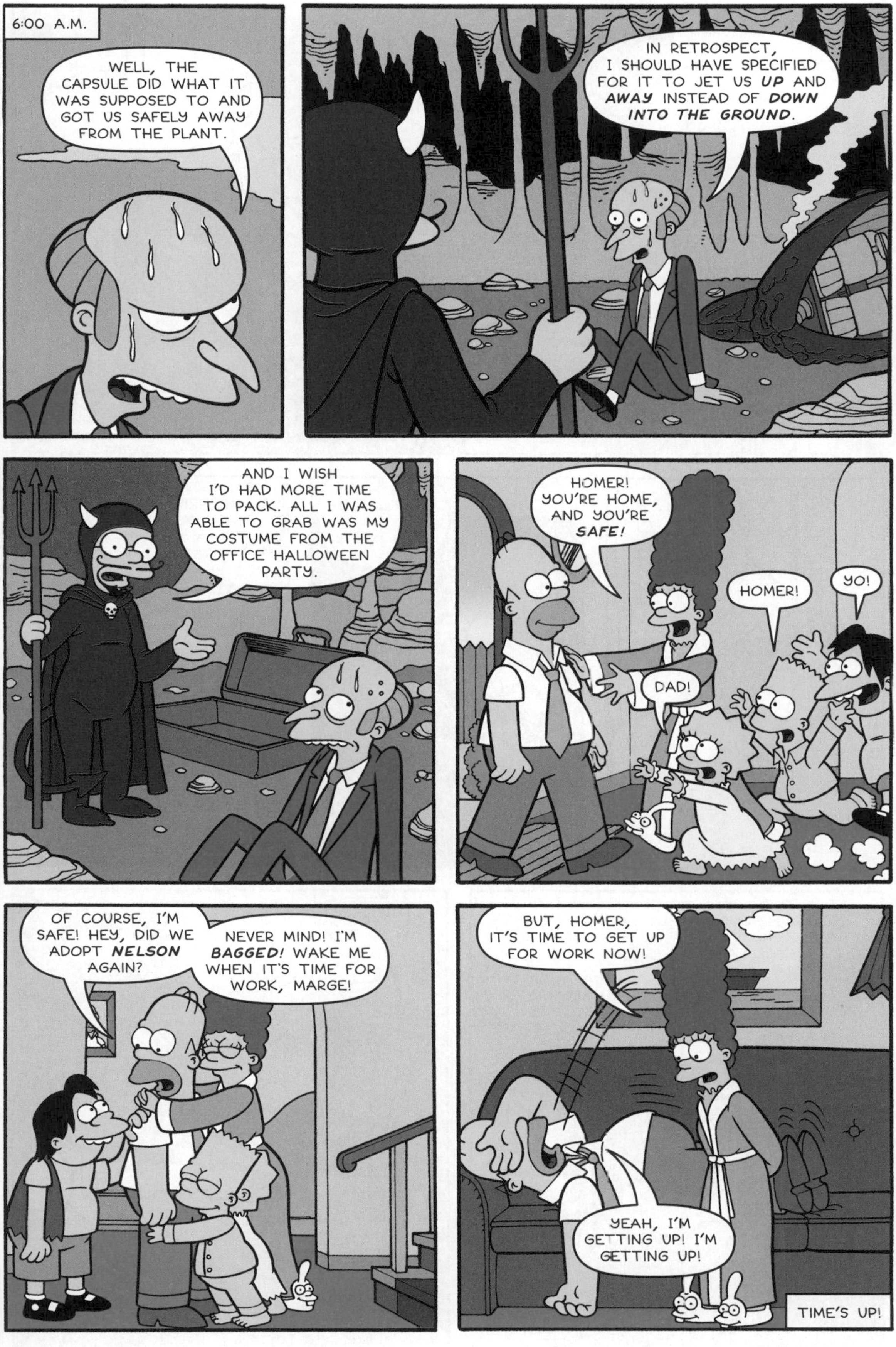
6:00 A.M.
WELL, THE CAPSULE DID WHAT IT WAS SUPPOSED TO AND GOT US SAFELY AWAY FROM THE PLANT.
IN RETROSPECT, I SHOULD HAVE SPECIFIED FOR IT TO JET US **UP** AND **AWAY** INSTEAD OF **DOWN INTO THE GROUND**.
AND I WISH I'D HAD MORE TIME TO PACK. ALL I WAS ABLE TO GRAB WAS MY COSTUME FROM THE OFFICE HALLOWEEN PARTY.
HOMER! YOU'RE HOME, AND YOU'RE **SAFE!**
HOMER!
YO!
DAD!
OF COURSE, I'M SAFE! HEY, DID WE ADOPT **NELSON** AGAIN?
NEVER MIND! I'M **BAGGED!** WAKE ME WHEN IT'S TIME FOR WORK, MARGE!
BUT, HOMER, IT'S TIME TO GET UP FOR WORK NOW!
YEAH, I'M GETTING UP! I'M GETTING UP!
TIME'S UP!

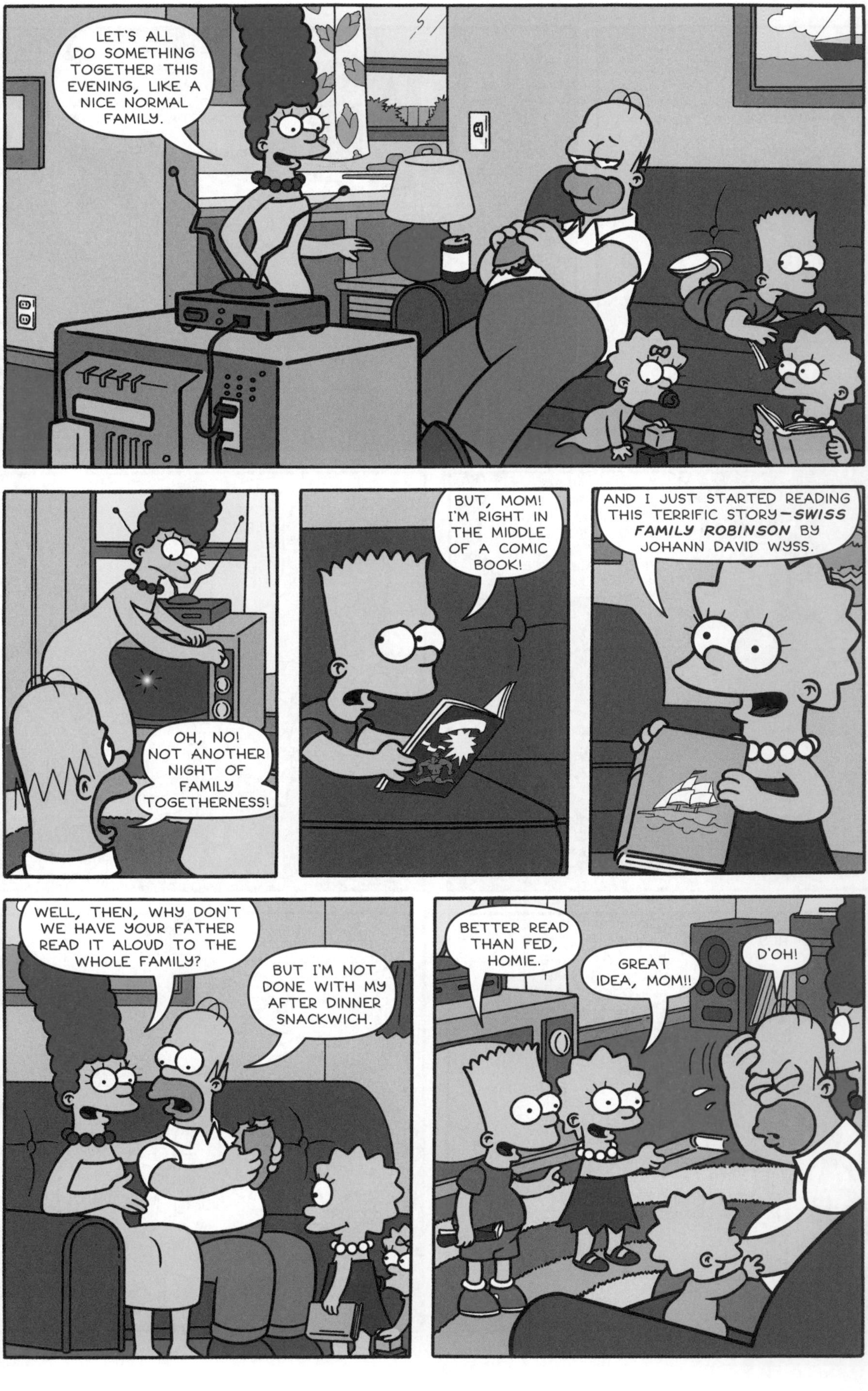
LET'S ALL DO SOMETHING TOGETHER THIS EVENING, LIKE A NICE NORMAL FAMILY.
OH, NO! NOT ANOTHER NIGHT OF FAMILY TOGETHERNESS!
BUT, MOM! I'M RIGHT IN THE MIDDLE OF A COMIC BOOK!
AND I JUST STARTED READING THIS TERRIFIC STORY—*SWISS FAMILY ROBINSON* BY JOHANN DAVID WYSS.
WELL, THEN, WHY DON'T WE HAVE YOUR FATHER READ IT ALOUD TO THE WHOLE FAMILY?
BUT I'M NOT DONE WITH MY AFTER DINNER SNACKWICH.
BETTER READ THAN FED, HOMIE.
GREAT IDEA, MOM!!
D'OH!

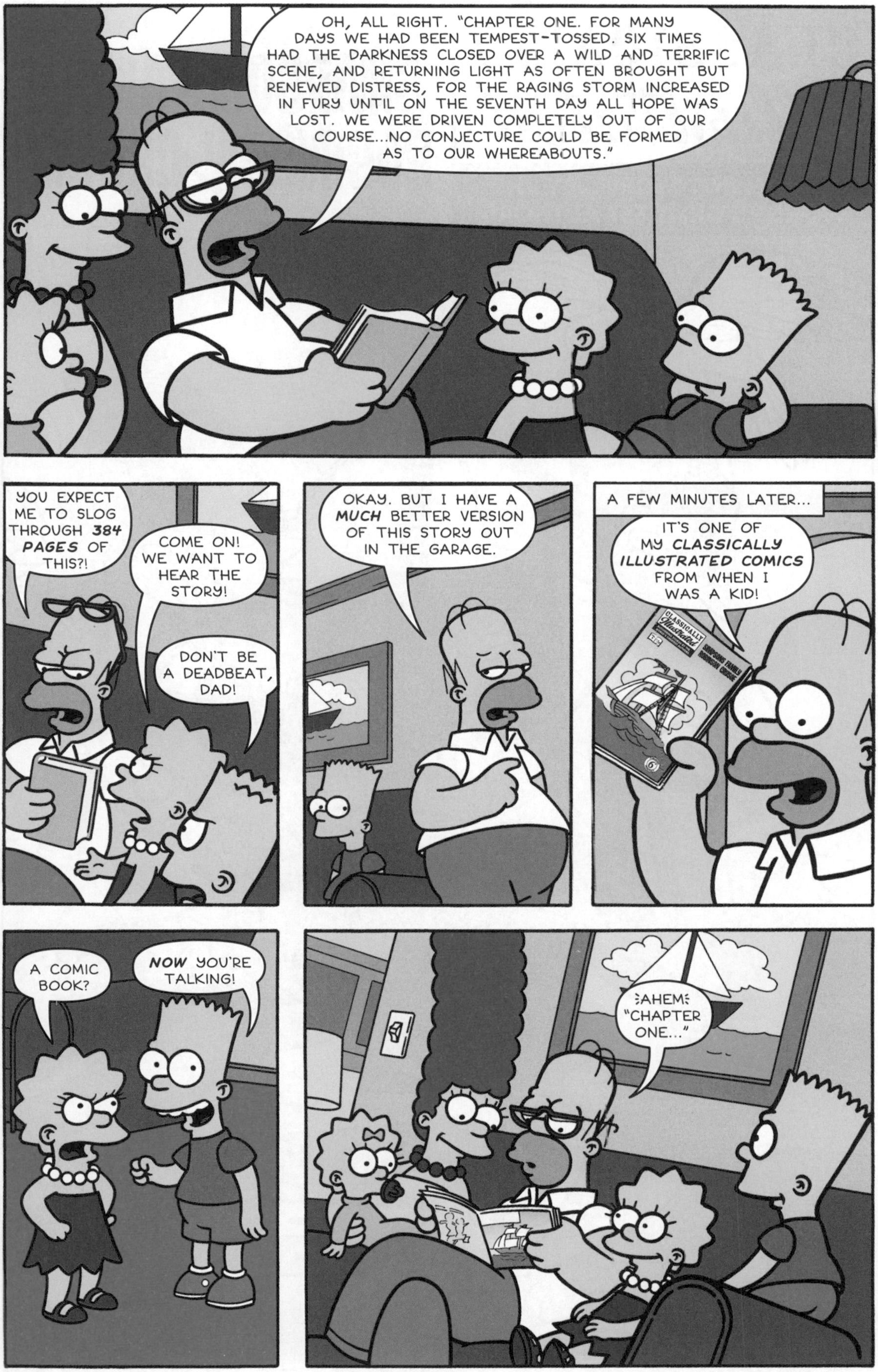

OH, ALL RIGHT. "CHAPTER ONE. FOR MANY DAYS WE HAD BEEN TEMPEST-TOSSED. SIX TIMES HAD THE DARKNESS CLOSED OVER A WILD AND TERRIFIC SCENE, AND RETURNING LIGHT AS OFTEN BROUGHT BUT RENEWED DISTRESS, FOR THE RAGING STORM INCREASED IN FURY UNTIL ON THE SEVENTH DAY ALL HOPE WAS LOST. WE WERE DRIVEN COMPLETELY OUT OF OUR COURSE...NO CONJECTURE COULD BE FORMED AS TO OUR WHEREABOUTS."
YOU EXPECT ME TO SLOG THROUGH **384 PAGES** OF THIS?!
COME ON! WE WANT TO HEAR THE STORY!
DON'T BE A DEADBEAT, DAD!
OKAY. BUT I HAVE A **MUCH** BETTER VERSION OF THIS STORY OUT IN THE GARAGE.
A FEW MINUTES LATER...
IT'S ONE OF MY **CLASSICALLY ILLUSTRATED COMICS** FROM WHEN I WAS A KID!
A COMIC BOOK?
NOW YOU'RE TALKING!
AHEM "CHAPTER ONE..."

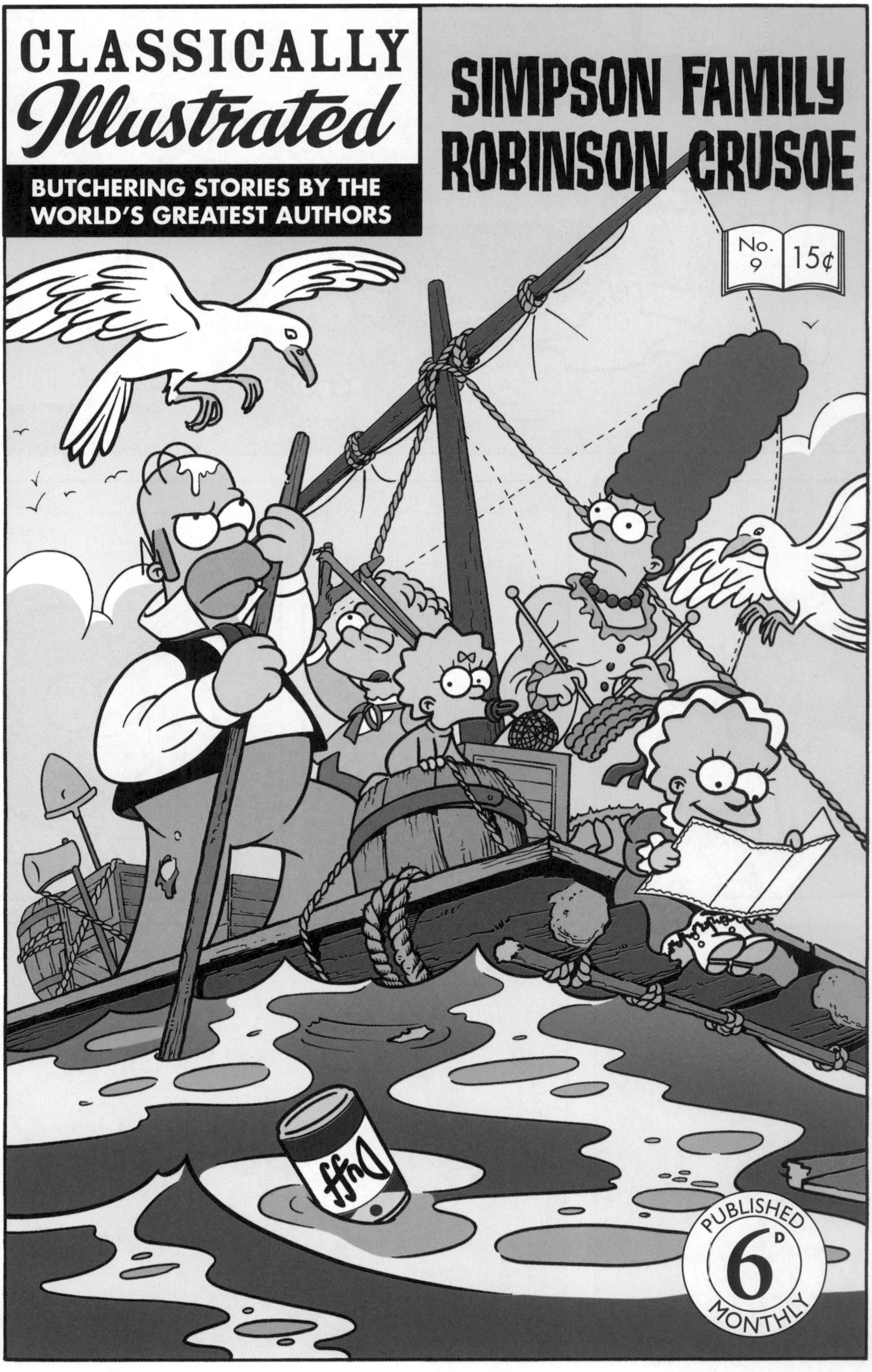
CLASSICALLY Illustrated
BUTCHERING STORIES BY THE WORLD'S GREATEST AUTHORS
SIMPSON FAMILY ROBINSON CRUSOE
No. 9
15¢
Duff
PUBLISHED 6D MONTHLY

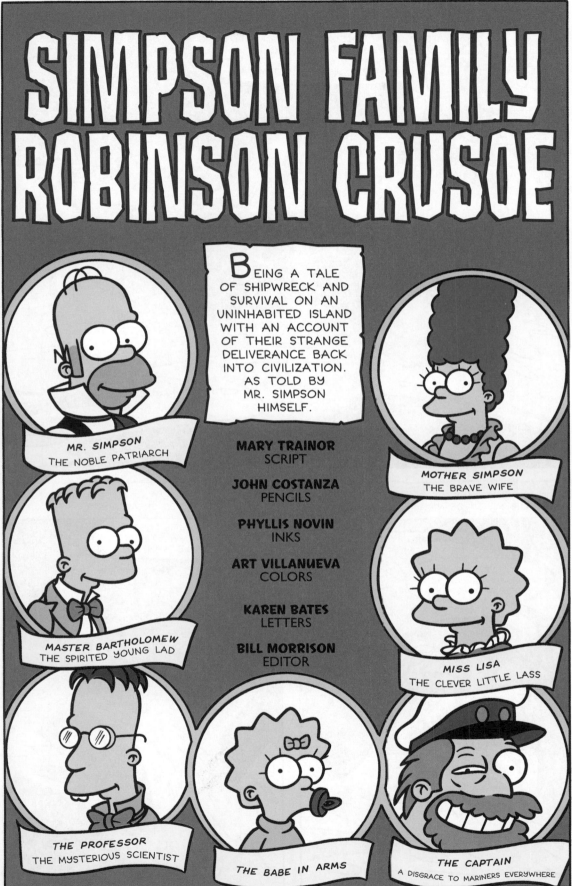

MATT GROENING presents

SIMPSON FAMILY ROBINSON CRUSOE

Being a tale of shipwreck and survival on an uninhabited island with an account of their strange deliverance back into civilization. As told by Mr. Simpson himself.

MR. SIMPSON
THE NOBLE PATRIARCH

MARY TRAINOR
SCRIPT

JOHN COSTANZA
PENCILS

PHYLLIS NOVIN
INKS

ART VILLANUEVA
COLORS

KAREN BATES
LETTERS

BILL MORRISON
EDITOR

MOTHER SIMPSON
THE BRAVE WIFE

MASTER BARTHOLOMEW
THE SPIRITED YOUNG LAD

MISS LISA
THE CLEVER LITTLE LASS

THE PROFESSOR
THE MYSTERIOUS SCIENTIST

THE BABE IN ARMS

THE CAPTAIN
A DISGRACE TO MARINERS EVERYWHERE

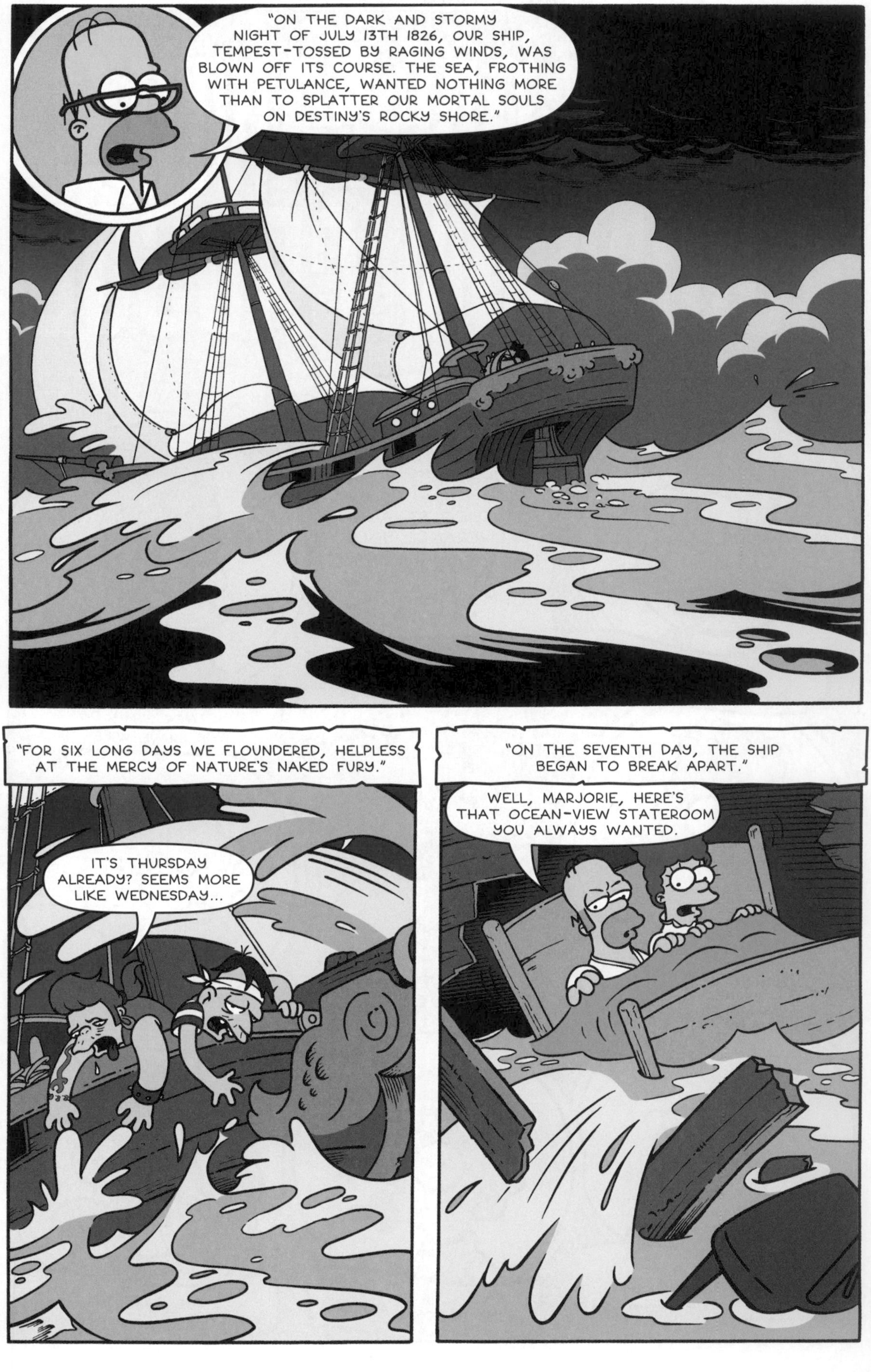
"ON THE DARK AND STORMY NIGHT OF JULY 13TH 1826, OUR SHIP, TEMPEST-TOSSED BY RAGING WINDS, WAS BLOWN OFF ITS COURSE. THE SEA, FROTHING WITH PETULANCE, WANTED NOTHING MORE THAN TO SPLATTER OUR MORTAL SOULS ON DESTINY'S ROCKY SHORE."
"FOR SIX LONG DAYS WE FLOUNDERED, HELPLESS AT THE MERCY OF NATURE'S NAKED FURY."
IT'S THURSDAY ALREADY? SEEMS MORE LIKE WEDNESDAY...
"ON THE SEVENTH DAY, THE SHIP BEGAN TO BREAK APART."
WELL, MARJORIE, HERE'S THAT OCEAN-VIEW STATEROOM YOU ALWAYS WANTED.

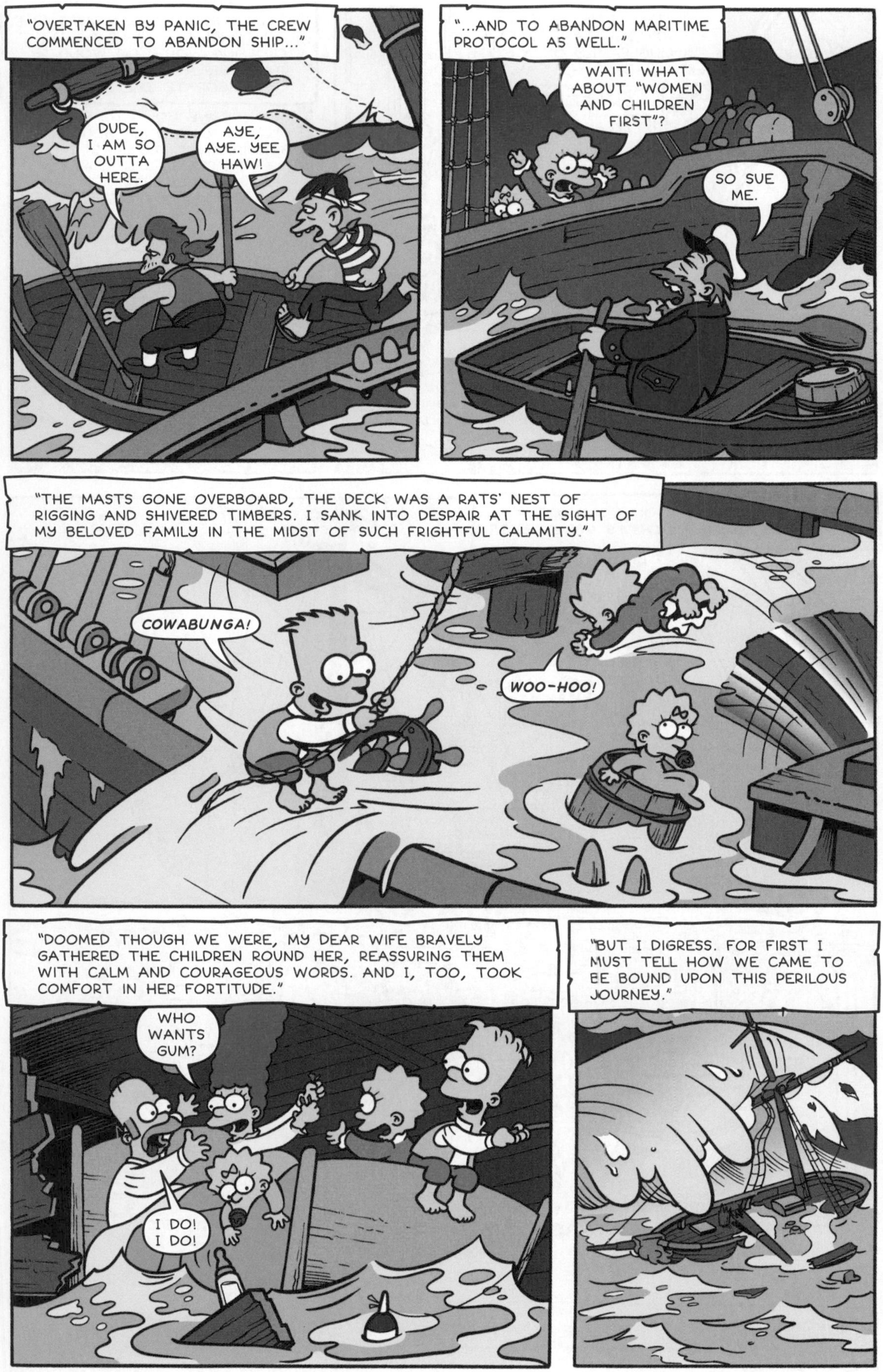
"OVERTAKEN BY PANIC, THE CREW COMMENCED TO ABANDON SHIP..."
DUDE, I AM SO OUTTA HERE.
AYE, AYE. YEE HAW!
"...AND TO ABANDON MARITIME PROTOCOL AS WELL."
WAIT! WHAT ABOUT "WOMEN AND CHILDREN FIRST"?
SO SUE ME.
"THE MASTS GONE OVERBOARD, THE DECK WAS A RATS' NEST OF RIGGING AND SHIVERED TIMBERS. I SANK INTO DESPAIR AT THE SIGHT OF MY BELOVED FAMILY IN THE MIDST OF SUCH FRIGHTFUL CALAMITY."
COWABUNGA!
WOO-HOO!
"DOOMED THOUGH WE WERE, MY DEAR WIFE BRAVELY GATHERED THE CHILDREN ROUND HER, REASSURING THEM WITH CALM AND COURAGEOUS WORDS. AND I, TOO, TOOK COMFORT IN HER FORTITUDE."
WHO WANTS GUM?
I DO! I DO!
"BUT I DIGRESS. FOR FIRST I MUST TELL HOW WE CAME TO BE BOUND UPON THIS PERILOUS JOURNEY."

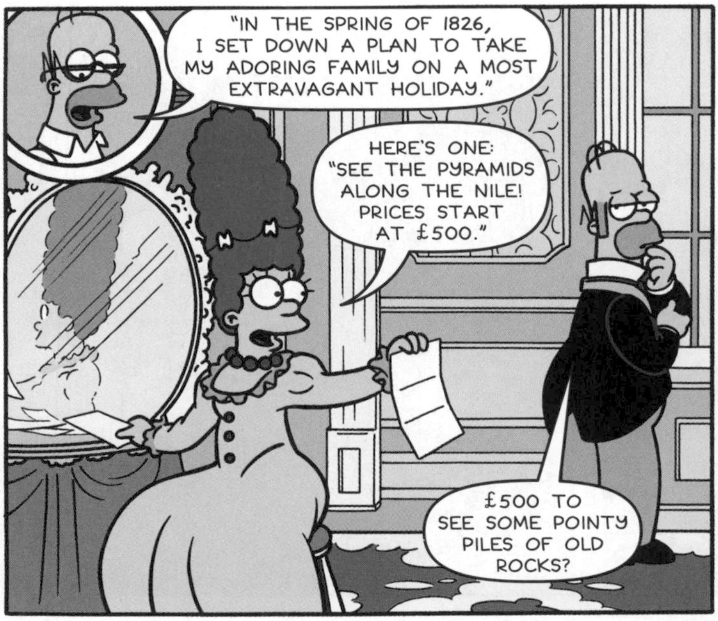
"IN THE SPRING OF 1826, I SET DOWN A PLAN TO TAKE MY ADORING FAMILY ON A MOST EXTRAVAGANT HOLIDAY."
HERE'S ONE: "SEE THE PYRAMIDS ALONG THE NILE! PRICES START AT £500."
£500 TO SEE SOME POINTY PILES OF OLD ROCKS?

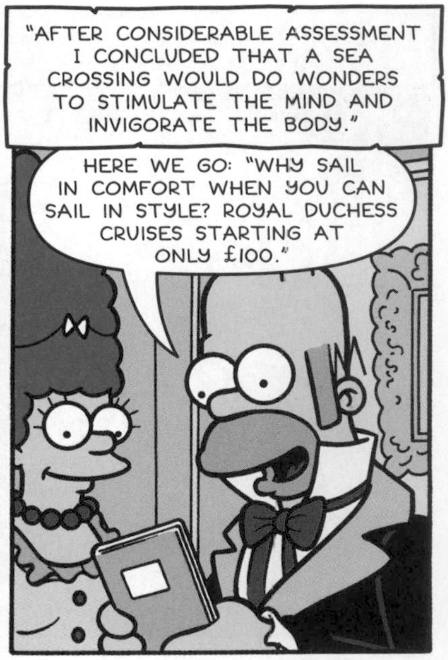
"AFTER CONSIDERABLE ASSESSMENT I CONCLUDED THAT A SEA CROSSING WOULD DO WONDERS TO STIMULATE THE MIND AND INVIGORATE THE BODY."
HERE WE GO: "WHY SAIL IN COMFORT WHEN YOU CAN SAIL IN STYLE? ROYAL DUCHESS CRUISES STARTING AT ONLY £100."

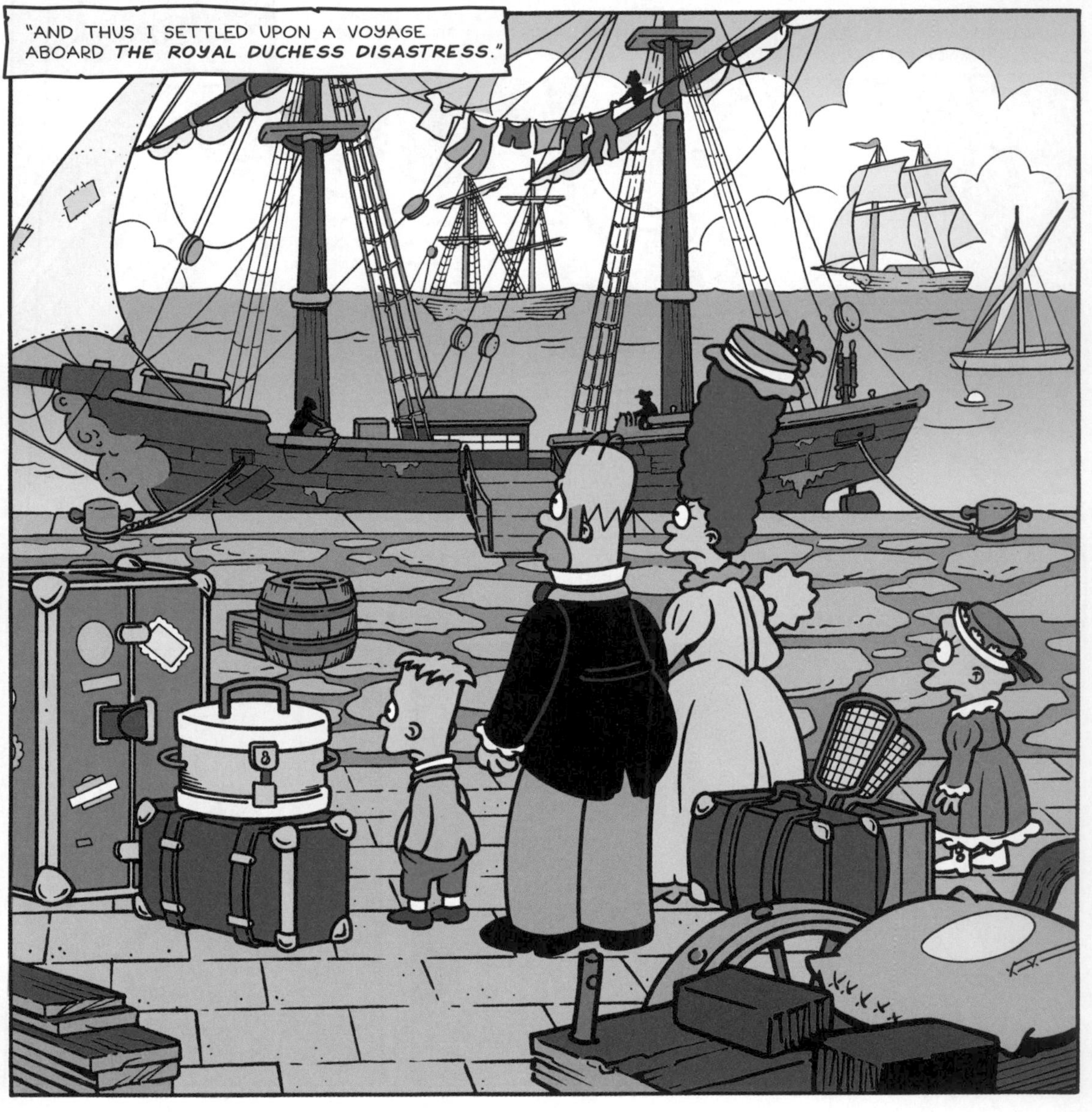
"AND THUS I SETTLED UPON A VOYAGE ABOARD ***THE ROYAL DUCHESS DISASTRESS***."

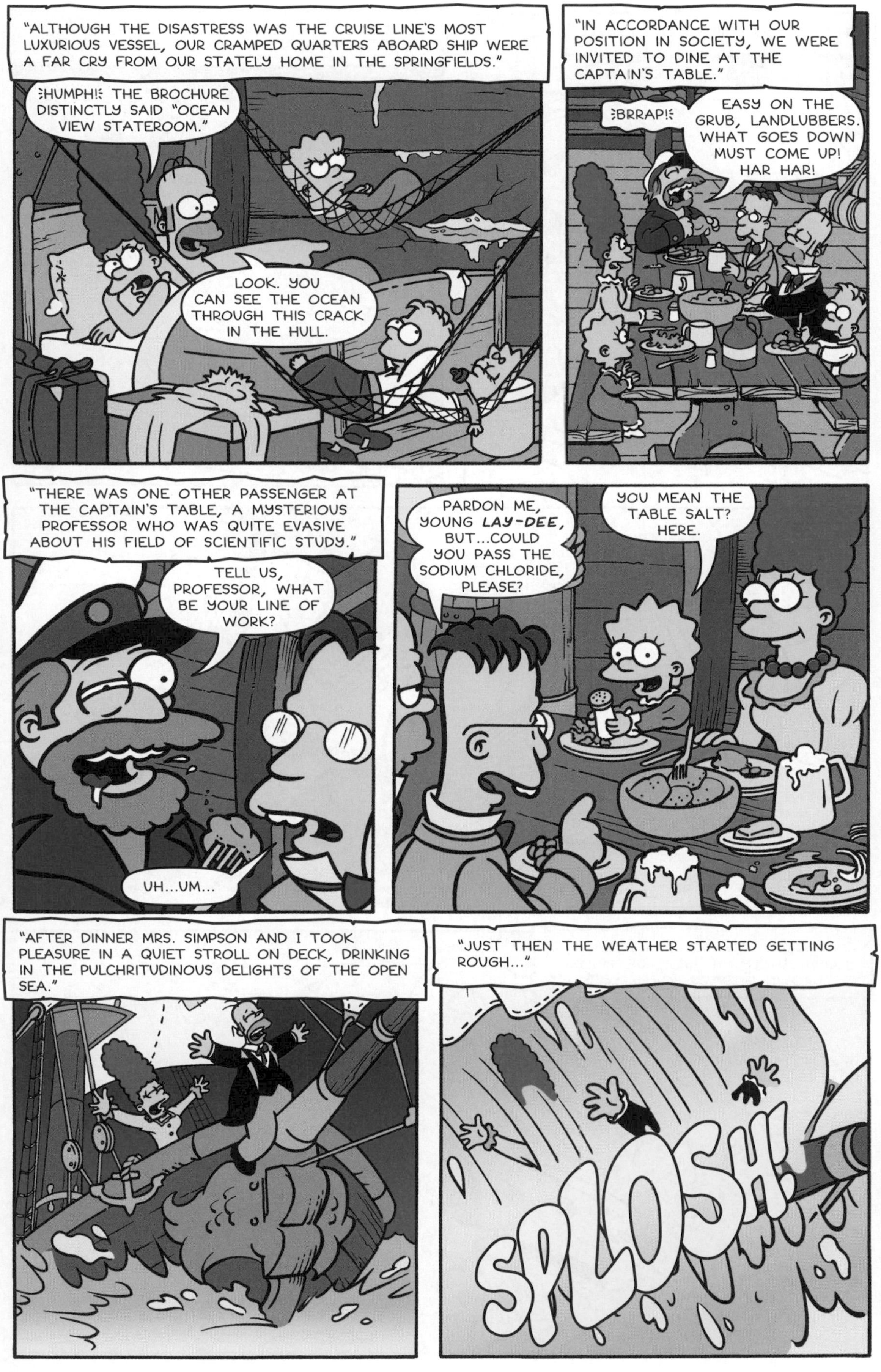
"ALTHOUGH THE DISASTRESS WAS THE CRUISE LINE'S MOST LUXURIOUS VESSEL, OUR CRAMPED QUARTERS ABOARD SHIP WERE A FAR CRY FROM OUR STATELY HOME IN THE SPRINGFIELDS."
HUMPH! THE BROCHURE DISTINCTLY SAID "OCEAN VIEW STATEROOM."
LOOK. YOU CAN SEE THE OCEAN THROUGH THIS CRACK IN THE HULL.
"IN ACCORDANCE WITH OUR POSITION IN SOCIETY, WE WERE INVITED TO DINE AT THE CAPTAIN'S TABLE."
BRRAP!
EASY ON THE GRUB, LANDLUBBERS. WHAT GOES DOWN MUST COME UP! HAR HAR!
"THERE WAS ONE OTHER PASSENGER AT THE CAPTAIN'S TABLE, A MYSTERIOUS PROFESSOR WHO WAS QUITE EVASIVE ABOUT HIS FIELD OF SCIENTIFIC STUDY."
TELL US, PROFESSOR, WHAT BE YOUR LINE OF WORK?
UH...UM...
PARDON ME, YOUNG ***LAY-DEE,*** BUT...COULD YOU PASS THE SODIUM CHLORIDE, PLEASE?
YOU MEAN THE TABLE SALT? HERE.
"AFTER DINNER MRS. SIMPSON AND I TOOK PLEASURE IN A QUIET STROLL ON DECK, DRINKING IN THE PULCHRITUDINOUS DELIGHTS OF THE OPEN SEA."
"JUST THEN THE WEATHER STARTED GETTING ROUGH..."
SPLOSH!

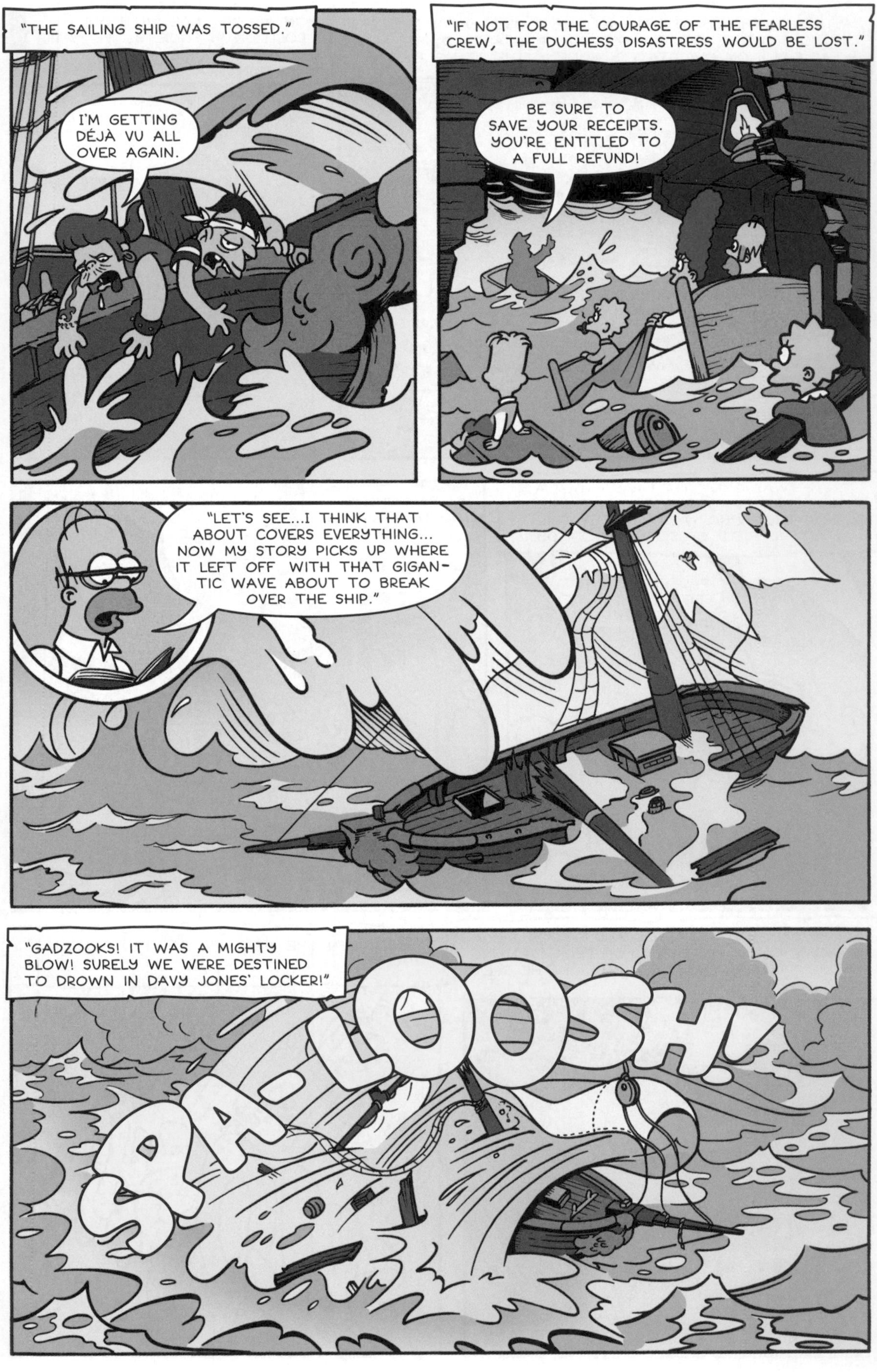
"THE SAILING SHIP WAS TOSSED."
I'M GETTING DÉJÀ VU ALL OVER AGAIN.
"IF NOT FOR THE COURAGE OF THE FEARLESS CREW, THE DUCHESS DISASTRESS WOULD BE LOST."
BE SURE TO SAVE YOUR RECEIPTS. YOU'RE ENTITLED TO A FULL REFUND!
"LET'S SEE...I THINK THAT ABOUT COVERS EVERYTHING... NOW MY STORY PICKS UP WHERE IT LEFT OFF WITH THAT GIGANTIC WAVE ABOUT TO BREAK OVER THE SHIP."
"GADZOOKS! IT WAS A MIGHTY BLOW! SURELY WE WERE DESTINED TO DROWN IN DAVY JONES' LOCKER!"
SPA-LOOSH!

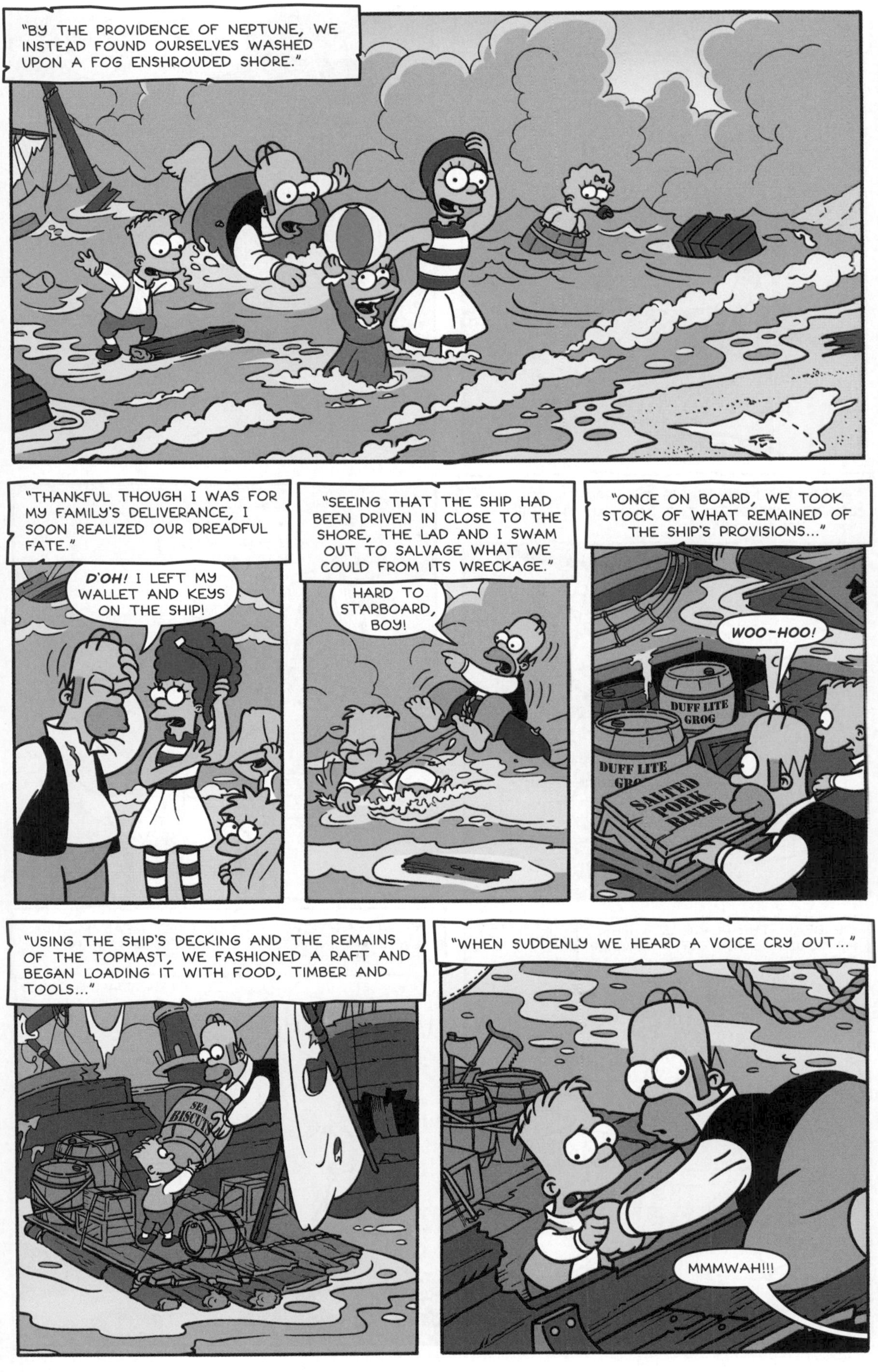
"BY THE PROVIDENCE OF NEPTUNE, WE INSTEAD FOUND OURSELVES WASHED UPON A FOG ENSHROUDED SHORE."
"THANKFUL THOUGH I WAS FOR MY FAMILY'S DELIVERANCE, I SOON REALIZED OUR DREADFUL FATE."
D'OH! I LEFT MY WALLET AND KEYS ON THE SHIP!
"SEEING THAT THE SHIP HAD BEEN DRIVEN IN CLOSE TO THE SHORE, THE LAD AND I SWAM OUT TO SALVAGE WHAT WE COULD FROM ITS WRECKAGE."
HARD TO STARBOARD, BOY!
"ONCE ON BOARD, WE TOOK STOCK OF WHAT REMAINED OF THE SHIP'S PROVISIONS..."
WOO-HOO!
DUFF LITE GROG
SALTED PORK RINDS
"USING THE SHIP'S DECKING AND THE REMAINS OF THE TOPMAST, WE FASHIONED A RAFT AND BEGAN LOADING IT WITH FOOD, TIMBER AND TOOLS..."
SEA BISCUITS
"WHEN SUDDENLY WE HEARD A VOICE CRY OUT..."
MMMWAH!!!

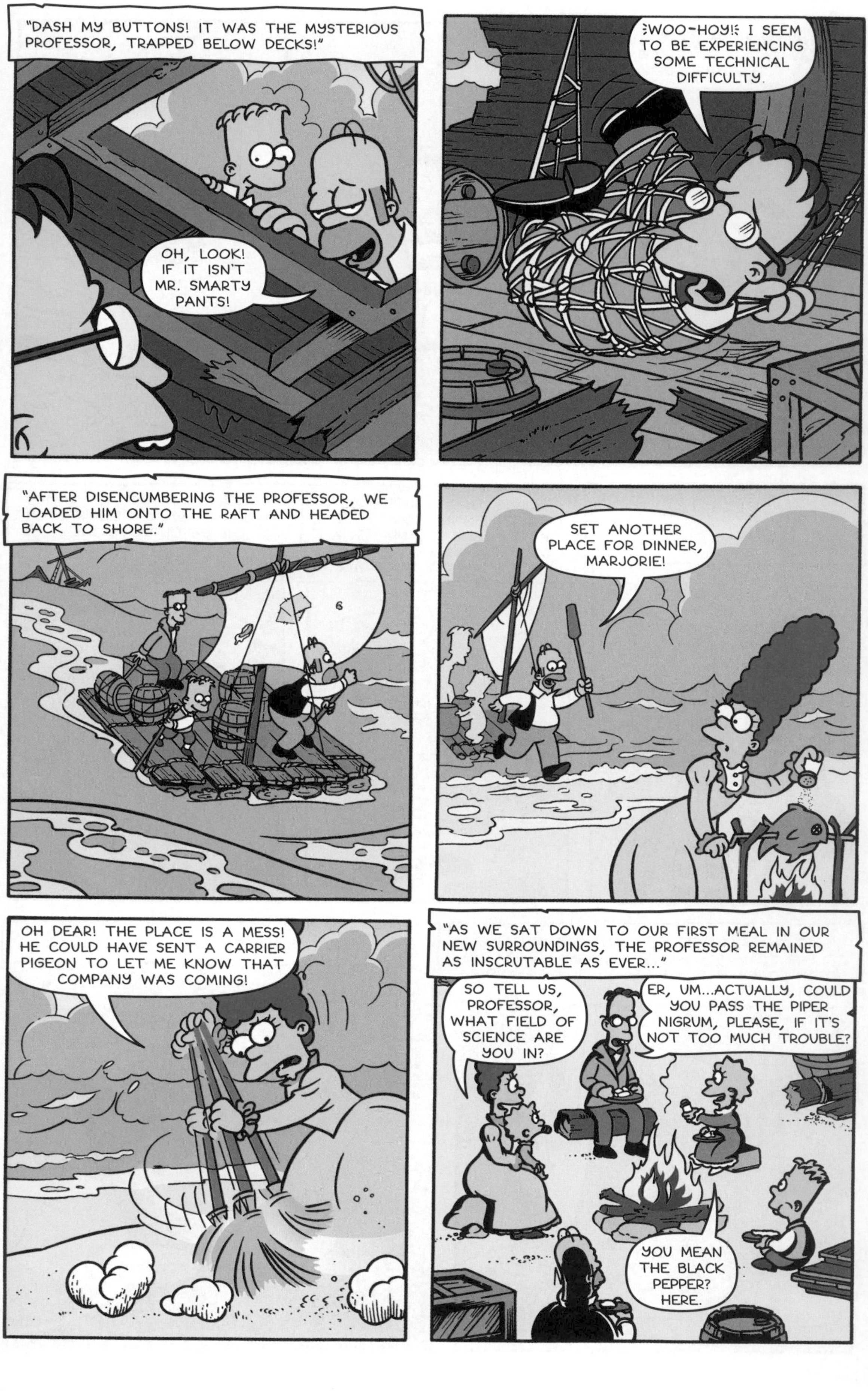
"DASH MY BUTTONS! IT WAS THE MYSTERIOUS PROFESSOR, TRAPPED BELOW DECKS!"
OH, LOOK! IF IT ISN'T MR. SMARTY PANTS!
WOO-HOO! I SEEM TO BE EXPERIENCING SOME TECHNICAL DIFFICULTY.
"AFTER DISENCUMBERING THE PROFESSOR, WE LOADED HIM ONTO THE RAFT AND HEADED BACK TO SHORE."
SET ANOTHER PLACE FOR DINNER, MARJORIE!
OH DEAR! THE PLACE IS A MESS! HE COULD HAVE SENT A CARRIER PIGEON TO LET ME KNOW THAT COMPANY WAS COMING!
"AS WE SAT DOWN TO OUR FIRST MEAL IN OUR NEW SURROUNDINGS, THE PROFESSOR REMAINED AS INSCRUTABLE AS EVER..."
SO TELL US, PROFESSOR, WHAT FIELD OF SCIENCE ARE YOU IN?
ER, UM...ACTUALLY, COULD YOU PASS THE PIPER NIGRUM, PLEASE, IF IT'S NOT TOO MUCH TROUBLE?
YOU MEAN THE BLACK PEPPER? HERE.

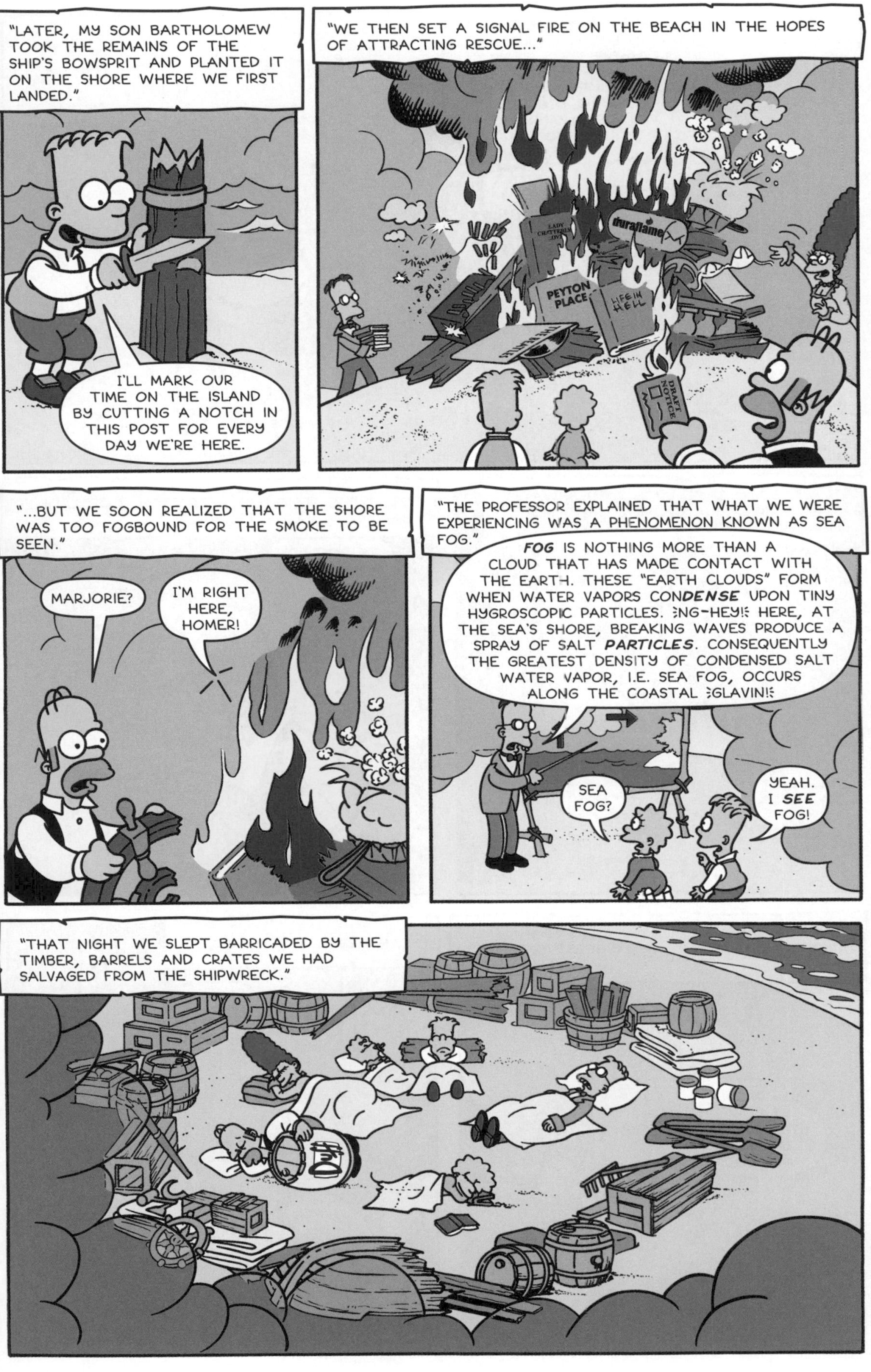

"LATER, MY SON BARTHOLOMEW TOOK THE REMAINS OF THE SHIP'S BOWSPRIT AND PLANTED IT ON THE SHORE WHERE WE FIRST LANDED."
I'LL MARK OUR TIME ON THE ISLAND BY CUTTING A NOTCH IN THIS POST FOR EVERY DAY WE'RE HERE.
"WE THEN SET A SIGNAL FIRE ON THE BEACH IN THE HOPES OF ATTRACTING RESCUE..."
duraflame
PEYTON PLACE
LIFE IN HELL
THE BEATLES
DRAFT NOTICE
"...BUT WE SOON REALIZED THAT THE SHORE WAS TOO FOGBOUND FOR THE SMOKE TO BE SEEN."
MARJORIE?
I'M RIGHT HERE, HOMER!
"THE PROFESSOR EXPLAINED THAT WHAT WE WERE EXPERIENCING WAS A PHENOMENON KNOWN AS SEA FOG."
FOG IS NOTHING MORE THAN A CLOUD THAT HAS MADE CONTACT WITH THE EARTH. THESE "EARTH CLOUDS" FORM WHEN WATER VAPORS CON*DENSE* UPON TINY HYGROSCOPIC PARTICLES. NG-HEY! HERE, AT THE SEA'S SHORE, BREAKING WAVES PRODUCE A SPRAY OF SALT *PARTICLES*. CONSEQUENTLY THE GREATEST DENSITY OF CONDENSED SALT WATER VAPOR, I.E. SEA FOG, OCCURS ALONG THE COASTAL GLAVIN!
SEA FOG?
YEAH. I *SEE* FOG!
"THAT NIGHT WE SLEPT BARRICADED BY THE TIMBER, BARRELS AND CRATES WE HAD SALVAGED FROM THE SHIPWRECK."

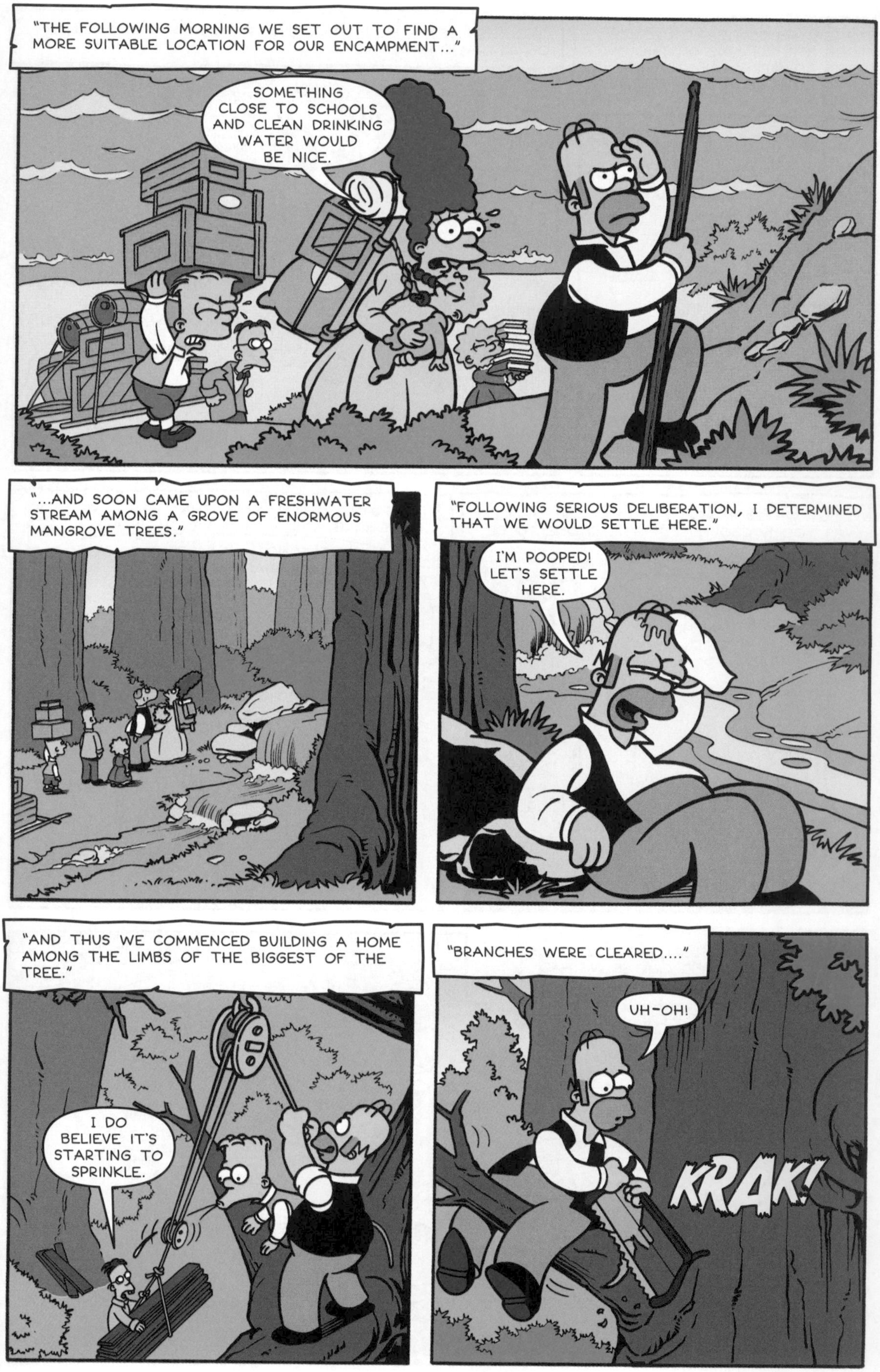
"THE FOLLOWING MORNING WE SET OUT TO FIND A MORE SUITABLE LOCATION FOR OUR ENCAMPMENT..."
SOMETHING CLOSE TO SCHOOLS AND CLEAN DRINKING WATER WOULD BE NICE.
"...AND SOON CAME UPON A FRESHWATER STREAM AMONG A GROVE OF ENORMOUS MANGROVE TREES."
"FOLLOWING SERIOUS DELIBERATION, I DETERMINED THAT WE WOULD SETTLE HERE."
I'M POOPED! LET'S SETTLE HERE.
"AND THUS WE COMMENCED BUILDING A HOME AMONG THE LIMBS OF THE BIGGEST OF THE TREE."
I DO BELIEVE IT'S STARTING TO SPRINKLE.
"BRANCHES WERE CLEARED...."
UH-OH!
KRAK!

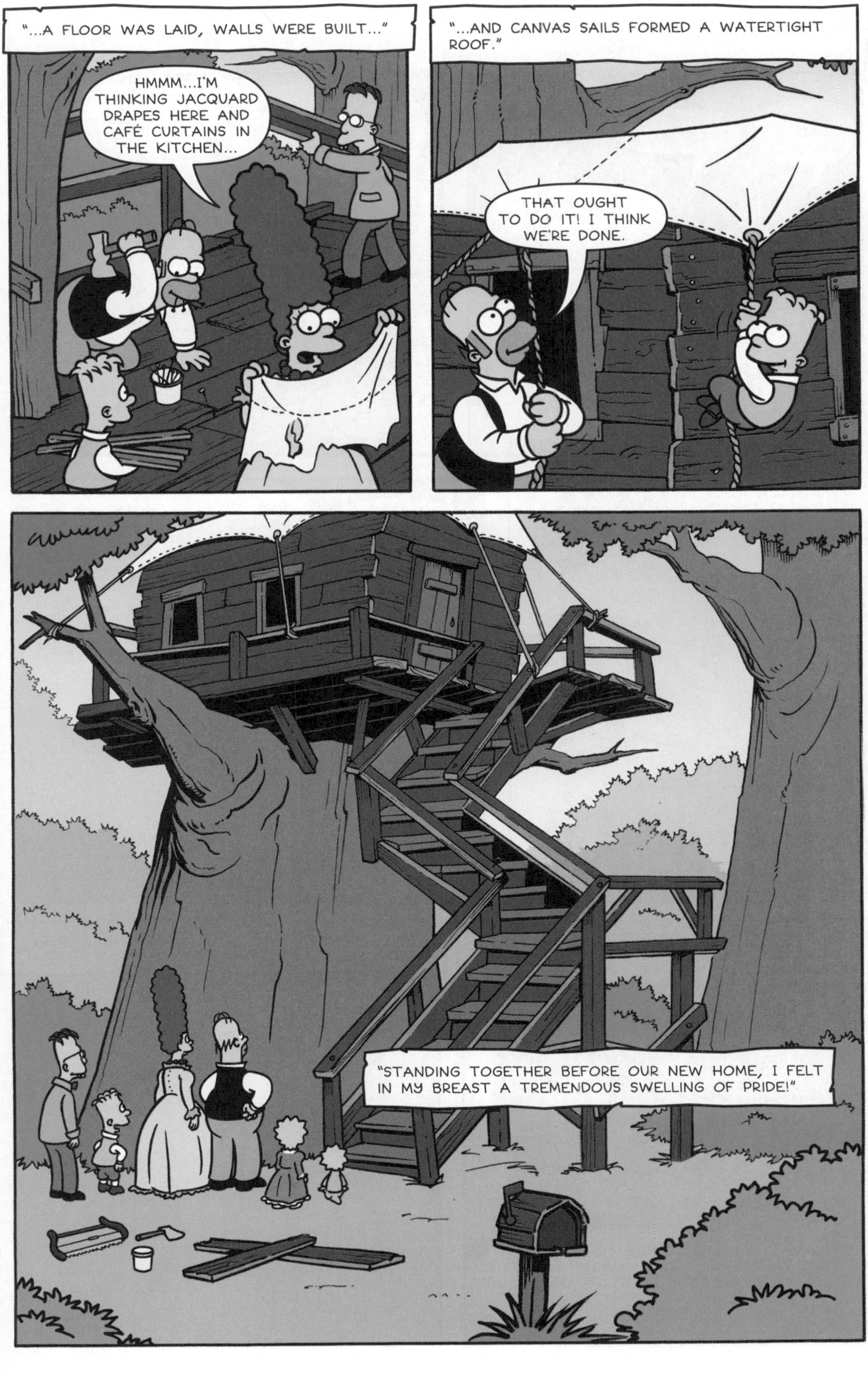
"...A FLOOR WAS LAID, WALLS WERE BUILT..."
HMMM...I'M THINKING JACQUARD DRAPES HERE AND CAFÉ CURTAINS IN THE KITCHEN...
"...AND CANVAS SAILS FORMED A WATERTIGHT ROOF."
THAT OUGHT TO DO IT! I THINK WE'RE DONE.
"STANDING TOGETHER BEFORE OUR NEW HOME, I FELT IN MY BREAST A TREMENDOUS SWELLING OF PRIDE!"

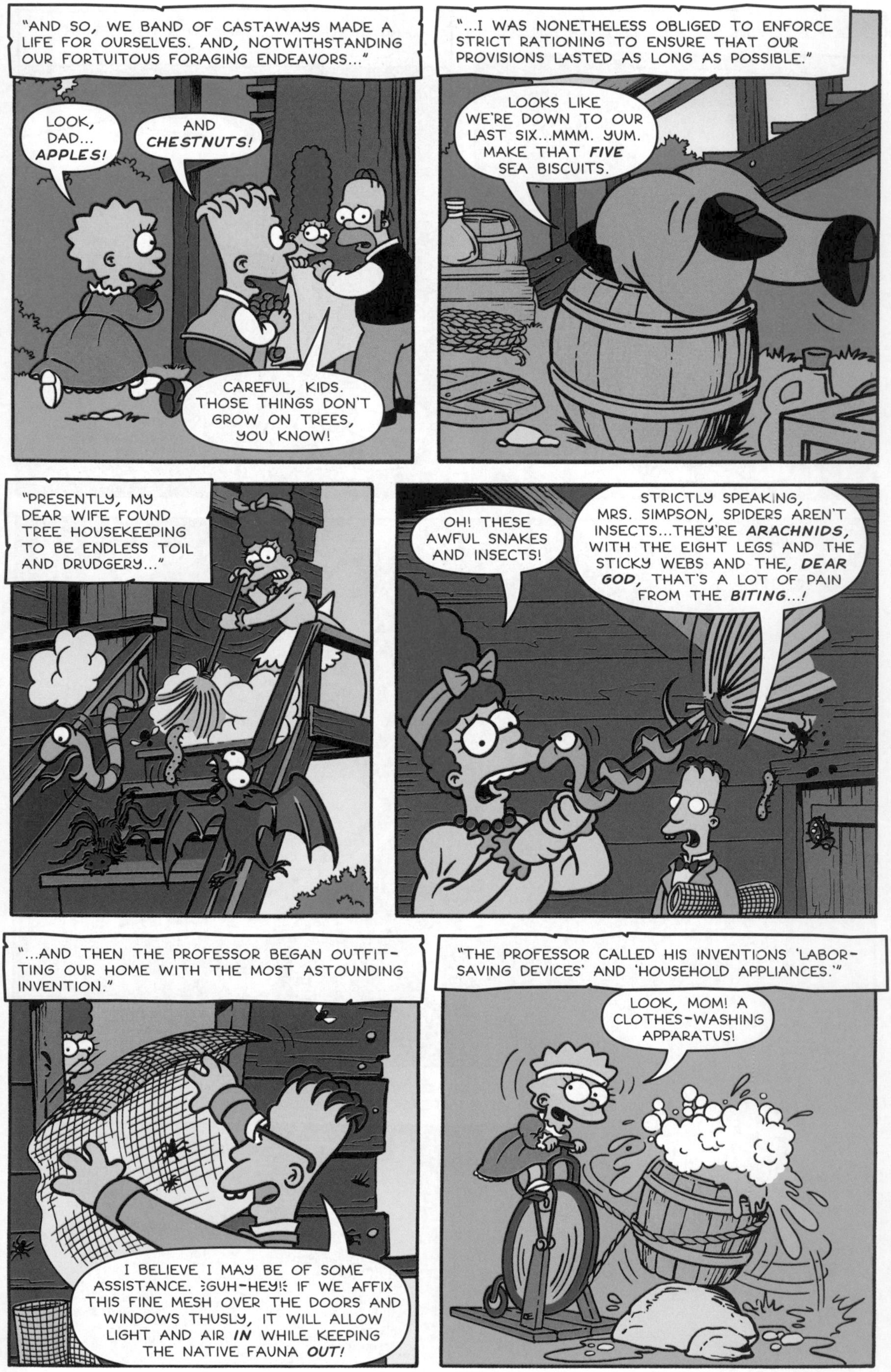
"AND SO, WE BAND OF CASTAWAYS MADE A LIFE FOR OURSELVES. AND, NOTWITHSTANDING OUR FORTUITOUS FORAGING ENDEAVORS..."
LOOK, DAD... **APPLES!**
AND **CHESTNUTS!**
CAREFUL, KIDS. THOSE THINGS DON'T GROW ON TREES, YOU KNOW!
"...I WAS NONETHELESS OBLIGED TO ENFORCE STRICT RATIONING TO ENSURE THAT OUR PROVISIONS LASTED AS LONG AS POSSIBLE."
LOOKS LIKE WE'RE DOWN TO OUR LAST SIX...MMM. YUM. MAKE THAT **FIVE** SEA BISCUITS.
"PRESENTLY, MY DEAR WIFE FOUND TREE HOUSEKEEPING TO BE ENDLESS TOIL AND DRUDGERY..."
OH! THESE AWFUL SNAKES AND INSECTS!
STRICTLY SPEAKING, MRS. SIMPSON, SPIDERS AREN'T INSECTS...THEY'RE **ARACHNIDS,** WITH THE EIGHT LEGS AND THE STICKY WEBS AND THE, **DEAR GOD,** THAT'S A LOT OF PAIN FROM THE **BITING**...!
"...AND THEN THE PROFESSOR BEGAN OUTFITTING OUR HOME WITH THE MOST ASTOUNDING INVENTION."
I BELIEVE I MAY BE OF SOME ASSISTANCE. ≷GUH-HEY!≶ IF WE AFFIX THIS FINE MESH OVER THE DOORS AND WINDOWS THUSLY, IT WILL ALLOW LIGHT AND AIR **IN** WHILE KEEPING THE NATIVE FAUNA **OUT!**
"THE PROFESSOR CALLED HIS INVENTIONS 'LABOR-SAVING DEVICES' AND 'HOUSEHOLD APPLIANCES.'"
LOOK, MOM! A CLOTHES-WASHING APPARATUS!

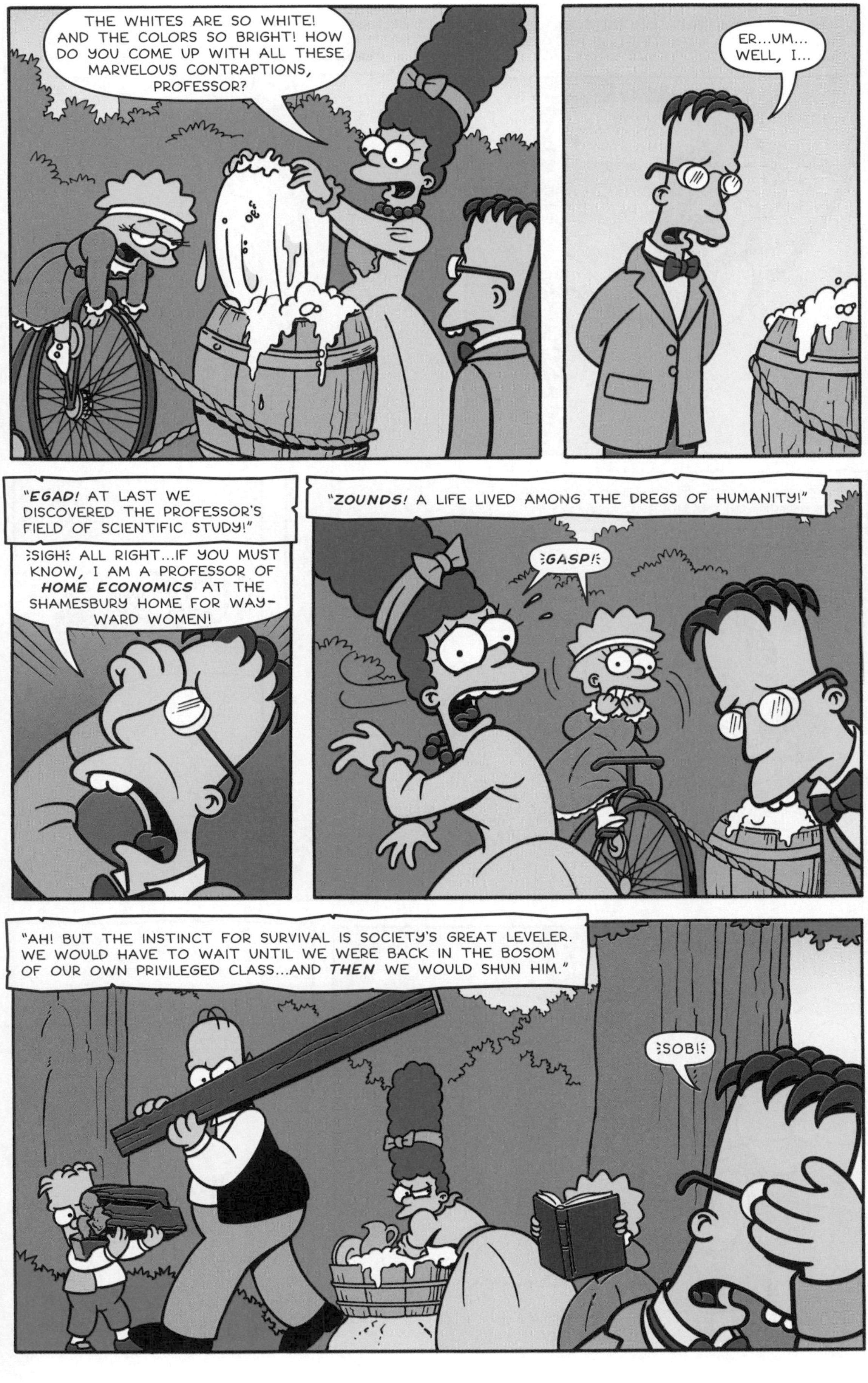
THE WHITES ARE SO WHITE! AND THE COLORS SO BRIGHT! HOW DO YOU COME UP WITH ALL THESE MARVELOUS CONTRAPTIONS, PROFESSOR?
ER...UM... WELL, I...
"EGAD! AT LAST WE DISCOVERED THE PROFESSOR'S FIELD OF SCIENTIFIC STUDY!"
SIGH ALL RIGHT...IF YOU MUST KNOW, I AM A PROFESSOR OF HOME ECONOMICS AT THE SHAMESBURY HOME FOR WAYWARD WOMEN!
"ZOUNDS! A LIFE LIVED AMONG THE DREGS OF HUMANITY!"
GASP!
"AH! BUT THE INSTINCT FOR SURVIVAL IS SOCIETY'S GREAT LEVELER. WE WOULD HAVE TO WAIT UNTIL WE WERE BACK IN THE BOSOM OF OUR OWN PRIVILEGED CLASS...AND THEN WE WOULD SHUN HIM."
SOB!

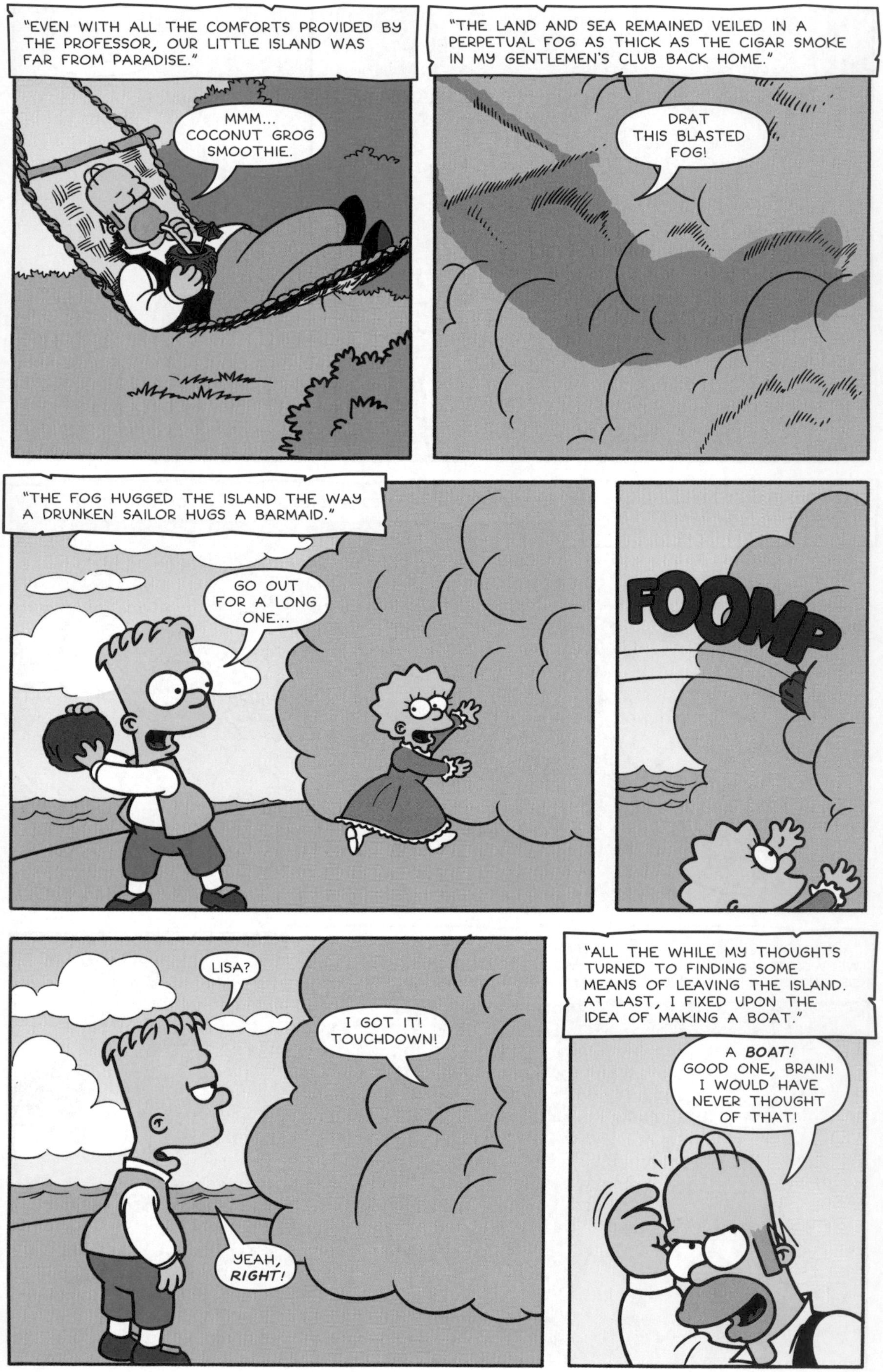
"EVEN WITH ALL THE COMFORTS PROVIDED BY THE PROFESSOR, OUR LITTLE ISLAND WAS FAR FROM PARADISE."
MMM... COCONUT GROG SMOOTHIE.
"THE LAND AND SEA REMAINED VEILED IN A PERPETUAL FOG AS THICK AS THE CIGAR SMOKE IN MY GENTLEMEN'S CLUB BACK HOME."
DRAT THIS BLASTED FOG!
"THE FOG HUGGED THE ISLAND THE WAY A DRUNKEN SAILOR HUGS A BARMAID."
GO OUT FOR A LONG ONE...
FOOMP
LISA?
I GOT IT! TOUCHDOWN!
YEAH, *RIGHT*!
"ALL THE WHILE MY THOUGHTS TURNED TO FINDING SOME MEANS OF LEAVING THE ISLAND. AT LAST, I FIXED UPON THE IDEA OF MAKING A BOAT."
A *BOAT*! GOOD ONE, BRAIN! I WOULD HAVE NEVER THOUGHT OF THAT!

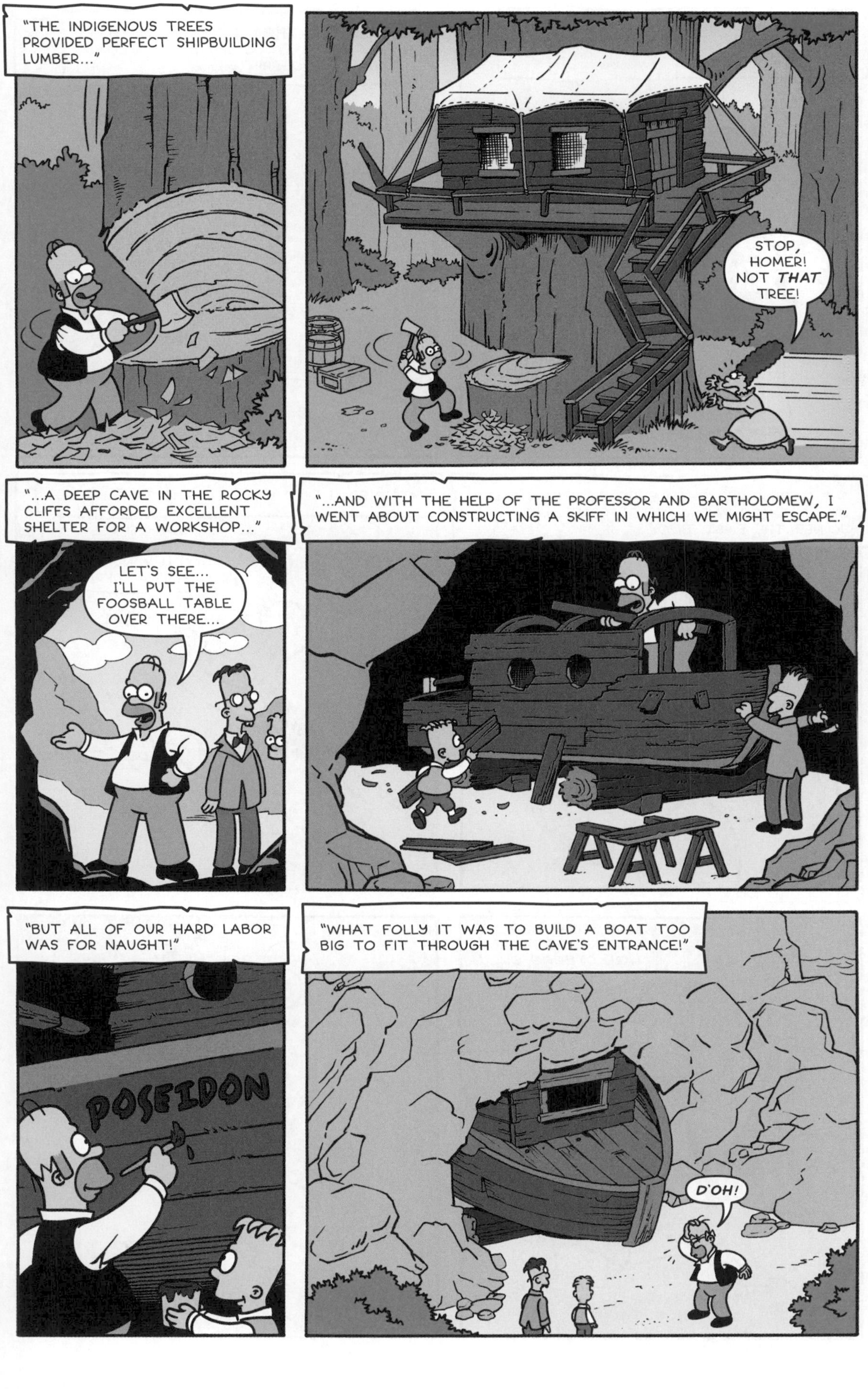
"THE INDIGENOUS TREES PROVIDED PERFECT SHIPBUILDING LUMBER..."
STOP, HOMER! NOT *THAT* TREE!
"...A DEEP CAVE IN THE ROCKY CLIFFS AFFORDED EXCELLENT SHELTER FOR A WORKSHOP..."
LET'S SEE... I'LL PUT THE FOOSBALL TABLE OVER THERE...
"...AND WITH THE HELP OF THE PROFESSOR AND BARTHOLOMEW, I WENT ABOUT CONSTRUCTING A SKIFF IN WHICH WE MIGHT ESCAPE."
"BUT ALL OF OUR HARD LABOR WAS FOR NAUGHT!"
POSEIDON
"WHAT FOLLY IT WAS TO BUILD A BOAT TOO BIG TO FIT THROUGH THE CAVE'S ENTRANCE!"
D'OH!

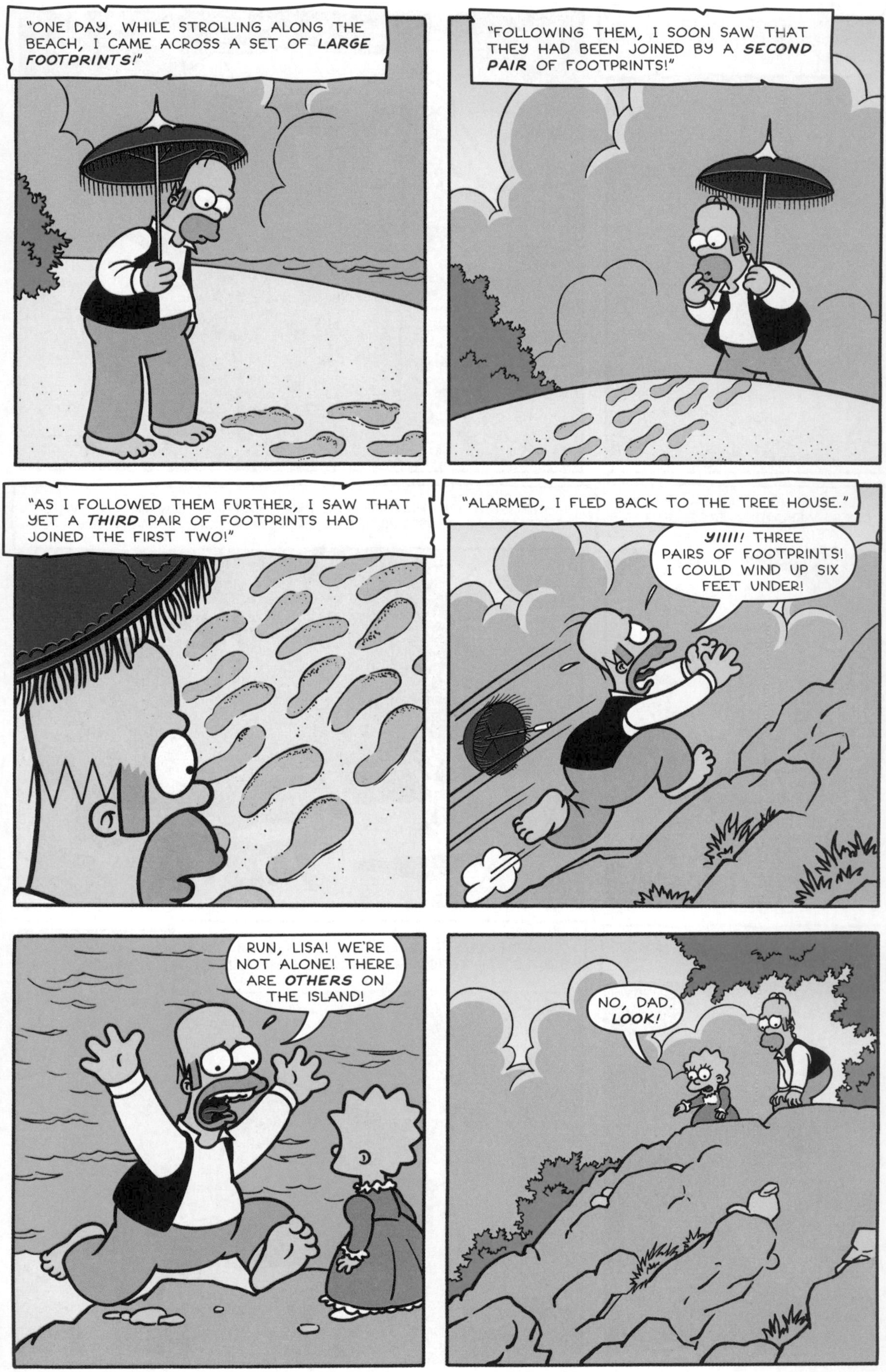
"ONE DAY, WHILE STROLLING ALONG THE BEACH, I CAME ACROSS A SET OF LARGE FOOTPRINTS!"
"FOLLOWING THEM, I SOON SAW THAT THEY HAD BEEN JOINED BY A SECOND PAIR OF FOOTPRINTS!"
"AS I FOLLOWED THEM FURTHER, I SAW THAT YET A THIRD PAIR OF FOOTPRINTS HAD JOINED THE FIRST TWO!"
"ALARMED, I FLED BACK TO THE TREE HOUSE."
YIIII! THREE PAIRS OF FOOTPRINTS! I COULD WIND UP SIX FEET UNDER!
RUN, LISA! WE'RE NOT ALONE! THERE ARE OTHERS ON THE ISLAND!
NO, DAD. LOOK!

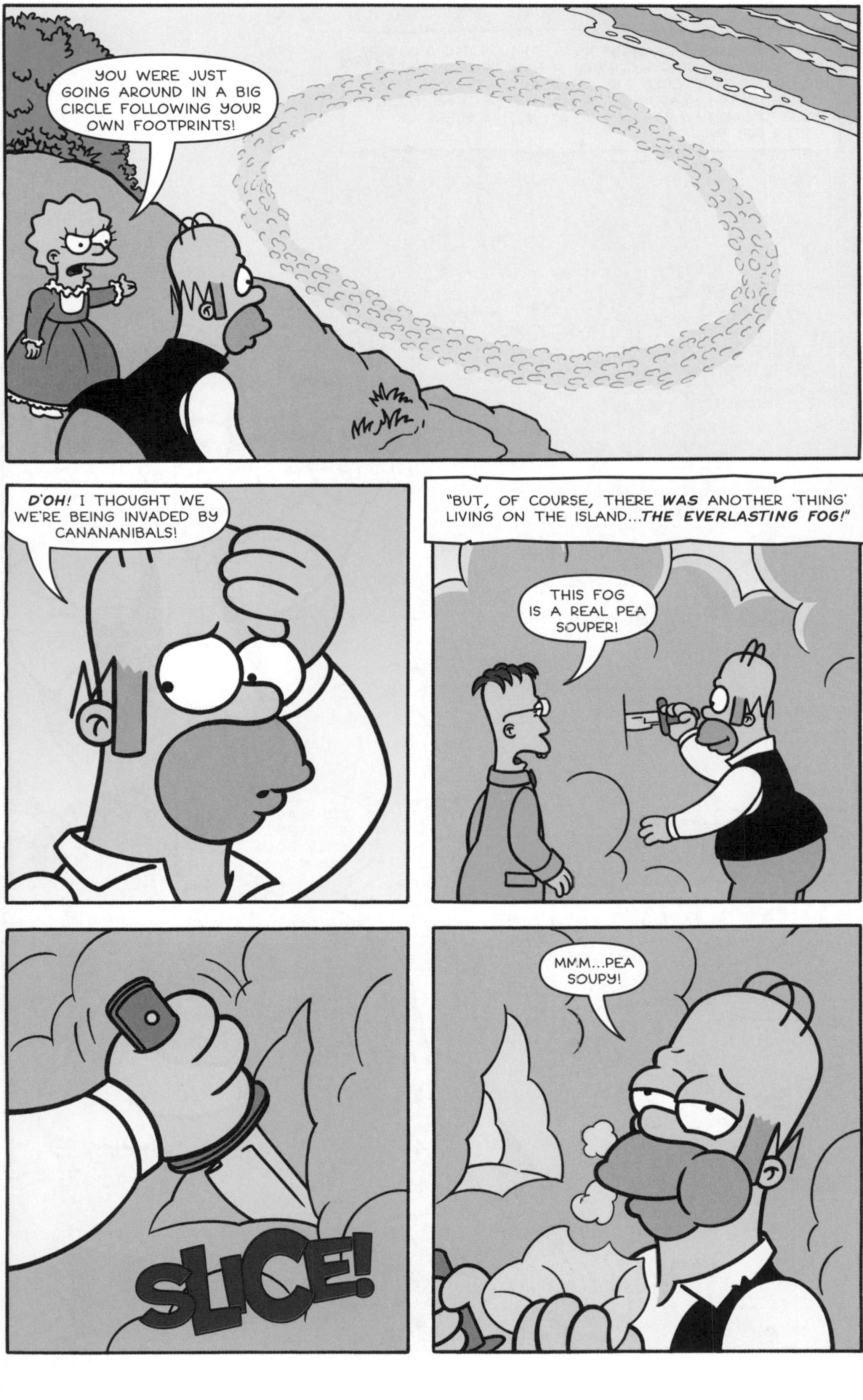
YOU WERE JUST GOING AROUND IN A BIG CIRCLE FOLLOWING YOUR OWN FOOTPRINTS!
D'OH! I THOUGHT WE WE'RE BEING INVADED BY CANANANIBALS!
"BUT, OF COURSE, THERE WAS ANOTHER 'THING' LIVING ON THE ISLAND...THE EVERLASTING FOG!"
THIS FOG IS A REAL PEA SOUPER!
SLICE!
MMM...PEA SOUPY!

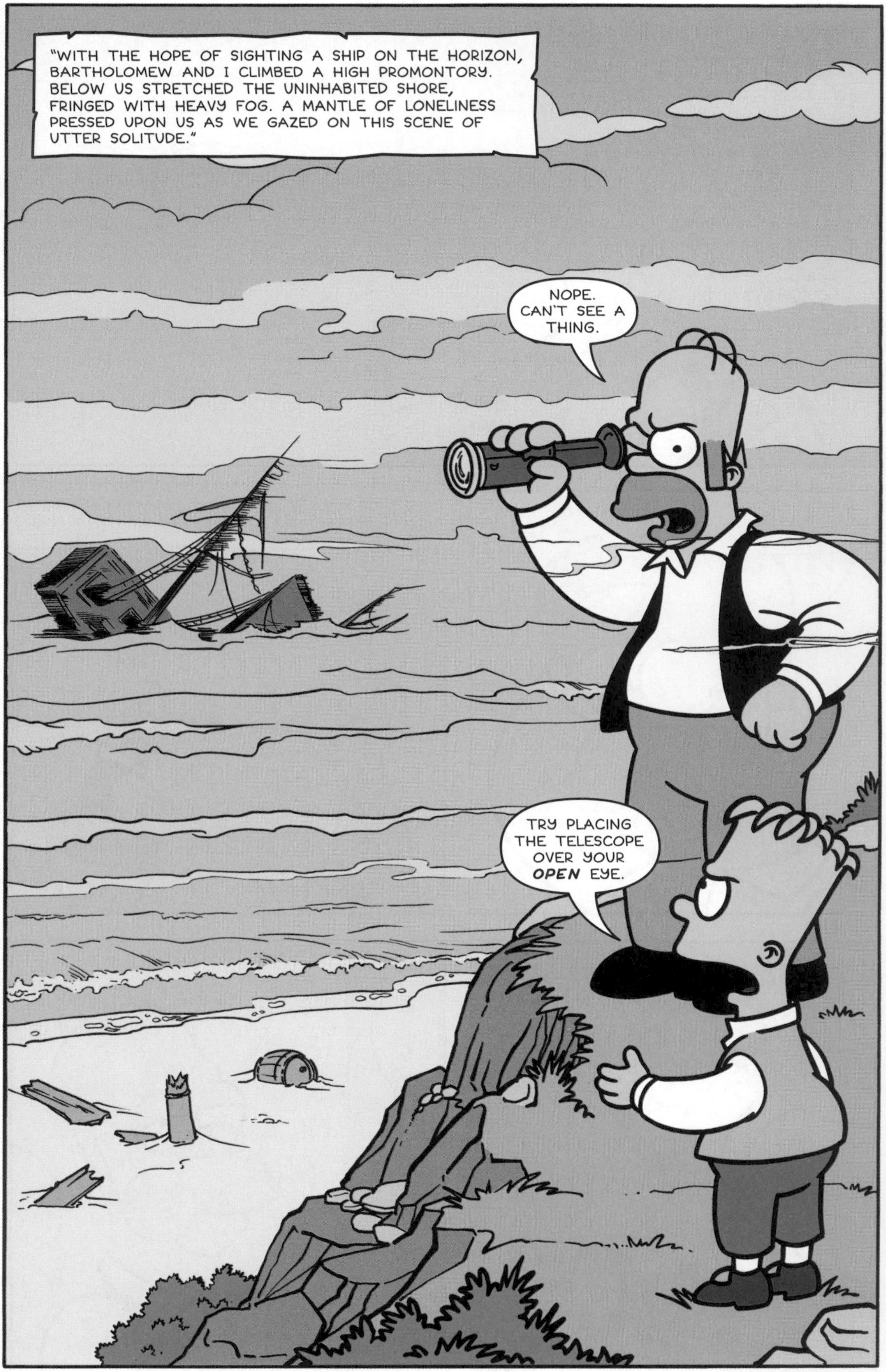
"WITH THE HOPE OF SIGHTING A SHIP ON THE HORIZON, BARTHOLOMEW AND I CLIMBED A HIGH PROMONTORY. BELOW US STRETCHED THE UNINHABITED SHORE, FRINGED WITH HEAVY FOG. A MANTLE OF LONELINESS PRESSED UPON US AS WE GAZED ON THIS SCENE OF UTTER SOLITUDE."
NOPE. CAN'T SEE A THING.
TRY PLACING THE TELESCOPE OVER YOUR *OPEN* EYE.

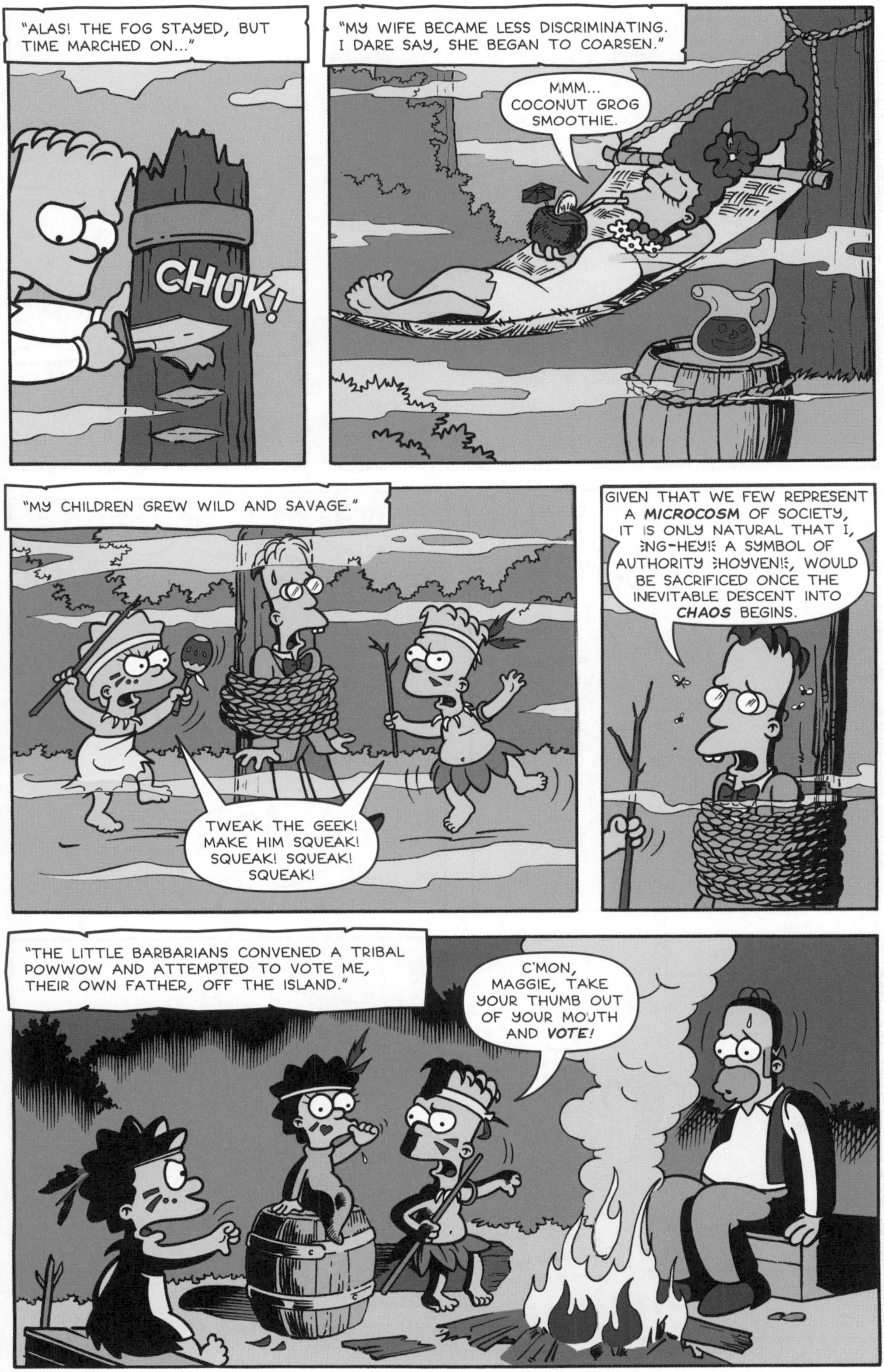

"ALAS! THE FOG STAYED, BUT TIME MARCHED ON..."
CHUK!
"MY WIFE BECAME LESS DISCRIMINATING. I DARE SAY, SHE BEGAN TO COARSEN."
MMM... COCONUT GROG SMOOTHIE.
"MY CHILDREN GREW WILD AND SAVAGE."
TWEAK THE GEEK! MAKE HIM SQUEAK! SQUEAK! SQUEAK! SQUEAK!
GIVEN THAT WE FEW REPRESENT A **MICROCOSM** OF SOCIETY, IT IS ONLY NATURAL THAT I, NG-HEY! A SYMBOL OF AUTHORITY HOYVEN!, WOULD BE SACRIFICED ONCE THE INEVITABLE DESCENT INTO **CHAOS** BEGINS.
"THE LITTLE BARBARIANS CONVENED A TRIBAL POWWOW AND ATTEMPTED TO VOTE ME, THEIR OWN FATHER, OFF THE ISLAND."
C'MON, MAGGIE, TAKE YOUR THUMB OUT OF YOUR MOUTH AND **VOTE!**

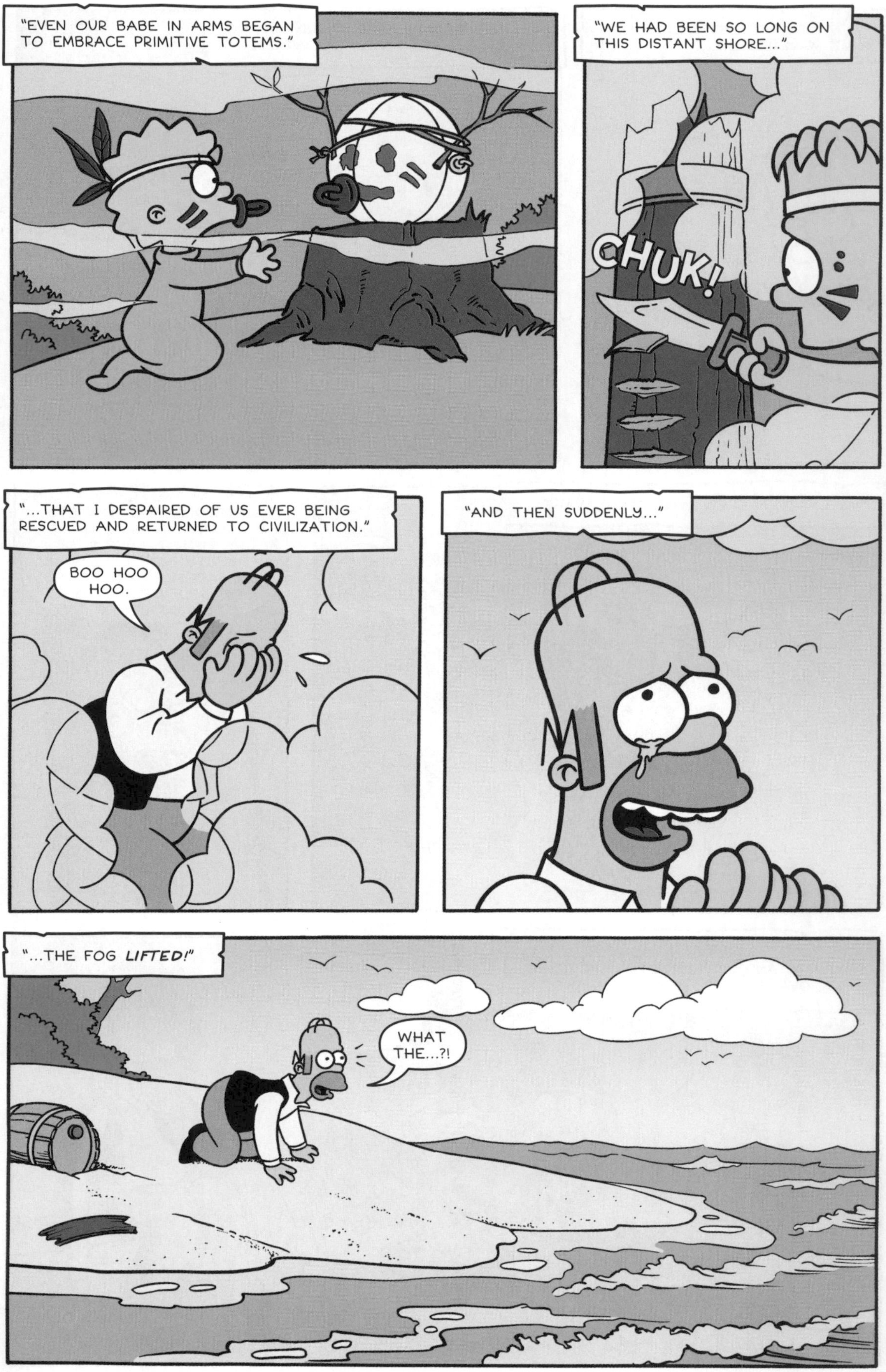
"EVEN OUR BABE IN ARMS BEGAN TO EMBRACE PRIMITIVE TOTEMS."
"WE HAD BEEN SO LONG ON THIS DISTANT SHORE..."
CHUK!
"...THAT I DESPAIRED OF US EVER BEING RESCUED AND RETURNED TO CIVILIZATION."
BOO HOO HOO.
"AND THEN SUDDENLY..."
"...THE FOG LIFTED!"
WHAT THE...?!

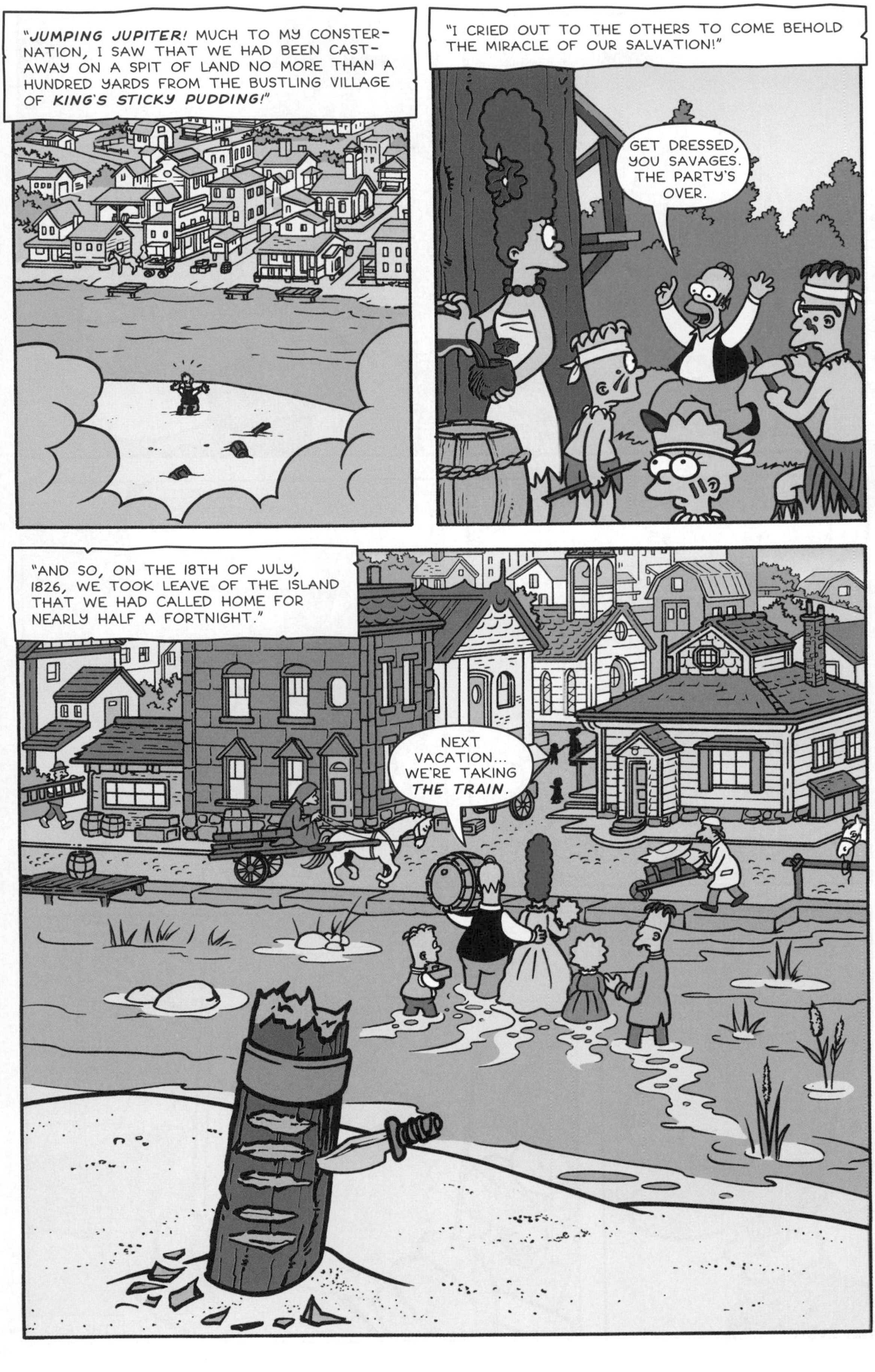
"JUMPING JUPITER! MUCH TO MY CONSTERNATION, I SAW THAT WE HAD BEEN CASTAWAY ON A SPIT OF LAND NO MORE THAN A HUNDRED YARDS FROM THE BUSTLING VILLAGE OF KING'S STICKY PUDDING!"
"I CRIED OUT TO THE OTHERS TO COME BEHOLD THE MIRACLE OF OUR SALVATION!"
GET DRESSED, YOU SAVAGES. THE PARTY'S OVER.
"AND SO, ON THE 18TH OF JULY, 1826, WE TOOK LEAVE OF THE ISLAND THAT WE HAD CALLED HOME FOR NEARLY HALF A FORTNIGHT."
NEXT VACATION... WE'RE TAKING THE TRAIN.

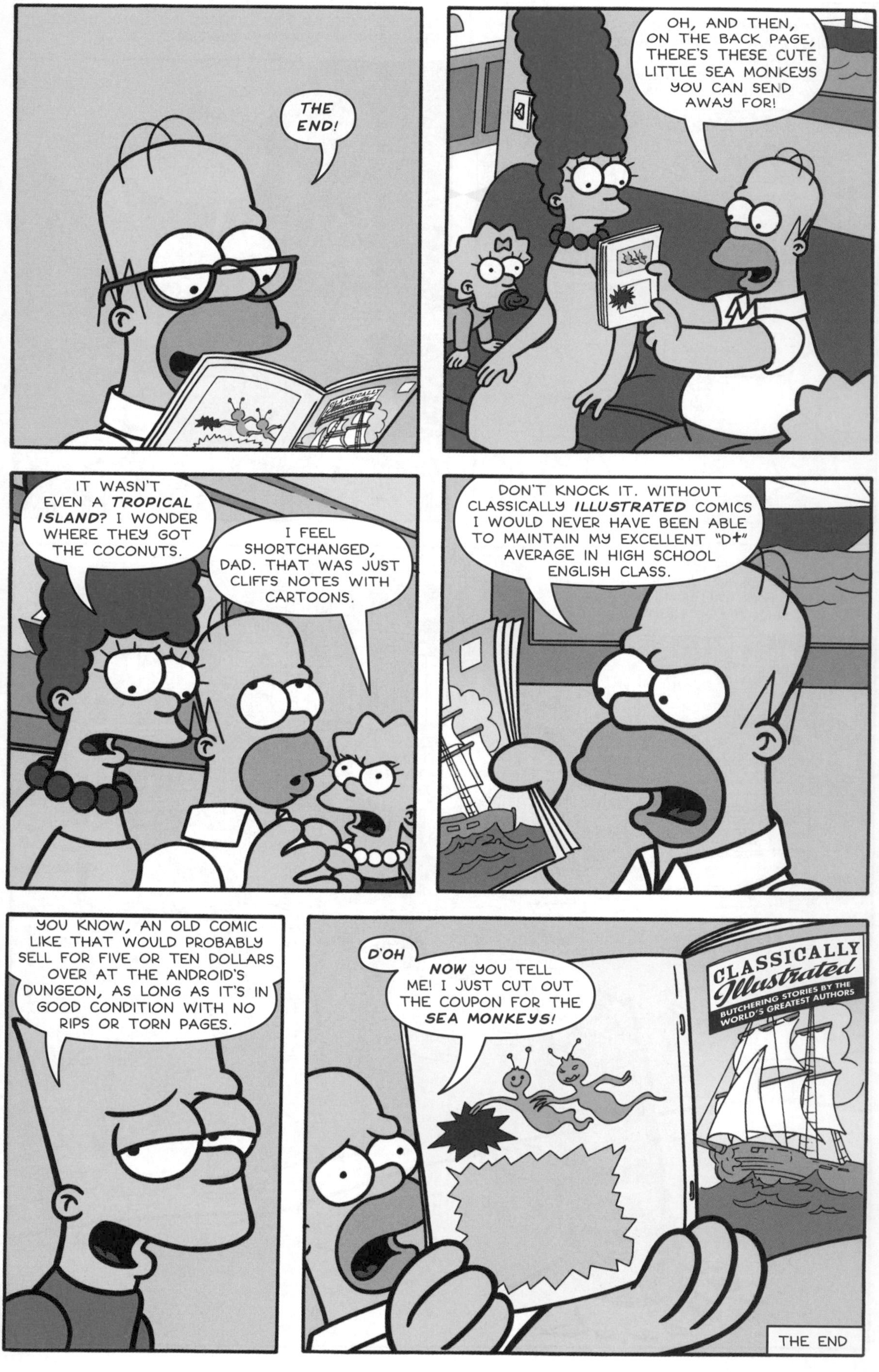
THE END!
OH, AND THEN, ON THE BACK PAGE, THERE'S THESE CUTE LITTLE SEA MONKEYS YOU CAN SEND AWAY FOR!
IT WASN'T EVEN A *TROPICAL ISLAND*? I WONDER WHERE THEY GOT THE COCONUTS.
I FEEL SHORTCHANGED, DAD. THAT WAS JUST CLIFFS NOTES WITH CARTOONS.
DON'T KNOCK IT. WITHOUT CLASSICALLY *ILLUSTRATED* COMICS I WOULD NEVER HAVE BEEN ABLE TO MAINTAIN MY EXCELLENT "D+" AVERAGE IN HIGH SCHOOL ENGLISH CLASS.
YOU KNOW, AN OLD COMIC LIKE THAT WOULD PROBABLY SELL FOR FIVE OR TEN DOLLARS OVER AT THE ANDROID'S DUNGEON, AS LONG AS IT'S IN GOOD CONDITION WITH NO RIPS OR TORN PAGES.
D'OH
NOW YOU TELL ME! I JUST CUT OUT THE COUPON FOR THE *SEA MONKEYS*!
CLASSICALLY Illustrated
BUTCHERING STORIES BY THE WORLD'S GREATEST AUTHORS
THE END

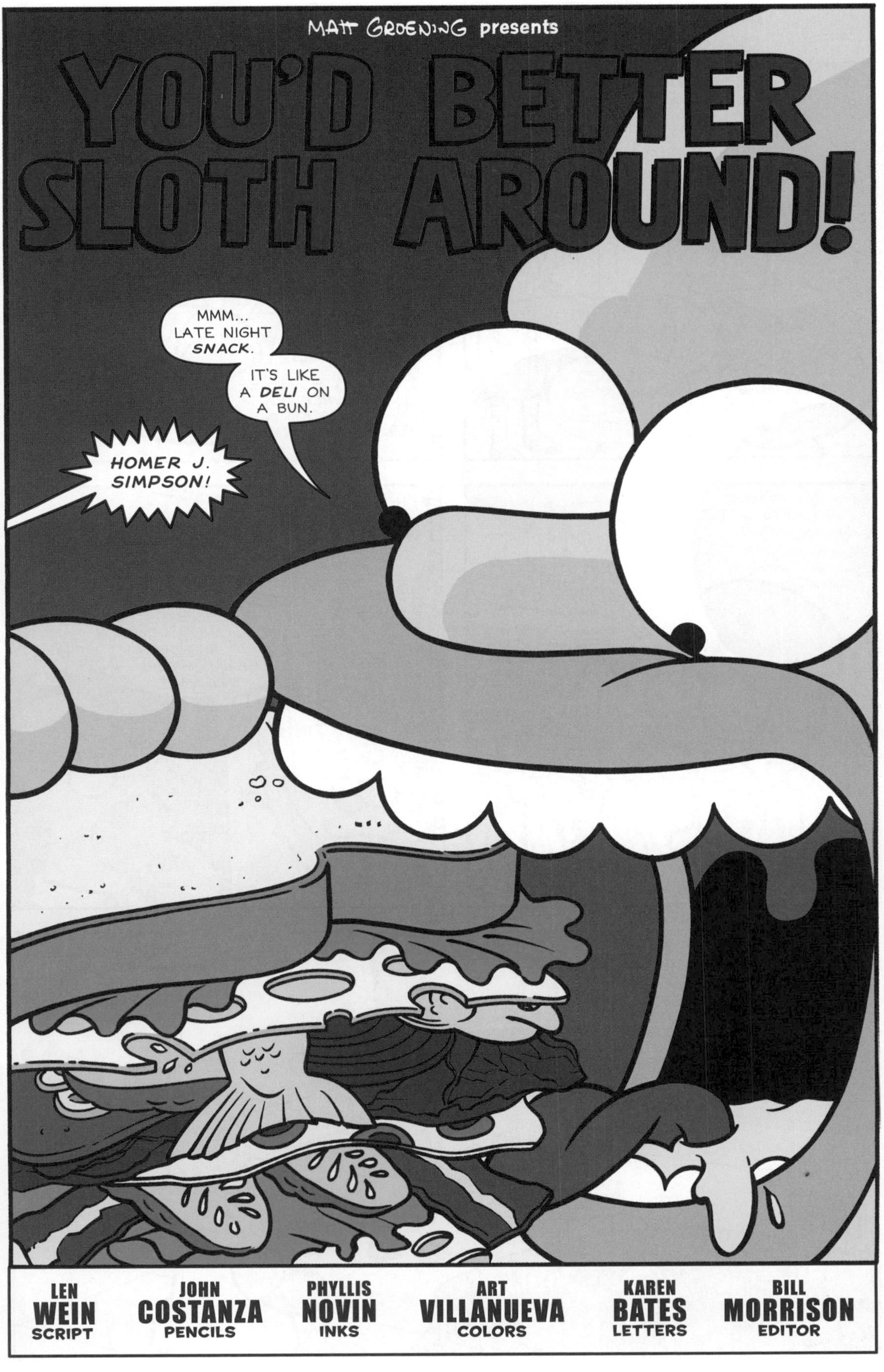
MATT GROENING presents
YOU'D BETTER SLOTH AROUND!
MMM... LATE NIGHT *SNACK*.
IT'S LIKE A *DELI* ON A BUN.
HOMER J. SIMPSON!

LEN WEIN SCRIPT | **JOHN COSTANZA** PENCILS | **PHYLLIS NOVIN** INKS | **ART VILLANUEVA** COLORS | **KAREN BATES** LETTERS | **BILL MORRISON** EDITOR

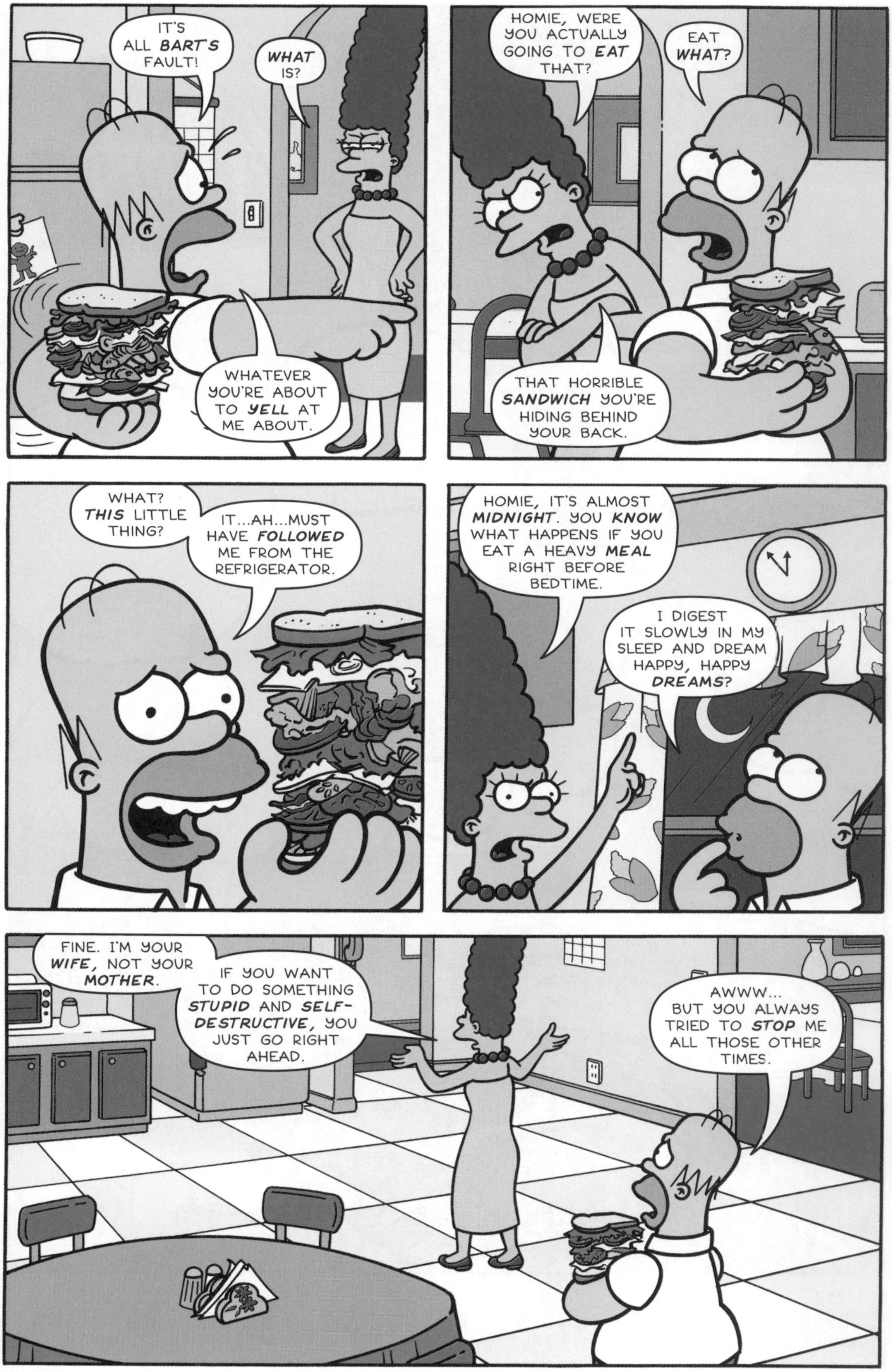
IT'S ALL BART'S FAULT!
WHAT IS?
WHATEVER YOU'RE ABOUT TO YELL AT ME ABOUT.
HOMIE, WERE YOU ACTUALLY GOING TO EAT THAT?
EAT WHAT?
THAT HORRIBLE SANDWICH YOU'RE HIDING BEHIND YOUR BACK.
WHAT? THIS LITTLE THING?
IT...AH...MUST HAVE FOLLOWED ME FROM THE REFRIGERATOR.
HOMIE, IT'S ALMOST MIDNIGHT. YOU KNOW WHAT HAPPENS IF YOU EAT A HEAVY MEAL RIGHT BEFORE BEDTIME.
I DIGEST IT SLOWLY IN MY SLEEP AND DREAM HAPPY, HAPPY DREAMS?
FINE. I'M YOUR WIFE, NOT YOUR MOTHER.
IF YOU WANT TO DO SOMETHING STUPID AND SELF-DESTRUCTIVE, YOU JUST GO RIGHT AHEAD.
AWWW... BUT YOU ALWAYS TRIED TO STOP ME ALL THOSE OTHER TIMES.

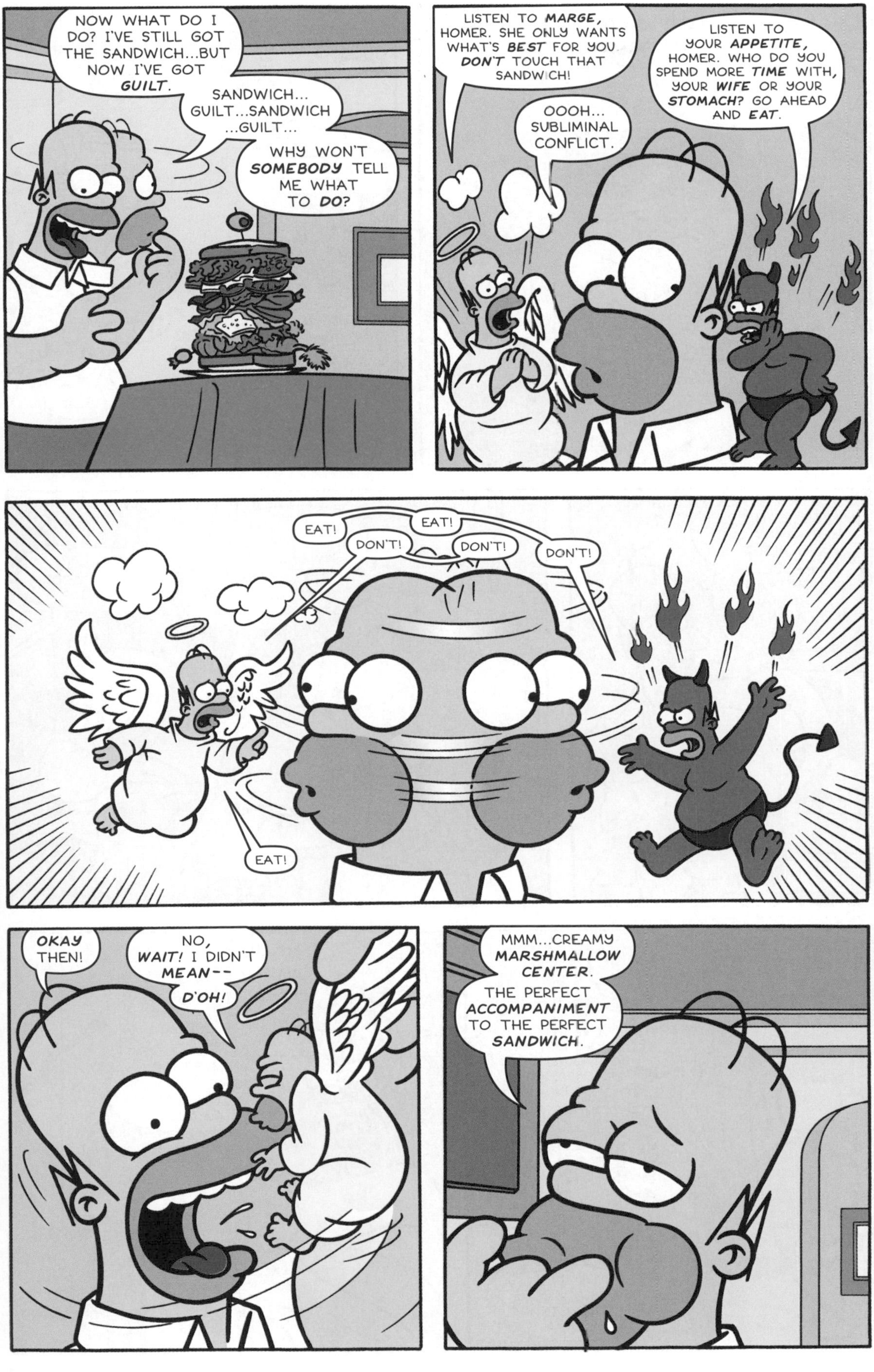
NOW WHAT DO I DO? I'VE STILL GOT THE SANDWICH...BUT NOW I'VE GOT GUILT.
SANDWICH... GUILT...SANDWICH ...GUILT...
WHY WON'T SOMEBODY TELL ME WHAT TO DO?
LISTEN TO MARGE, HOMER. SHE ONLY WANTS WHAT'S BEST FOR YOU. DON'T TOUCH THAT SANDWICH!
OOOH... SUBLIMINAL CONFLICT.
LISTEN TO YOUR APPETITE, HOMER. WHO DO YOU SPEND MORE TIME WITH, YOUR WIFE OR YOUR STOMACH? GO AHEAD AND EAT.
EAT!
EAT!
DON'T!
DON'T!
DON'T!
EAT!
OKAY THEN!
NO, WAIT! I DIDN'T MEAN--
D'OH!
MMM...CREAMY MARSHMALLOW CENTER.
THE PERFECT ACCOMPANIMENT TO THE PERFECT SANDWICH.

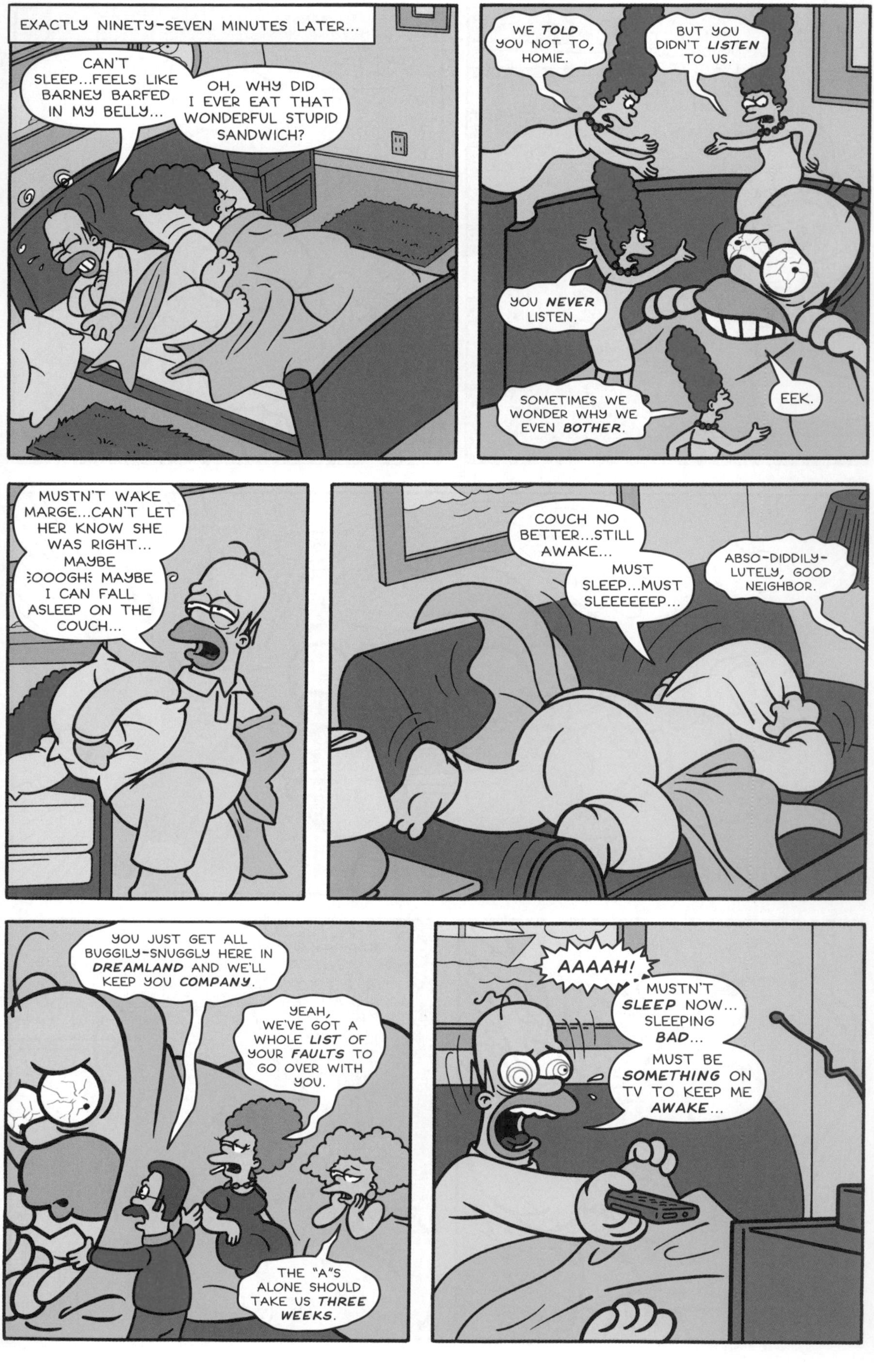
EXACTLY NINETY-SEVEN MINUTES LATER...
CAN'T SLEEP...FEELS LIKE BARNEY BARFED IN MY BELLY...
OH, WHY DID I EVER EAT THAT WONDERFUL STUPID SANDWICH?
WE TOLD YOU NOT TO, HOMIE.
BUT YOU DIDN'T LISTEN TO US.
YOU NEVER LISTEN.
SOMETIMES WE WONDER WHY WE EVEN BOTHER.
EEK.
MUSTN'T WAKE MARGE...CAN'T LET HER KNOW SHE WAS RIGHT... MAYBE ŠOOOGHŠ MAYBE I CAN FALL ASLEEP ON THE COUCH...
COUCH NO BETTER...STILL AWAKE...
MUST SLEEP...MUST SLEEEEEEP...
ABSO-DIDDILY-LUTELY, GOOD NEIGHBOR.
YOU JUST GET ALL BUGGILY-SNUGGLY HERE IN DREAMLAND AND WE'LL KEEP YOU COMPANY.
YEAH, WE'VE GOT A WHOLE LIST OF YOUR FAULTS TO GO OVER WITH YOU.
THE "A"S ALONE SHOULD TAKE US THREE WEEKS.
AAAAH!
MUSTN'T SLEEP NOW... SLEEPING BAD...
MUST BE SOMETHING ON TV TO KEEP ME AWAKE...

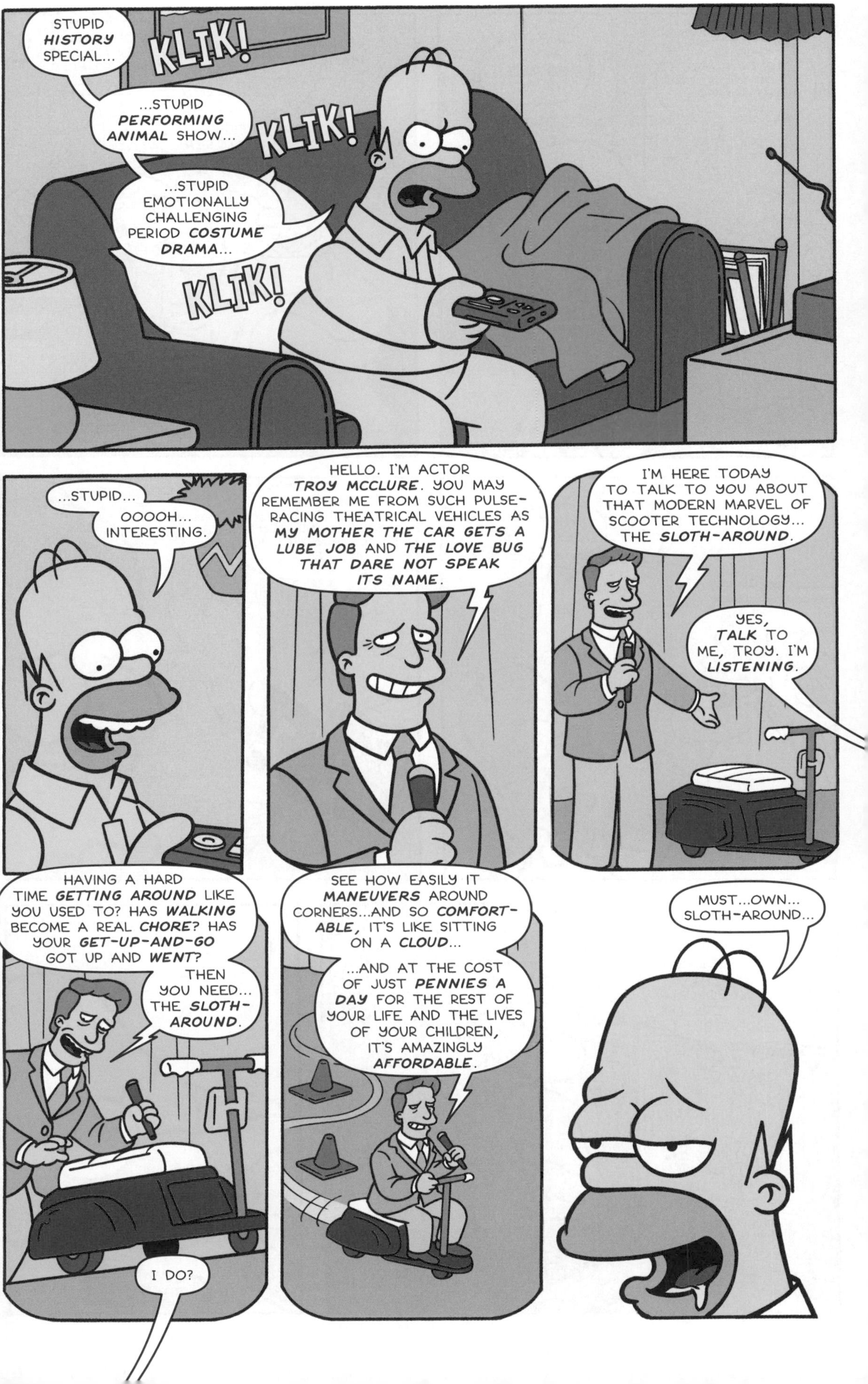

STUPID HISTORY SPECIAL...
KLIK!
...STUPID PERFORMING ANIMAL SHOW...
KLIK!
...STUPID EMOTIONALLY CHALLENGING PERIOD COSTUME DRAMA...
KLIK!
...STUPID...
OOOOH... INTERESTING.
HELLO. I'M ACTOR TROY MCCLURE. YOU MAY REMEMBER ME FROM SUCH PULSE-RACING THEATRICAL VEHICLES AS MY MOTHER THE CAR GETS A LUBE JOB AND THE LOVE BUG THAT DARE NOT SPEAK ITS NAME.
I'M HERE TODAY TO TALK TO YOU ABOUT THAT MODERN MARVEL OF SCOOTER TECHNOLOGY... THE SLOTH-AROUND.
YES, TALK TO ME, TROY. I'M LISTENING.
HAVING A HARD TIME GETTING AROUND LIKE YOU USED TO? HAS WALKING BECOME A REAL CHORE? HAS YOUR GET-UP-AND-GO GOT UP AND WENT?
THEN YOU NEED... THE SLOTH-AROUND.
I DO?
SEE HOW EASILY IT MANEUVERS AROUND CORNERS...AND SO COMFORT-ABLE, IT'S LIKE SITTING ON A CLOUD...
...AND AT THE COST OF JUST PENNIES A DAY FOR THE REST OF YOUR LIFE AND THE LIVES OF YOUR CHILDREN, IT'S AMAZINGLY AFFORDABLE.
MUST...OWN... SLOTH-AROUND...

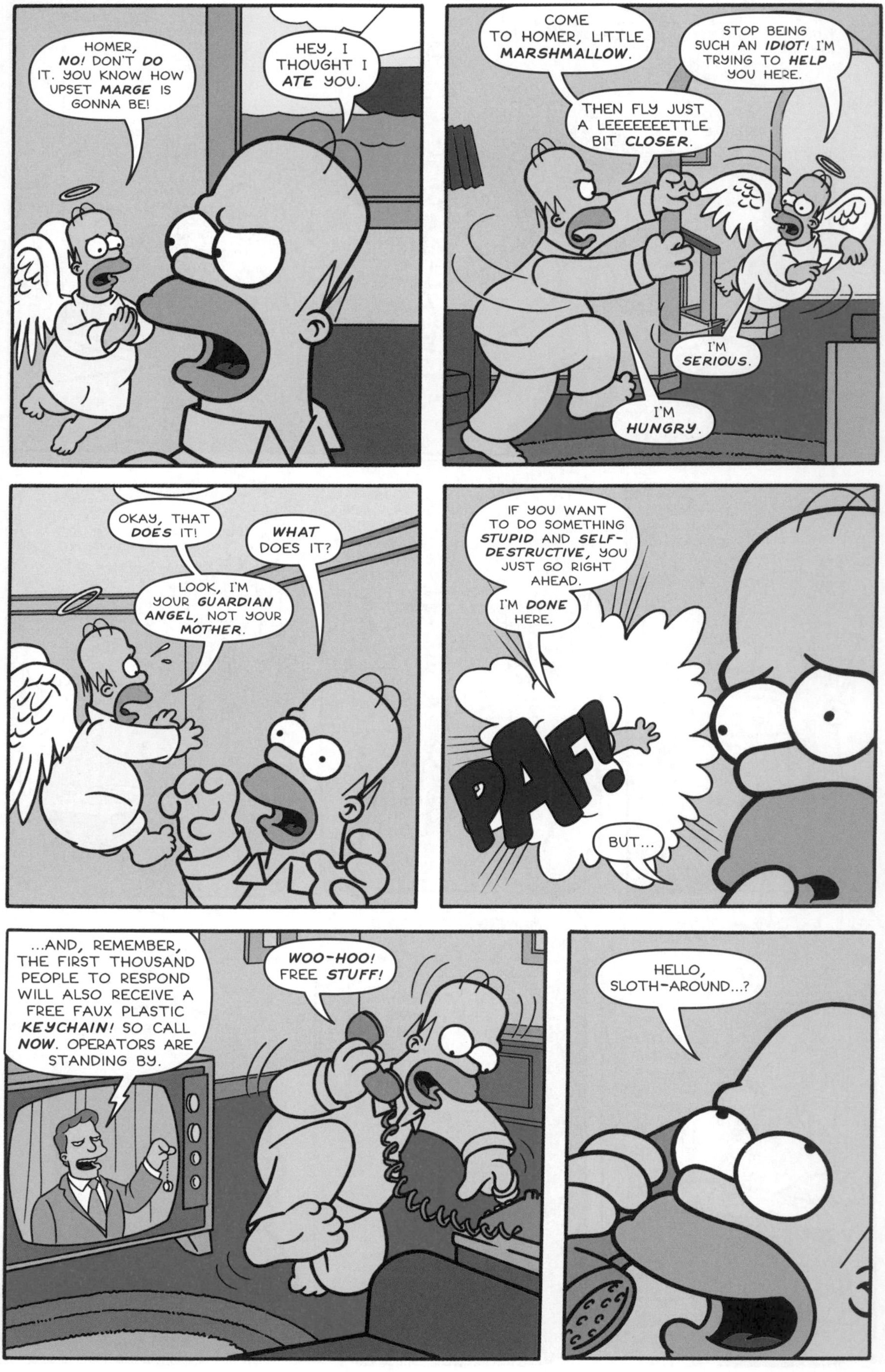
HOMER, NO! DON'T DO IT. YOU KNOW HOW UPSET MARGE IS GONNA BE!
HEY, I THOUGHT I ATE YOU.
COME TO HOMER, LITTLE MARSHMALLOW.
STOP BEING SUCH AN IDIOT! I'M TRYING TO HELP YOU HERE.
THEN FLY JUST A LEEEEEEETTLE BIT CLOSER.
I'M SERIOUS.
I'M HUNGRY.
OKAY, THAT DOES IT!
WHAT DOES IT?
LOOK, I'M YOUR GUARDIAN ANGEL, NOT YOUR MOTHER.
IF YOU WANT TO DO SOMETHING STUPID AND SELF-DESTRUCTIVE, YOU JUST GO RIGHT AHEAD.
I'M DONE HERE.
PAF!
BUT...
...AND, REMEMBER, THE FIRST THOUSAND PEOPLE TO RESPOND WILL ALSO RECEIVE A FREE FAUX PLASTIC KEYCHAIN! SO CALL NOW. OPERATORS ARE STANDING BY.
WOO-HOO! FREE STUFF!
HELLO, SLOTH-AROUND...?

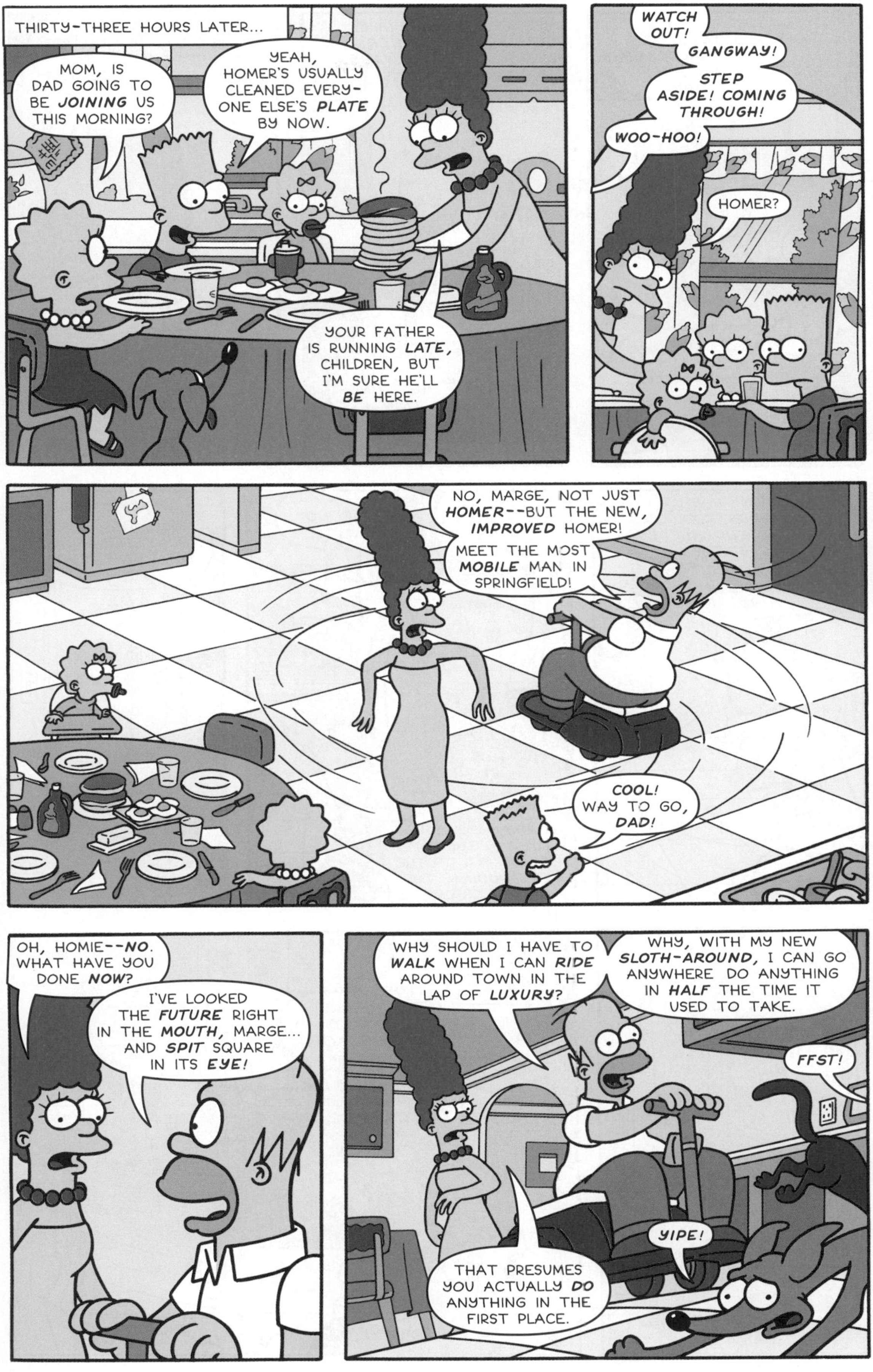
THIRTY-THREE HOURS LATER...
MOM, IS DAD GOING TO BE JOINING US THIS MORNING?
YEAH, HOMER'S USUALLY CLEANED EVERY-ONE ELSE'S PLATE BY NOW.
YOUR FATHER IS RUNNING LATE, CHILDREN, BUT I'M SURE HE'LL BE HERE.
WATCH OUT!
GANGWAY!
STEP ASIDE! COMING THROUGH!
WOO-HOO!
HOMER?
NO, MARGE, NOT JUST HOMER--BUT THE NEW, IMPROVED HOMER!
MEET THE MOST MOBILE MAN IN SPRINGFIELD!
COOL! WAY TO GO, DAD!
OH, HOMIE--NO. WHAT HAVE YOU DONE NOW?
I'VE LOOKED THE FUTURE RIGHT IN THE MOUTH, MARGE... AND SPIT SQUARE IN ITS EYE!
WHY SHOULD I HAVE TO WALK WHEN I CAN RIDE AROUND TOWN IN THE LAP OF LUXURY?
WHY, WITH MY NEW SLOTH-AROUND, I CAN GO ANYWHERE DO ANYTHING IN HALF THE TIME IT USED TO TAKE.
FFST!
YIPE!
THAT PRESUMES YOU ACTUALLY DO ANYTHING IN THE FIRST PLACE.

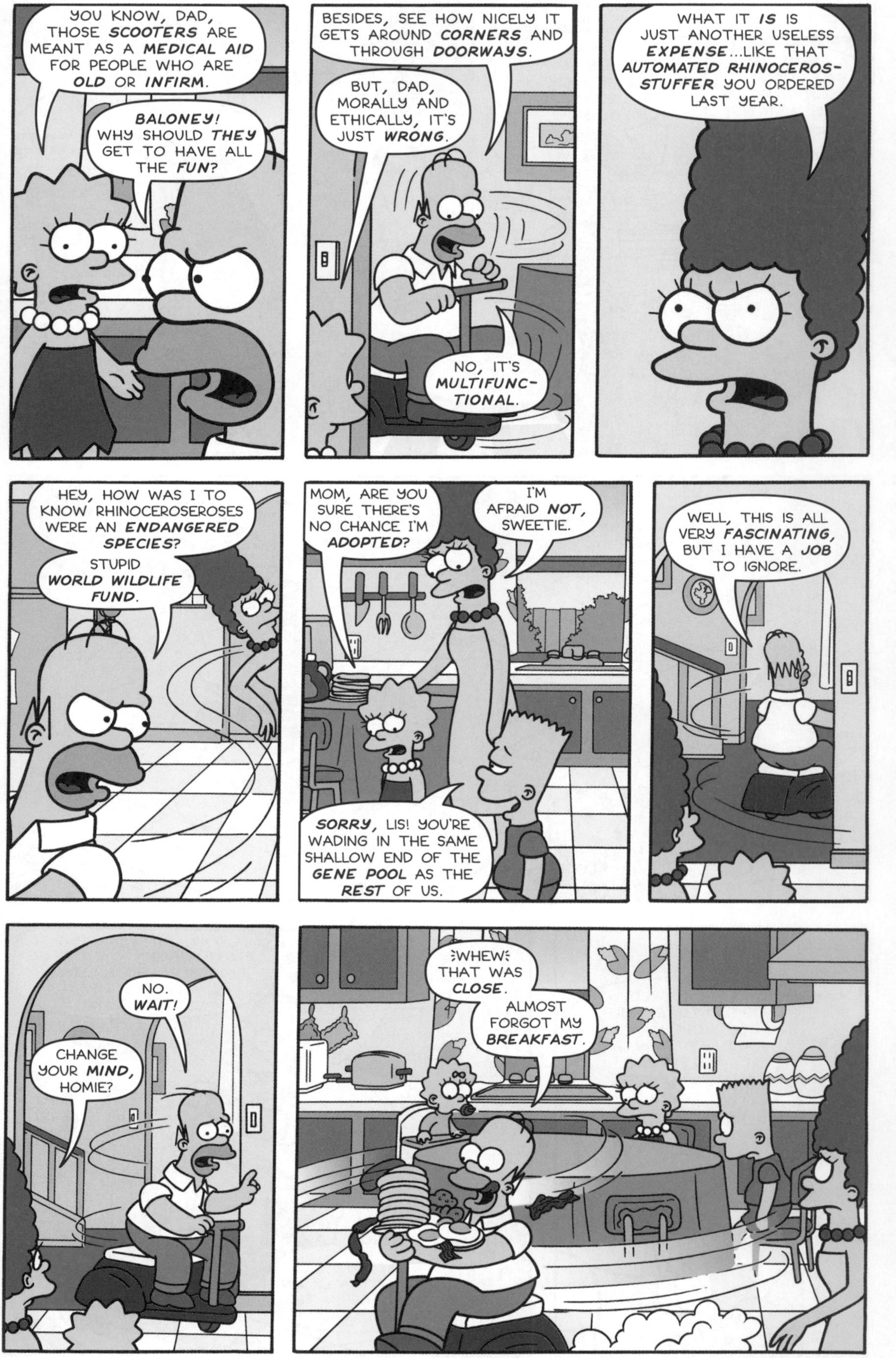
YOU KNOW, DAD, THOSE SCOOTERS ARE MEANT AS A MEDICAL AID FOR PEOPLE WHO ARE OLD OR INFIRM.
BALONEY! WHY SHOULD THEY GET TO HAVE ALL THE FUN?
BESIDES, SEE HOW NICELY IT GETS AROUND CORNERS AND THROUGH DOORWAYS.
BUT, DAD, MORALLY AND ETHICALLY, IT'S JUST WRONG.
NO, IT'S MULTIFUNCTIONAL.
WHAT IT IS IS JUST ANOTHER USELESS EXPENSE...LIKE THAT AUTOMATED RHINOCEROS-STUFFER YOU ORDERED LAST YEAR.
HEY, HOW WAS I TO KNOW RHINOCEROSEROSES WERE AN ENDANGERED SPECIES?
STUPID WORLD WILDLIFE FUND.
MOM, ARE YOU SURE THERE'S NO CHANCE I'M ADOPTED?
I'M AFRAID NOT, SWEETIE.
SORRY, LIS! YOU'RE WADING IN THE SAME SHALLOW END OF THE GENE POOL AS THE REST OF US.
WELL, THIS IS ALL VERY FASCINATING, BUT I HAVE A JOB TO IGNORE.
NO. WAIT!
CHANGE YOUR MIND, HOMIE?
WHEW THAT WAS CLOSE.
ALMOST FORGOT MY BREAKFAST.

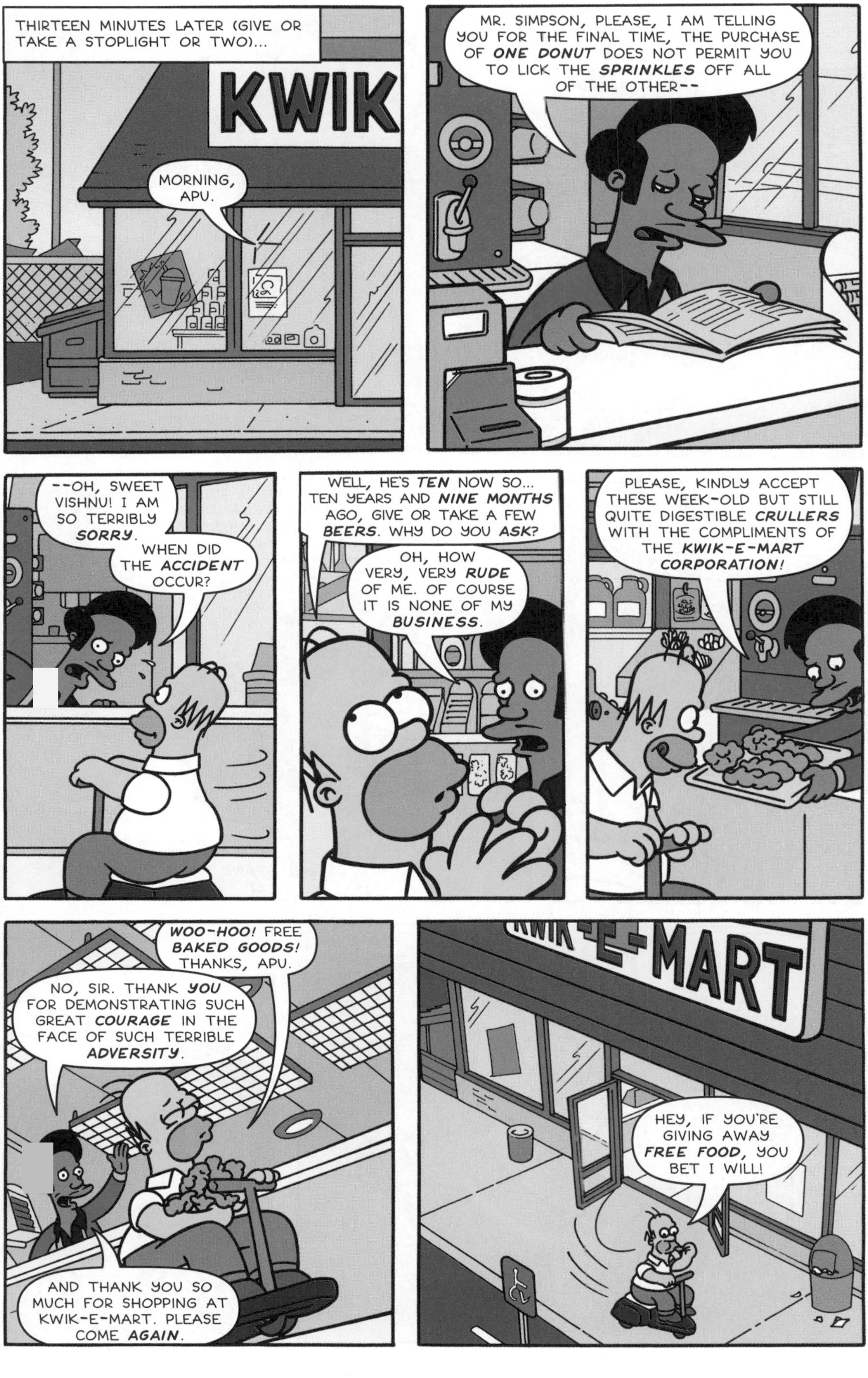
THIRTEEN MINUTES LATER (GIVE OR TAKE A STOPLIGHT OR TWO)...
KWIK
MORNING, APU.
MR. SIMPSON, PLEASE, I AM TELLING YOU FOR THE FINAL TIME, THE PURCHASE OF ONE DONUT DOES NOT PERMIT YOU TO LICK THE SPRINKLES OFF ALL OF THE OTHER--
--OH, SWEET VISHNU! I AM SO TERRIBLY SORRY.
WHEN DID THE ACCIDENT OCCUR?
WELL, HE'S TEN NOW SO... TEN YEARS AND NINE MONTHS AGO, GIVE OR TAKE A FEW BEERS. WHY DO YOU ASK?
OH, HOW VERY, VERY RUDE OF ME. OF COURSE IT IS NONE OF MY BUSINESS.
PLEASE, KINDLY ACCEPT THESE WEEK-OLD BUT STILL QUITE DIGESTIBLE CRULLERS WITH THE COMPLIMENTS OF THE KWIK-E-MART CORPORATION!
WOO-HOO! FREE BAKED GOODS! THANKS, APU.
NO, SIR. THANK YOU FOR DEMONSTRATING SUCH GREAT COURAGE IN THE FACE OF SUCH TERRIBLE ADVERSITY.
AND THANK YOU SO MUCH FOR SHOPPING AT KWIK-E-MART. PLEASE COME AGAIN.
KWIK-E-MART
HEY, IF YOU'RE GIVING AWAY FREE FOOD, YOU BET I WILL!

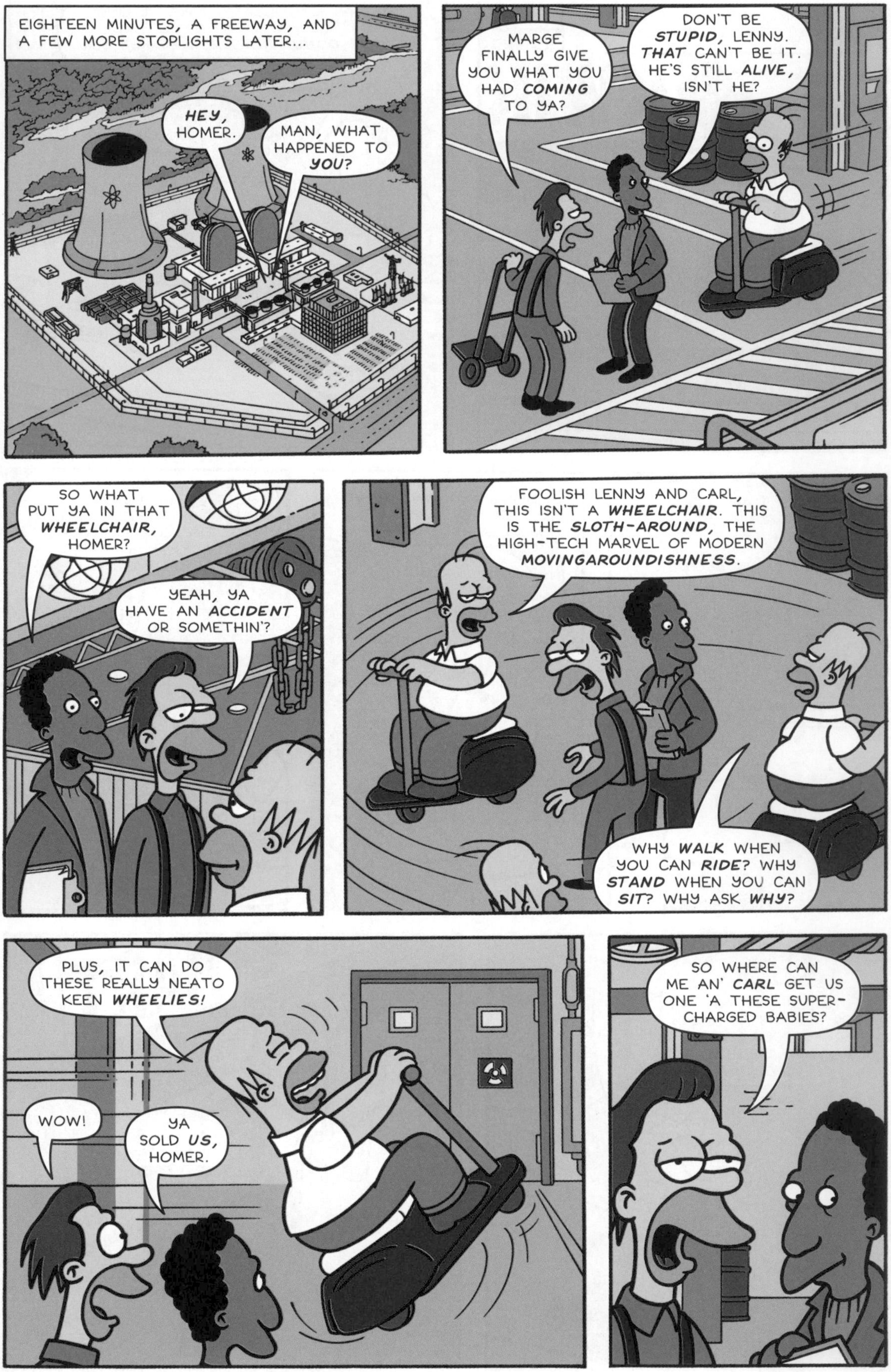
EIGHTEEN MINUTES, A FREEWAY, AND A FEW MORE STOPLIGHTS LATER...
HEY, HOMER.
MAN, WHAT HAPPENED TO YOU?
MARGE FINALLY GIVE YOU WHAT YOU HAD COMING TO YA?
DON'T BE STUPID, LENNY. THAT CAN'T BE IT. HE'S STILL ALIVE, ISN'T HE?
SO WHAT PUT YA IN THAT WHEELCHAIR, HOMER?
YEAH, YA HAVE AN ACCIDENT OR SOMETHIN'?
FOOLISH LENNY AND CARL, THIS ISN'T A WHEELCHAIR. THIS IS THE SLOTH-AROUND, THE HIGH-TECH MARVEL OF MODERN MOVINGAROUNDISHNESS.
WHY WALK WHEN YOU CAN RIDE? WHY STAND WHEN YOU CAN SIT? WHY ASK WHY?
PLUS, IT CAN DO THESE REALLY NEATO KEEN WHEELIES!
WOW!
YA SOLD US, HOMER.
SO WHERE CAN ME AN' CARL GET US ONE 'A THESE SUPER-CHARGED BABIES?

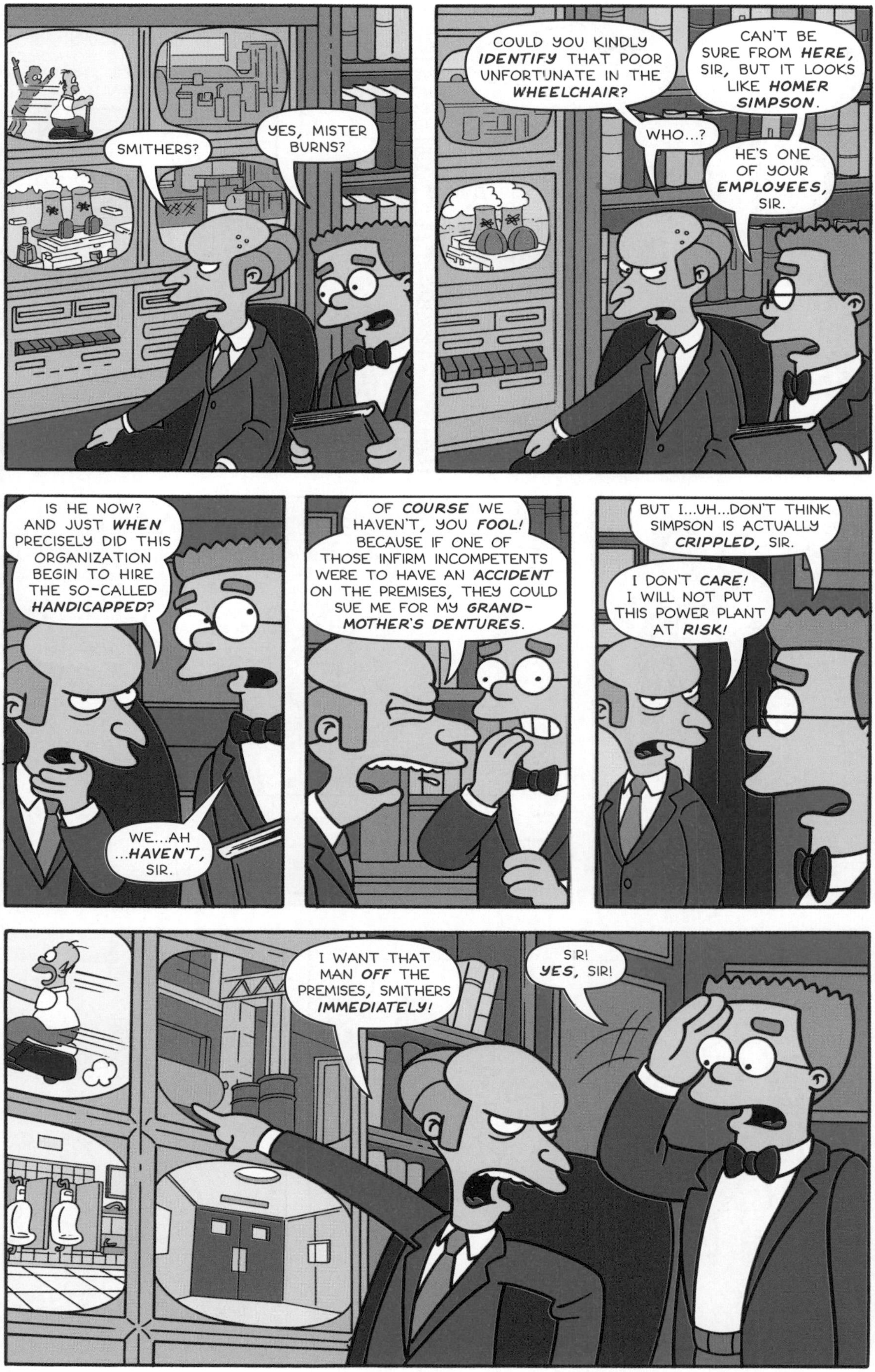
SMITHERS?
YES, MISTER BURNS?
COULD YOU KINDLY IDENTIFY THAT POOR UNFORTUNATE IN THE WHEELCHAIR?
WHO...?
CAN'T BE SURE FROM HERE, SIR, BUT IT LOOKS LIKE HOMER SIMPSON.
HE'S ONE OF YOUR EMPLOYEES, SIR.
IS HE NOW? AND JUST WHEN PRECISELY DID THIS ORGANIZATION BEGIN TO HIRE THE SO-CALLED HANDICAPPED?
WE...AH ...HAVEN'T, SIR.
OF COURSE WE HAVEN'T, YOU FOOL! BECAUSE IF ONE OF THOSE INFIRM INCOMPETENTS WERE TO HAVE AN ACCIDENT ON THE PREMISES, THEY COULD SUE ME FOR MY GRAND-MOTHER'S DENTURES.
BUT I...UH...DON'T THINK SIMPSON IS ACTUALLY CRIPPLED, SIR.
I DON'T CARE! I WILL NOT PUT THIS POWER PLANT AT RISK!
I WANT THAT MAN OFF THE PREMISES, SMITHERS IMMEDIATELY!
SIR! YES, SIR!

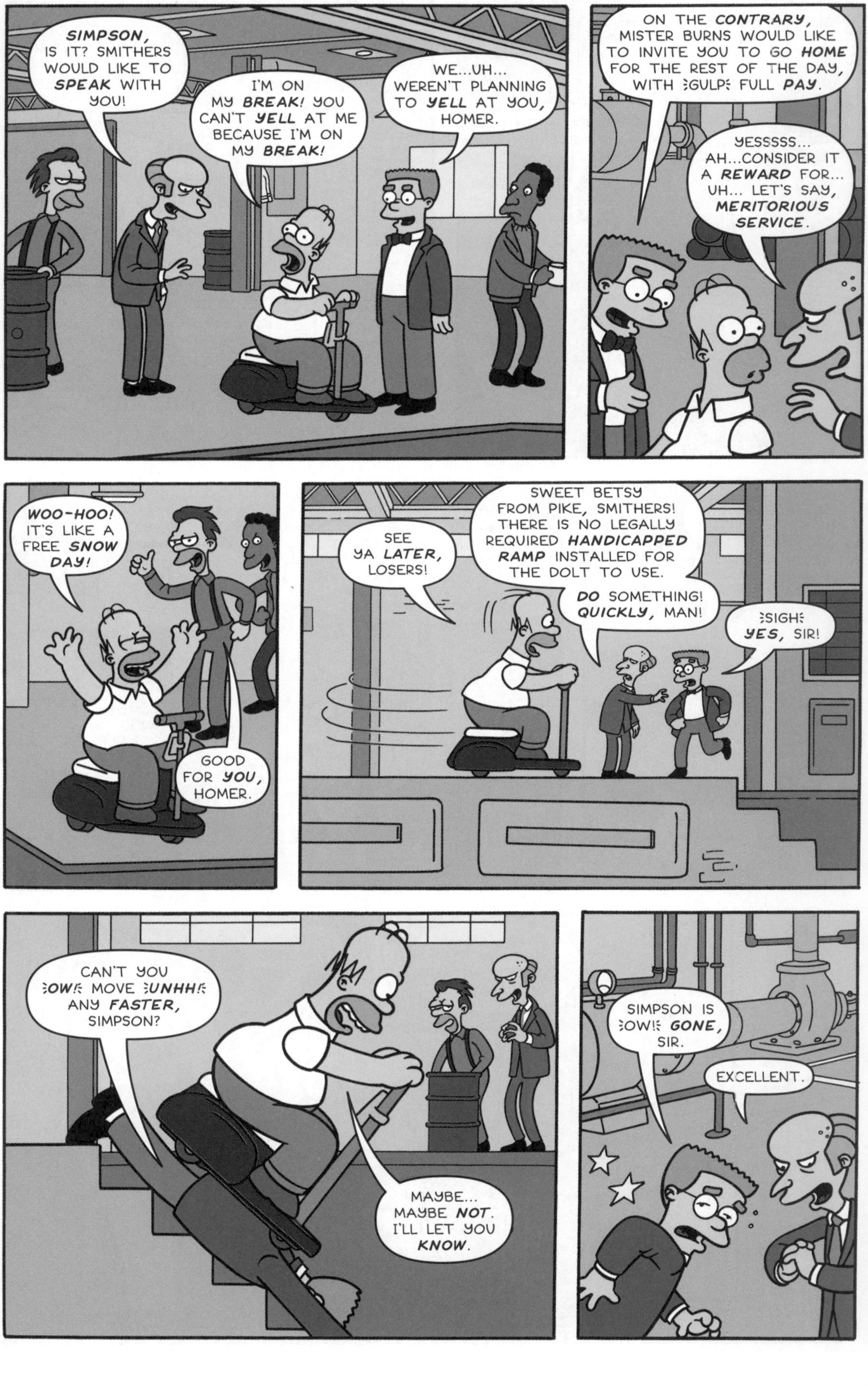

SIMPSON, IS IT? SMITHERS WOULD LIKE TO SPEAK WITH YOU!
I'M ON MY BREAK! YOU CAN'T YELL AT ME BECAUSE I'M ON MY BREAK!
WE...UH... WEREN'T PLANNING TO YELL AT YOU, HOMER.
ON THE CONTRARY, MISTER BURNS WOULD LIKE TO INVITE YOU TO GO HOME FOR THE REST OF THE DAY, WITH ⁝GULP⁝ FULL PAY.
YESSSSS... AH...CONSIDER IT A REWARD FOR... UH... LET'S SAY, MERITORIOUS SERVICE.
WOO-HOO! IT'S LIKE A FREE SNOW DAY!
GOOD FOR YOU, HOMER.
SEE YA LATER, LOSERS!
SWEET BETSY FROM PIKE, SMITHERS! THERE IS NO LEGALLY REQUIRED HANDICAPPED RAMP INSTALLED FOR THE DOLT TO USE.
DO SOMETHING! QUICKLY, MAN!
⁝SIGH⁝ YES, SIR!
CAN'T YOU ⁝OW!⁝ MOVE ⁝UNHH!⁝ ANY FASTER, SIMPSON?
MAYBE... MAYBE NOT. I'LL LET YOU KNOW.
SIMPSON IS ⁝OW!⁝ GONE, SIR.
EXCELLENT.

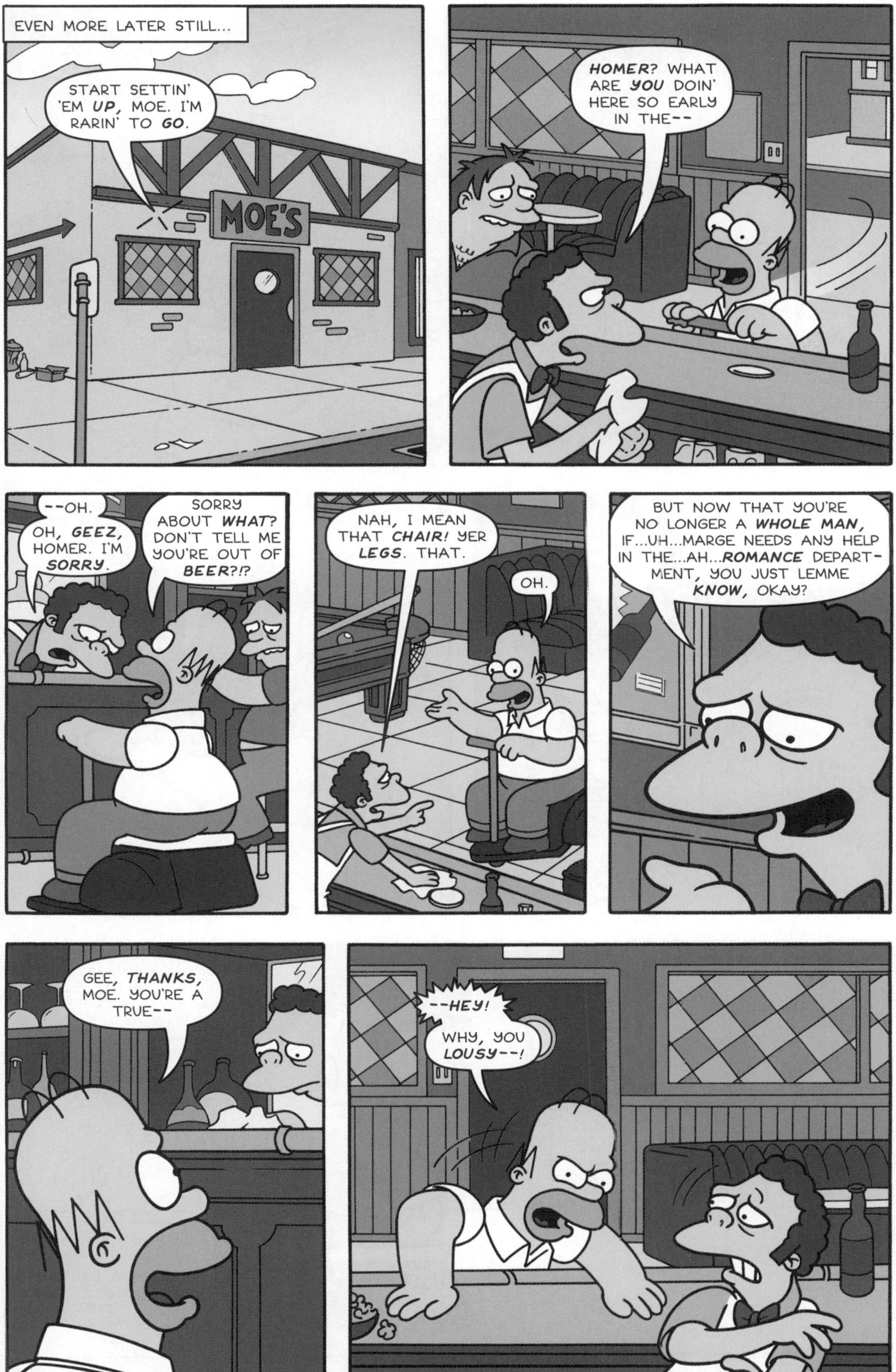
EVEN MORE LATER STILL...
START SETTIN' 'EM UP, MOE. I'M RARIN' TO GO.
MOE'S
HOMER? WHAT ARE YOU DOIN' HERE SO EARLY IN THE--
--OH.
OH, GEEZ, HOMER. I'M SORRY.
SORRY ABOUT WHAT? DON'T TELL ME YOU'RE OUT OF BEER?!?
NAH, I MEAN THAT CHAIR! YER LEGS. THAT.
OH.
BUT NOW THAT YOU'RE NO LONGER A WHOLE MAN, IF...UH...MARGE NEEDS ANY HELP IN THE...AH...ROMANCE DEPARTMENT, YOU JUST LEMME KNOW, OKAY?
GEE, THANKS, MOE. YOU'RE A TRUE--
--HEY!
WHY, YOU LOUSY--!

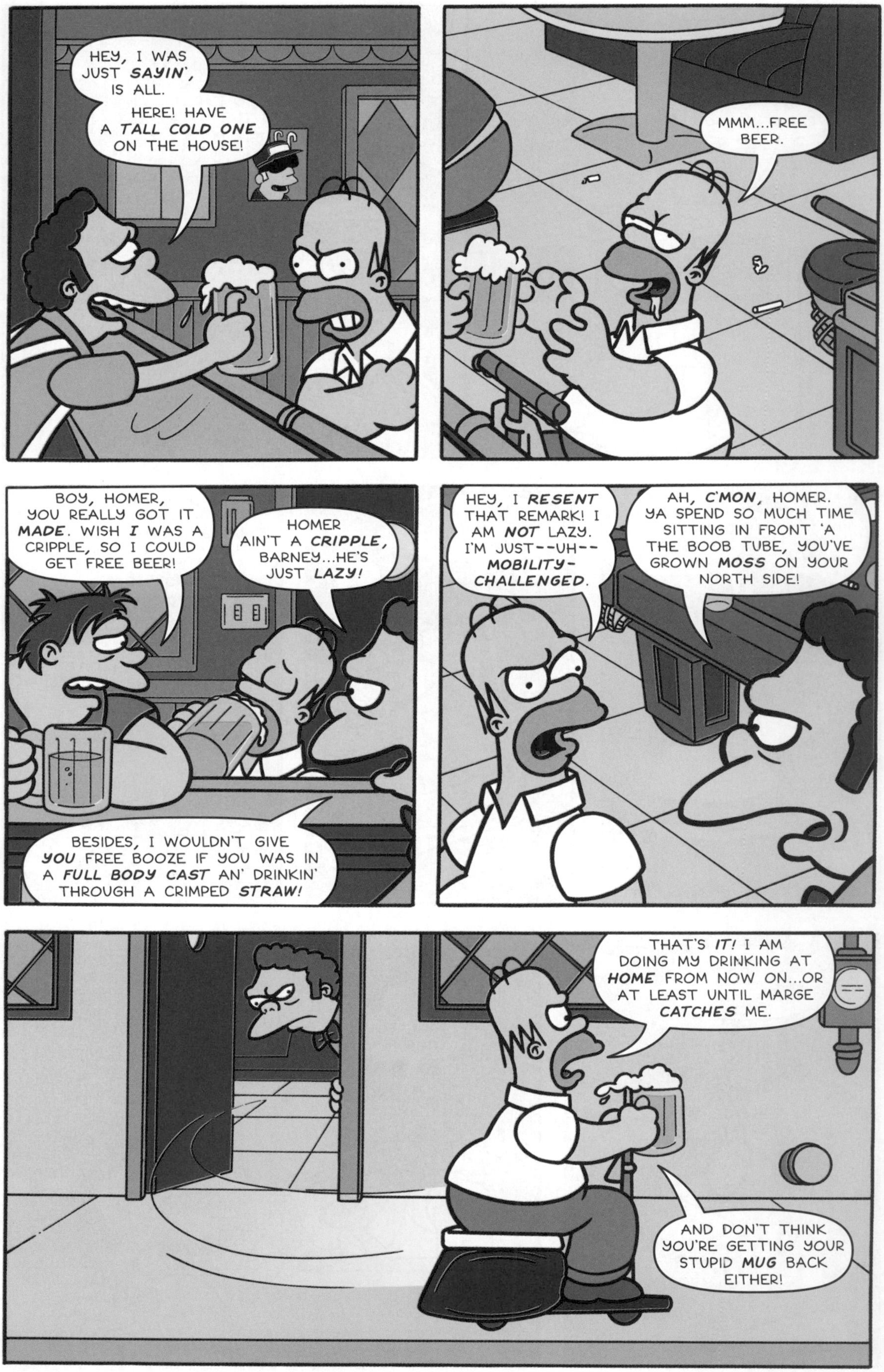
HEY, I WAS JUST SAYIN', IS ALL.
HERE! HAVE A TALL COLD ONE ON THE HOUSE!
MMM...FREE BEER.
BOY, HOMER, YOU REALLY GOT IT MADE. WISH I WAS A CRIPPLE, SO I COULD GET FREE BEER!
HOMER AIN'T A CRIPPLE, BARNEY...HE'S JUST LAZY!
BESIDES, I WOULDN'T GIVE YOU FREE BOOZE IF YOU WAS IN A FULL BODY CAST AN' DRINKIN' THROUGH A CRIMPED STRAW!
HEY, I RESENT THAT REMARK! I AM NOT LAZY. I'M JUST--UH--MOBILITY-CHALLENGED.
AH, C'MON, HOMER. YA SPEND SO MUCH TIME SITTING IN FRONT 'A THE BOOB TUBE, YOU'VE GROWN MOSS ON YOUR NORTH SIDE!
THAT'S IT! I AM DOING MY DRINKING AT HOME FROM NOW ON...OR AT LEAST UNTIL MARGE CATCHES ME.
AND DON'T THINK YOU'RE GETTING YOUR STUPID MUG BACK EITHER!

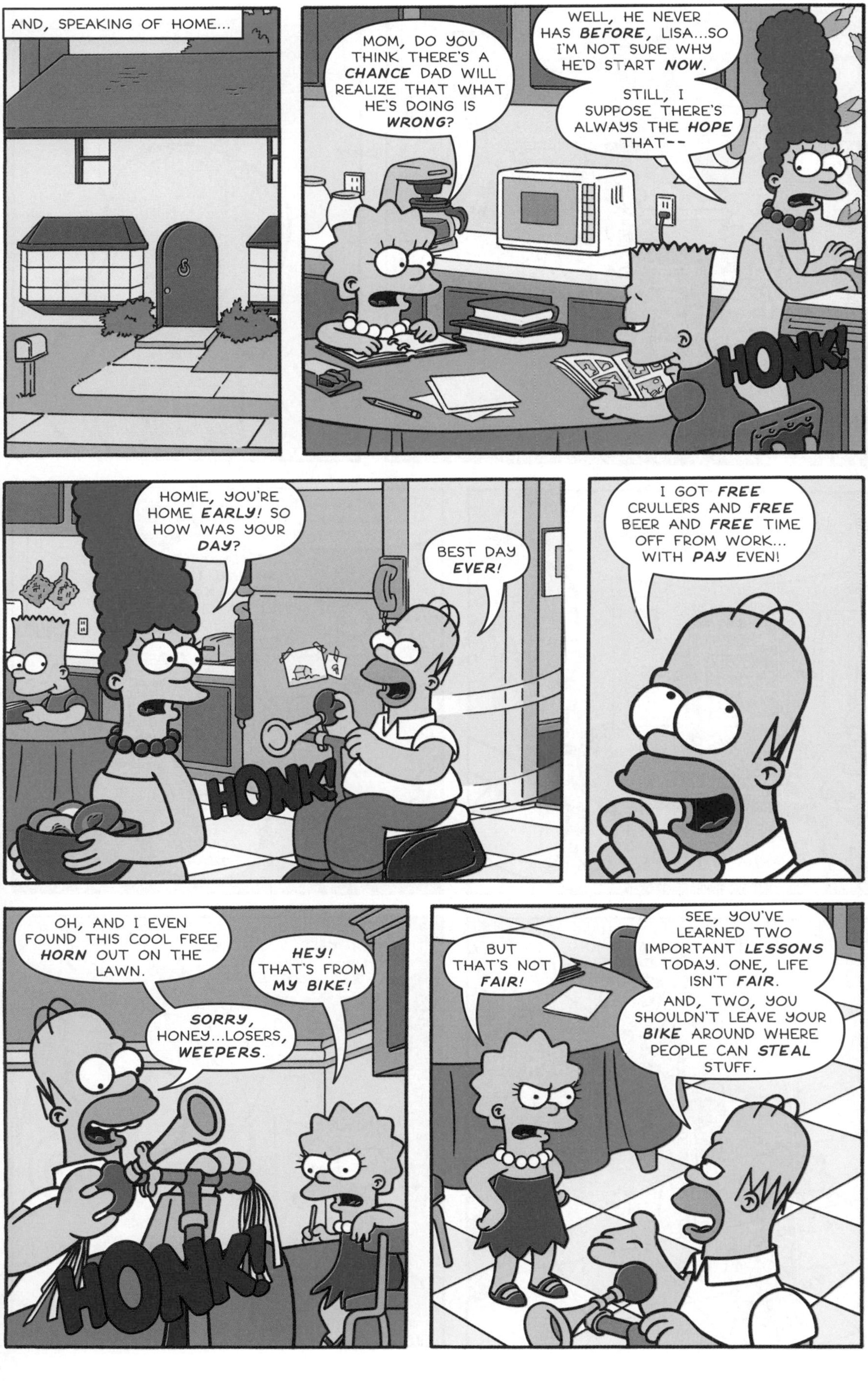
AND, SPEAKING OF HOME...
MOM, DO YOU THINK THERE'S A CHANCE DAD WILL REALIZE THAT WHAT HE'S DOING IS WRONG?
WELL, HE NEVER HAS BEFORE, LISA...SO I'M NOT SURE WHY HE'D START NOW.
STILL, I SUPPOSE THERE'S ALWAYS THE HOPE THAT--
HONK!
HOMIE, YOU'RE HOME EARLY! SO HOW WAS YOUR DAY?
BEST DAY EVER!
HONK!
I GOT FREE CRULLERS AND FREE BEER AND FREE TIME OFF FROM WORK... WITH PAY EVEN!
OH, AND I EVEN FOUND THIS COOL FREE HORN OUT ON THE LAWN.
HEY! THAT'S FROM MY BIKE!
SORRY, HONEY...LOSERS, WEEPERS.
HONK!
BUT THAT'S NOT FAIR!
SEE, YOU'VE LEARNED TWO IMPORTANT LESSONS TODAY. ONE, LIFE ISN'T FAIR.
AND, TWO, YOU SHOULDN'T LEAVE YOUR BIKE AROUND WHERE PEOPLE CAN STEAL STUFF.

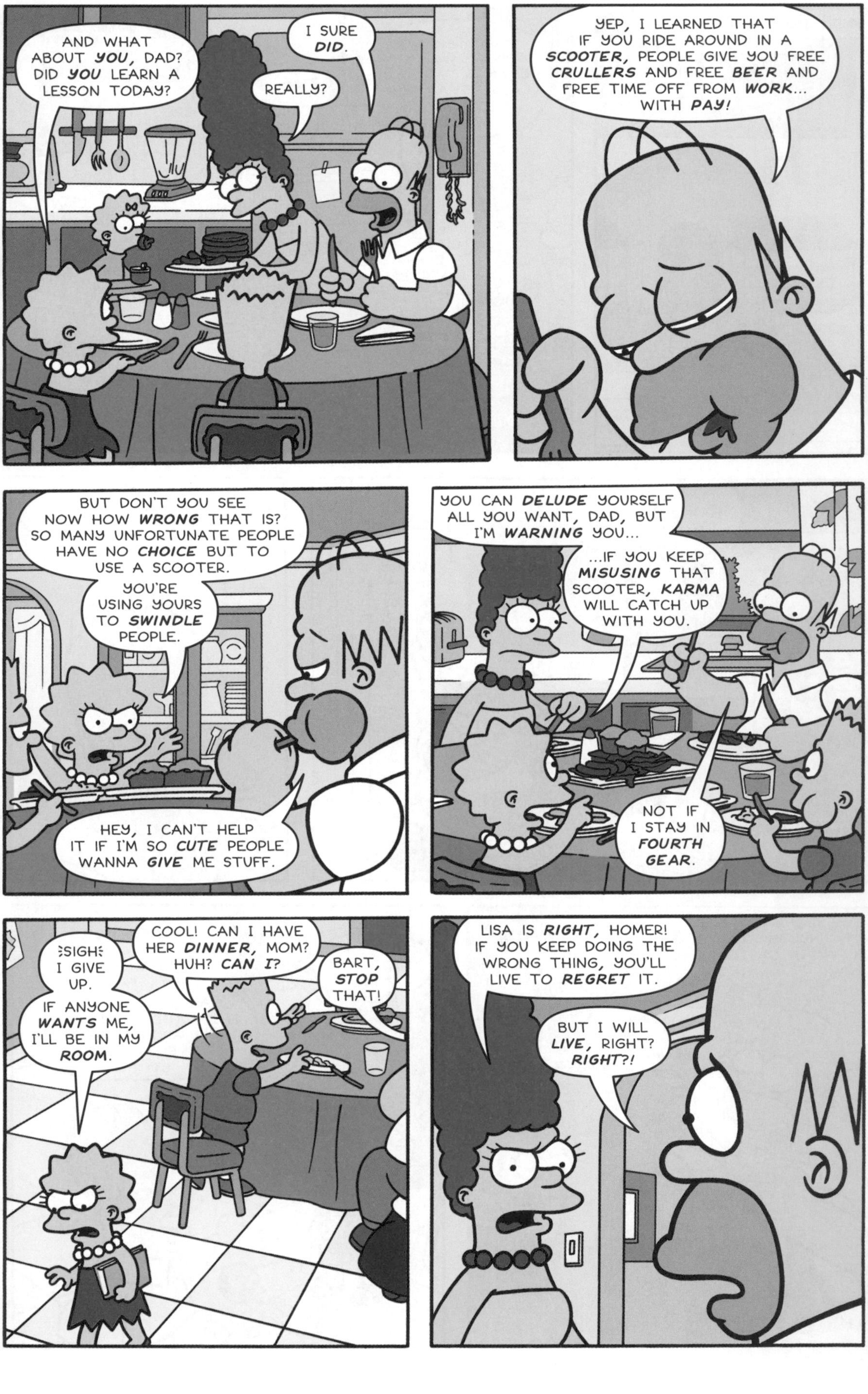
AND WHAT ABOUT YOU, DAD? DID YOU LEARN A LESSON TODAY?
REALLY?
I SURE DID.
YEP, I LEARNED THAT IF YOU RIDE AROUND IN A SCOOTER, PEOPLE GIVE YOU FREE CRULLERS AND FREE BEER AND FREE TIME OFF FROM WORK... WITH PAY!
BUT DON'T YOU SEE NOW HOW WRONG THAT IS? SO MANY UNFORTUNATE PEOPLE HAVE NO CHOICE BUT TO USE A SCOOTER.
YOU'RE USING YOURS TO SWINDLE PEOPLE.
HEY, I CAN'T HELP IT IF I'M SO CUTE PEOPLE WANNA GIVE ME STUFF.
YOU CAN DELUDE YOURSELF ALL YOU WANT, DAD, BUT I'M WARNING YOU...
...IF YOU KEEP MISUSING THAT SCOOTER, KARMA WILL CATCH UP WITH YOU.
NOT IF I STAY IN FOURTH GEAR.
SIGH I GIVE UP.
IF ANYONE WANTS ME, I'LL BE IN MY ROOM.
COOL! CAN I HAVE HER DINNER, MOM? HUH? CAN I?
BART, STOP THAT!
LISA IS RIGHT, HOMER! IF YOU KEEP DOING THE WRONG THING, YOU'LL LIVE TO REGRET IT.
BUT I WILL LIVE, RIGHT? RIGHT?!

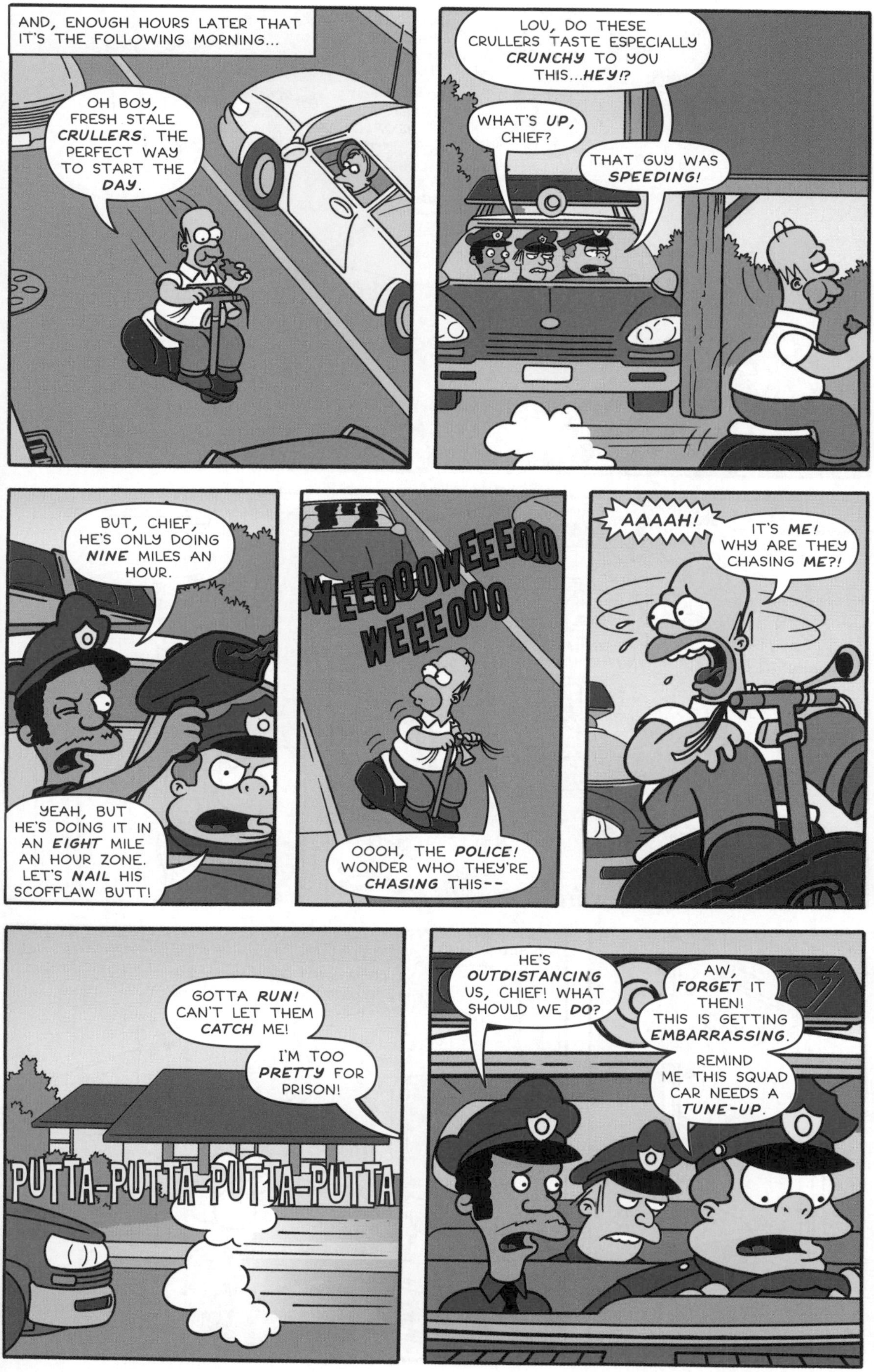
AND, ENOUGH HOURS LATER THAT IT'S THE FOLLOWING MORNING...
OH BOY, FRESH STALE CRULLERS. THE PERFECT WAY TO START THE DAY.
LOU, DO THESE CRULLERS TASTE ESPECIALLY CRUNCHY TO YOU THIS...HEY!?
WHAT'S UP, CHIEF?
THAT GUY WAS SPEEDING!
BUT, CHIEF, HE'S ONLY DOING NINE MILES AN HOUR.
YEAH, BUT HE'S DOING IT IN AN EIGHT MILE AN HOUR ZONE. LET'S NAIL HIS SCOFFLAW BUTT!
WEEOOOWEEEOO
WEEEOOO
OOOH, THE POLICE! WONDER WHO THEY'RE CHASING THIS--
AAAAH!
IT'S ME! WHY ARE THEY CHASING ME?!
GOTTA RUN! CAN'T LET THEM CATCH ME!
I'M TOO PRETTY FOR PRISON!
PUTTA-PUTTA-PUTTA-PUTTA
HE'S OUTDISTANCING US, CHIEF! WHAT SHOULD WE DO?
AW, FORGET IT THEN! THIS IS GETTING EMBARRASSING.
REMIND ME THIS SQUAD CAR NEEDS A TUNE-UP.

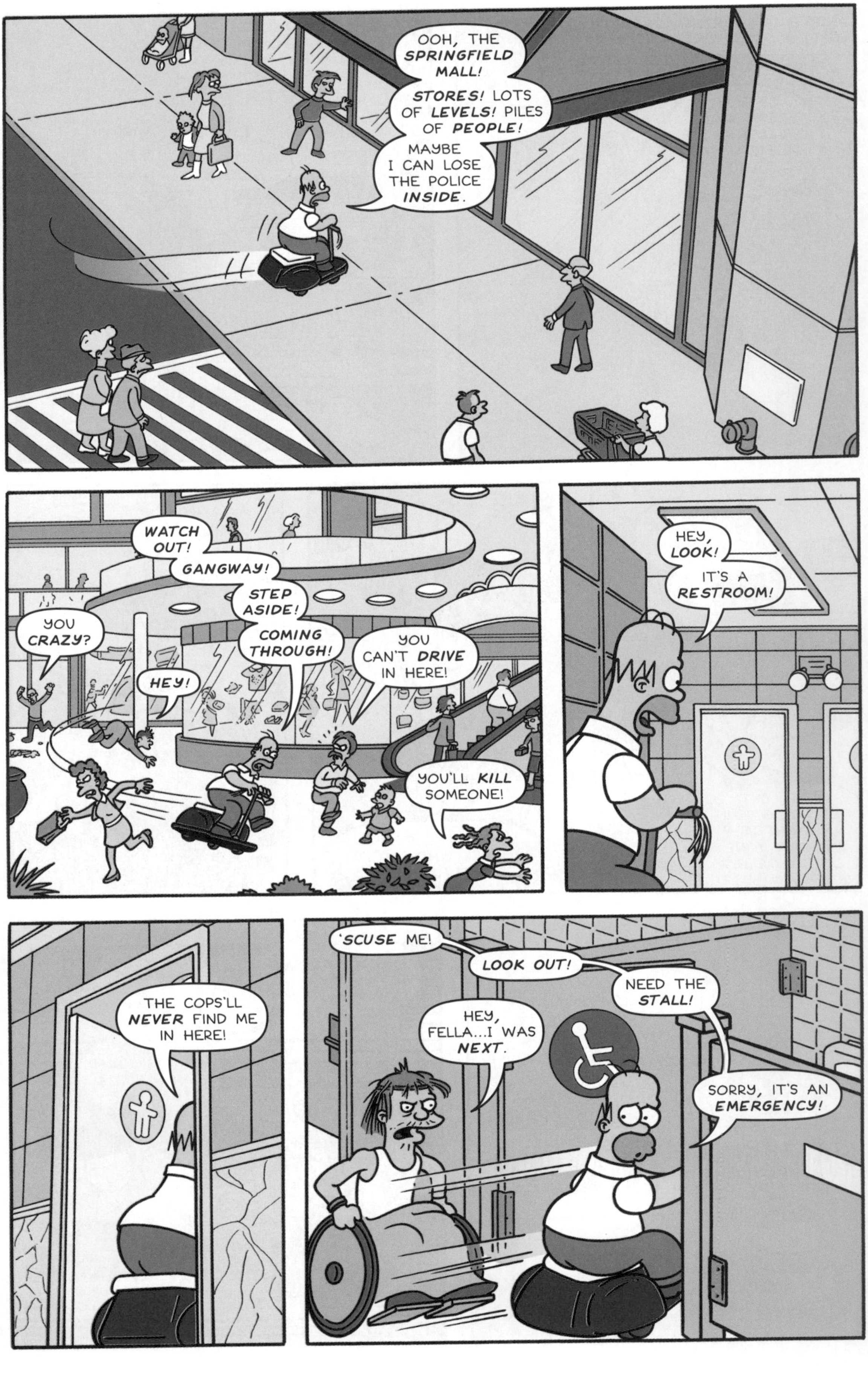
OOH, THE SPRINGFIELD MALL!
STORES! LOTS OF LEVELS! PILES OF PEOPLE!
MAYBE I CAN LOSE THE POLICE INSIDE.
WATCH OUT!
GANGWAY!
STEP ASIDE!
COMING THROUGH!
YOU CRAZY?
HEY!
YOU CAN'T DRIVE IN HERE!
YOU'LL KILL SOMEONE!
HEY, LOOK!
IT'S A RESTROOM!
THE COPS'LL NEVER FIND ME IN HERE!
'SCUSE ME!
LOOK OUT!
NEED THE STALL!
HEY, FELLA...I WAS NEXT.
SORRY, IT'S AN EMERGENCY!

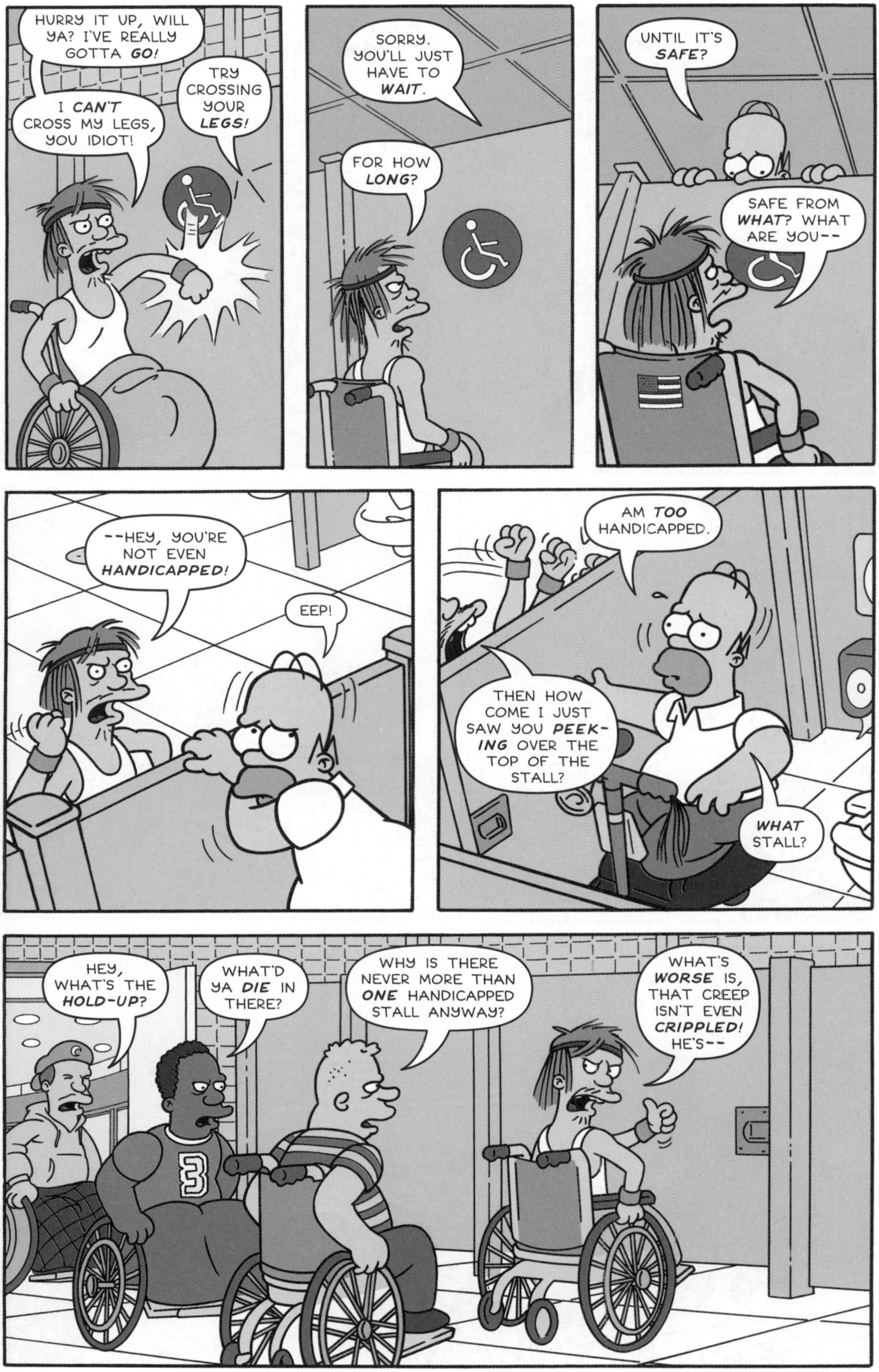
HURRY IT UP, WILL YA? I'VE REALLY GOTTA GO!
I CAN'T CROSS MY LEGS, YOU IDIOT!
TRY CROSSING YOUR LEGS!
SORRY. YOU'LL JUST HAVE TO WAIT.
FOR HOW LONG?
UNTIL IT'S SAFE?
SAFE FROM WHAT? WHAT ARE YOU--
--HEY, YOU'RE NOT EVEN HANDICAPPED!
EEP!
AM TOO HANDICAPPED.
THEN HOW COME I JUST SAW YOU PEEKING OVER THE TOP OF THE STALL?
WHAT STALL?
HEY, WHAT'S THE HOLD-UP?
WHAT'D YA DIE IN THERE?
WHY IS THERE NEVER MORE THAN ONE HANDICAPPED STALL ANYWAY?
WHAT'S WORSE IS, THAT CREEP ISN'T EVEN CRIPPLED! HE'S--

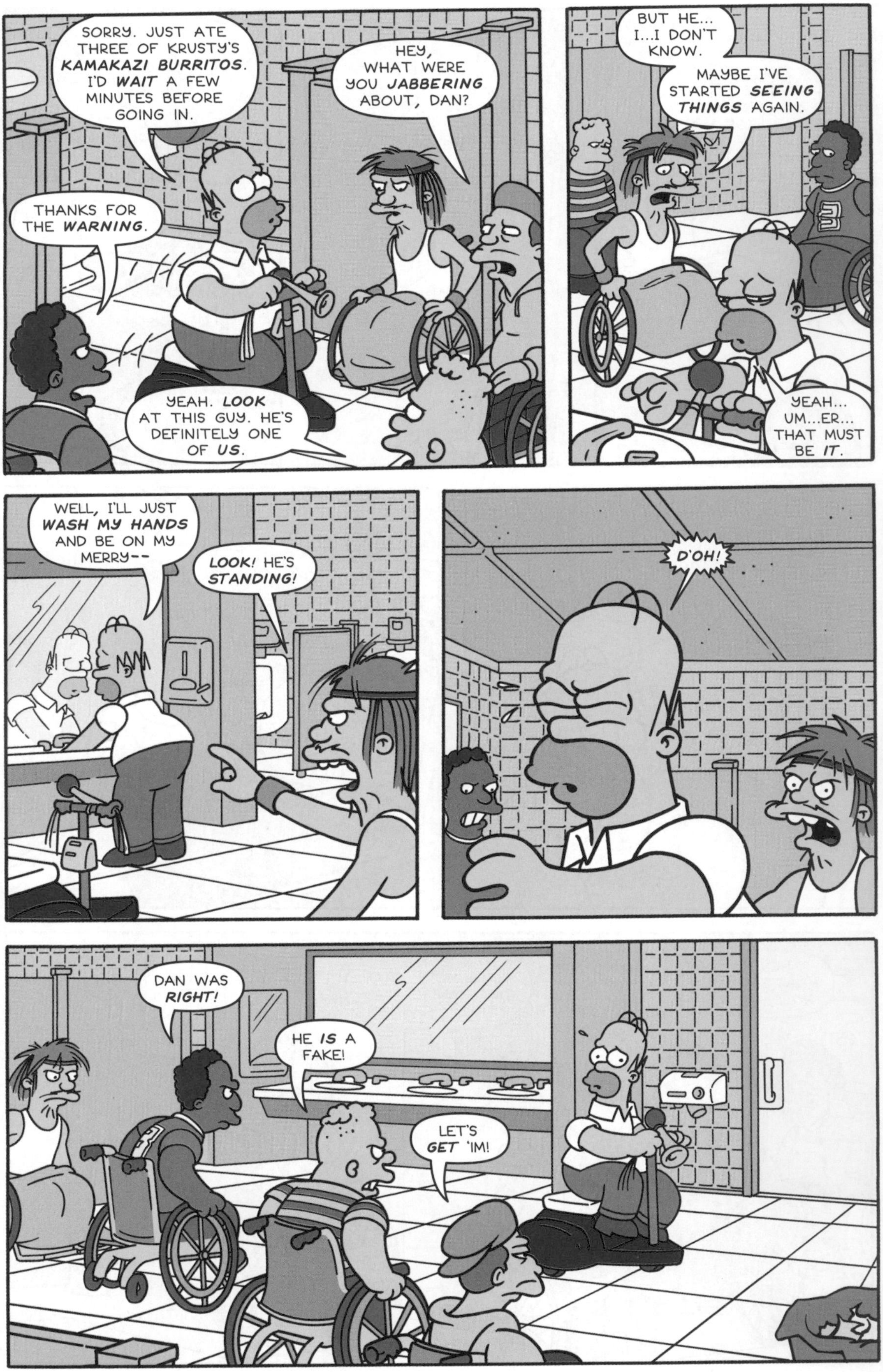
SORRY. JUST ATE THREE OF KRUSTY'S KAMAKAZI BURRITOS. I'D WAIT A FEW MINUTES BEFORE GOING IN.
HEY, WHAT WERE YOU JABBERING ABOUT, DAN?
THANKS FOR THE WARNING.
YEAH. LOOK AT THIS GUY. HE'S DEFINITELY ONE OF US.
BUT HE... I...I DON'T KNOW.
MAYBE I'VE STARTED SEEING THINGS AGAIN.
YEAH... UM...ER... THAT MUST BE IT.
WELL, I'LL JUST WASH MY HANDS AND BE ON MY MERRY--
LOOK! HE'S STANDING!
D'OH!
DAN WAS RIGHT!
HE IS A FAKE!
LET'S GET 'IM!

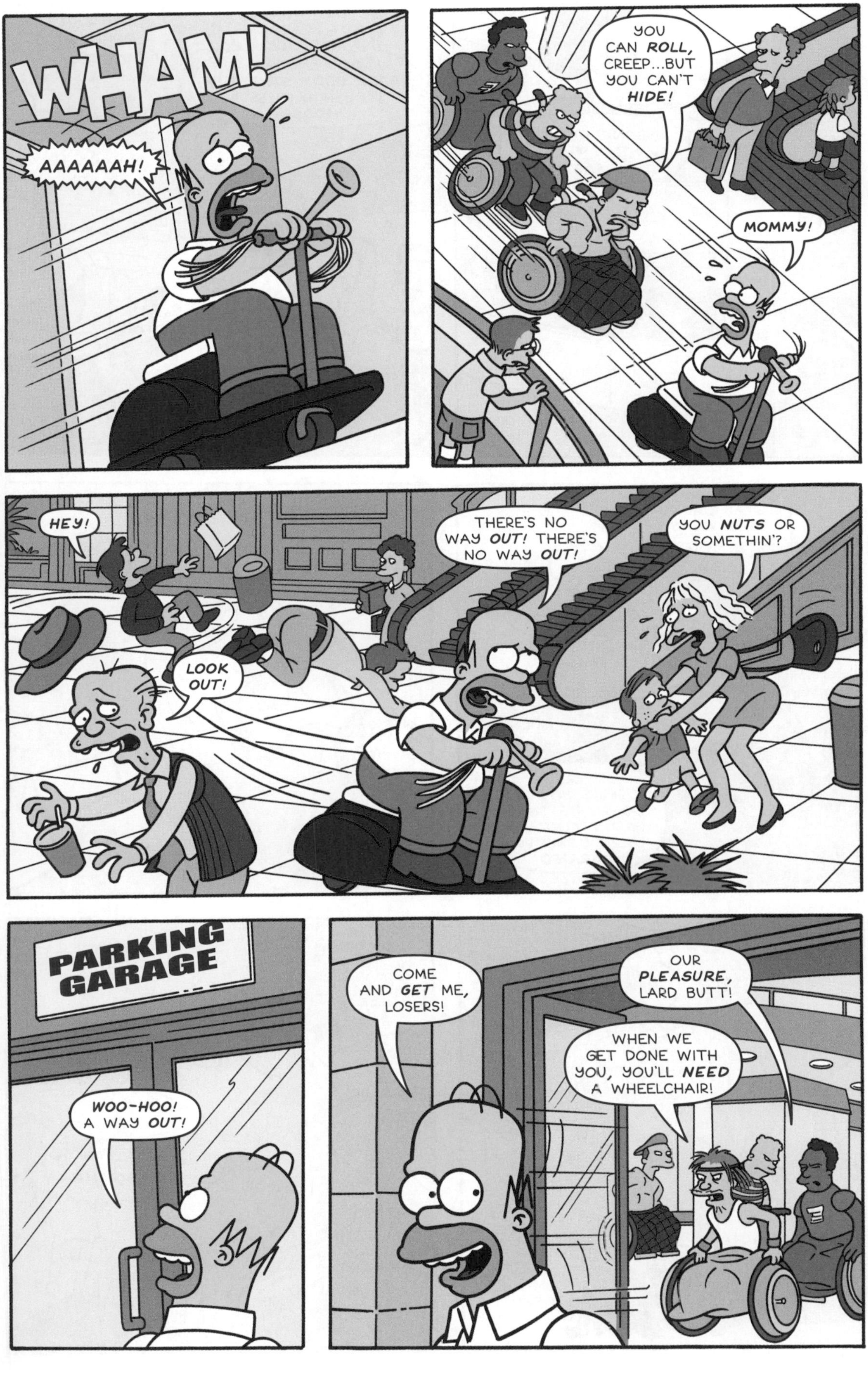
WHAM!
AAAAAAH!
YOU CAN ROLL, CREEP...BUT YOU CAN'T HIDE!
MOMMY!
HEY!
THERE'S NO WAY OUT! THERE'S NO WAY OUT!
YOU NUTS OR SOMETHIN'?
LOOK OUT!
PARKING GARAGE
WOO-HOO! A WAY OUT!
COME AND GET ME, LOSERS!
OUR PLEASURE, LARD BUTT!
WHEN WE GET DONE WITH YOU, YOU'LL NEED A WHEELCHAIR!

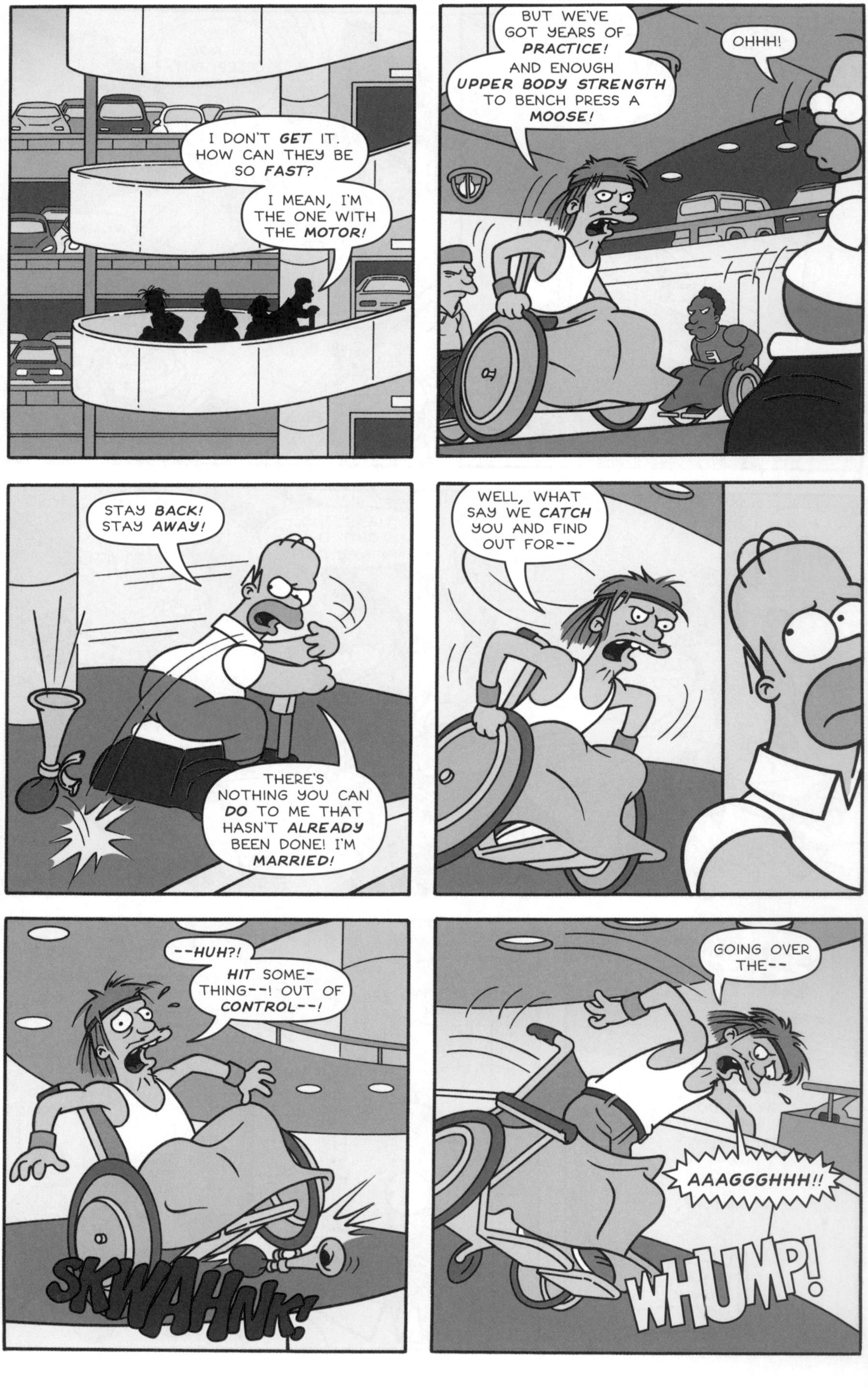
I DON'T GET IT. HOW CAN THEY BE SO FAST?
I MEAN, I'M THE ONE WITH THE MOTOR!
BUT WE'VE GOT YEARS OF PRACTICE! AND ENOUGH UPPER BODY STRENGTH TO BENCH PRESS A MOOSE!
OHHH!
STAY BACK! STAY AWAY!
THERE'S NOTHING YOU CAN DO TO ME THAT HASN'T ALREADY BEEN DONE! I'M MARRIED!
WELL, WHAT SAY WE CATCH YOU AND FIND OUT FOR--
--HUH?!
HIT SOME-THING--! OUT OF CONTROL--!
SKWAHNK!
GOING OVER THE--
AAAGGGHHH!!
WHUMP!

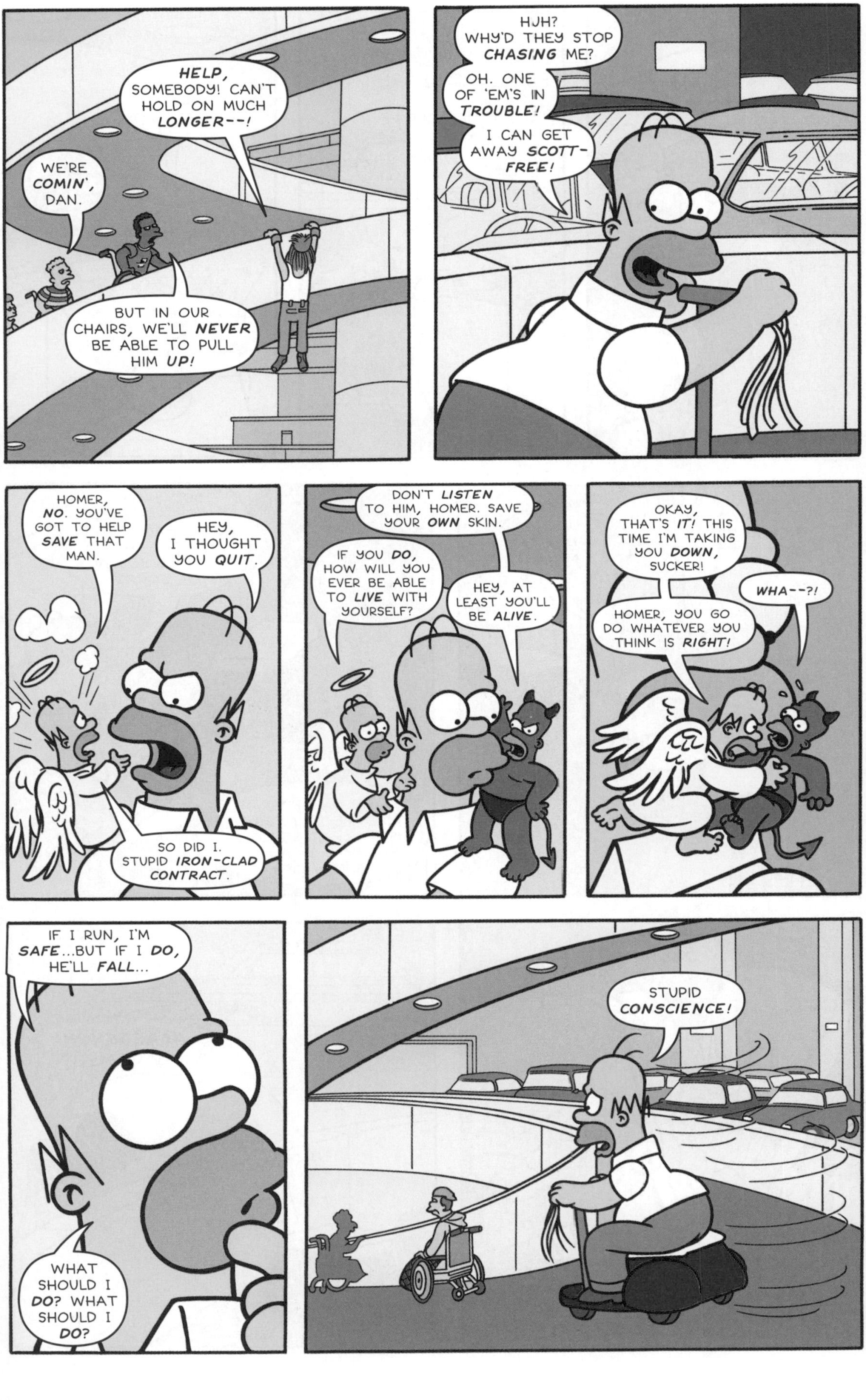
HELP, SOMEBODY! CAN'T HOLD ON MUCH LONGER--!
WE'RE COMIN', DAN.
BUT IN OUR CHAIRS, WE'LL NEVER BE ABLE TO PULL HIM UP!
HUH? WHY'D THEY STOP CHASING ME?
OH. ONE OF 'EM'S IN TROUBLE!
I CAN GET AWAY SCOTT-FREE!
HOMER, NO. YOU'VE GOT TO HELP SAVE THAT MAN.
HEY, I THOUGHT YOU QUIT.
SO DID I. STUPID IRON-CLAD CONTRACT.
DON'T LISTEN TO HIM, HOMER. SAVE YOUR OWN SKIN.
IF YOU DO, HOW WILL YOU EVER BE ABLE TO LIVE WITH YOURSELF?
HEY, AT LEAST YOU'LL BE ALIVE.
OKAY, THAT'S IT! THIS TIME I'M TAKING YOU DOWN, SUCKER!
WHA--?!
HOMER, YOU GO DO WHATEVER YOU THINK IS RIGHT!
IF I RUN, I'M SAFE...BUT IF I DO, HE'LL FALL...
WHAT SHOULD I DO? WHAT SHOULD I DO?
STUPID CONSCIENCE!

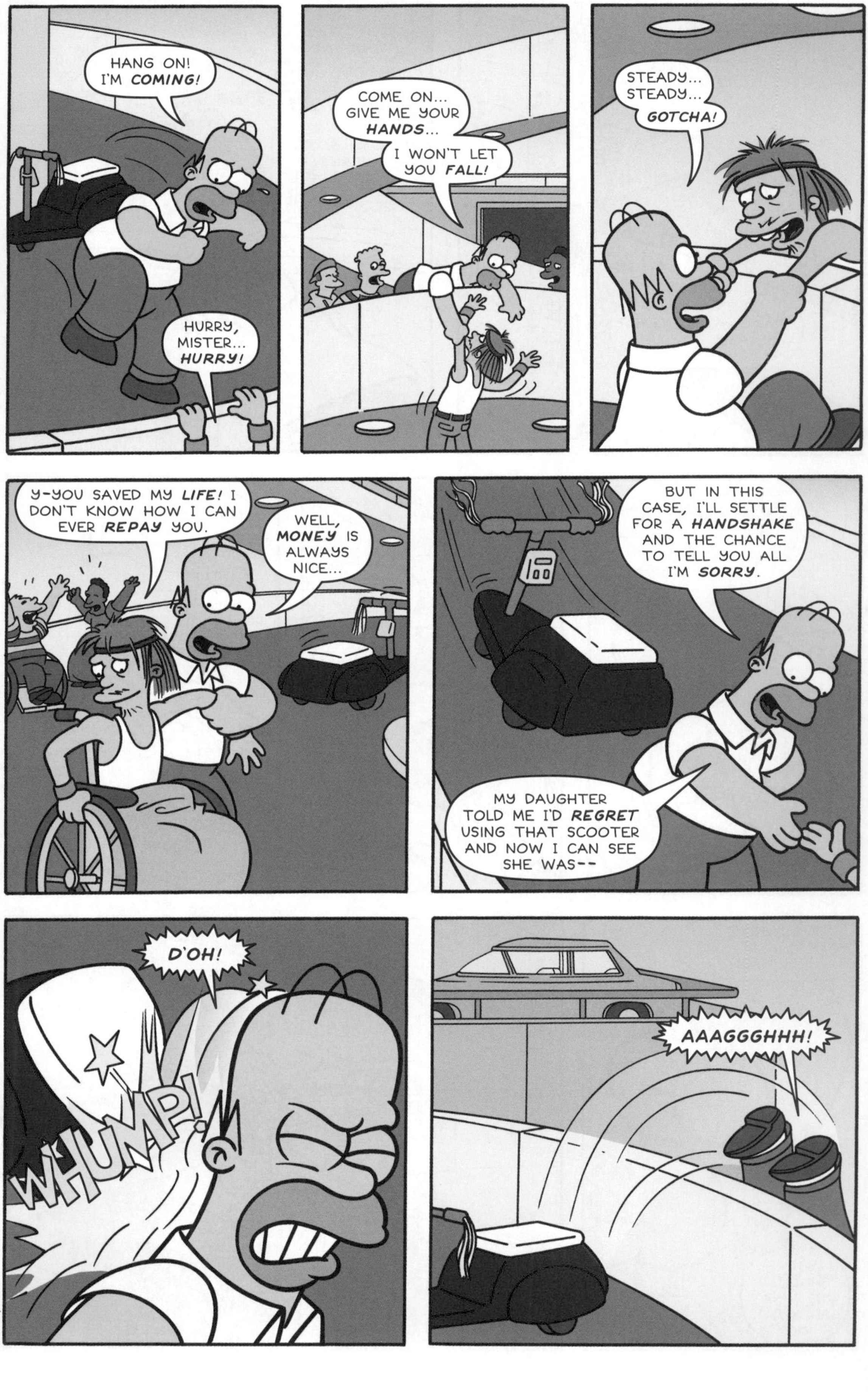
HANG ON! I'M COMING!
HURRY, MISTER... HURRY!
COME ON... GIVE ME YOUR HANDS...
I WON'T LET YOU FALL!
STEADY... STEADY... GOTCHA!
Y-YOU SAVED MY LIFE! I DON'T KNOW HOW I CAN EVER REPAY YOU.
WELL, MONEY IS ALWAYS NICE...
BUT IN THIS CASE, I'LL SETTLE FOR A HANDSHAKE AND THE CHANCE TO TELL YOU ALL I'M SORRY.
MY DAUGHTER TOLD ME I'D REGRET USING THAT SCOOTER AND NOW I CAN SEE SHE WAS--
D'OH!
WHUMP!
AAAGGGHHH!

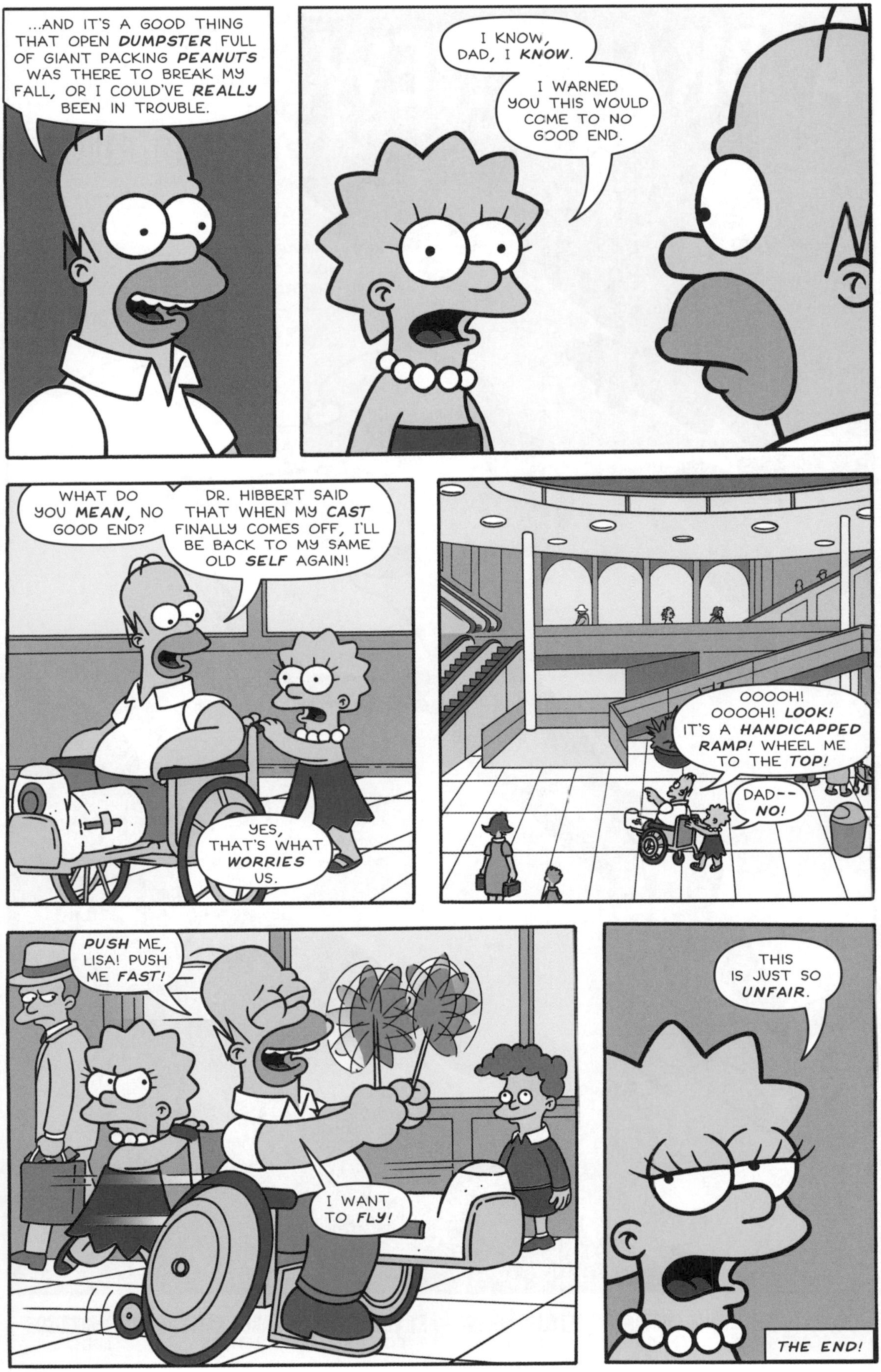
...AND IT'S A GOOD THING THAT OPEN DUMPSTER FULL OF GIANT PACKING PEANUTS WAS THERE TO BREAK MY FALL, OR I COULD'VE REALLY BEEN IN TROUBLE.
I KNOW, DAD, I KNOW.
I WARNED YOU THIS WOULD COME TO NO GOOD END.
WHAT DO YOU MEAN, NO GOOD END?
DR. HIBBERT SAID THAT WHEN MY CAST FINALLY COMES OFF, I'LL BE BACK TO MY SAME OLD SELF AGAIN!
YES, THAT'S WHAT WORRIES US.
OOOOH! OOOOH! LOOK! IT'S A HANDICAPPED RAMP! WHEEL ME TO THE TOP!
DAD-- NO!
PUSH ME, LISA! PUSH ME FAST!
I WANT TO FLY!
THIS IS JUST SO UNFAIR.
THE END!

MATT GROENING presents

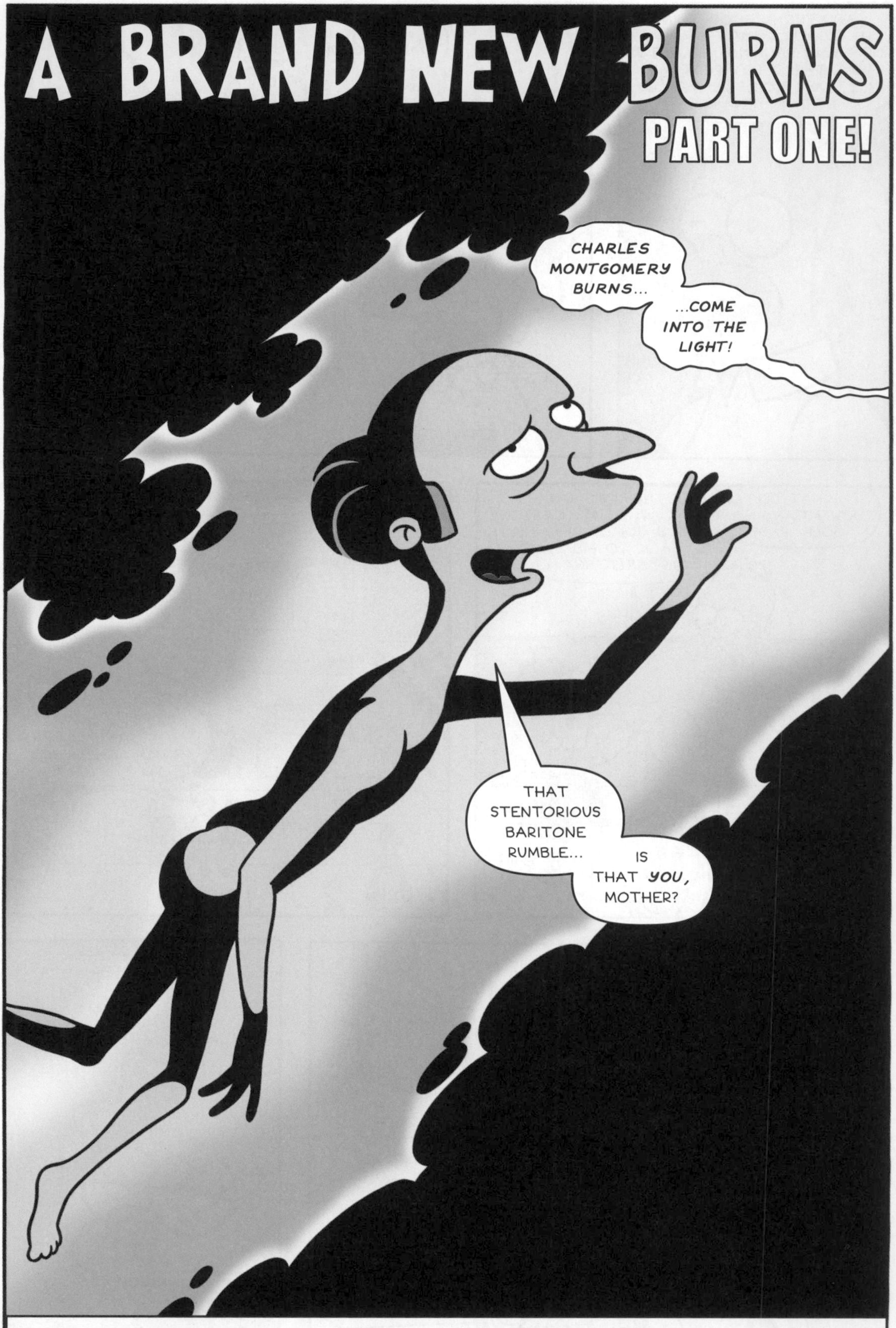
A BRAND NEW BURNS
PART ONE!
CHARLES MONTGOMERY BURNS...
...COME INTO THE LIGHT!
THAT STENTORIOUS BARITONE RUMBLE...
IS THAT *YOU*, MOTHER?

CHUCK DIXON SCRIPT | **JOHN COSTANZA** PENCILS | **PHYLLIS NOVIN** INKS | **ART VILLANUEVA** COLORS | **KAREN BATES** LETTERS | **BILL MORRISON** EDITOR

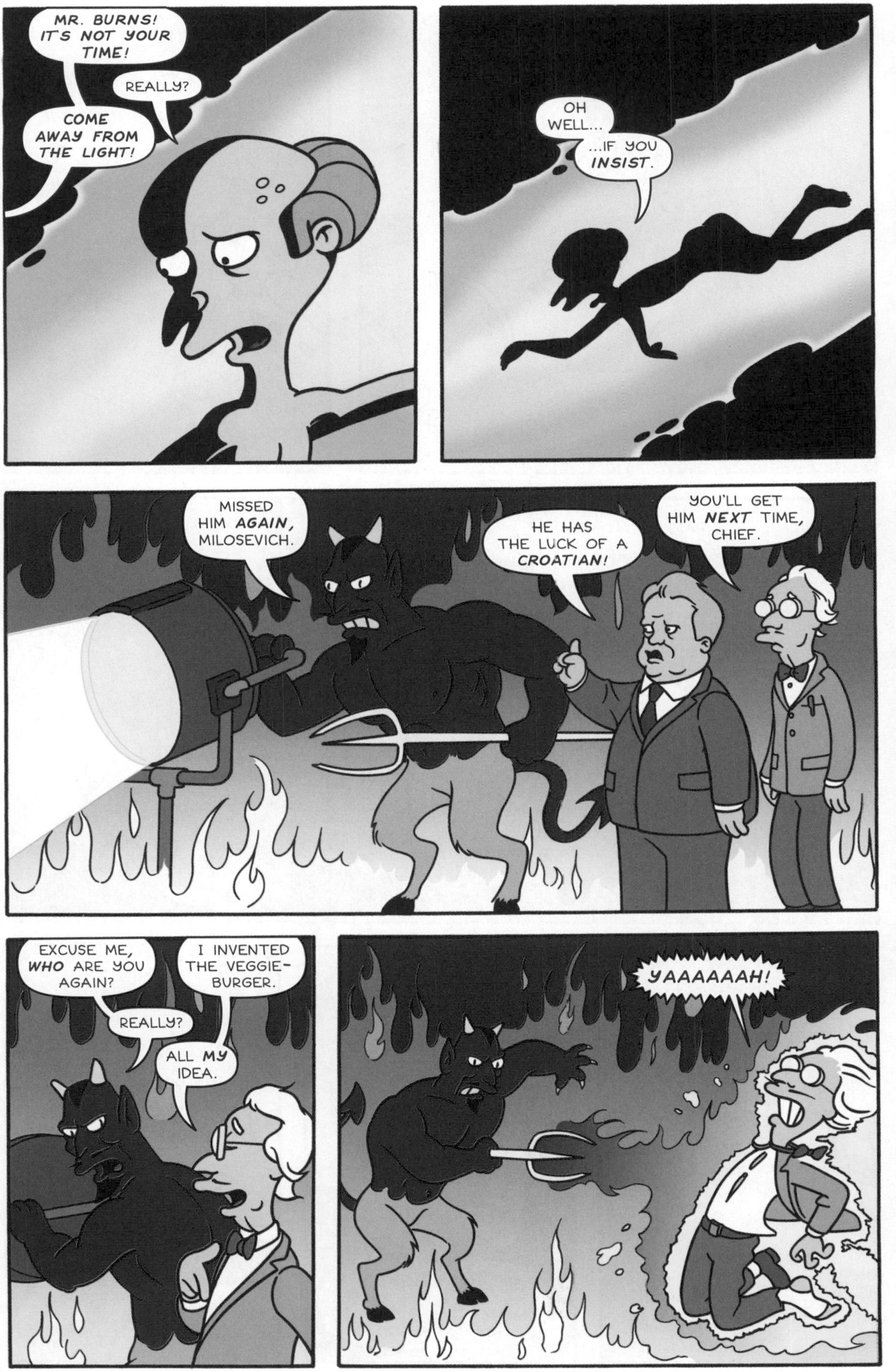
MR. BURNS! IT'S NOT YOUR TIME!
REALLY?
COME AWAY FROM THE LIGHT!
OH WELL...
...IF YOU INSIST.
MISSED HIM AGAIN, MILOSEVICH.
HE HAS THE LUCK OF A CROATIAN!
YOU'LL GET HIM NEXT TIME, CHIEF.
EXCUSE ME, WHO ARE YOU AGAIN?
I INVENTED THE VEGGIE-BURGER.
REALLY?
ALL MY IDEA.
YAAAAAAH!

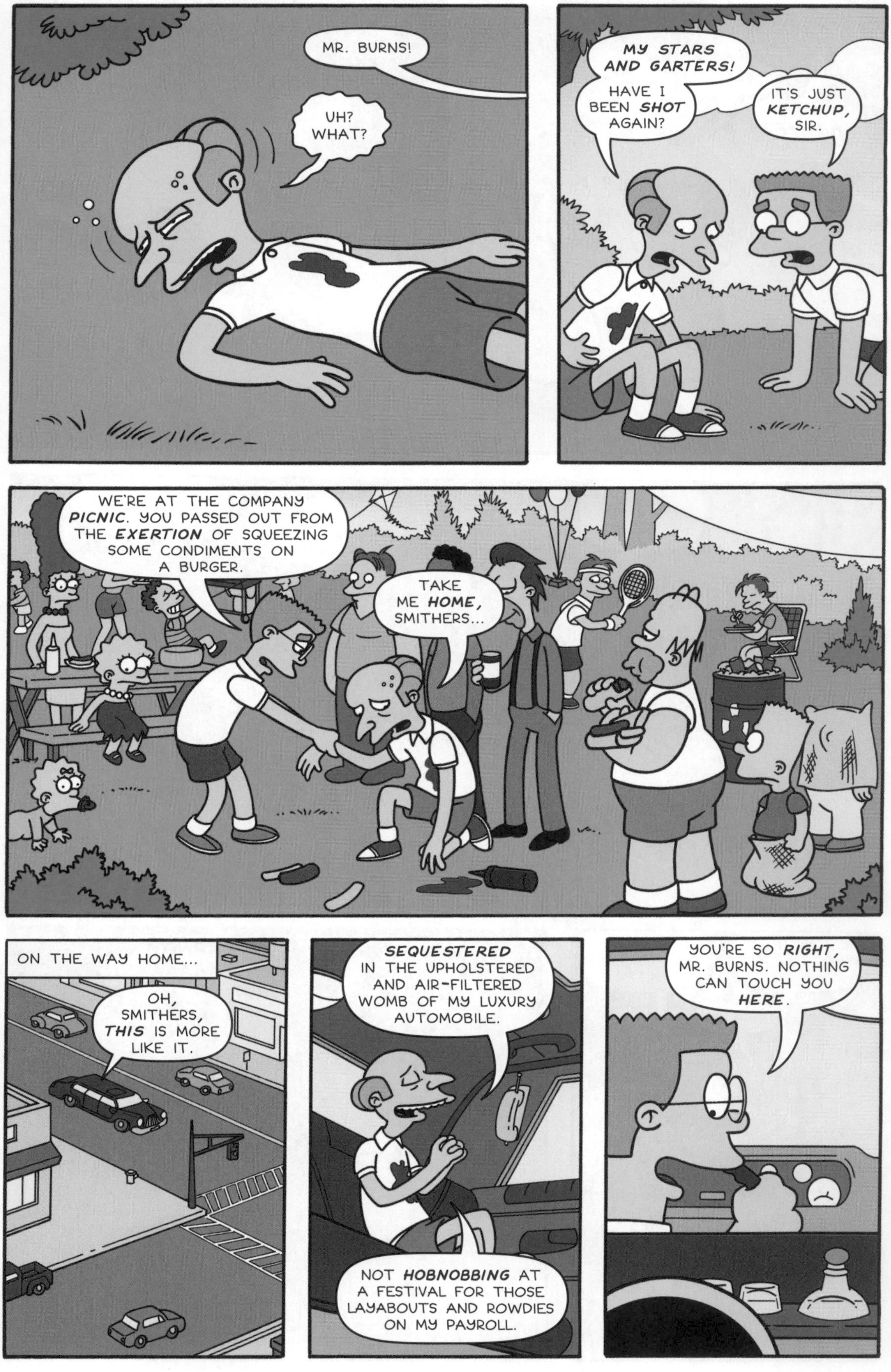

MR. BURNS!
UH? WHAT?
MY STARS AND GARTERS!
HAVE I BEEN SHOT AGAIN?
IT'S JUST KETCHUP, SIR.
WE'RE AT THE COMPANY PICNIC. YOU PASSED OUT FROM THE EXERTION OF SQUEEZING SOME CONDIMENTS ON A BURGER.
TAKE ME HOME, SMITHERS...
ON THE WAY HOME...
OH, SMITHERS, THIS IS MORE LIKE IT.
SEQUESTERED IN THE UPHOLSTERED AND AIR-FILTERED WOMB OF MY LUXURY AUTOMOBILE.
NOT HOBNOBBING AT A FESTIVAL FOR THOSE LAYABOUTS AND ROWDIES ON MY PAYROLL.
YOU'RE SO RIGHT, MR. BURNS. NOTHING CAN TOUCH YOU HERE.

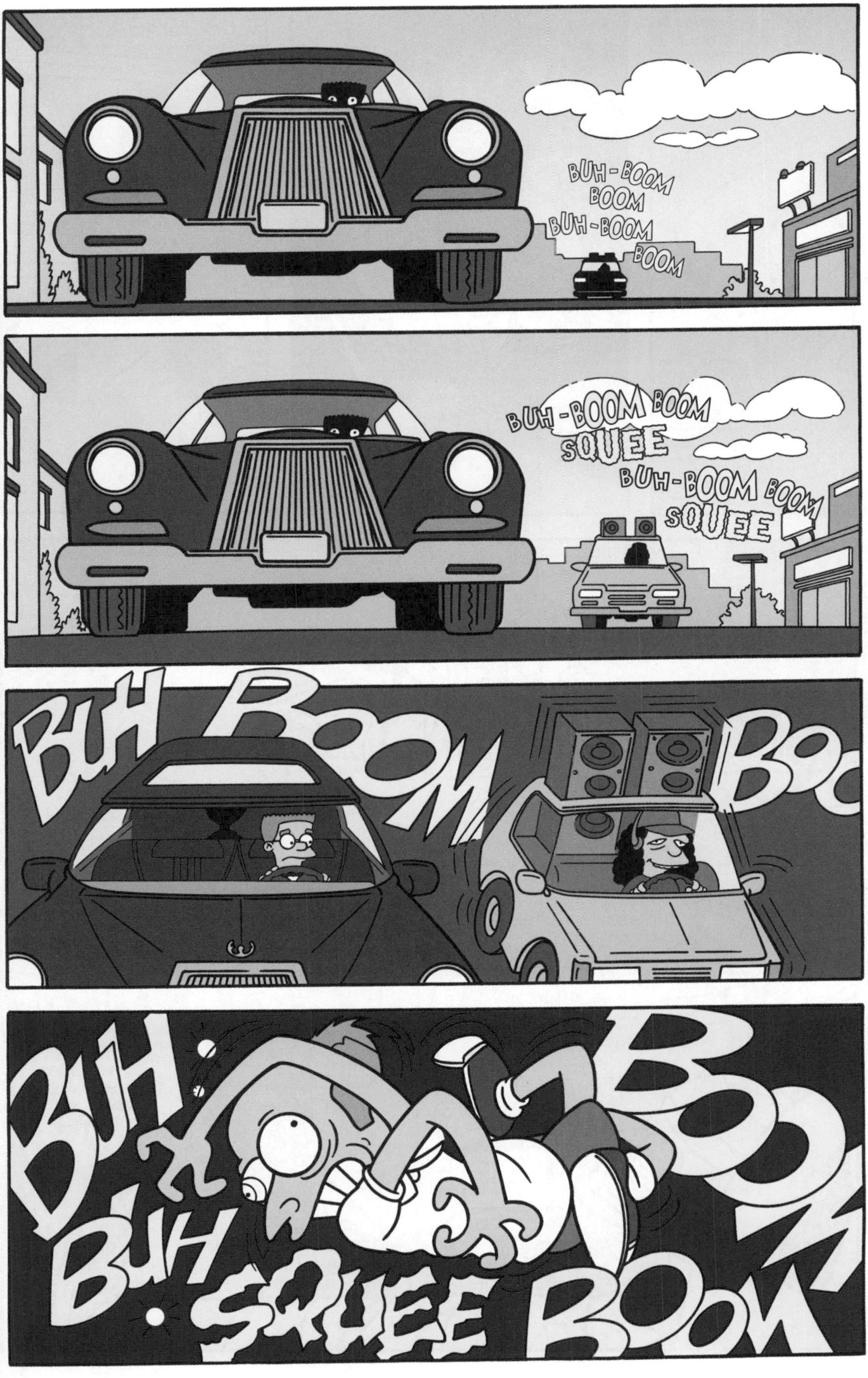
BUH-BOOM
BOOM
BUH-BOOM
BOOM
BUH-BOOM BOOM
SQUEE
BUH-BOOM BOOM
SQUEE
BUH BOOM
BOO
BUH
BUH
SQUEE
BOOM
BOOM

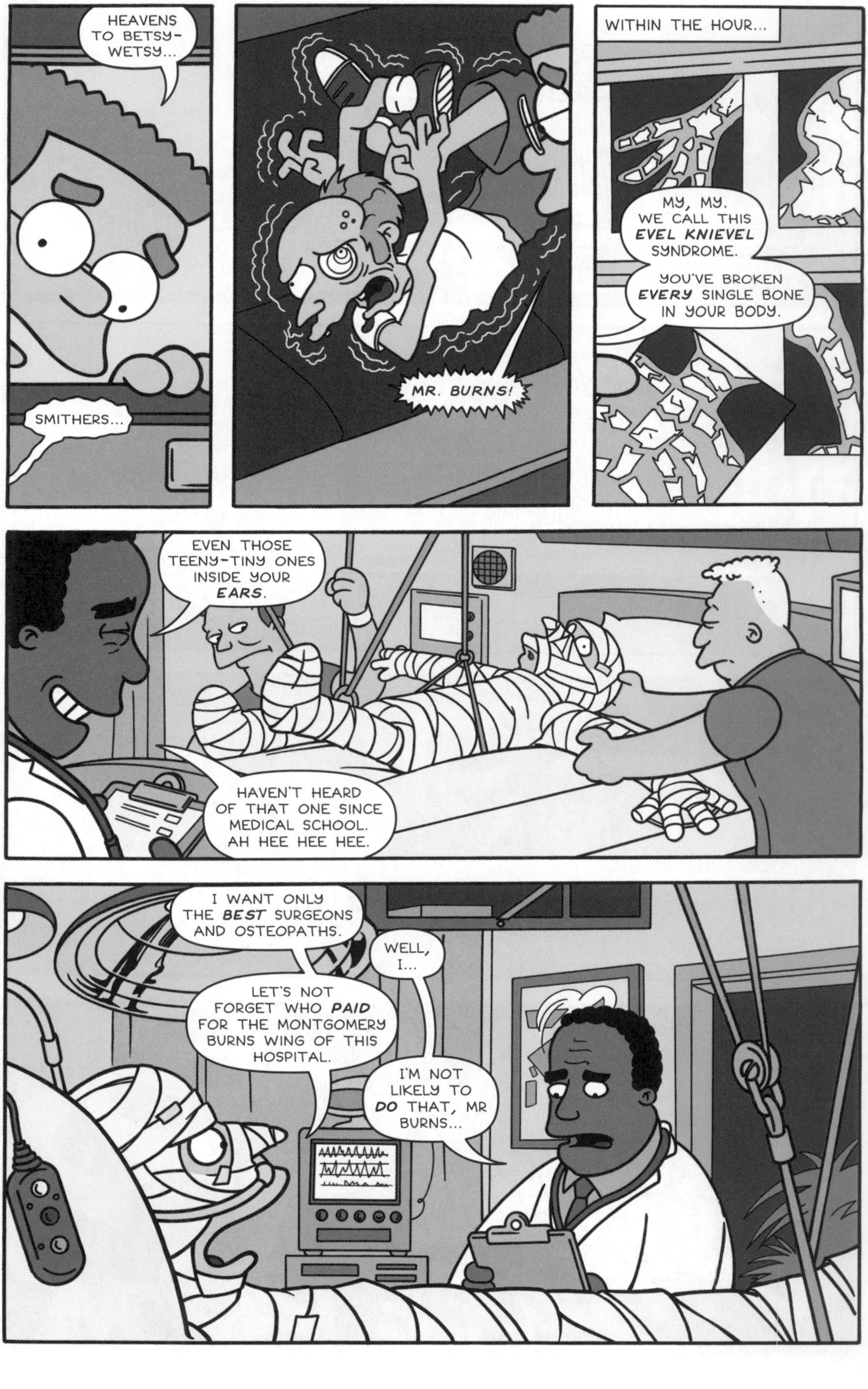

HEAVENS TO BETSY-WETSY...
SMITHERS...
MR. BURNS!
WITHIN THE HOUR...
MY, MY. WE CALL THIS EVEL KNIEVEL SYNDROME.
YOU'VE BROKEN EVERY SINGLE BONE IN YOUR BODY.
EVEN THOSE TEENY-TINY ONES INSIDE YOUR EARS.
HAVEN'T HEARD OF THAT ONE SINCE MEDICAL SCHOOL. AH HEE HEE HEE.
I WANT ONLY THE BEST SURGEONS AND OSTEOPATHS.
WELL, I...
LET'S NOT FORGET WHO PAID FOR THE MONTGOMERY BURNS WING OF THIS HOSPITAL.
I'M NOT LIKELY TO DO THAT, MR BURNS...

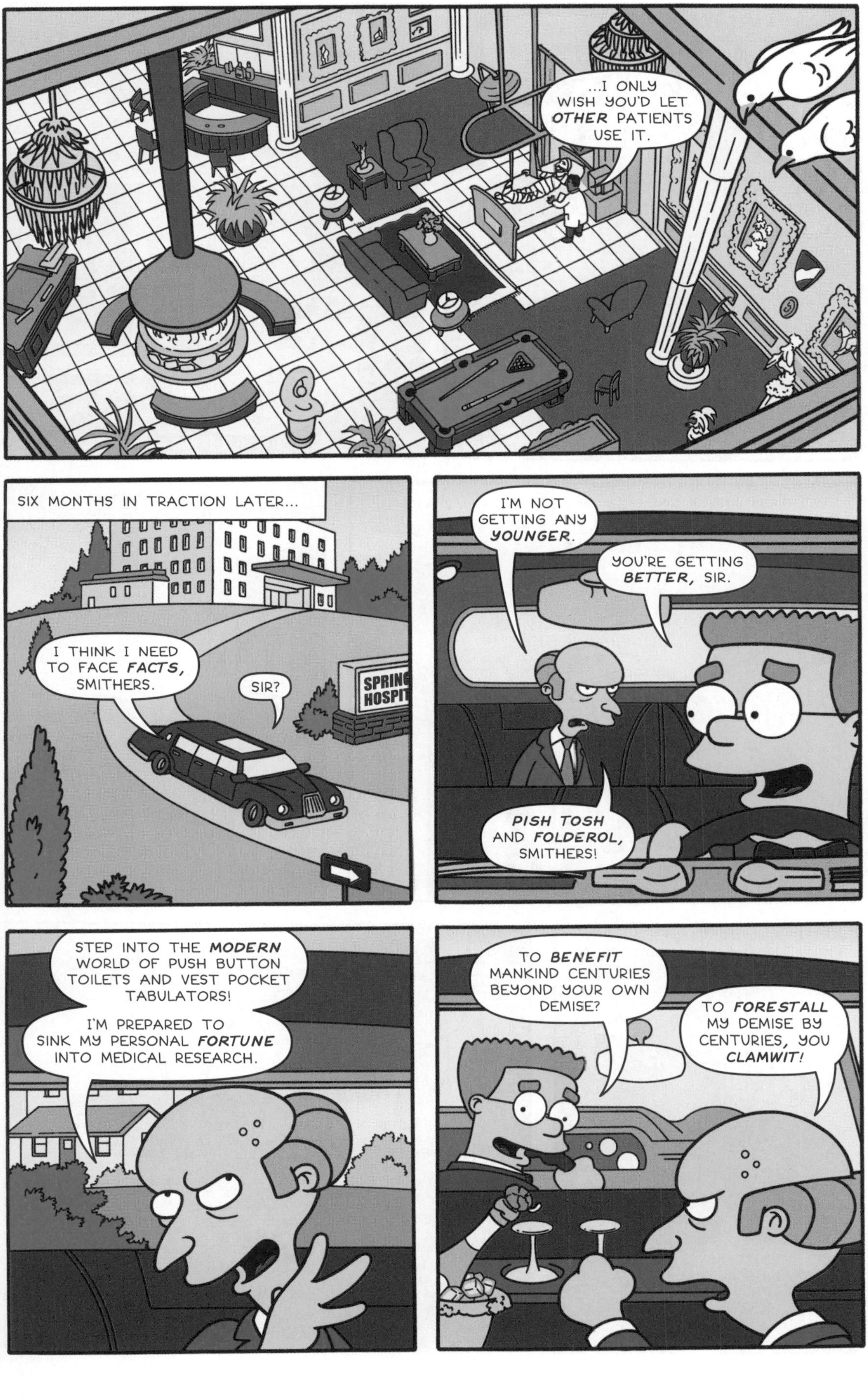

...I ONLY WISH YOU'D LET *OTHER* PATIENTS USE IT.
SIX MONTHS IN TRACTION LATER...
I THINK I NEED TO FACE *FACTS,* SMITHERS.
SIR?
I'M NOT GETTING ANY *YOUNGER*.
YOU'RE GETTING *BETTER,* SIR.
PISH TOSH AND *FOLDEROL,* SMITHERS!
STEP INTO THE *MODERN* WORLD OF PUSH BUTTON TOILETS AND VEST POCKET TABULATORS!
I'M PREPARED TO SINK MY PERSONAL *FORTUNE* INTO MEDICAL RESEARCH.
TO *BENEFIT* MANKIND CENTURIES BEYOND YOUR OWN DEMISE?
TO *FORESTALL* MY DEMISE BY CENTURIES, YOU *CLAMWIT!*

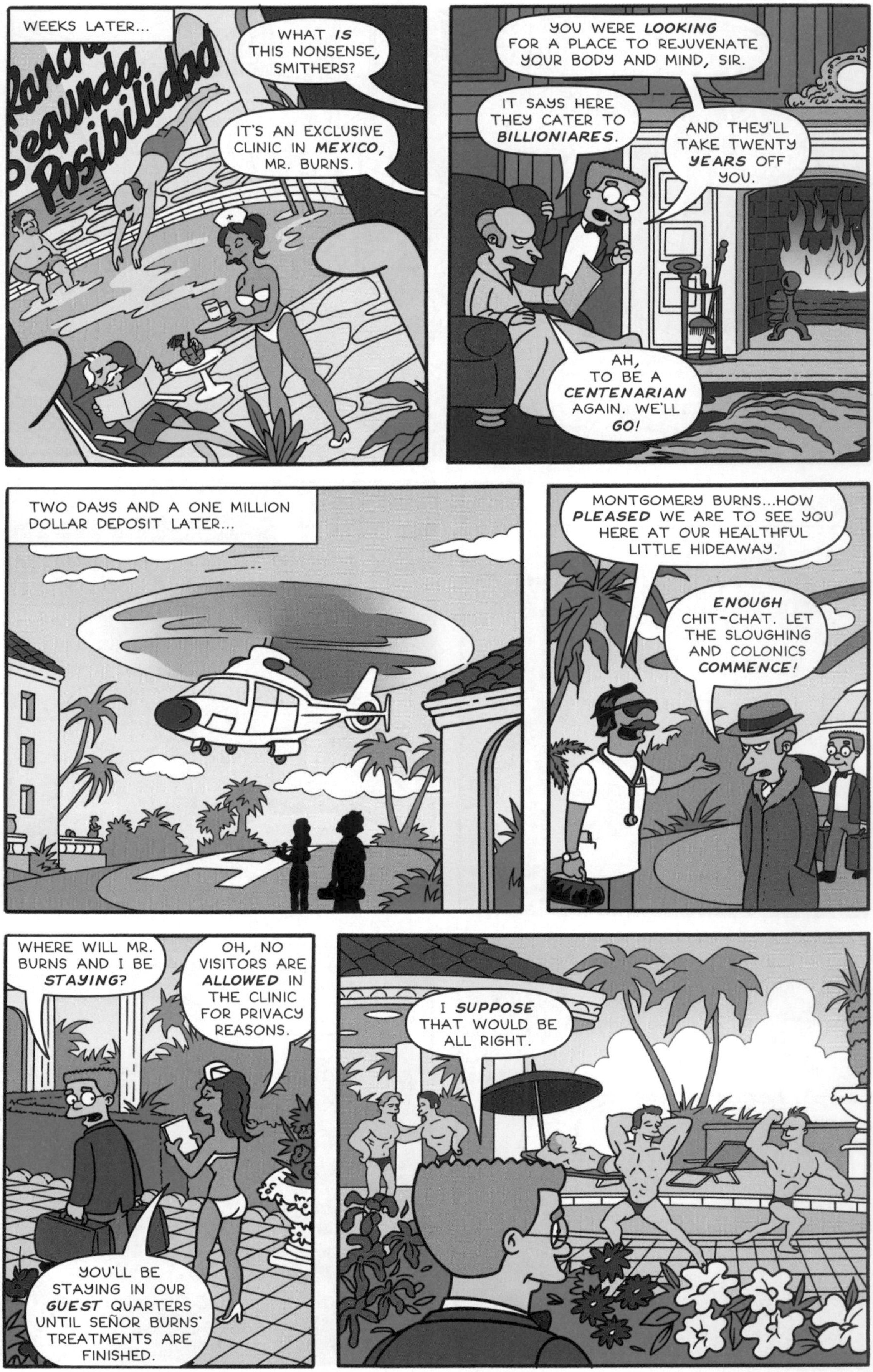
WEEKS LATER...
Rancho Segunda Posibilidad
WHAT IS THIS NONSENSE, SMITHERS?
IT'S AN EXCLUSIVE CLINIC IN MEXICO, MR. BURNS.
YOU WERE LOOKING FOR A PLACE TO REJUVENATE YOUR BODY AND MIND, SIR.
IT SAYS HERE THEY CATER TO BILLIONIARES.
AND THEY'LL TAKE TWENTY YEARS OFF YOU.
AH, TO BE A CENTENARIAN AGAIN. WE'LL GO!
TWO DAYS AND A ONE MILLION DOLLAR DEPOSIT LATER...
MONTGOMERY BURNS...HOW PLEASED WE ARE TO SEE YOU HERE AT OUR HEALTHFUL LITTLE HIDEAWAY.
ENOUGH CHIT-CHAT. LET THE SLOUGHING AND COLONICS COMMENCE!
WHERE WILL MR. BURNS AND I BE STAYING?
OH, NO VISITORS ARE ALLOWED IN THE CLINIC FOR PRIVACY REASONS.
YOU'LL BE STAYING IN OUR GUEST QUARTERS UNTIL SEÑOR BURNS' TREATMENTS ARE FINISHED.
I SUPPOSE THAT WOULD BE ALL RIGHT.

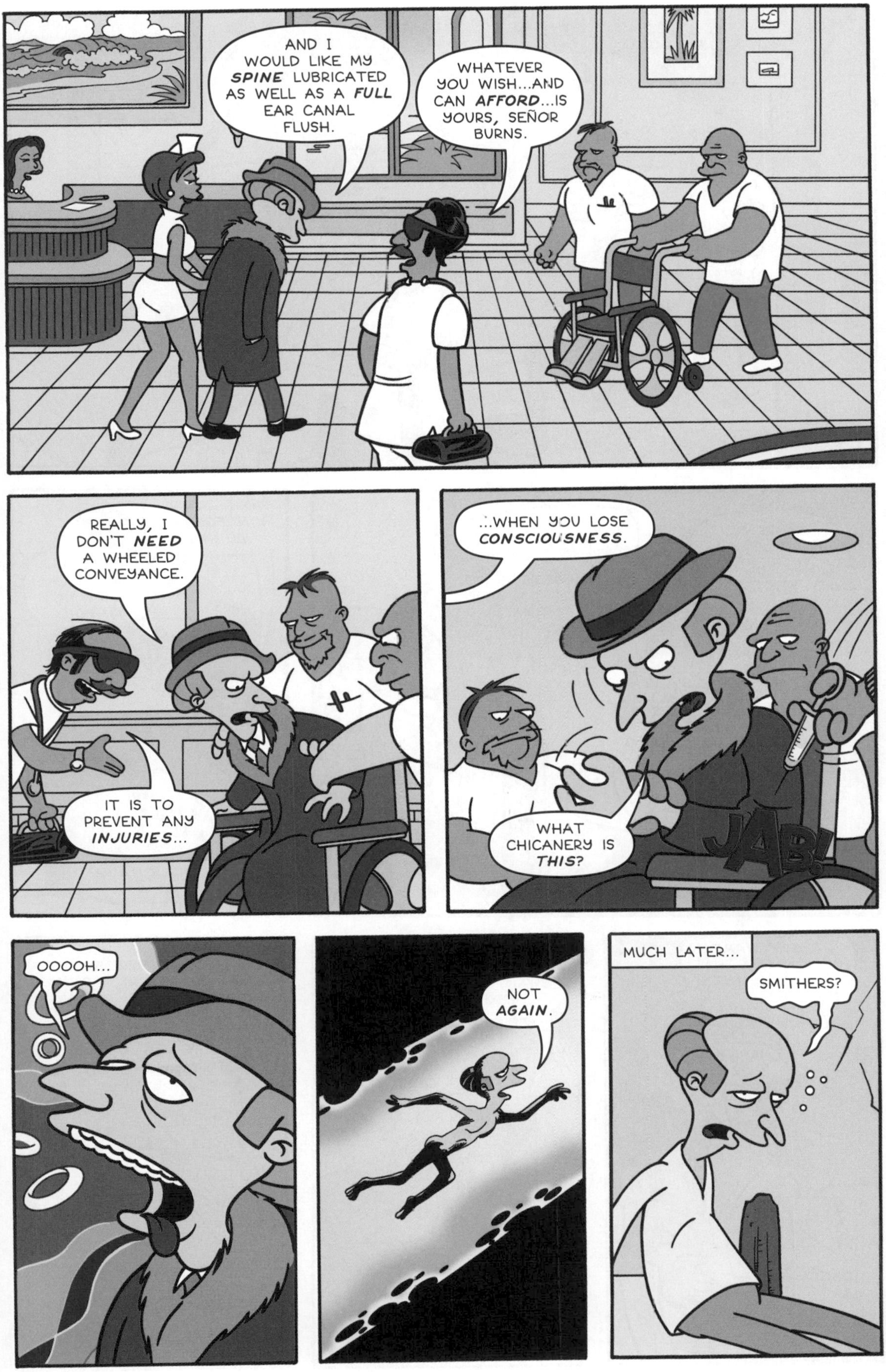
AND I WOULD LIKE MY SPINE LUBRICATED AS WELL AS A FULL EAR CANAL FLUSH.
WHATEVER YOU WISH...AND CAN AFFORD...IS YOURS, SEÑOR BURNS.
REALLY, I DON'T NEED A WHEELED CONVEYANCE.
IT IS TO PREVENT ANY INJURIES...
...WHEN YOU LOSE CONSCIOUSNESS.
WHAT CHICANERY IS THIS?
JAB!
OOOOH...
NOT AGAIN.
MUCH LATER...
SMITHERS?

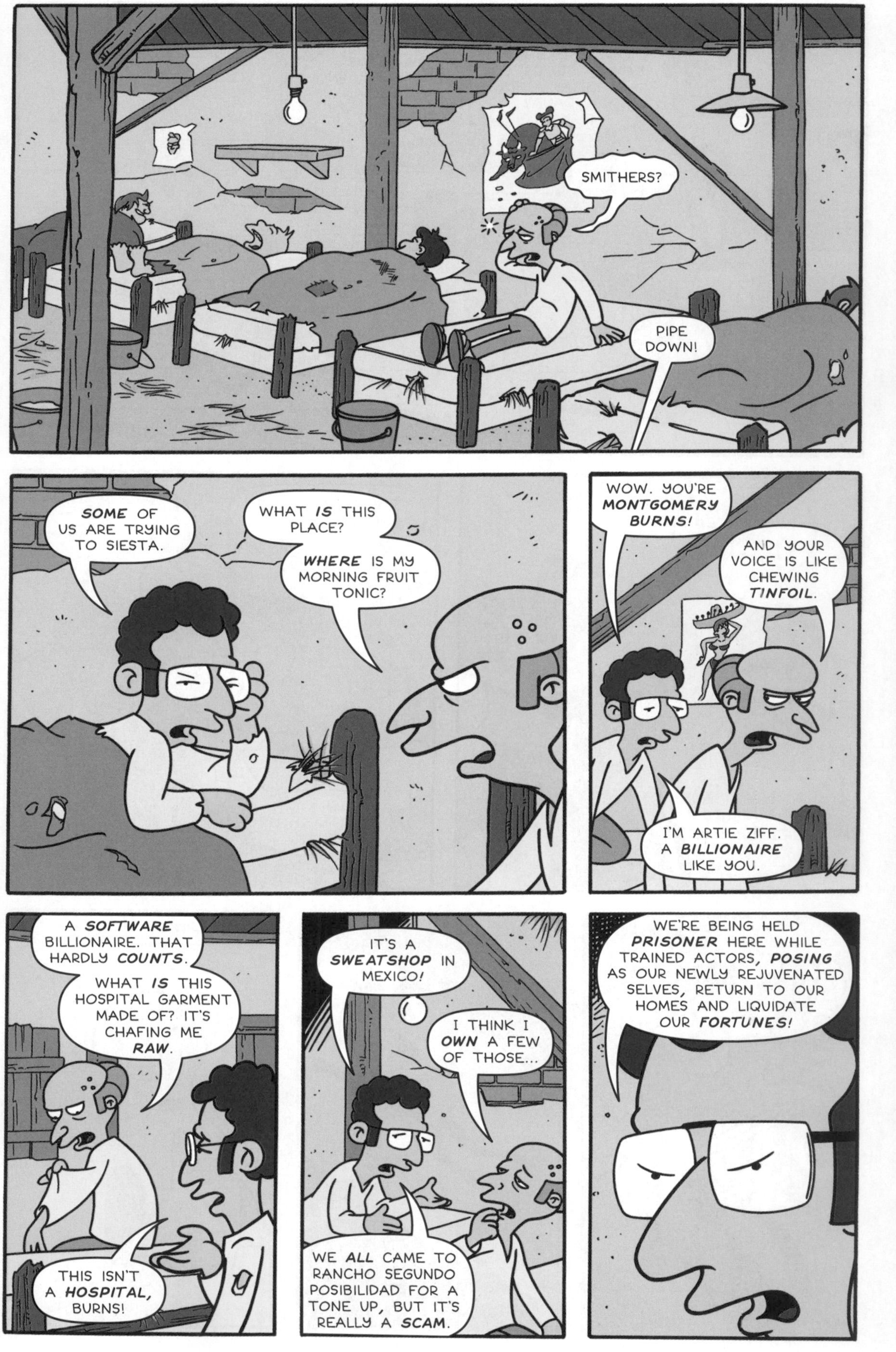
SMITHERS?
PIPE DOWN!
SOME OF US ARE TRYING TO SIESTA.
WHAT IS THIS PLACE?
WHERE IS MY MORNING FRUIT TONIC?
WOW. YOU'RE MONTGOMERY BURNS!
AND YOUR VOICE IS LIKE CHEWING TINFOIL.
I'M ARTIE ZIFF. A BILLIONAIRE LIKE YOU.
A SOFTWARE BILLIONAIRE. THAT HARDLY COUNTS.
WHAT IS THIS HOSPITAL GARMENT MADE OF? IT'S CHAFING ME RAW.
THIS ISN'T A HOSPITAL, BURNS!
IT'S A SWEATSHOP IN MEXICO!
I THINK I OWN A FEW OF THOSE...
WE ALL CAME TO RANCHO SEGUNDO POSIBILIDAD FOR A TONE UP, BUT IT'S REALLY A SCAM.
WE'RE BEING HELD PRISONER HERE WHILE TRAINED ACTORS, POSING AS OUR NEWLY REJUVENATED SELVES, RETURN TO OUR HOMES AND LIQUIDATE OUR FORTUNES!

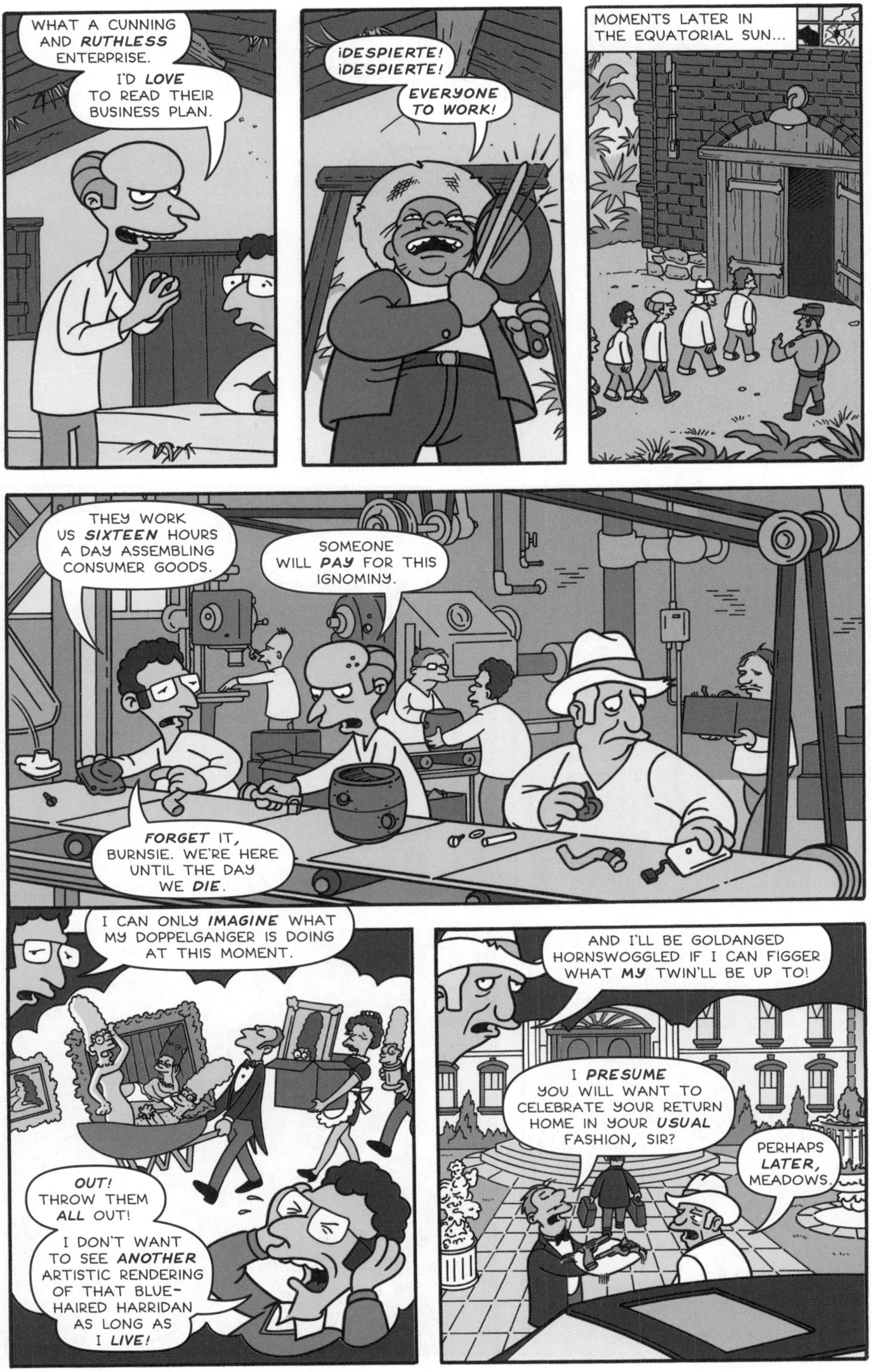
WHAT A CUNNING AND RUTHLESS ENTERPRISE.
I'D LOVE TO READ THEIR BUSINESS PLAN.
¡DESPIERTE! ¡DESPIERTE!
EVERYONE TO WORK!
MOMENTS LATER IN THE EQUATORIAL SUN...
THEY WORK US SIXTEEN HOURS A DAY ASSEMBLING CONSUMER GOODS.
SOMEONE WILL PAY FOR THIS IGNOMINY.
FORGET IT, BURNSIE. WE'RE HERE UNTIL THE DAY WE DIE.
I CAN ONLY IMAGINE WHAT MY DOPPELGANGER IS DOING AT THIS MOMENT.
OUT! THROW THEM ALL OUT!
I DON'T WANT TO SEE ANOTHER ARTISTIC RENDERING OF THAT BLUE-HAIRED HARRIDAN AS LONG AS I LIVE!
AND I'LL BE GOLDANGED HORNSWOGGLED IF I CAN FIGGER WHAT MY TWIN'LL BE UP TO!
I PRESUME YOU WILL WANT TO CELEBRATE YOUR RETURN HOME IN YOUR USUAL FASHION, SIR?
PERHAPS LATER, MEADOWS.

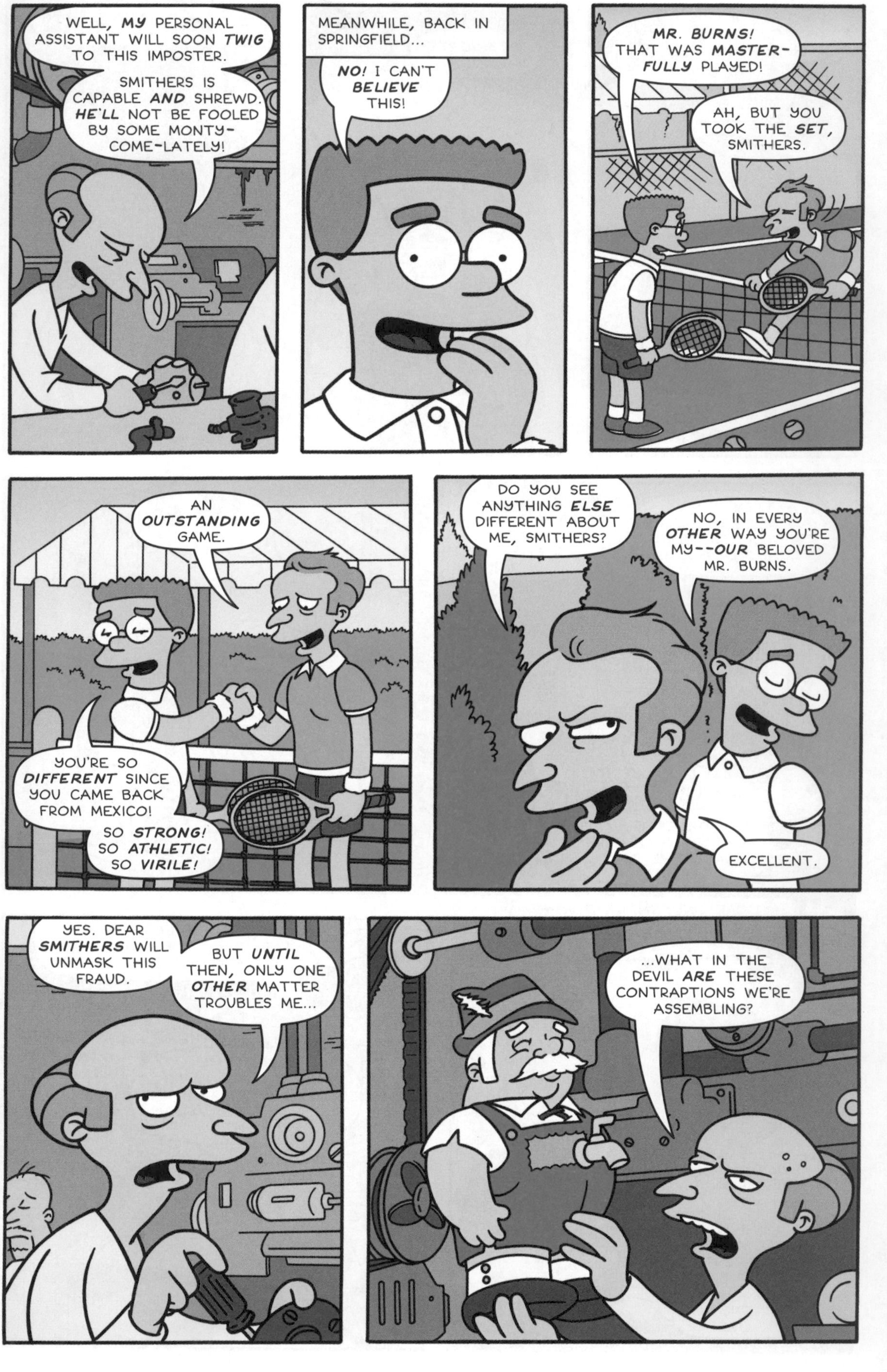
WELL, MY PERSONAL ASSISTANT WILL SOON TWIG TO THIS IMPOSTER.
SMITHERS IS CAPABLE AND SHREWD. HE'LL NOT BE FOOLED BY SOME MONTY-COME-LATELY!
MEANWHILE, BACK IN SPRINGFIELD...
NO! I CAN'T BELIEVE THIS!
MR. BURNS! THAT WAS MASTER-FULLY PLAYED!
AH, BUT YOU TOOK THE SET, SMITHERS.
AN OUTSTANDING GAME.
YOU'RE SO DIFFERENT SINCE YOU CAME BACK FROM MEXICO!
SO STRONG! SO ATHLETIC! SO VIRILE!
DO YOU SEE ANYTHING ELSE DIFFERENT ABOUT ME, SMITHERS?
NO, IN EVERY OTHER WAY YOU'RE MY--OUR BELOVED MR. BURNS.
EXCELLENT.
YES. DEAR SMITHERS WILL UNMASK THIS FRAUD.
BUT UNTIL THEN, ONLY ONE OTHER MATTER TROUBLES ME...
...WHAT IN THE DEVIL ARE THESE CONTRAPTIONS WE'RE ASSEMBLING?

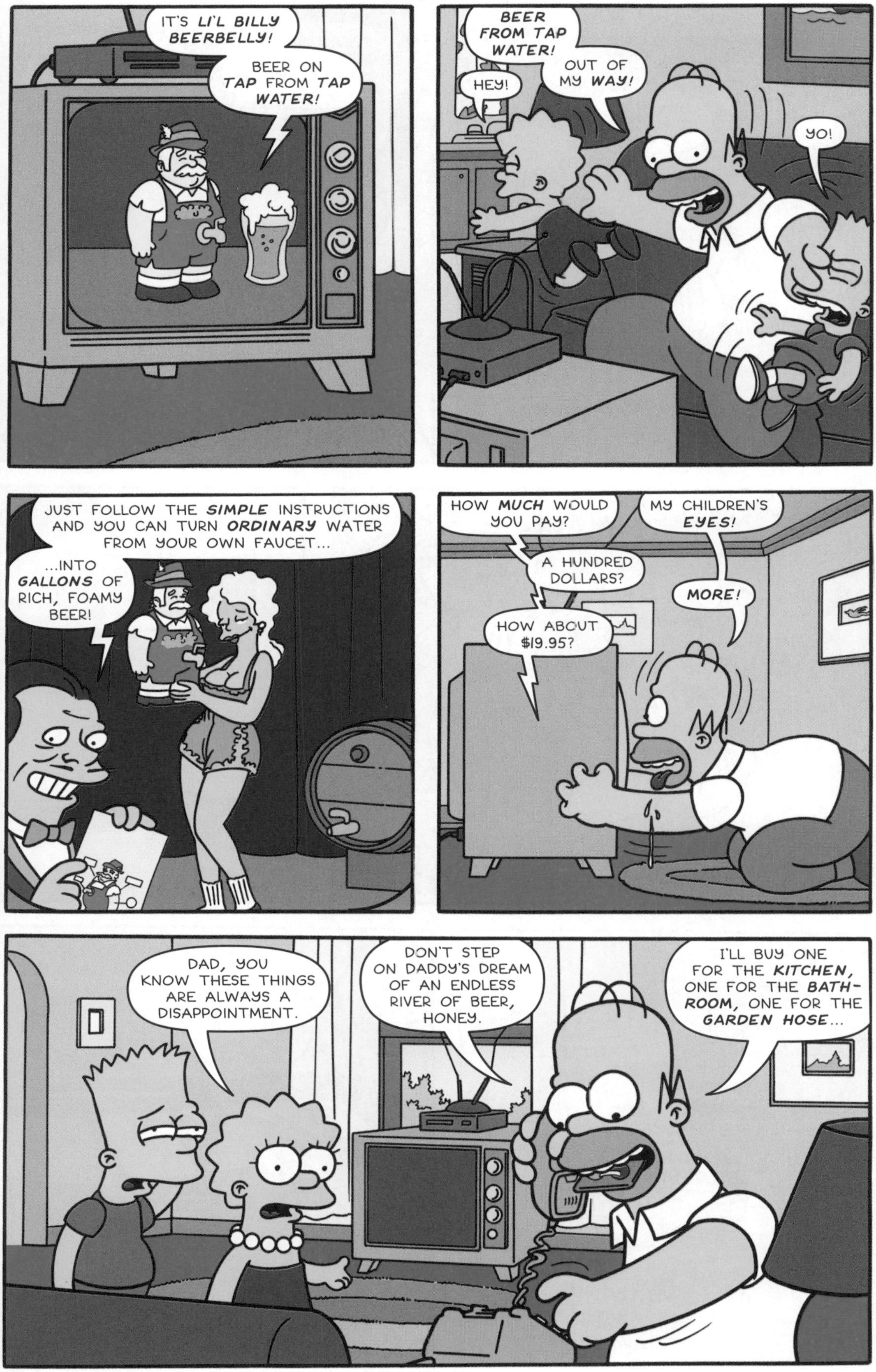
IT'S LI'L BILLY BEERBELLY!
BEER ON TAP FROM TAP WATER!
BEER FROM TAP WATER!
HEY!
OUT OF MY WAY!
YO!
JUST FOLLOW THE SIMPLE INSTRUCTIONS AND YOU CAN TURN ORDINARY WATER FROM YOUR OWN FAUCET...
...INTO GALLONS OF RICH, FOAMY BEER!
HOW MUCH WOULD YOU PAY?
A HUNDRED DOLLARS?
HOW ABOUT $19.95?
MY CHILDREN'S EYES!
MORE!
DAD, YOU KNOW THESE THINGS ARE ALWAYS A DISAPPOINTMENT.
DON'T STEP ON DADDY'S DREAM OF AN ENDLESS RIVER OF BEER, HONEY.
I'LL BUY ONE FOR THE KITCHEN, ONE FOR THE BATHROOM, ONE FOR THE GARDEN HOSE...

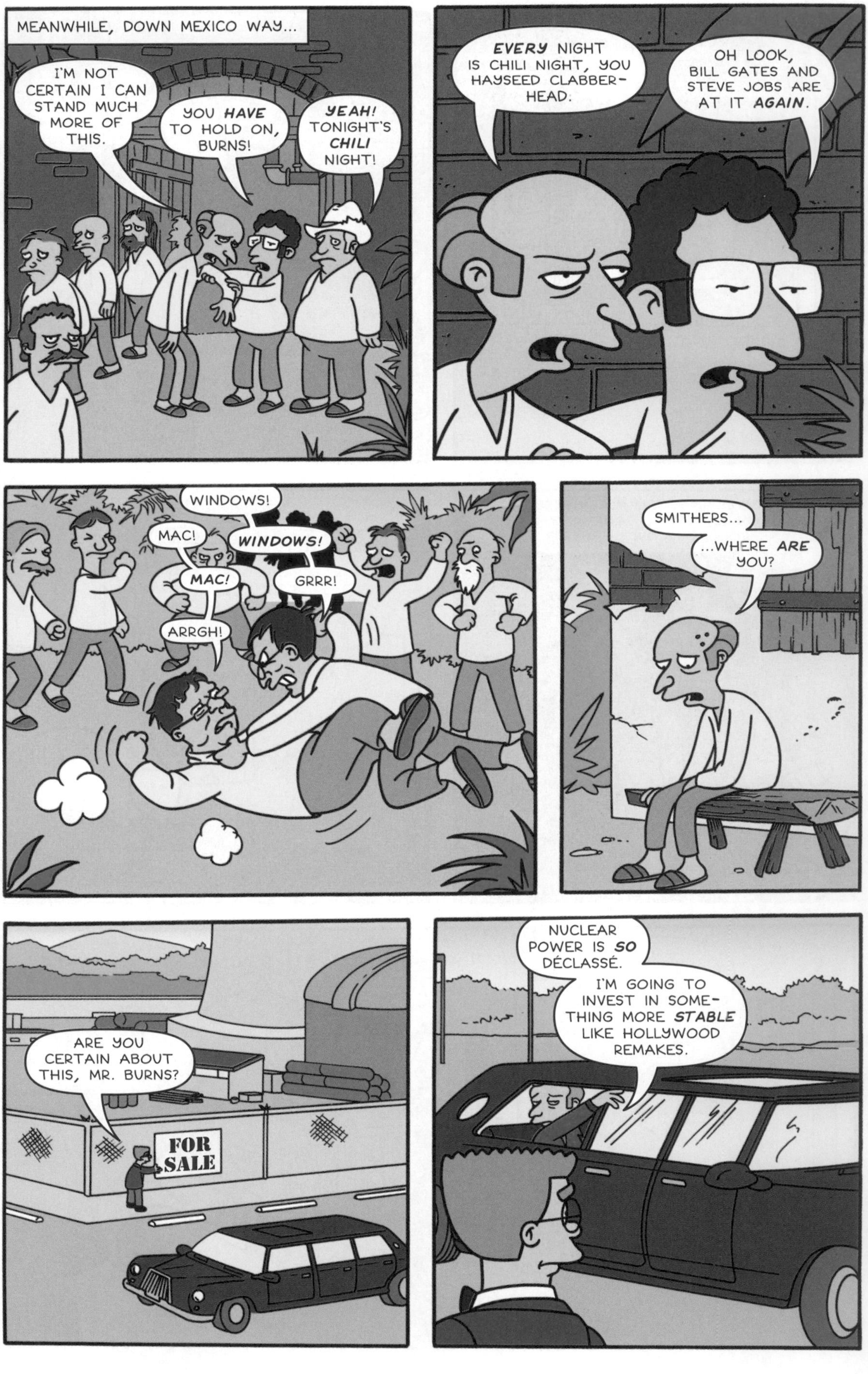

MEANWHILE, DOWN MEXICO WAY...
I'M NOT CERTAIN I CAN STAND MUCH MORE OF THIS.
YOU HAVE TO HOLD ON, BURNS!
YEAH! TONIGHT'S CHILI NIGHT!
EVERY NIGHT IS CHILI NIGHT, YOU HAYSEED CLABBER-HEAD.
OH LOOK, BILL GATES AND STEVE JOBS ARE AT IT AGAIN.
WINDOWS!
MAC!
WINDOWS!
MAC!
GRRR!
ARRGH!
SMITHERS...
...WHERE ARE YOU?
ARE YOU CERTAIN ABOUT THIS, MR. BURNS?
FOR SALE
NUCLEAR POWER IS SO DÉCLASSÉ.
I'M GOING TO INVEST IN SOME-THING MORE STABLE LIKE HOLLYWOOD REMAKES.

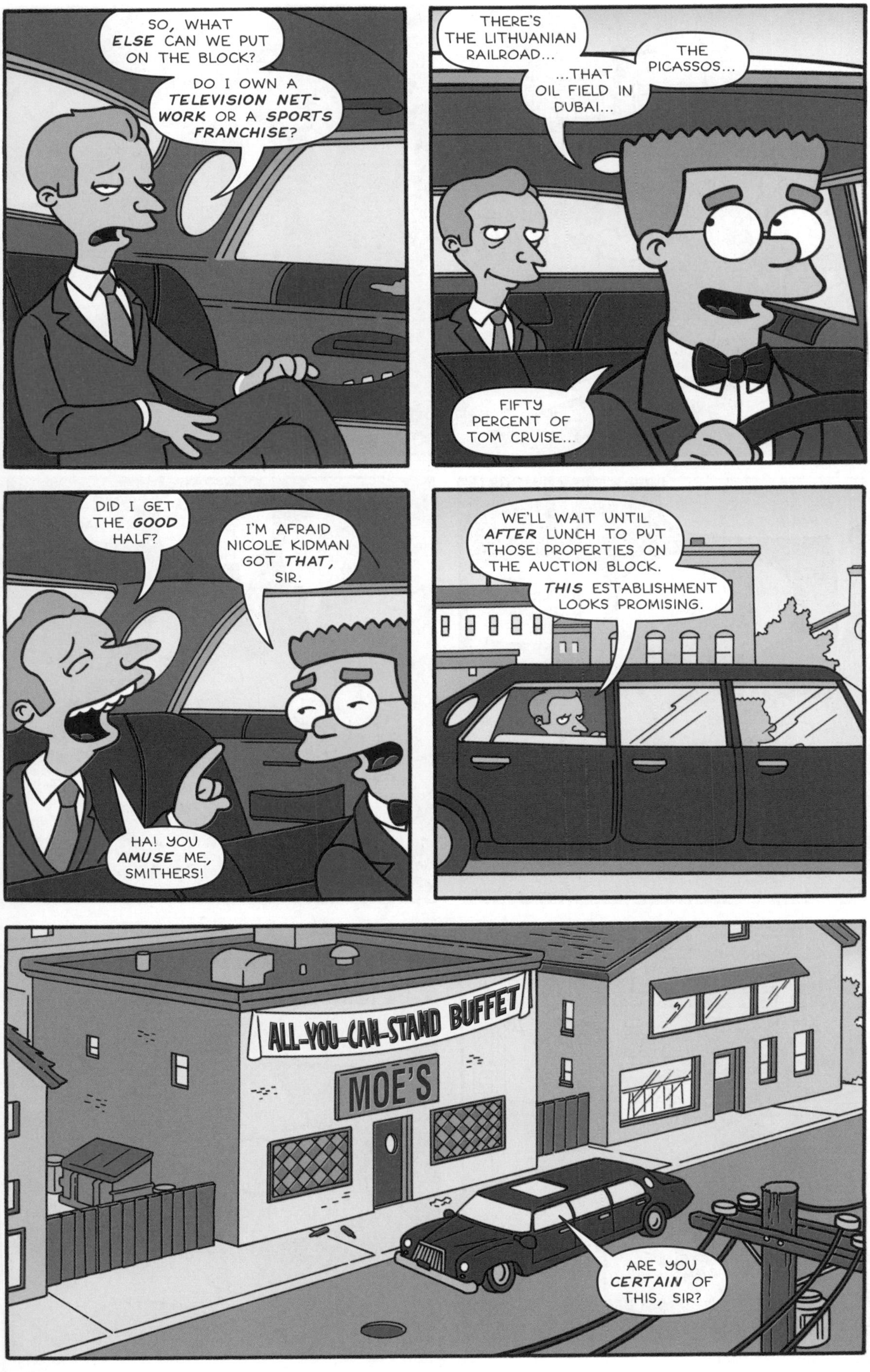
SO, WHAT *ELSE* CAN WE PUT ON THE BLOCK?
DO I OWN A *TELEVISION NETWORK* OR A *SPORTS FRANCHISE*?
THERE'S THE LITHUANIAN RAILROAD...
...THAT OIL FIELD IN DUBAI...
THE PICASSOS...
FIFTY PERCENT OF TOM CRUISE...
DID I GET THE *GOOD* HALF?
I'M AFRAID NICOLE KIDMAN GOT *THAT,* SIR.
HA! YOU *AMUSE* ME, SMITHERS!
WE'LL WAIT UNTIL *AFTER* LUNCH TO PUT THOSE PROPERTIES ON THE AUCTION BLOCK.
THIS ESTABLISHMENT LOOKS PROMISING.
ALL-YOU-CAN-STAND BUFFET
MOE'S
ARE YOU *CERTAIN* OF THIS, SIR?

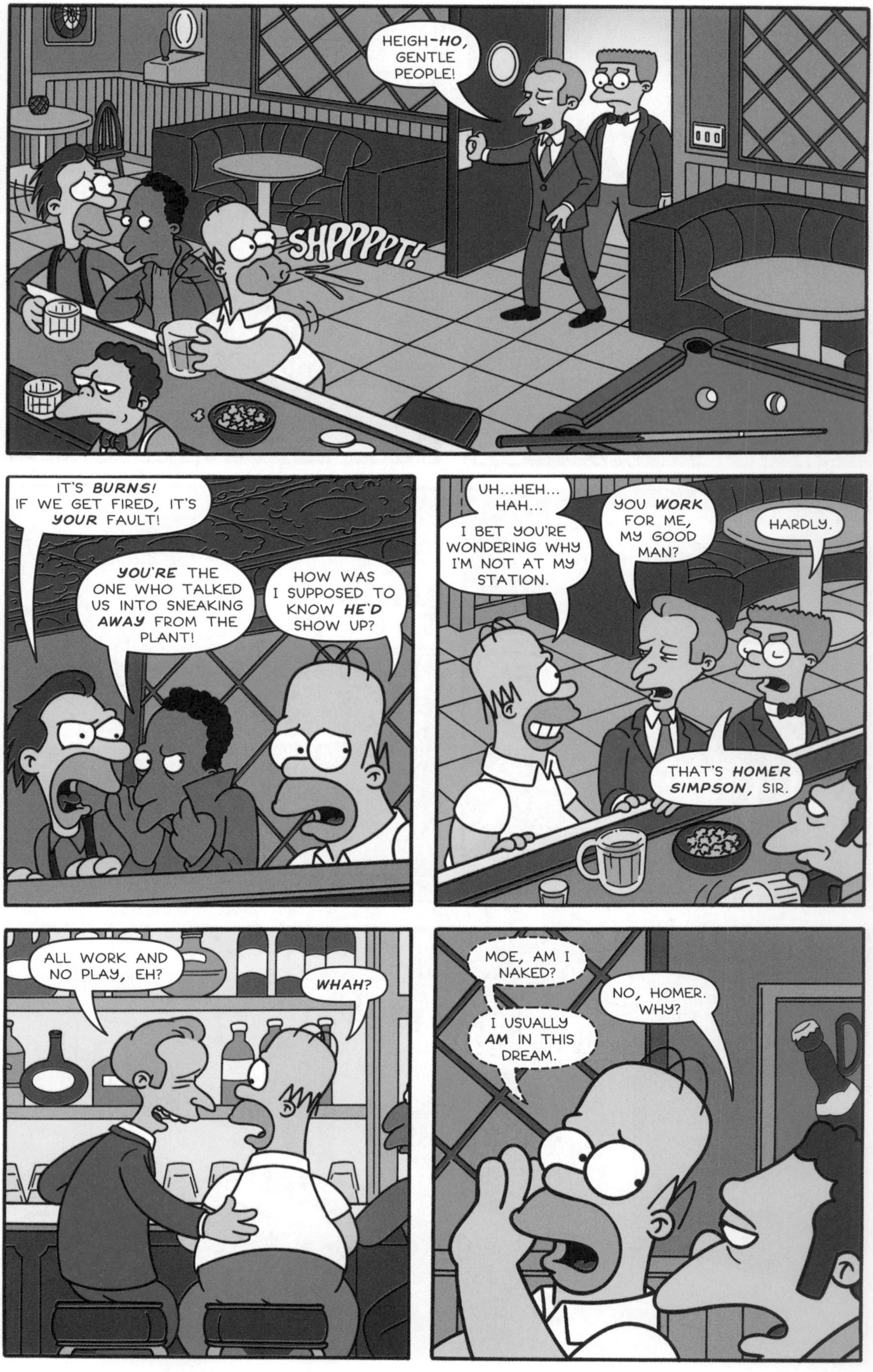
HEIGH-HO, GENTLE PEOPLE!
SHPPPPT!
IT'S BURNS! IF WE GET FIRED, IT'S YOUR FAULT!
YOU'RE THE ONE WHO TALKED US INTO SNEAKING AWAY FROM THE PLANT!
HOW WAS I SUPPOSED TO KNOW HE'D SHOW UP?
UH...HEH... HAH...
I BET YOU'RE WONDERING WHY I'M NOT AT MY STATION.
YOU WORK FOR ME, MY GOOD MAN?
HARDLY.
THAT'S HOMER SIMPSON, SIR.
ALL WORK AND NO PLAY, EH?
WHAH?
MOE, AM I NAKED?
I USUALLY AM IN THIS DREAM.
NO, HOMER. WHY?

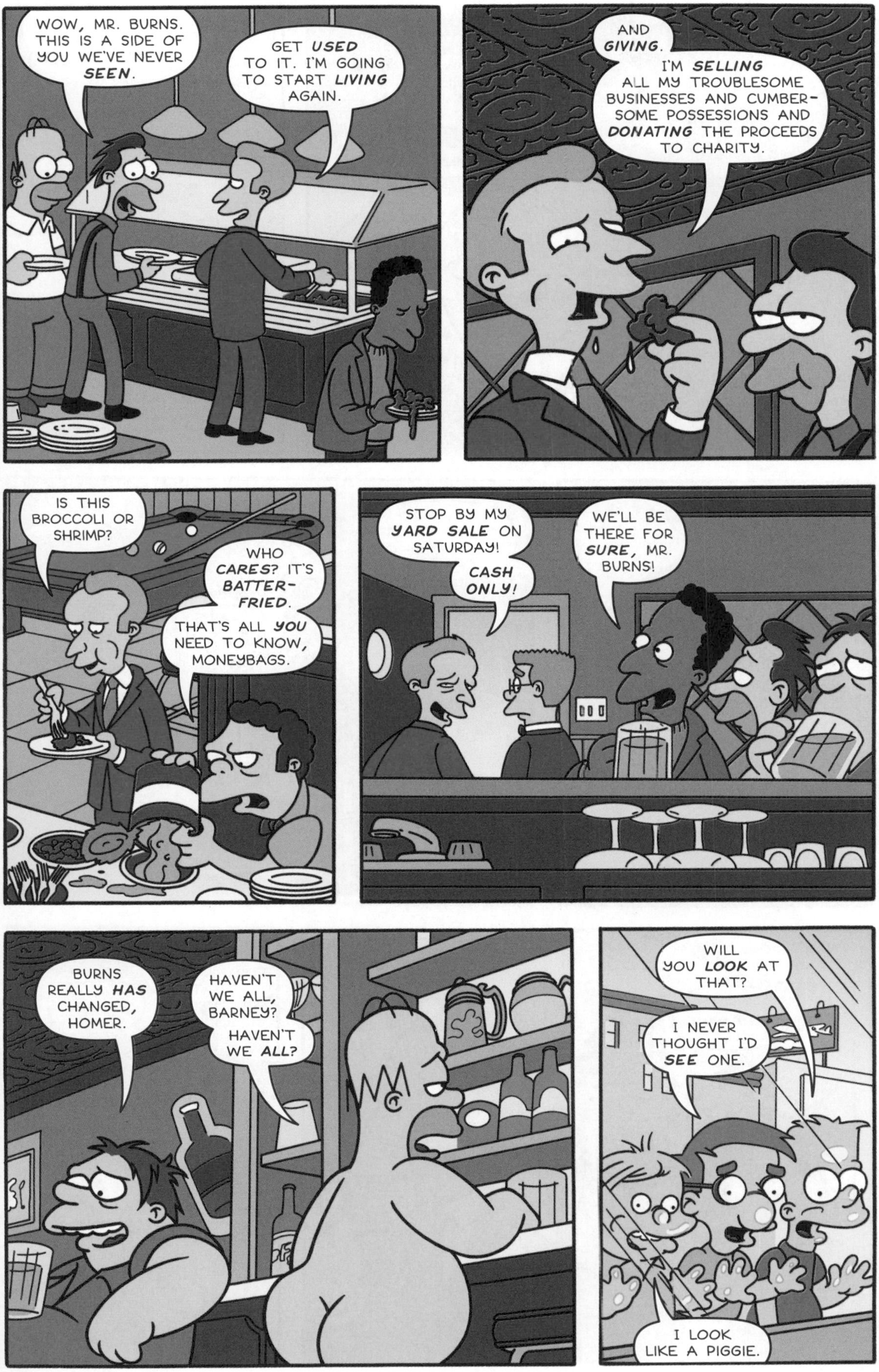
WOW, MR. BURNS. THIS IS A SIDE OF YOU WE'VE NEVER SEEN.
GET USED TO IT. I'M GOING TO START LIVING AGAIN.
AND GIVING.
I'M SELLING ALL MY TROUBLESOME BUSINESSES AND CUMBER-SOME POSSESSIONS AND DONATING THE PROCEEDS TO CHARITY.
IS THIS BROCCOLI OR SHRIMP?
WHO CARES? IT'S BATTER-FRIED.
THAT'S ALL YOU NEED TO KNOW, MONEYBAGS.
STOP BY MY YARD SALE ON SATURDAY!
CASH ONLY!
WE'LL BE THERE FOR SURE, MR. BURNS!
BURNS REALLY HAS CHANGED, HOMER.
HAVEN'T WE ALL, BARNEY?
HAVEN'T WE ALL?
WILL YOU LOOK AT THAT?
I NEVER THOUGHT I'D SEE ONE.
I LOOK LIKE A PIGGIE.

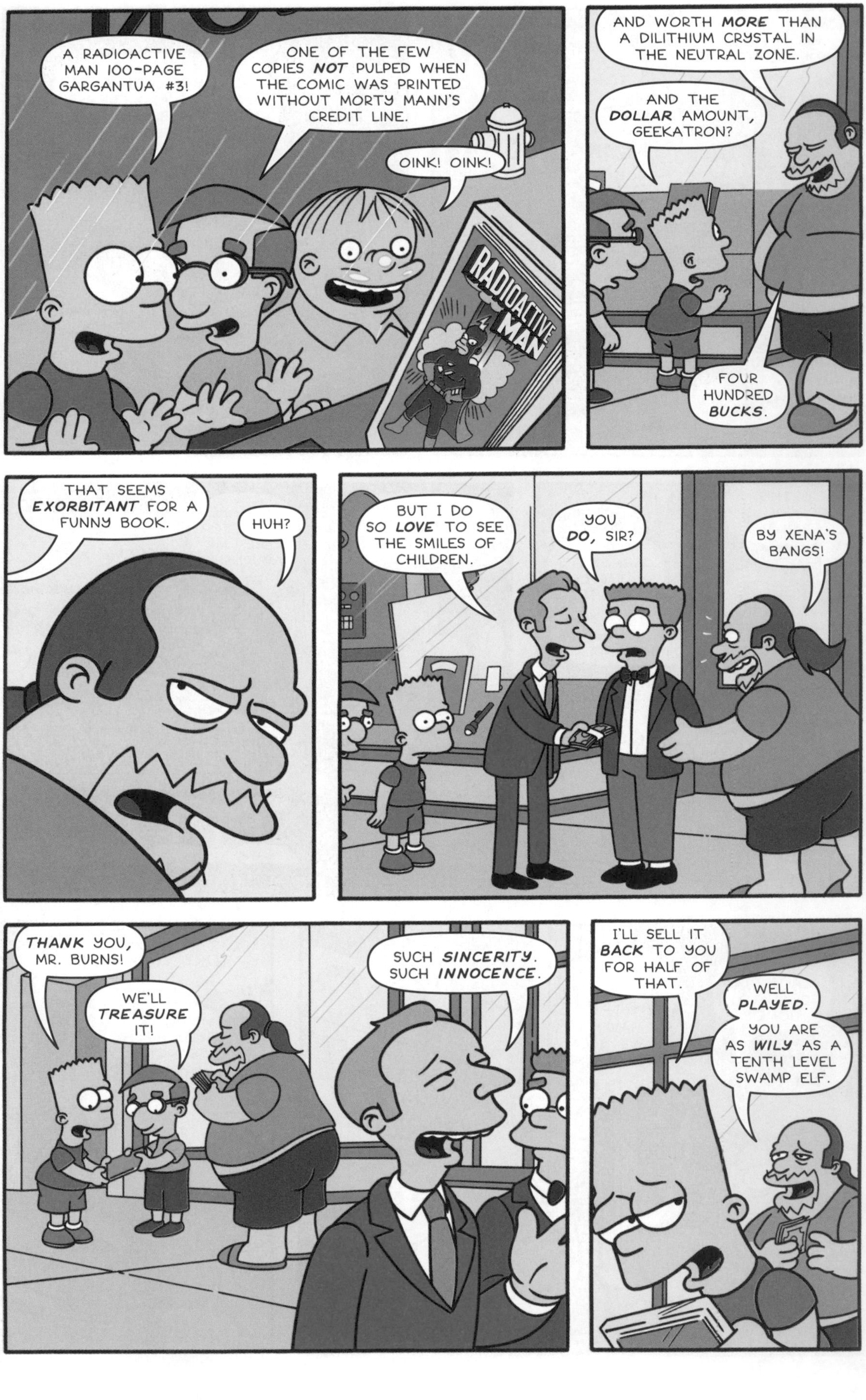

A RADIOACTIVE MAN 100-PAGE GARGANTUA #3!
ONE OF THE FEW COPIES **NOT** PULPED WHEN THE COMIC WAS PRINTED WITHOUT MORTY MANN'S CREDIT LINE.
OINK! OINK!
RADIOACTIVE MAN
AND WORTH **MORE** THAN A DILITHIUM CRYSTAL IN THE NEUTRAL ZONE.
AND THE **DOLLAR** AMOUNT, GEEKATRON?
FOUR HUNDRED **BUCKS**.
THAT SEEMS **EXORBITANT** FOR A FUNNY BOOK.
HUH?
BUT I DO SO **LOVE** TO SEE THE SMILES OF CHILDREN.
YOU **DO**, SIR?
BY XENA'S BANGS!
THANK YOU, MR. BURNS!
WE'LL **TREASURE** IT!
SUCH **SINCERITY**. SUCH **INNOCENCE**.
I'LL SELL IT **BACK** TO YOU FOR HALF OF THAT.
WELL **PLAYED**.
YOU ARE AS **WILY** AS A TENTH LEVEL SWAMP ELF.

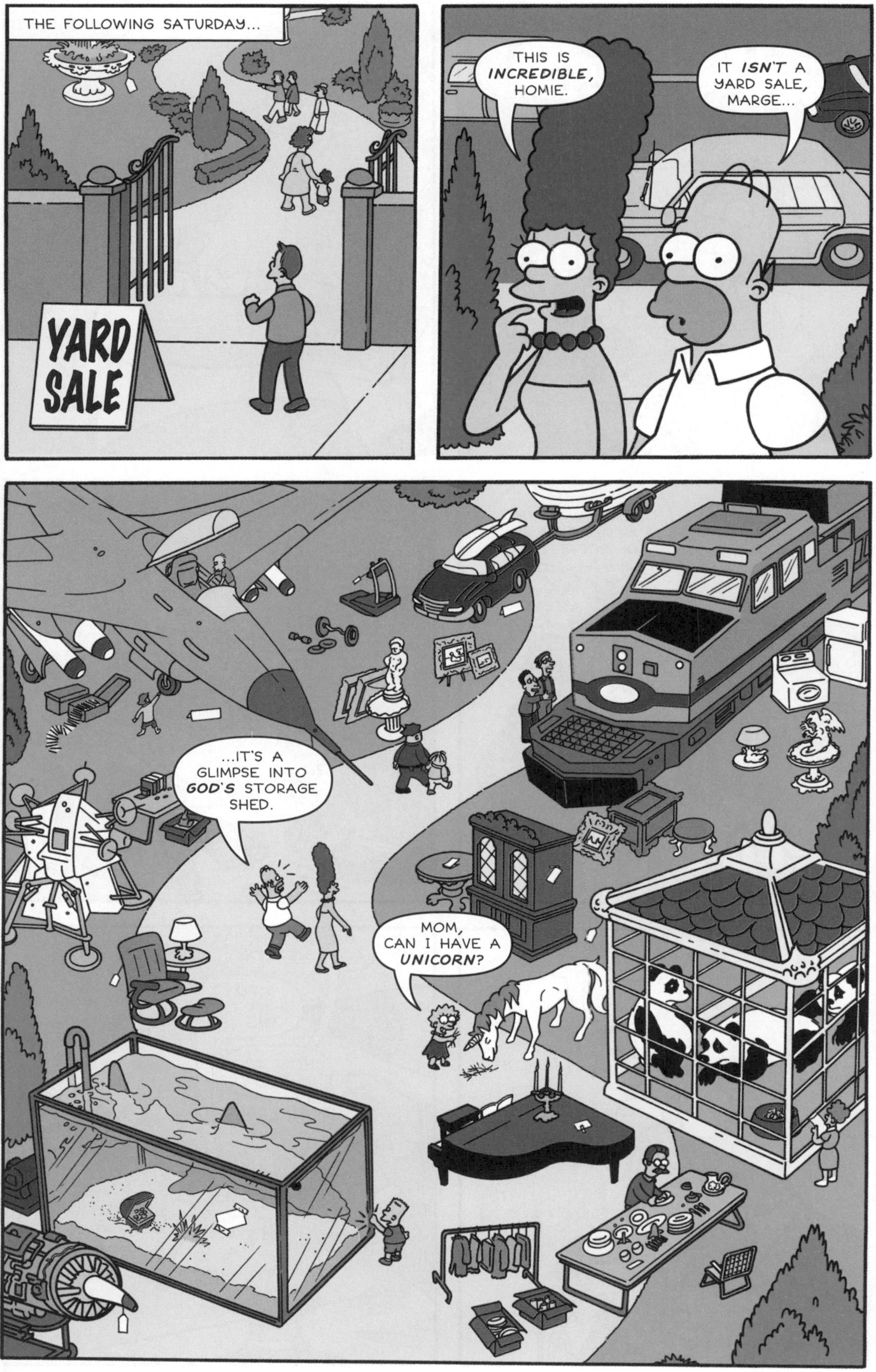
THE FOLLOWING SATURDAY...
YARD SALE
THIS IS *INCREDIBLE*, HOMIE.
IT *ISN'T* A YARD SALE, MARGE...
...IT'S A GLIMPSE INTO *GOD'S* STORAGE SHED.
MOM, CAN I HAVE A *UNICORN*?

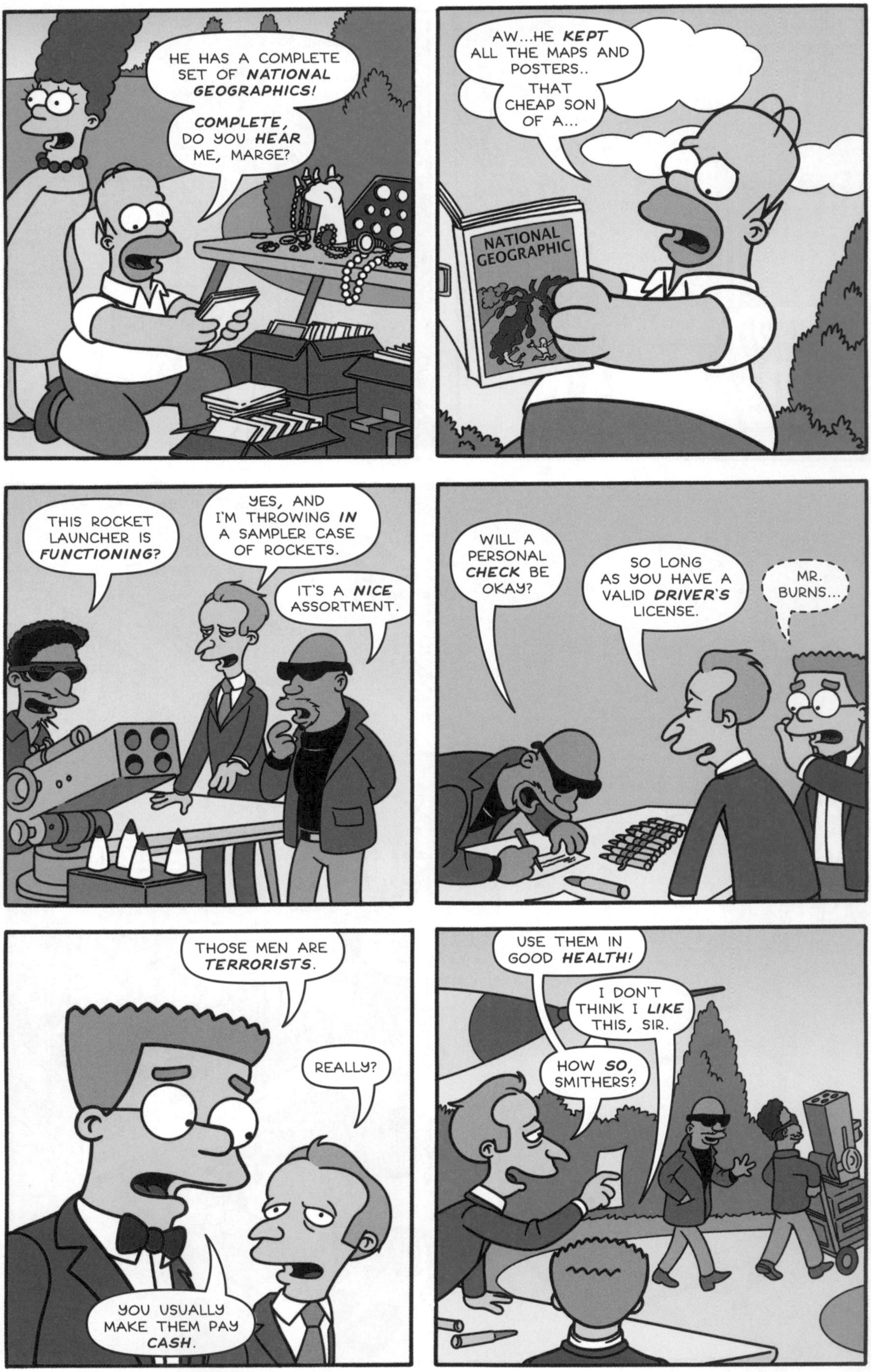
HE HAS A COMPLETE SET OF NATIONAL GEOGRAPHICS!
COMPLETE, DO YOU HEAR ME, MARGE?
AW...HE KEPT ALL THE MAPS AND POSTERS..
THAT CHEAP SON OF A...
NATIONAL GEOGRAPHIC
THIS ROCKET LAUNCHER IS FUNCTIONING?
YES, AND I'M THROWING IN A SAMPLER CASE OF ROCKETS.
IT'S A NICE ASSORTMENT.
WILL A PERSONAL CHECK BE OKAY?
SO LONG AS YOU HAVE A VALID DRIVER'S LICENSE.
MR. BURNS...
THOSE MEN ARE TERRORISTS.
REALLY?
YOU USUALLY MAKE THEM PAY CASH.
USE THEM IN GOOD HEALTH!
I DON'T THINK I LIKE THIS, SIR.
HOW SO, SMITHERS?

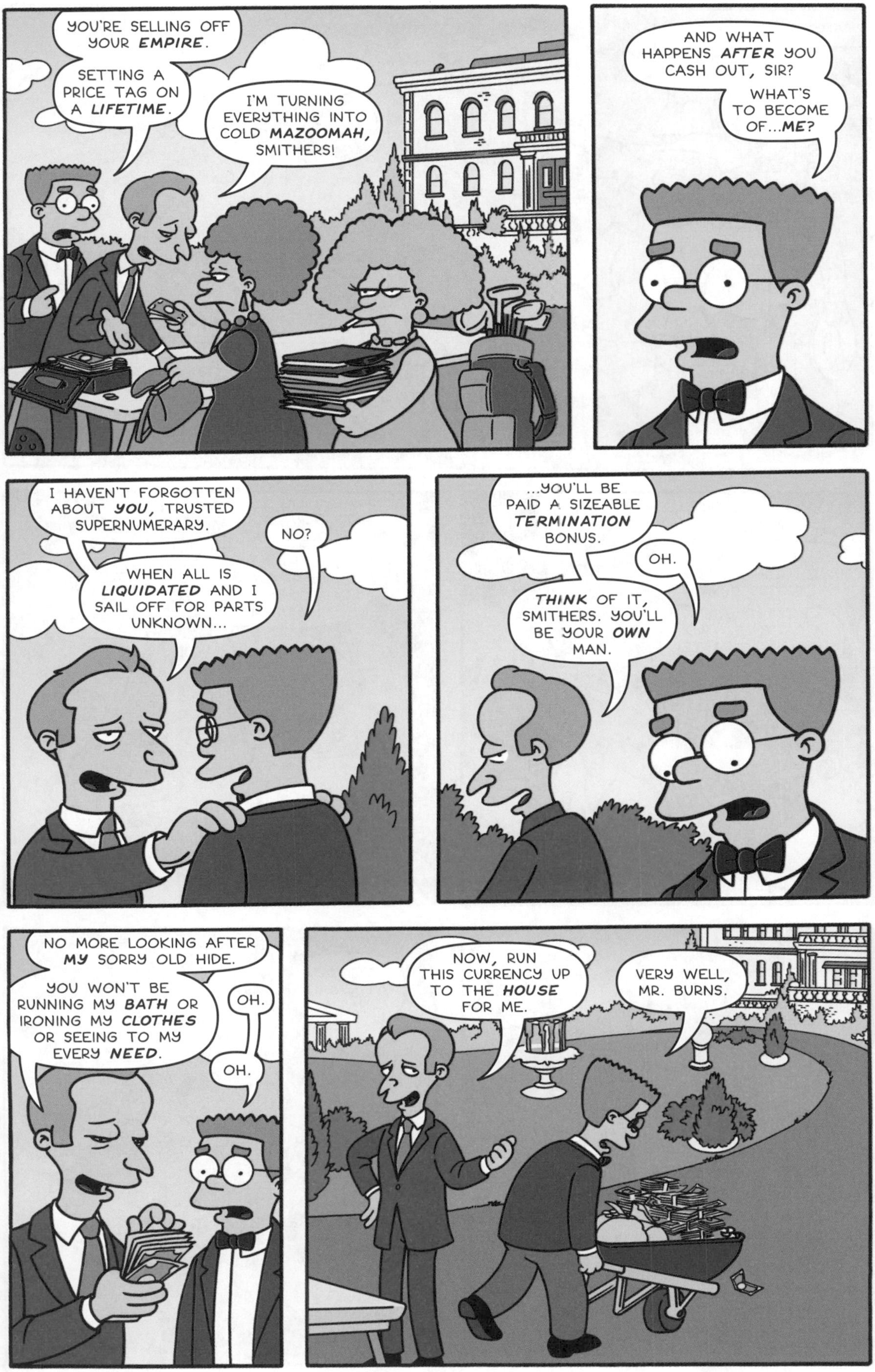
YOU'RE SELLING OFF YOUR EMPIRE.
SETTING A PRICE TAG ON A LIFETIME.
I'M TURNING EVERYTHING INTO COLD MAZOOMAH, SMITHERS!
AND WHAT HAPPENS AFTER YOU CASH OUT, SIR?
WHAT'S TO BECOME OF...ME?
I HAVEN'T FORGOTTEN ABOUT YOU, TRUSTED SUPERNUMERARY.
NO?
WHEN ALL IS LIQUIDATED AND I SAIL OFF FOR PARTS UNKNOWN...
...YOU'LL BE PAID A SIZEABLE TERMINATION BONUS.
OH.
THINK OF IT, SMITHERS. YOU'LL BE YOUR OWN MAN.
NO MORE LOOKING AFTER MY SORRY OLD HIDE.
YOU WON'T BE RUNNING MY BATH OR IRONING MY CLOTHES OR SEEING TO MY EVERY NEED.
OH.
OH.
NOW, RUN THIS CURRENCY UP TO THE HOUSE FOR ME.
VERY WELL, MR. BURNS.

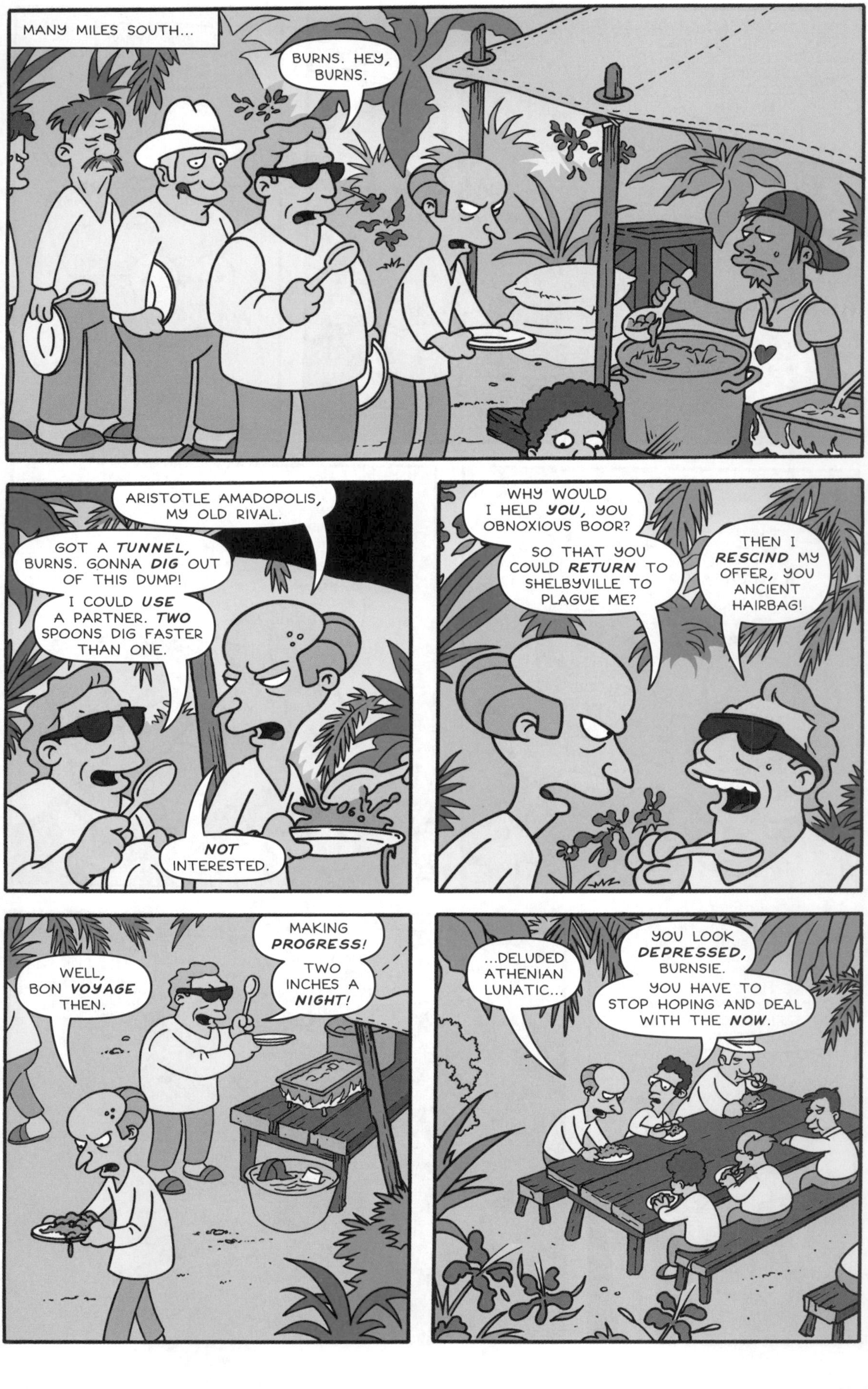

MANY MILES SOUTH...
BURNS. HEY, BURNS.
ARISTOTLE AMADOPOLIS, MY OLD RIVAL.
GOT A TUNNEL, BURNS. GONNA DIG OUT OF THIS DUMP!
I COULD USE A PARTNER. TWO SPOONS DIG FASTER THAN ONE.
NOT INTERESTED.
WHY WOULD I HELP YOU, YOU OBNOXIOUS BOOR?
SO THAT YOU COULD RETURN TO SHELBYVILLE TO PLAGUE ME?
THEN I RESCIND MY OFFER, YOU ANCIENT HAIRBAG!
WELL, BON VOYAGE THEN.
MAKING PROGRESS!
TWO INCHES A NIGHT!
...DELUDED ATHENIAN LUNATIC...
YOU LOOK DEPRESSED, BURNSIE.
YOU HAVE TO STOP HOPING AND DEAL WITH THE NOW.

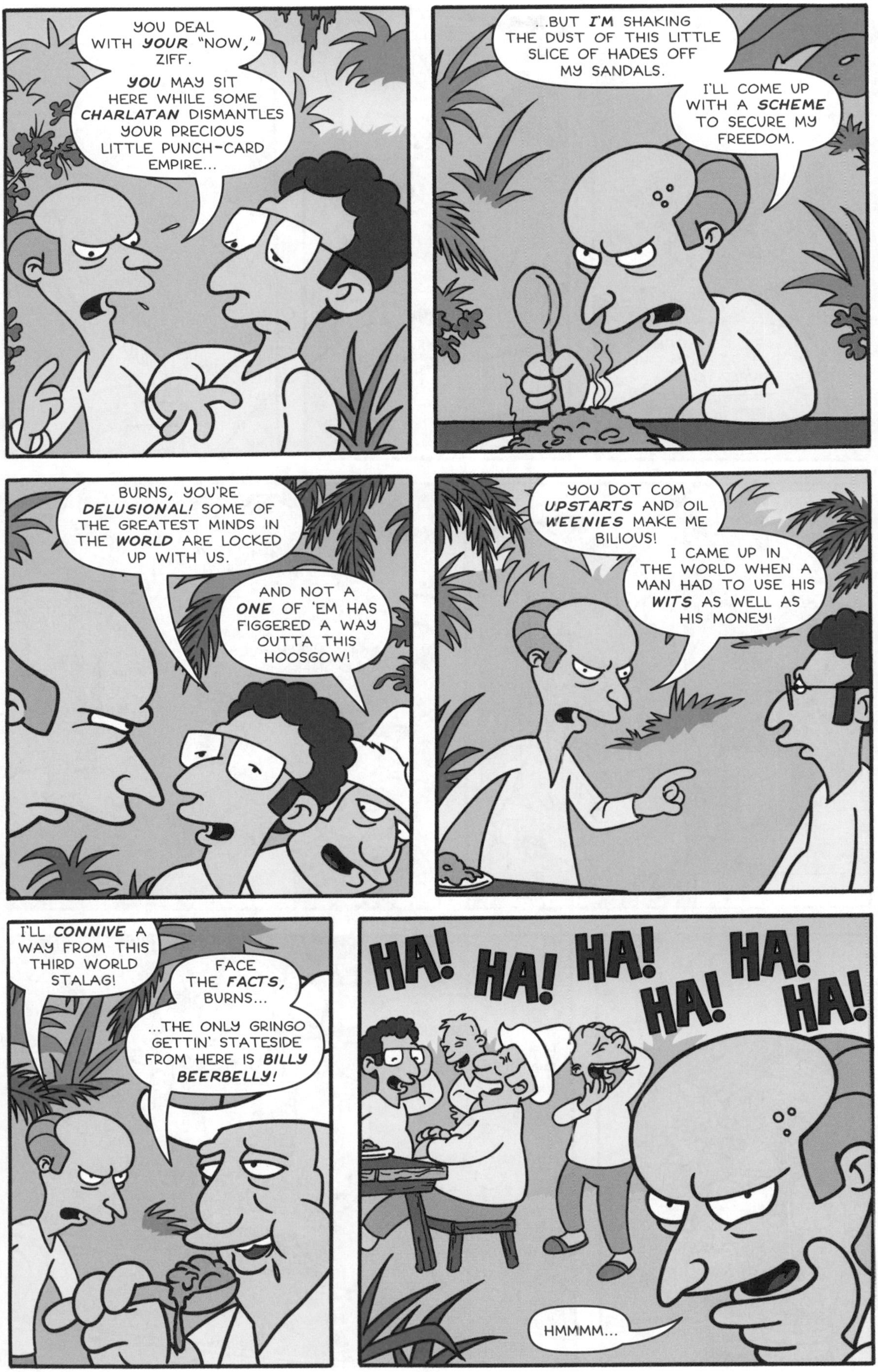
YOU DEAL WITH YOUR "NOW," ZIFF.
YOU MAY SIT HERE WHILE SOME CHARLATAN DISMANTLES YOUR PRECIOUS LITTLE PUNCH-CARD EMPIRE...
..BUT I'M SHAKING THE DUST OF THIS LITTLE SLICE OF HADES OFF MY SANDALS.
I'LL COME UP WITH A SCHEME TO SECURE MY FREEDOM.
BURNS, YOU'RE DELUSIONAL! SOME OF THE GREATEST MINDS IN THE WORLD ARE LOCKED UP WITH US.
AND NOT A ONE OF 'EM HAS FIGGERED A WAY OUTTA THIS HOOSGOW!
YOU DOT COM UPSTARTS AND OIL WEENIES MAKE ME BILIOUS!
I CAME UP IN THE WORLD WHEN A MAN HAD TO USE HIS WITS AS WELL AS HIS MONEY!
I'LL CONNIVE A WAY FROM THIS THIRD WORLD STALAG!
FACE THE FACTS, BURNS...
...THE ONLY GRINGO GETTIN' STATESIDE FROM HERE IS BILLY BEERBELLY!
HA! HA! HA! HA! HA! HA!
HMMMM...

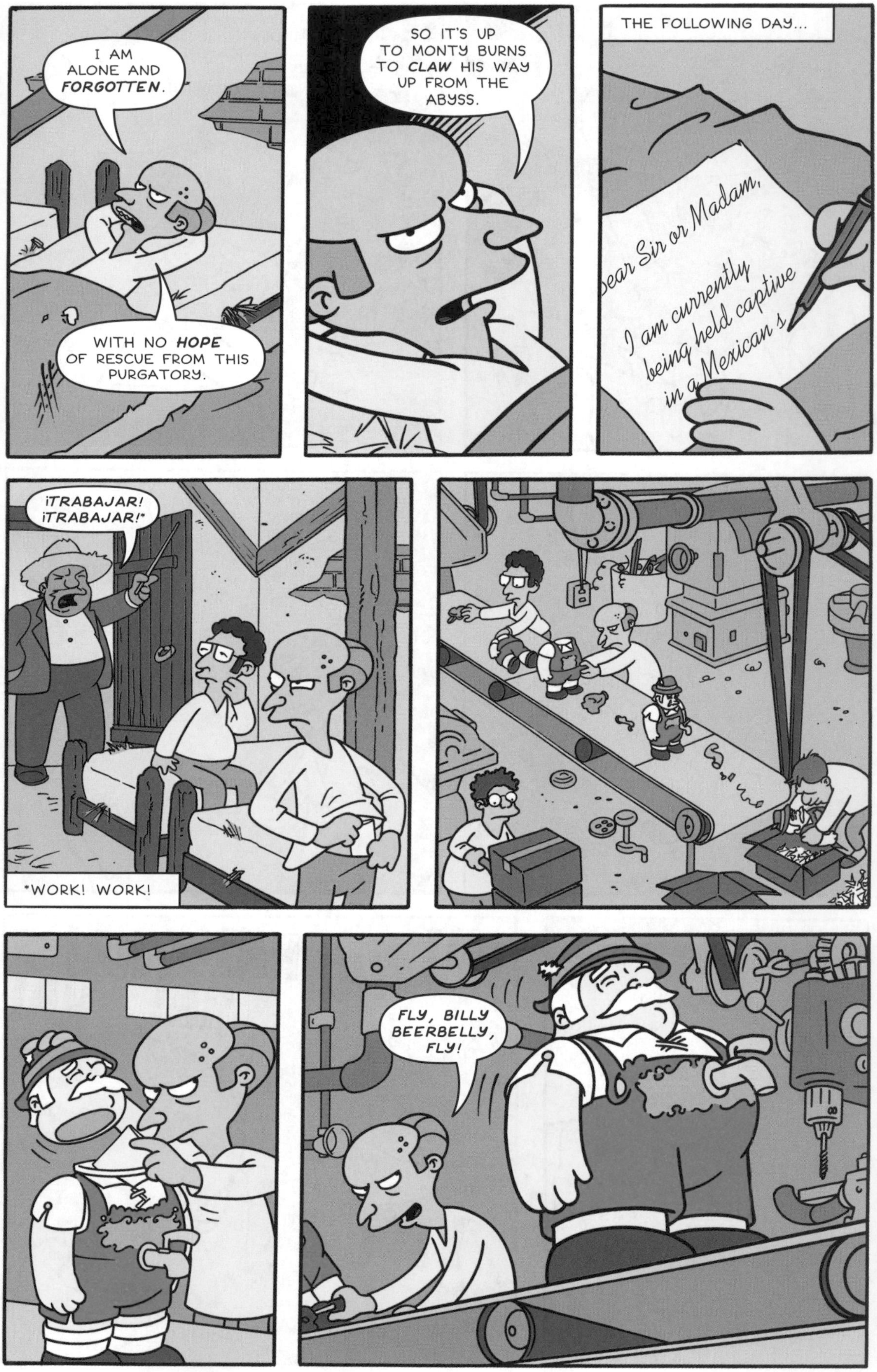
I AM ALONE AND FORGOTTEN.
WITH NO HOPE OF RESCUE FROM THIS PURGATORY.
SO IT'S UP TO MONTY BURNS TO CLAW HIS WAY UP FROM THE ABYSS.
THE FOLLOWING DAY...
Dear Sir or Madam,
I am currently being held captive in a Mexican s
¡TRABAJAR! ¡TRABAJAR!*
*WORK! WORK!
FLY, BILLY BEERBELLY, FLY!

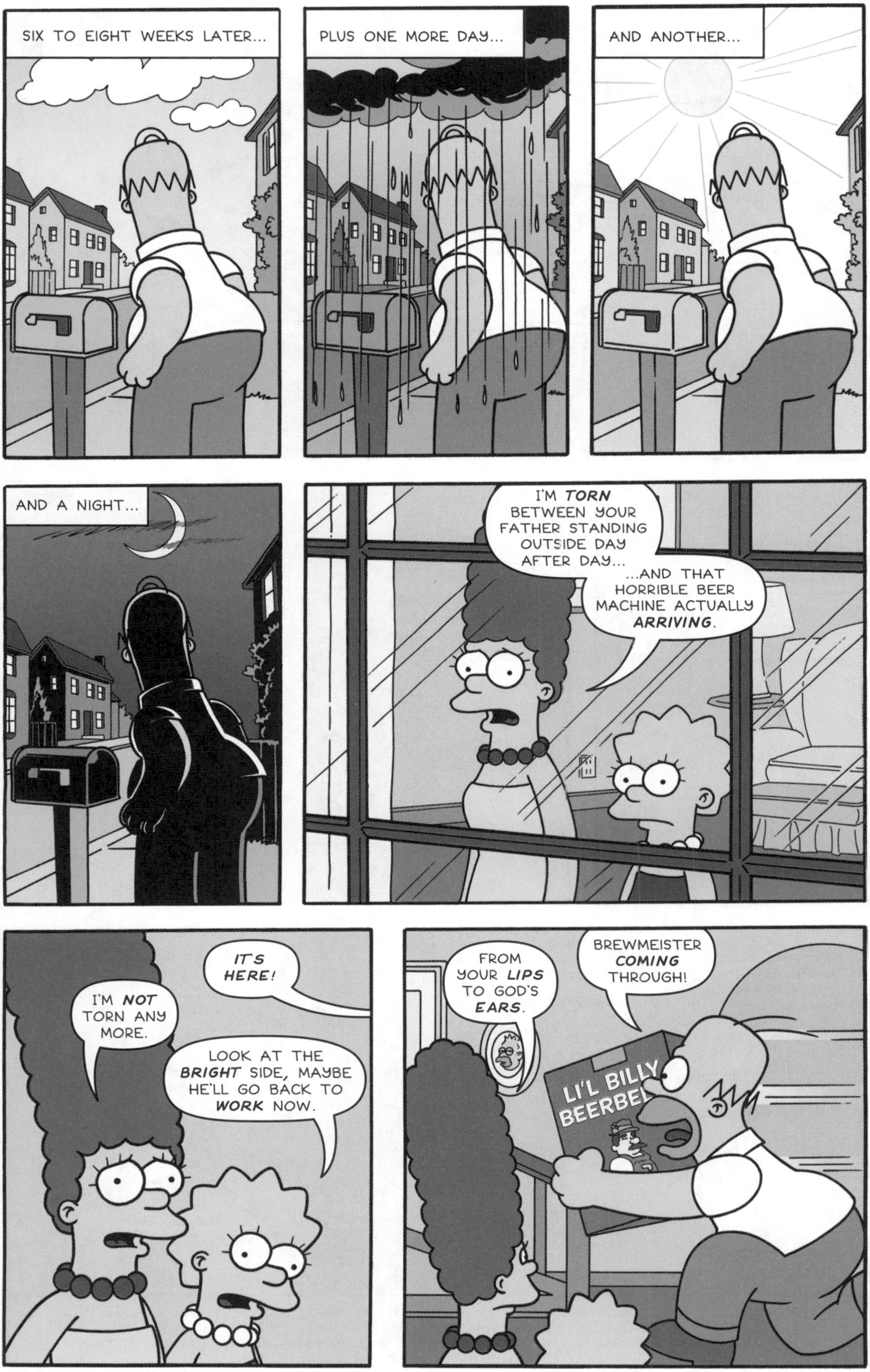
SIX TO EIGHT WEEKS LATER...
PLUS ONE MORE DAY...
AND ANOTHER...
AND A NIGHT...
I'M TORN BETWEEN YOUR FATHER STANDING OUTSIDE DAY AFTER DAY...
...AND THAT HORRIBLE BEER MACHINE ACTUALLY ARRIVING.
I'M NOT TORN ANY MORE.
IT'S HERE!
LOOK AT THE BRIGHT SIDE, MAYBE HE'LL GO BACK TO WORK NOW.
FROM YOUR LIPS TO GOD'S EARS.
BREWMEISTER COMING THROUGH!
LI'L BILLY BEERBE

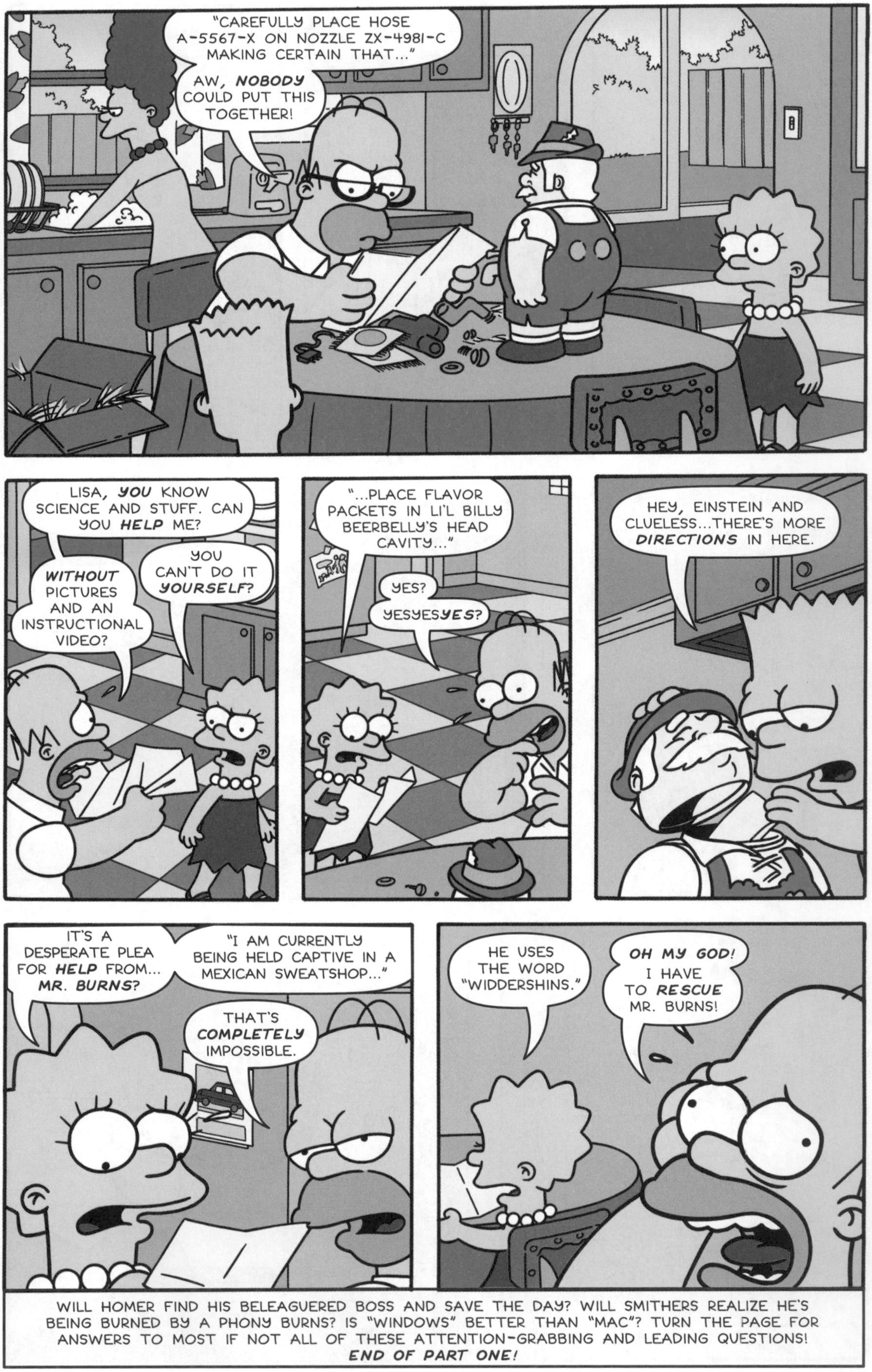
"CAREFULLY PLACE HOSE A-5567-X ON NOZZLE ZX-4981-C MAKING CERTAIN THAT..."
AW, NOBODY COULD PUT THIS TOGETHER!
LISA, YOU KNOW SCIENCE AND STUFF. CAN YOU HELP ME?
YOU CAN'T DO IT YOURSELF?
WITHOUT PICTURES AND AN INSTRUCTIONAL VIDEO?
"...PLACE FLAVOR PACKETS IN LI'L BILLY BEERBELLY'S HEAD CAVITY..."
YES?
YESYESYES?
HEY, EINSTEIN AND CLUELESS...THERE'S MORE DIRECTIONS IN HERE.
IT'S A DESPERATE PLEA FOR HELP FROM... MR. BURNS?
"I AM CURRENTLY BEING HELD CAPTIVE IN A MEXICAN SWEATSHOP..."
THAT'S COMPLETELY IMPOSSIBLE.
HE USES THE WORD "WIDDERSHINS."
OH MY GOD! I HAVE TO RESCUE MR. BURNS!
WILL HOMER FIND HIS BELEAGUERED BOSS AND SAVE THE DAY? WILL SMITHERS REALIZE HE'S BEING BURNED BY A PHONY BURNS? IS "WINDOWS" BETTER THAN "MAC"? TURN THE PAGE FOR ANSWERS TO MOST IF NOT ALL OF THESE ATTENTION-GRABBING AND LEADING QUESTIONS!
END OF PART ONE!

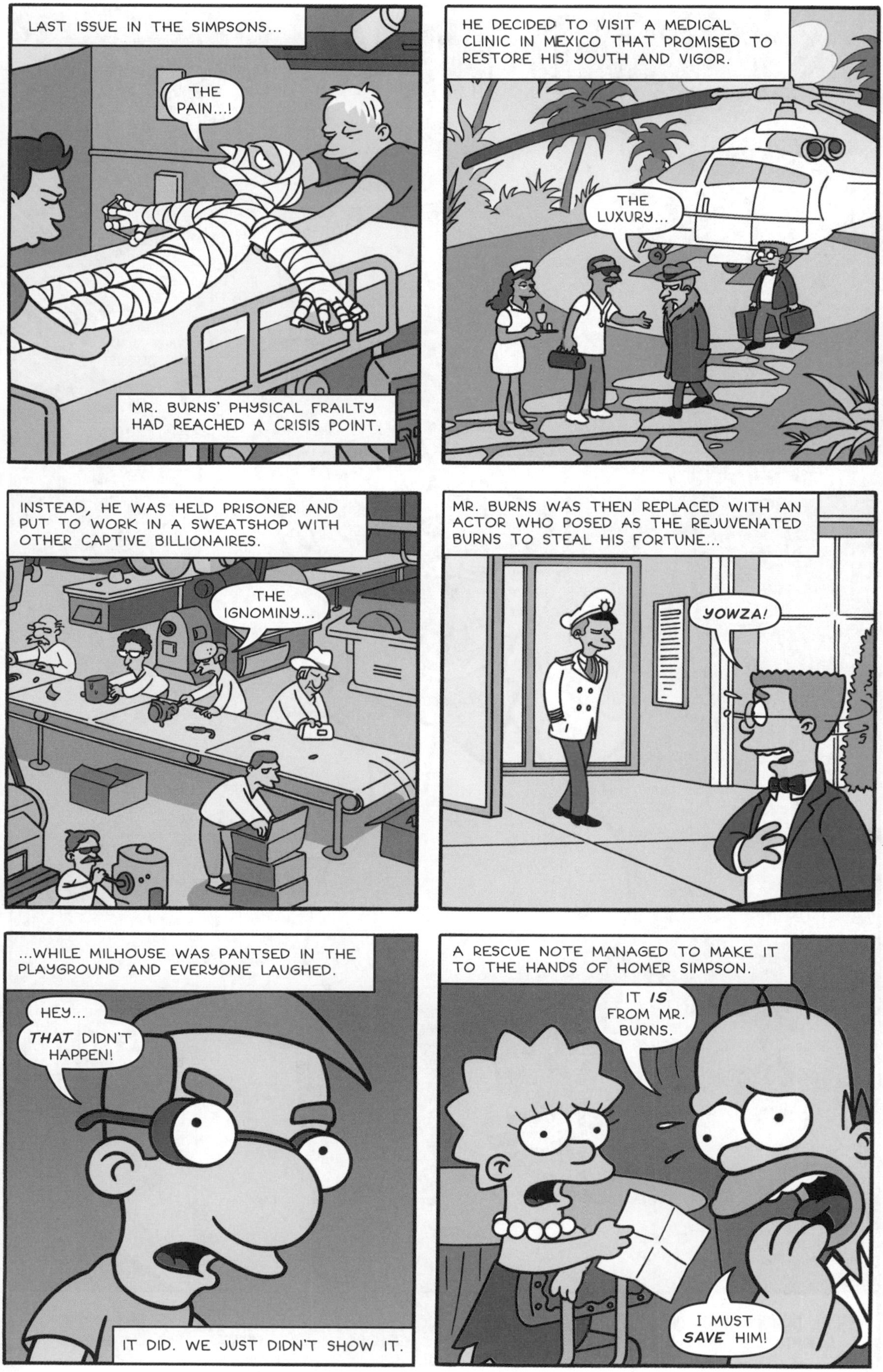
LAST ISSUE IN THE SIMPSONS...
THE PAIN...!
MR. BURNS' PHYSICAL FRAILTY HAD REACHED A CRISIS POINT.
HE DECIDED TO VISIT A MEDICAL CLINIC IN MEXICO THAT PROMISED TO RESTORE HIS YOUTH AND VIGOR.
THE LUXURY...
INSTEAD, HE WAS HELD PRISONER AND PUT TO WORK IN A SWEATSHOP WITH OTHER CAPTIVE BILLIONAIRES.
THE IGNOMINY...
MR. BURNS WAS THEN REPLACED WITH AN ACTOR WHO POSED AS THE REJUVENATED BURNS TO STEAL HIS FORTUNE...
YOWZA!
...WHILE MILHOUSE WAS PANTSED IN THE PLAYGROUND AND EVERYONE LAUGHED.
HEY... THAT DIDN'T HAPPEN!
IT DID. WE JUST DIDN'T SHOW IT.
A RESCUE NOTE MANAGED TO MAKE IT TO THE HANDS OF HOMER SIMPSON.
IT IS FROM MR. BURNS.
I MUST SAVE HIM!

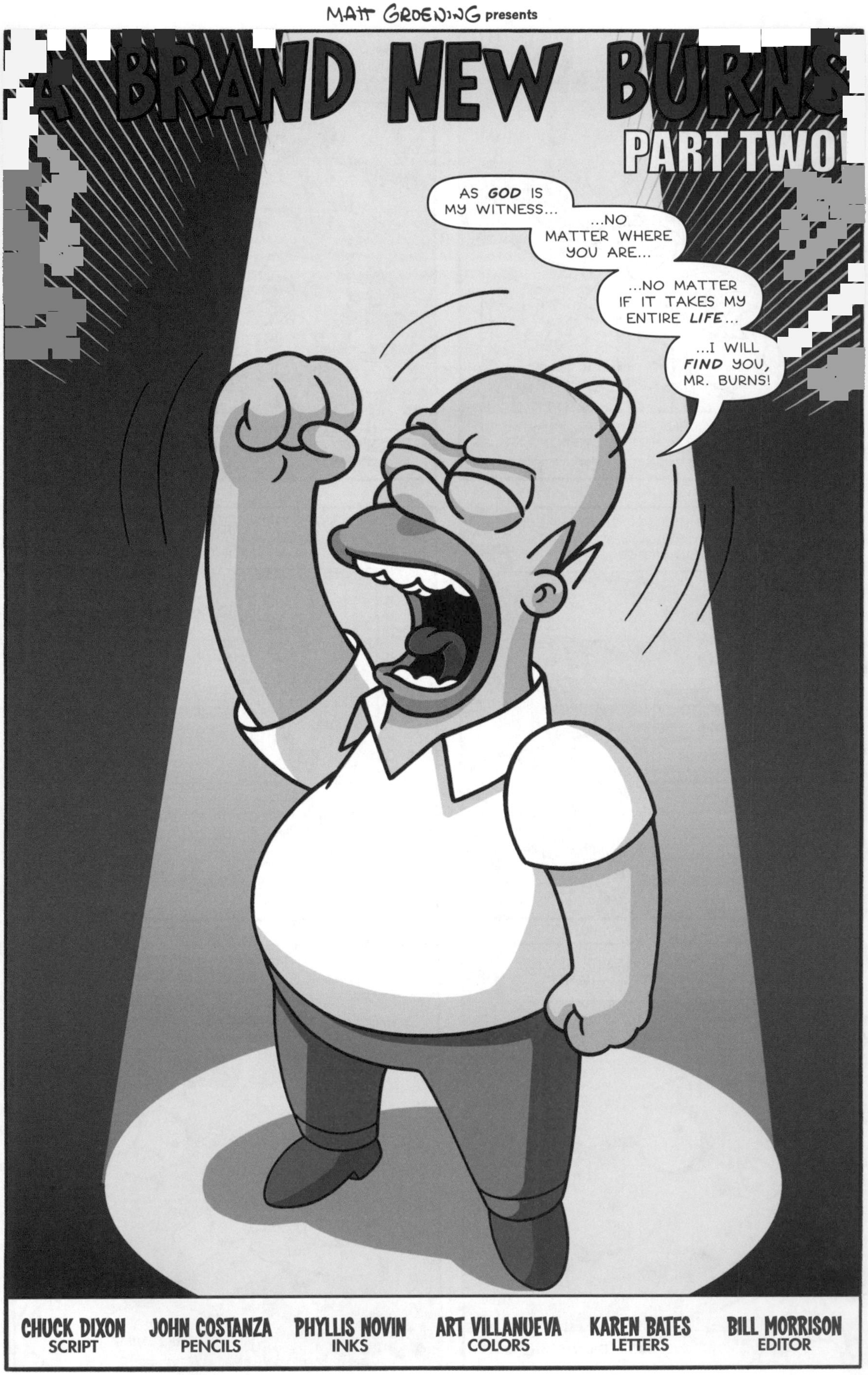
MATT GROENING presents
A BRAND NEW BURNS
PART TWO
AS GOD IS MY WITNESS...
...NO MATTER WHERE YOU ARE...
...NO MATTER IF IT TAKES MY ENTIRE LIFE...
...I WILL FIND YOU, MR. BURNS!
CHUCK DIXON SCRIPT
JOHN COSTANZA PENCILS
PHYLLIS NOVIN INKS
ART VILLANUEVA COLORS
KAREN BATES LETTERS
BILL MORRISON EDITOR

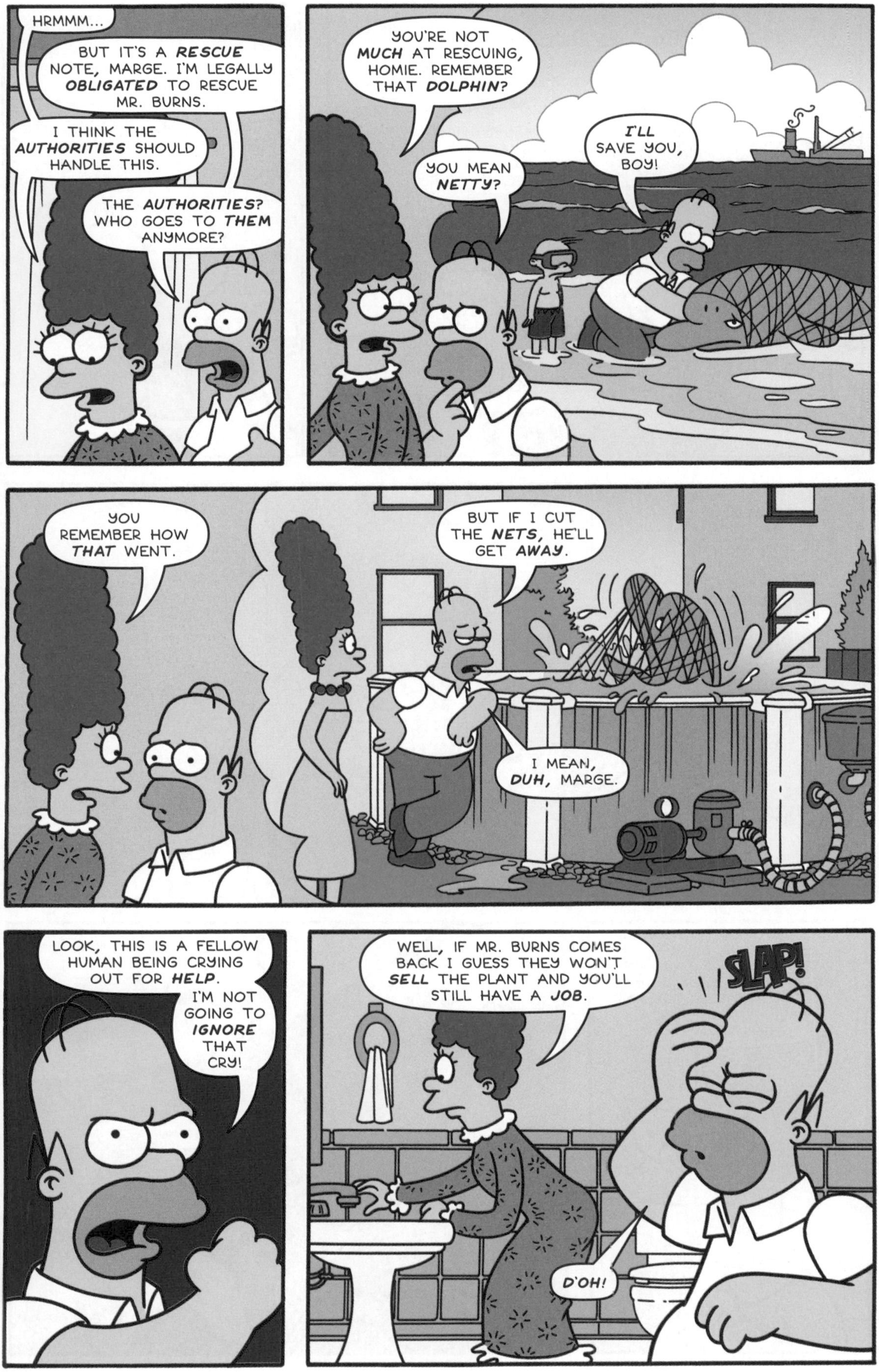

HRMMM...
BUT IT'S A RESCUE NOTE, MARGE. I'M LEGALLY OBLIGATED TO RESCUE MR. BURNS.
I THINK THE AUTHORITIES SHOULD HANDLE THIS.
THE AUTHORITIES? WHO GOES TO THEM ANYMORE?
YOU'RE NOT MUCH AT RESCUING, HOMIE. REMEMBER THAT DOLPHIN?
YOU MEAN NETTY?
I'LL SAVE YOU, BOY!
YOU REMEMBER HOW THAT WENT.
BUT IF I CUT THE NETS, HE'LL GET AWAY.
I MEAN, DUH, MARGE.
LOOK, THIS IS A FELLOW HUMAN BEING CRYING OUT FOR HELP.
I'M NOT GOING TO IGNORE THAT CRY!
WELL, IF MR. BURNS COMES BACK I GUESS THEY WON'T SELL THE PLANT AND YOU'LL STILL HAVE A JOB.
SLAP!
D'OH!

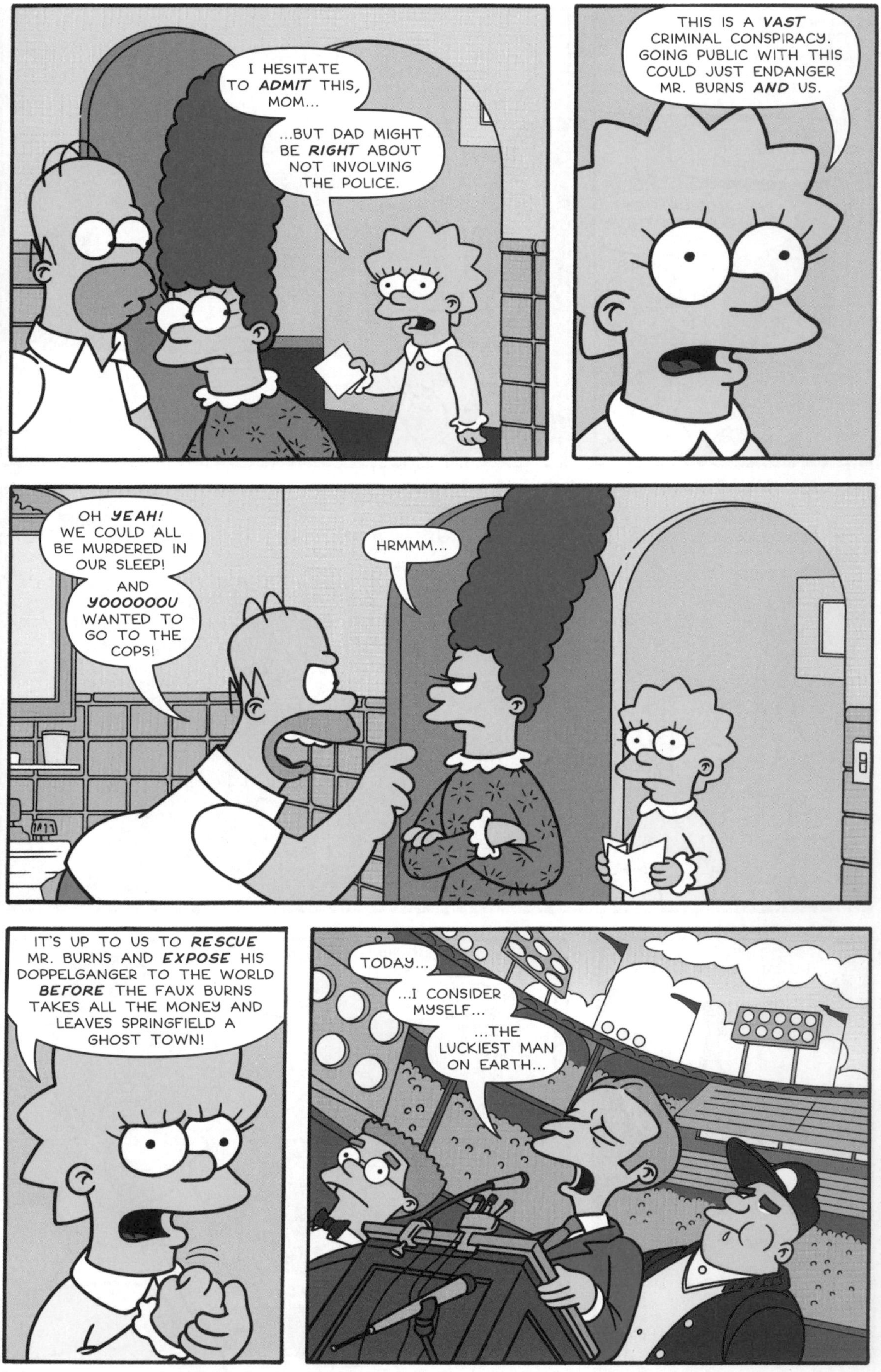
I HESITATE TO ADMIT THIS, MOM...
...BUT DAD MIGHT BE RIGHT ABOUT NOT INVOLVING THE POLICE.
THIS IS A VAST CRIMINAL CONSPIRACY. GOING PUBLIC WITH THIS COULD JUST ENDANGER MR. BURNS AND US.
OH YEAH! WE COULD ALL BE MURDERED IN OUR SLEEP!
AND YOOOOOOU WANTED TO GO TO THE COPS!
HRMMM...
IT'S UP TO US TO RESCUE MR. BURNS AND EXPOSE HIS DOPPELGANGER TO THE WORLD BEFORE THE FAUX BURNS TAKES ALL THE MONEY AND LEAVES SPRINGFIELD A GHOST TOWN!
TODAY...
...I CONSIDER MYSELF...
...THE LUCKIEST MAN ON EARTH...

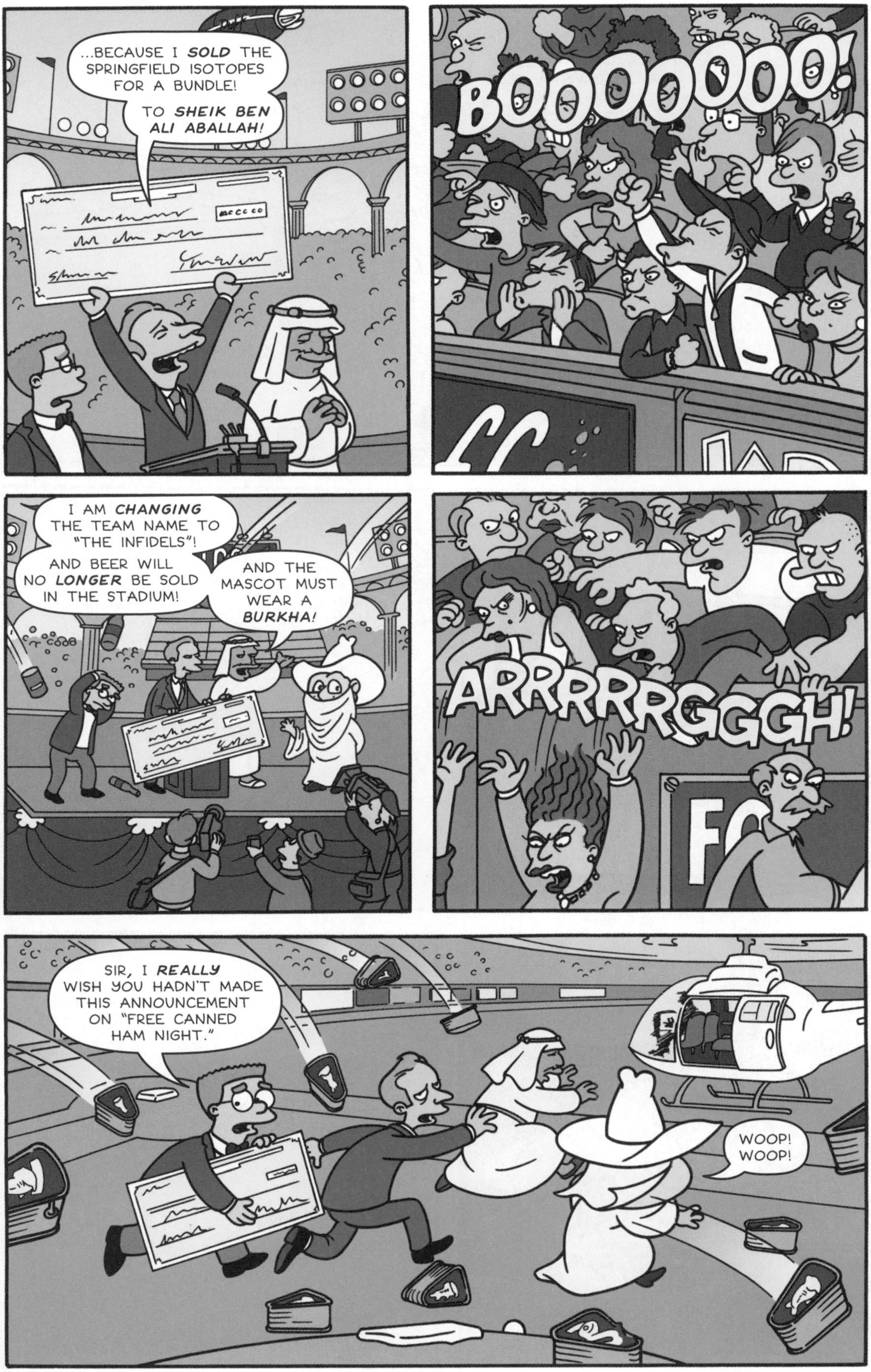
...BECAUSE I SOLD THE SPRINGFIELD ISOTOPES FOR A BUNDLE!
TO SHEIK BEN ALI ABALLAH!
BOOOOOOO!
I AM CHANGING THE TEAM NAME TO "THE INFIDELS"!
AND BEER WILL NO LONGER BE SOLD IN THE STADIUM!
AND THE MASCOT MUST WEAR A BURKHA!
ARRRRRGGGH!
SIR, I REALLY WISH YOU HADN'T MADE THIS ANNOUNCEMENT ON "FREE CANNED HAM NIGHT."
WOOP! WOOP!

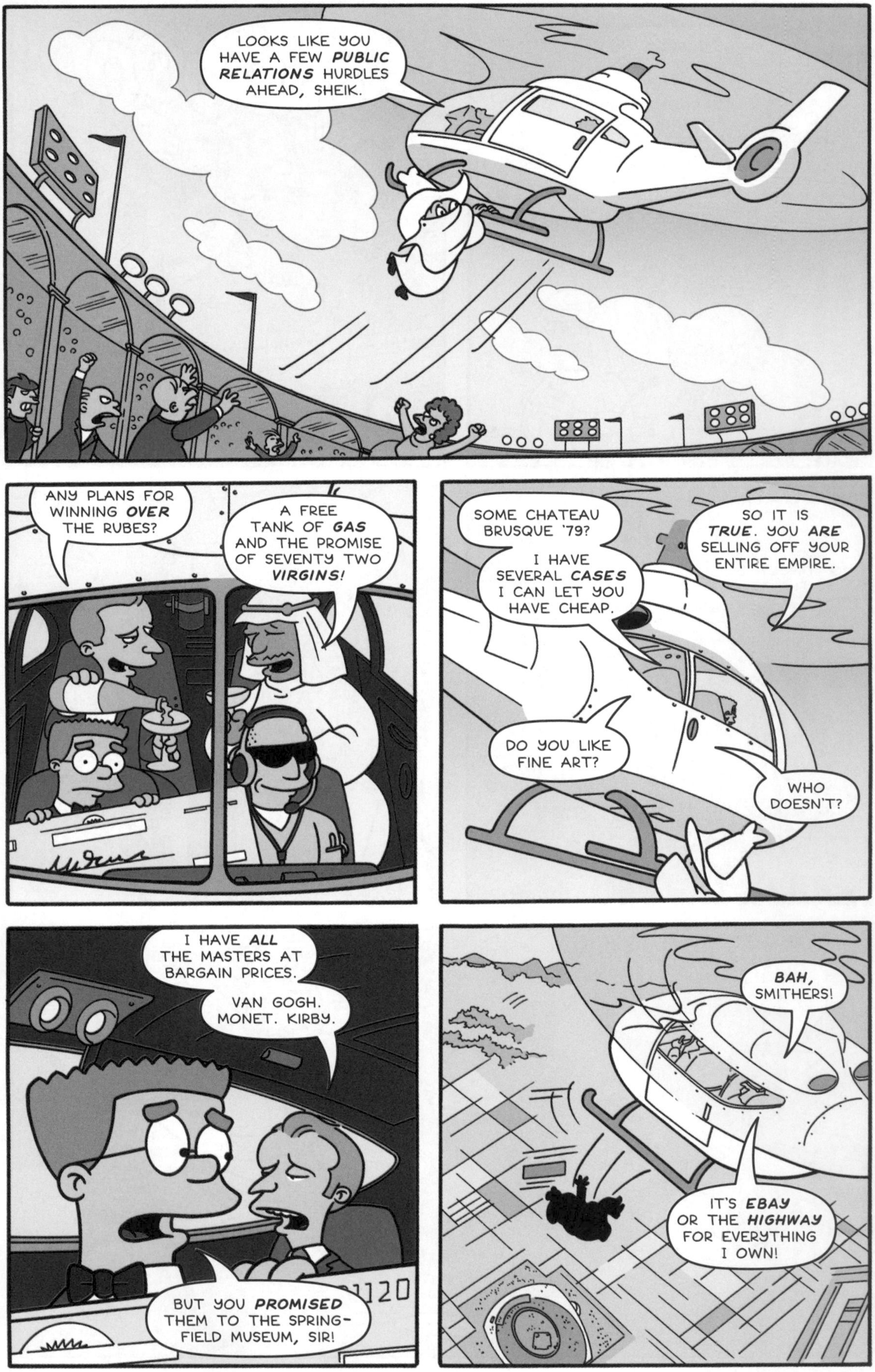
LOOKS LIKE YOU HAVE A FEW **PUBLIC RELATIONS** HURDLES AHEAD, SHEIK.
ANY PLANS FOR WINNING **OVER** THE RUBES?
A FREE TANK OF **GAS** AND THE PROMISE OF SEVENTY TWO **VIRGINS**!
SOME CHATEAU BRUSQUE '79?
I HAVE SEVERAL **CASES** I CAN LET YOU HAVE CHEAP.
SO IT IS **TRUE**. YOU **ARE** SELLING OFF YOUR ENTIRE EMPIRE.
DO YOU LIKE FINE ART?
WHO DOESN'T?
I HAVE **ALL** THE MASTERS AT BARGAIN PRICES.
VAN GOGH. MONET. KIRBY.
BUT YOU **PROMISED** THEM TO THE SPRING-FIELD MUSEUM, SIR!
BAH, SMITHERS!
IT'S **EBAY** OR THE **HIGHWAY** FOR EVERYTHING I OWN!

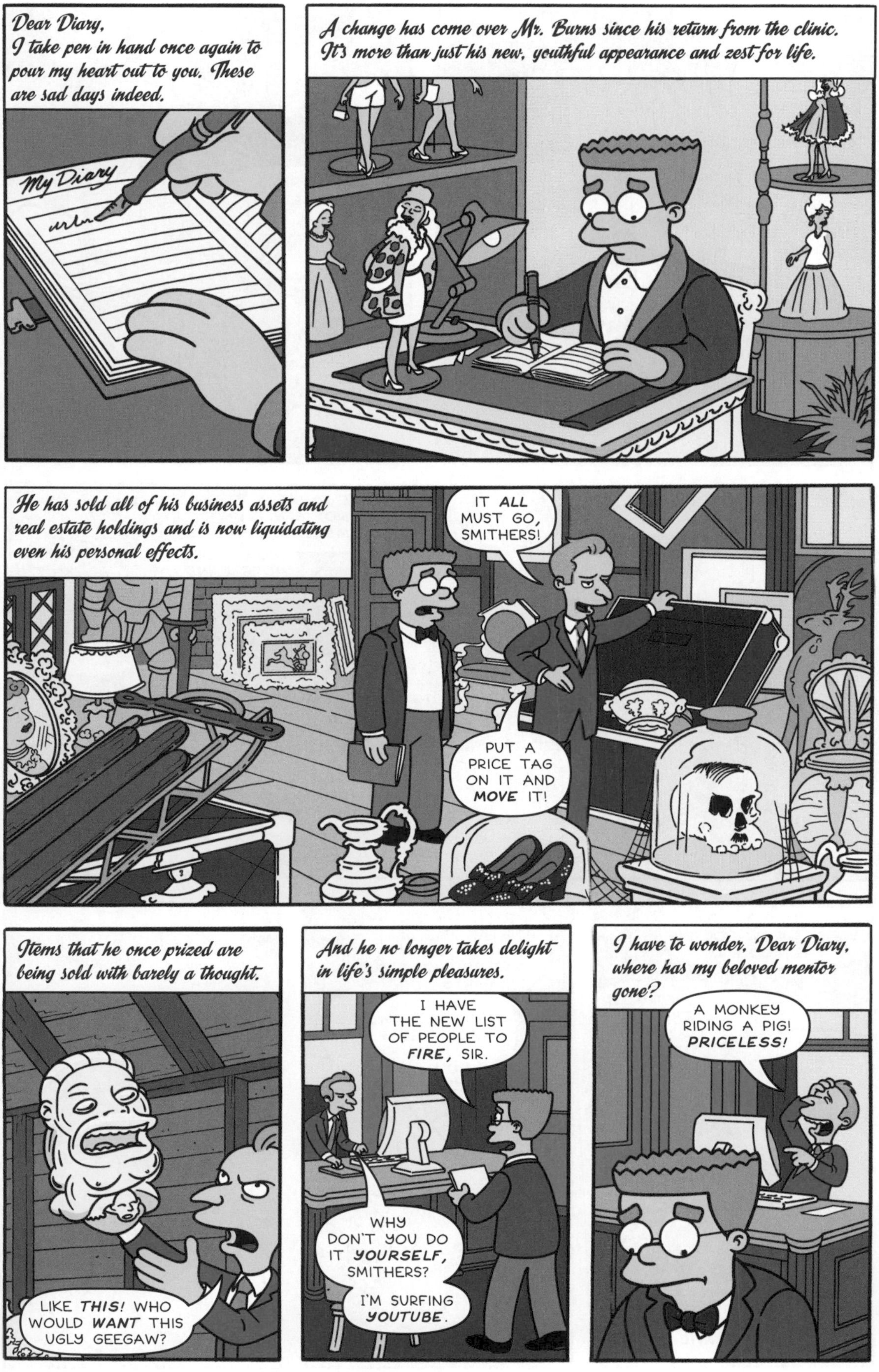
Dear Diary,
I take pen in hand once again to pour my heart out to you. These are sad days indeed.
My Diary
A change has come over Mr. Burns since his return from the clinic. It's more than just his new, youthful appearance and zest for life.
He has sold all of his business assets and real estate holdings and is now liquidating even his personal effects.
IT ALL MUST GO, SMITHERS!
PUT A PRICE TAG ON IT AND MOVE IT!
Items that he once prized are being sold with barely a thought.
LIKE THIS! WHO WOULD WANT THIS UGLY GEEGAW?
And he no longer takes delight in life's simple pleasures.
I HAVE THE NEW LIST OF PEOPLE TO FIRE, SIR.
WHY DON'T YOU DO IT YOURSELF, SMITHERS?
I'M SURFING YOUTUBE.
I have to wonder, Dear Diary, where has my beloved mentor gone?
A MONKEY RIDING A PIG! PRICELESS!

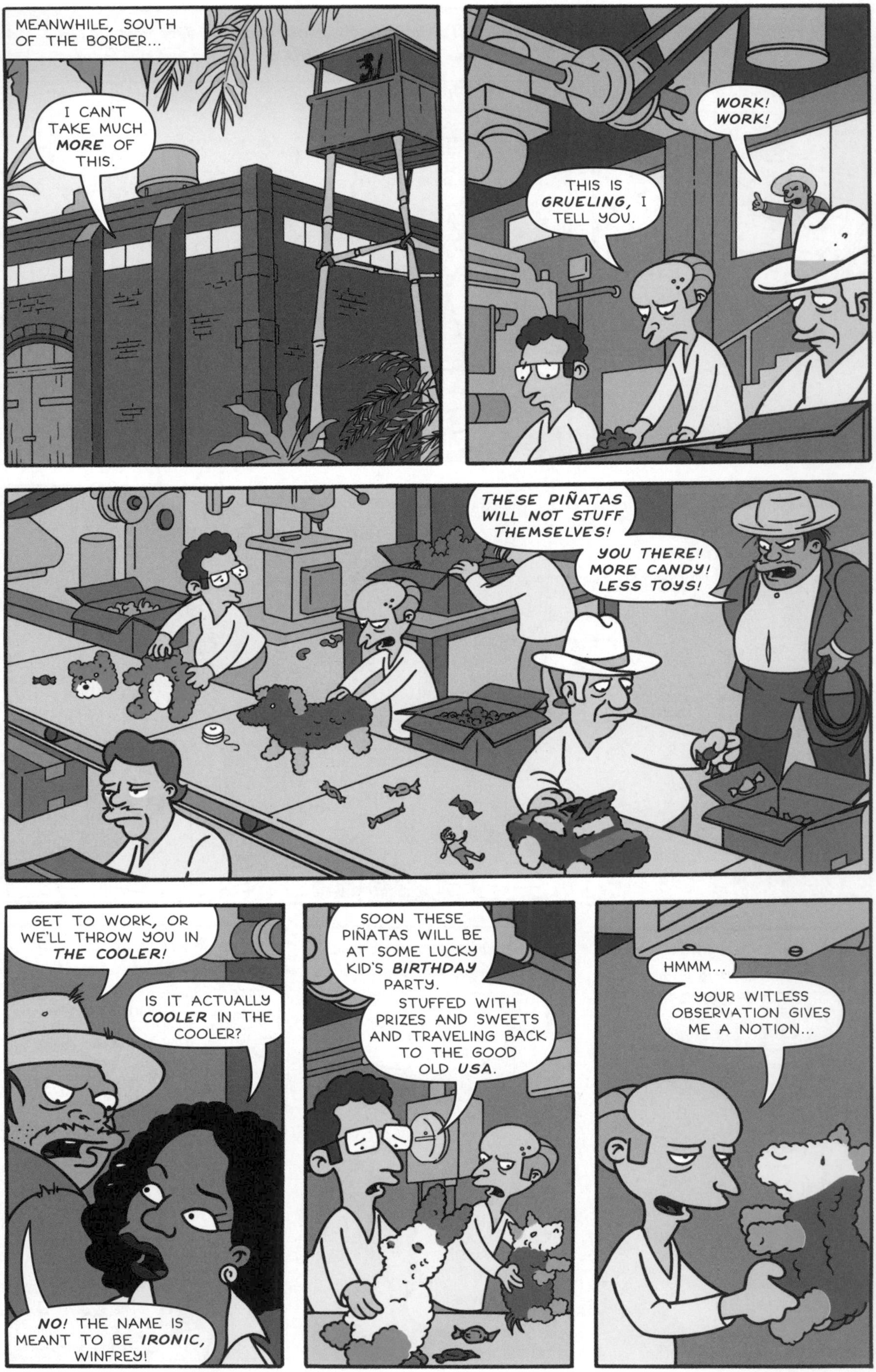
MEANWHILE, SOUTH OF THE BORDER...
I CAN'T TAKE MUCH MORE OF THIS.
WORK! WORK!
THIS IS GRUELING, I TELL YOU.
THESE PIÑATAS WILL NOT STUFF THEMSELVES!
YOU THERE! MORE CANDY! LESS TOYS!
GET TO WORK, OR WE'LL THROW YOU IN THE COOLER!
IS IT ACTUALLY COOLER IN THE COOLER?
NO! THE NAME IS MEANT TO BE IRONIC, WINFREY!
SOON THESE PIÑATAS WILL BE AT SOME LUCKY KID'S BIRTHDAY PARTY.
STUFFED WITH PRIZES AND SWEETS AND TRAVELING BACK TO THE GOOD OLD USA.
HMMM...
YOUR WITLESS OBSERVATION GIVES ME A NOTION...

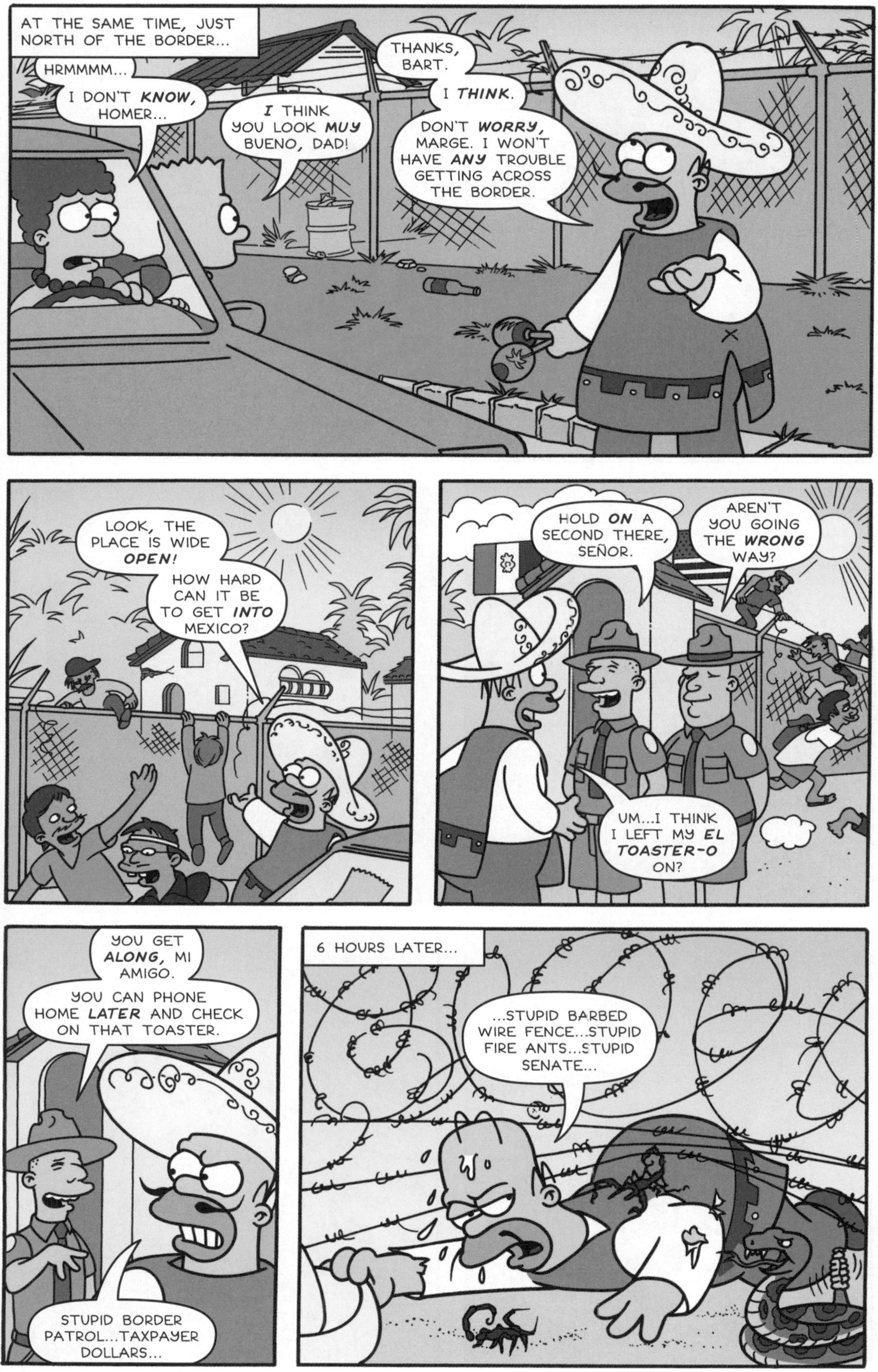
AT THE SAME TIME, JUST NORTH OF THE BORDER...
HRMMMM...
I DON'T **KNOW,** HOMER...
I THINK YOU LOOK **MUY** BUENO, DAD!
THANKS, BART.
I **THINK**.
DON'T **WORRY,** MARGE. I WON'T HAVE **ANY** TROUBLE GETTING ACROSS THE BORDER.
LOOK, THE PLACE IS WIDE **OPEN!**
HOW HARD CAN IT BE TO GET **INTO** MEXICO?
HOLD **ON** A SECOND THERE, SEÑOR.
AREN'T YOU GOING THE **WRONG** WAY?
UM...I THINK I LEFT MY **EL TOASTER-O** ON?
YOU GET **ALONG,** MI AMIGO.
YOU CAN PHONE HOME **LATER** AND CHECK ON THAT TOASTER.
STUPID BORDER PATROL...TAXPAYER DOLLARS...
6 HOURS LATER...
...STUPID BARBED WIRE FENCE...STUPID FIRE ANTS...STUPID SENATE...

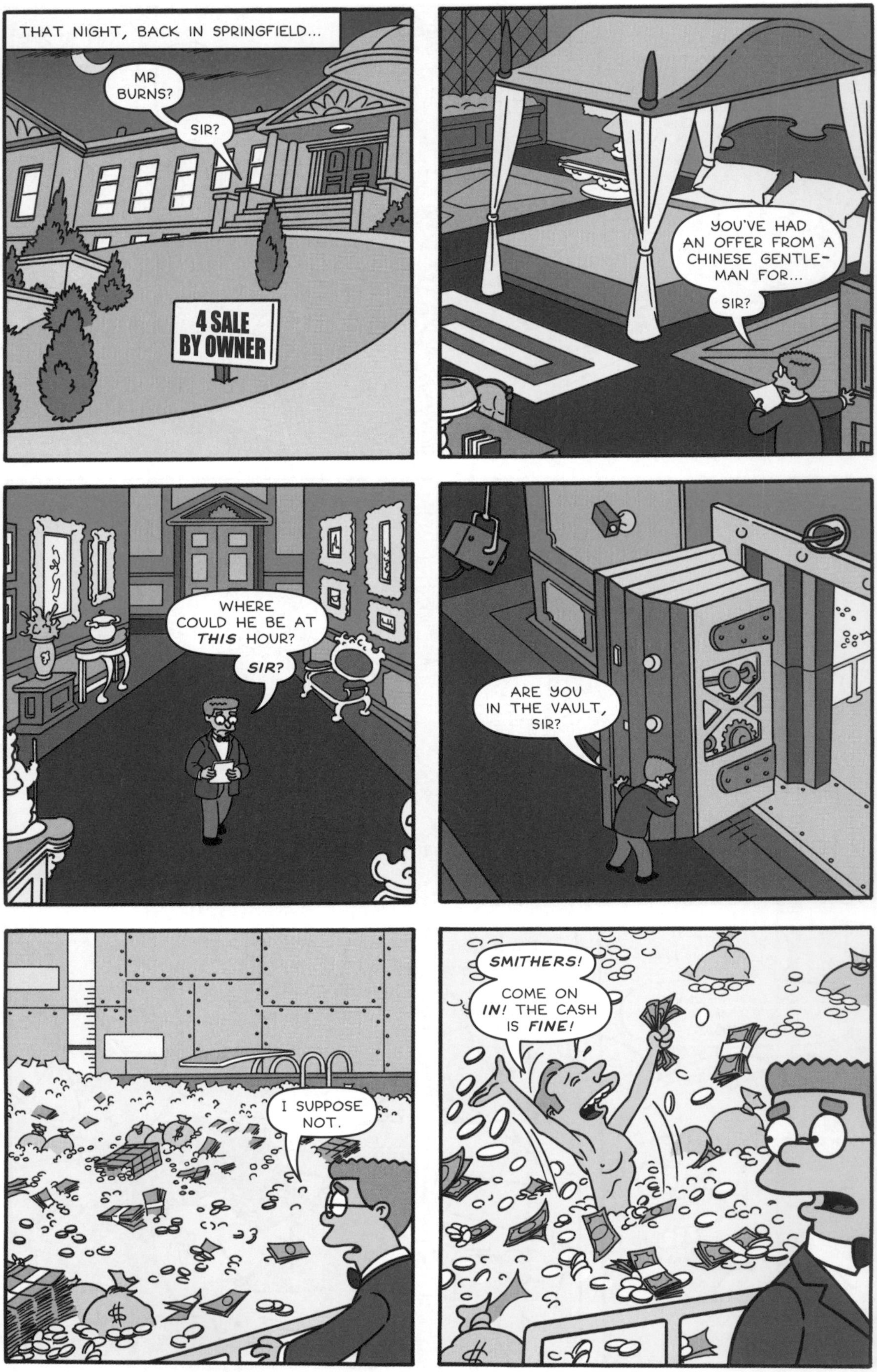
THAT NIGHT, BACK IN SPRINGFIELD...
MR BURNS?
SIR?
4 SALE BY OWNER
YOU'VE HAD AN OFFER FROM A CHINESE GENTLE-MAN FOR...
SIR?
WHERE COULD HE BE AT THIS HOUR?
SIR?
ARE YOU IN THE VAULT, SIR?
I SUPPOSE NOT.
SMITHERS!
COME ON IN! THE CASH IS FINE!

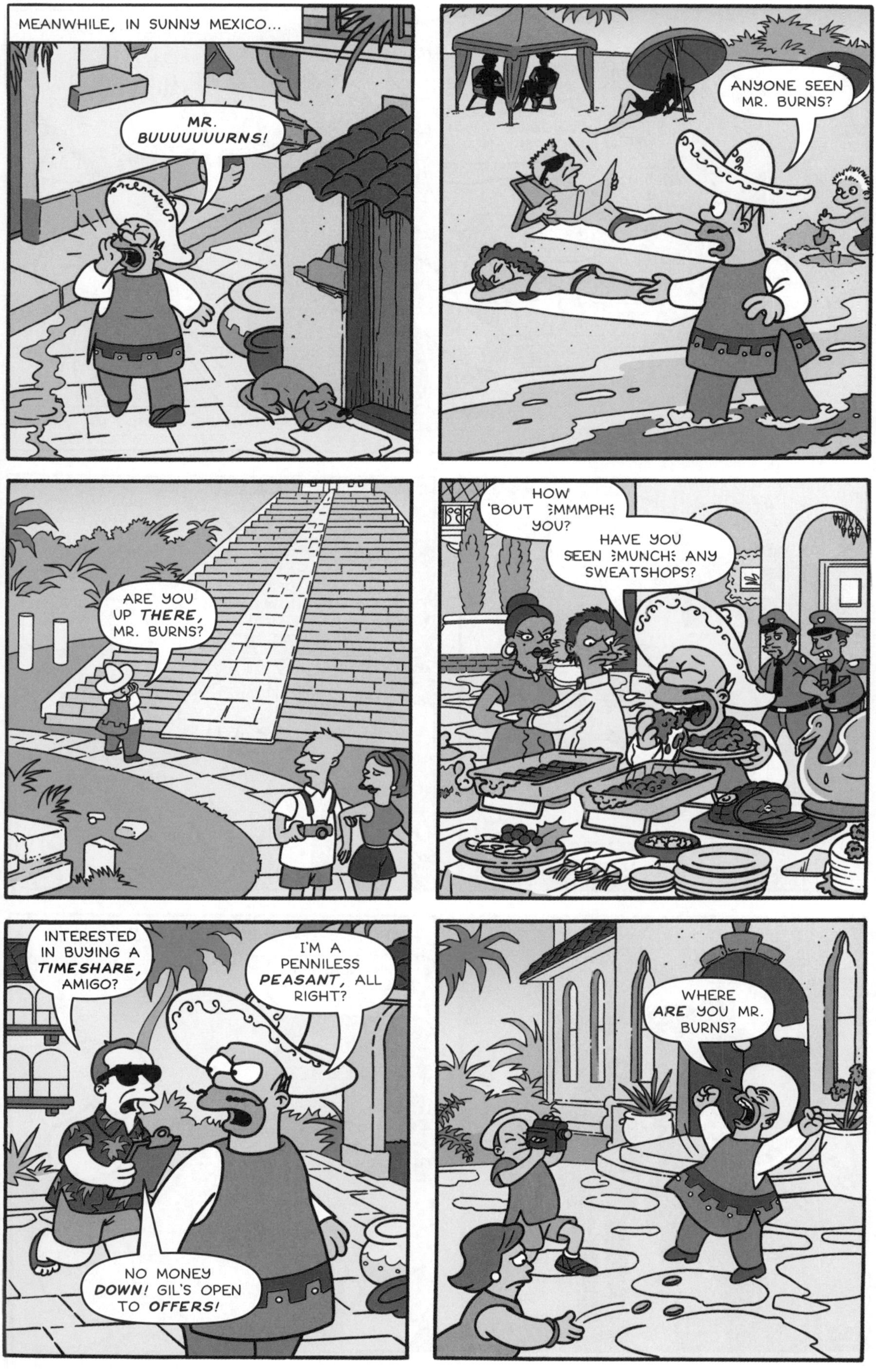
MEANWHILE, IN SUNNY MEXICO...
MR. BUUUUUUURNS!
ANYONE SEEN MR. BURNS?
ARE YOU UP THERE, MR. BURNS?
HOW 'BOUT ⁝MMMPH⁝ YOU?
HAVE YOU SEEN ⁝MUNCH⁝ ANY SWEATSHOPS?
INTERESTED IN BUYING A TIMESHARE, AMIGO?
I'M A PENNILESS PEASANT, ALL RIGHT?
NO MONEY DOWN! GIL'S OPEN TO OFFERS!
WHERE ARE YOU MR. BURNS?

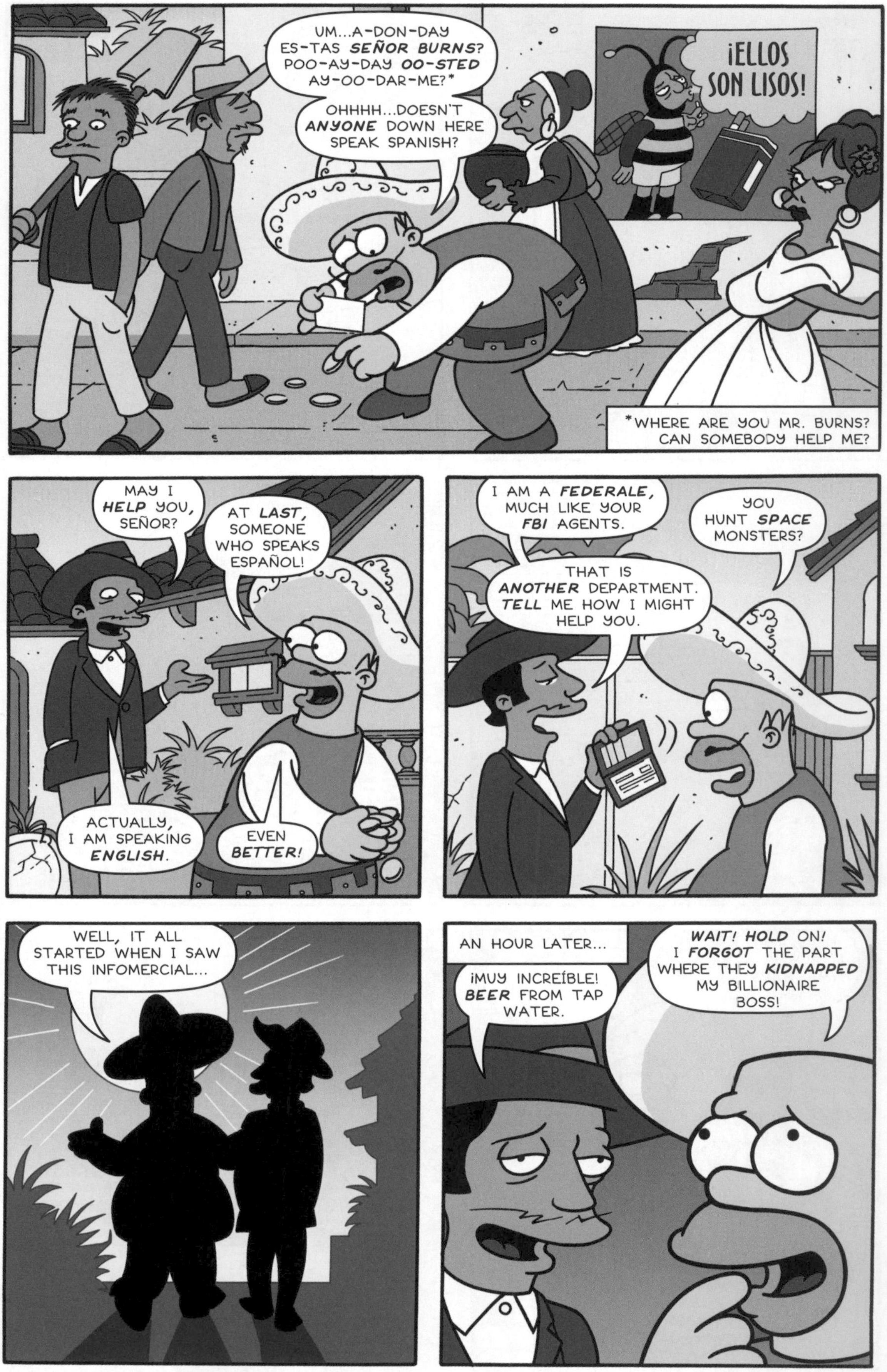
UM...A-DON-DAY ES-TAS **SEÑOR BURNS**? POO-AY-DAY **OO-STED** AY-OO-DAR-ME?*
OHHHH...DOESN'T **ANYONE** DOWN HERE SPEAK SPANISH?
¡ELLOS SON LISOS!
*WHERE ARE YOU MR. BURNS? CAN SOMEBODY HELP ME?
MAY I **HELP** YOU, SEÑOR?
AT **LAST**, SOMEONE WHO SPEAKS ESPAÑOL!
ACTUALLY, I AM SPEAKING **ENGLISH**.
EVEN **BETTER**!
I AM A **FEDERALE**, MUCH LIKE YOUR **FBI** AGENTS.
YOU HUNT **SPACE** MONSTERS?
THAT IS **ANOTHER** DEPARTMENT. **TELL** ME HOW I MIGHT HELP YOU.
WELL, IT ALL STARTED WHEN I SAW THIS INFOMERCIAL...
AN HOUR LATER...
¡MUY INCREÍBLE! **BEER** FROM TAP WATER.
WAIT! HOLD ON! I **FORGOT** THE PART WHERE THEY **KIDNAPPED** MY BILLIONAIRE BOSS!

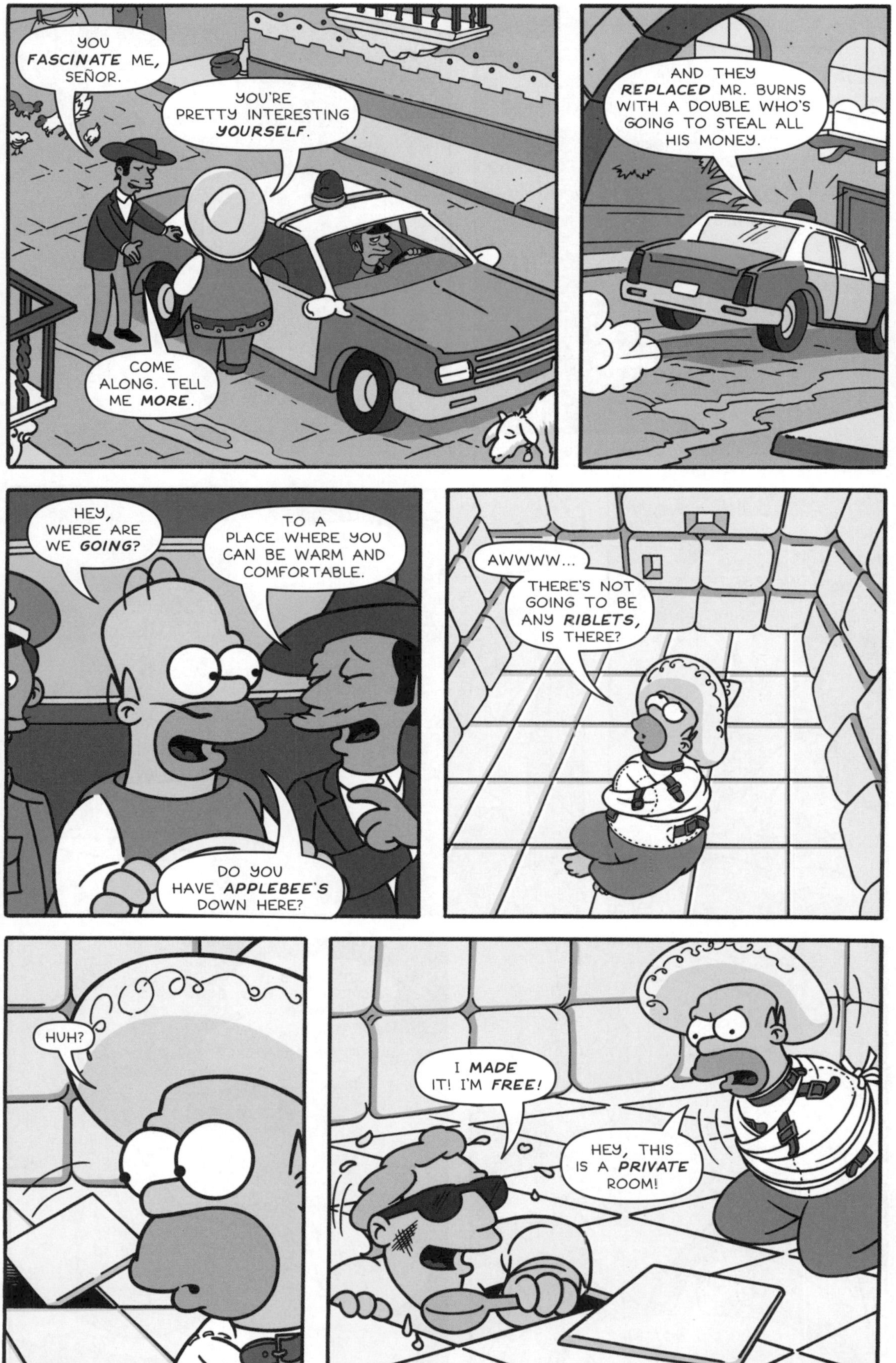
YOU **FASCINATE** ME, SEÑOR.
YOU'RE PRETTY INTERESTING **YOURSELF**.
COME ALONG. TELL ME **MORE**.
AND THEY **REPLACED** MR. BURNS WITH A DOUBLE WHO'S GOING TO STEAL ALL HIS MONEY.
HEY, WHERE ARE WE **GOING**?
TO A PLACE WHERE YOU CAN BE WARM AND COMFORTABLE.
DO YOU HAVE **APPLEBEE'S** DOWN HERE?
AWWWW...
THERE'S NOT GOING TO BE ANY **RIBLETS**, IS THERE?
HUH?
I **MADE** IT! I'M **FREE**!
HEY, THIS IS A **PRIVATE** ROOM!

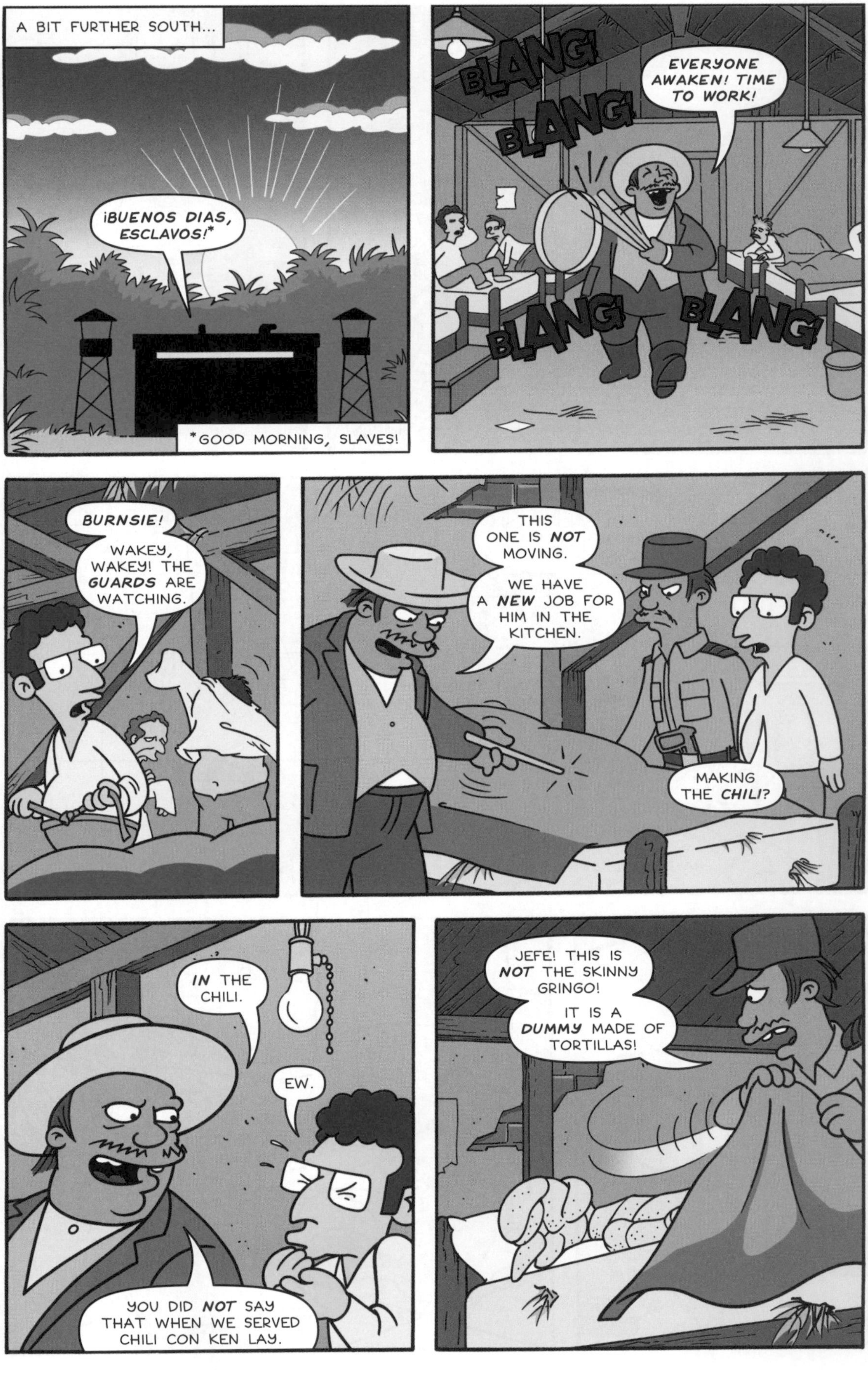
A BIT FURTHER SOUTH...
¡BUENOS DIAS, ESCLAVOS!*
*GOOD MORNING, SLAVES!
BLANG! BLANG!
EVERYONE AWAKEN! TIME TO WORK!
BLANG! BLANG!
BURNSIE!
WAKEY, WAKEY! THE GUARDS ARE WATCHING.
THIS ONE IS NOT MOVING.
WE HAVE A NEW JOB FOR HIM IN THE KITCHEN.
MAKING THE CHILI?
IN THE CHILI.
EW.
YOU DID NOT SAY THAT WHEN WE SERVED CHILI CON KEN LAY.
JEFE! THIS IS NOT THE SKINNY GRINGO!
IT IS A DUMMY MADE OF TORTILLAS!

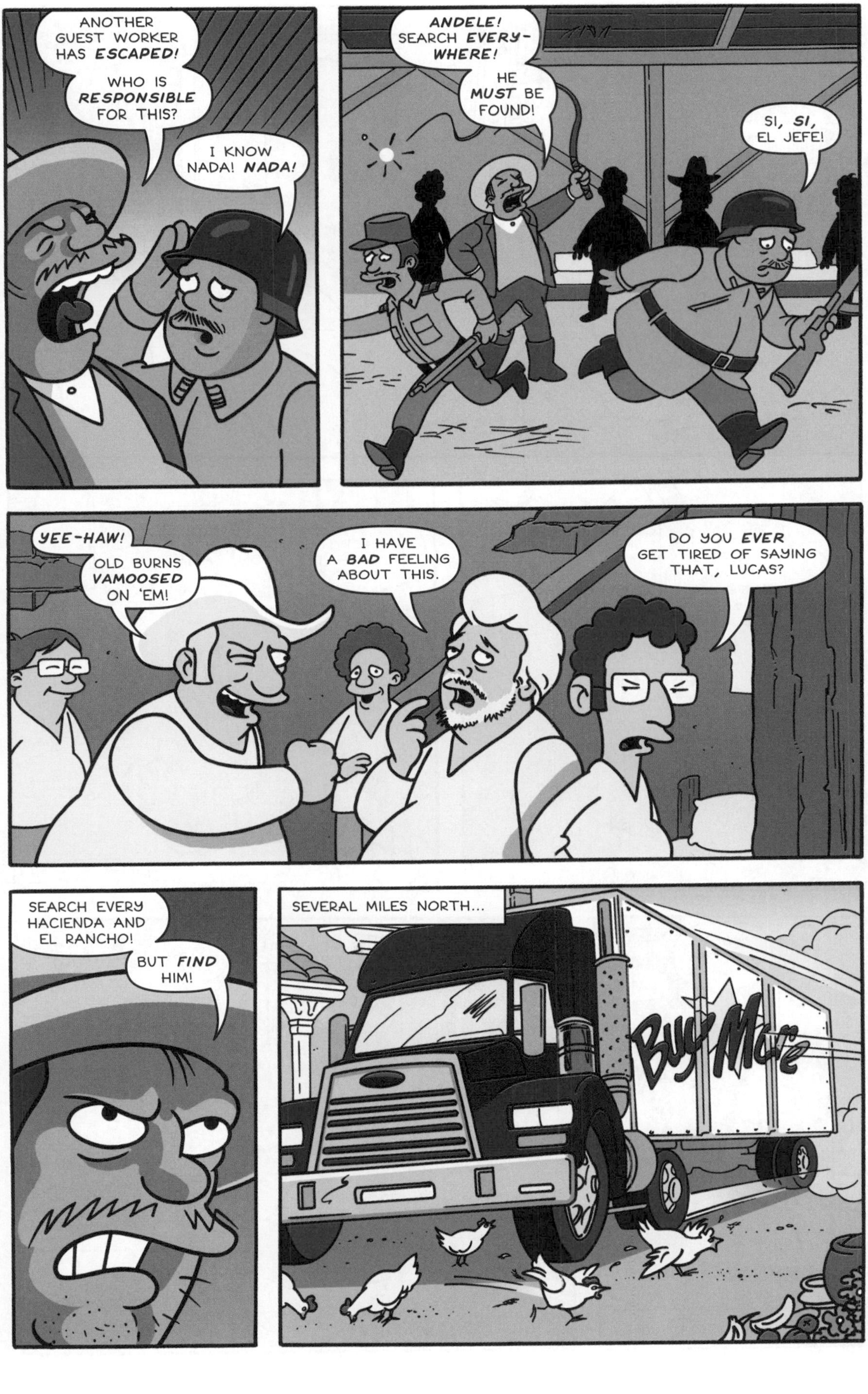
ANOTHER GUEST WORKER HAS ESCAPED!
WHO IS RESPONSIBLE FOR THIS?
I KNOW NADA! NADA!
ANDELE! SEARCH EVERY-WHERE!
HE MUST BE FOUND!
SI, SI, EL JEFE!
YEE-HAW!
OLD BURNS VAMOOSED ON 'EM!
I HAVE A BAD FEELING ABOUT THIS.
DO YOU EVER GET TIRED OF SAYING THAT, LUCAS?
SEARCH EVERY HACIENDA AND EL RANCHO!
BUT FIND HIM!
SEVERAL MILES NORTH...
Buy More

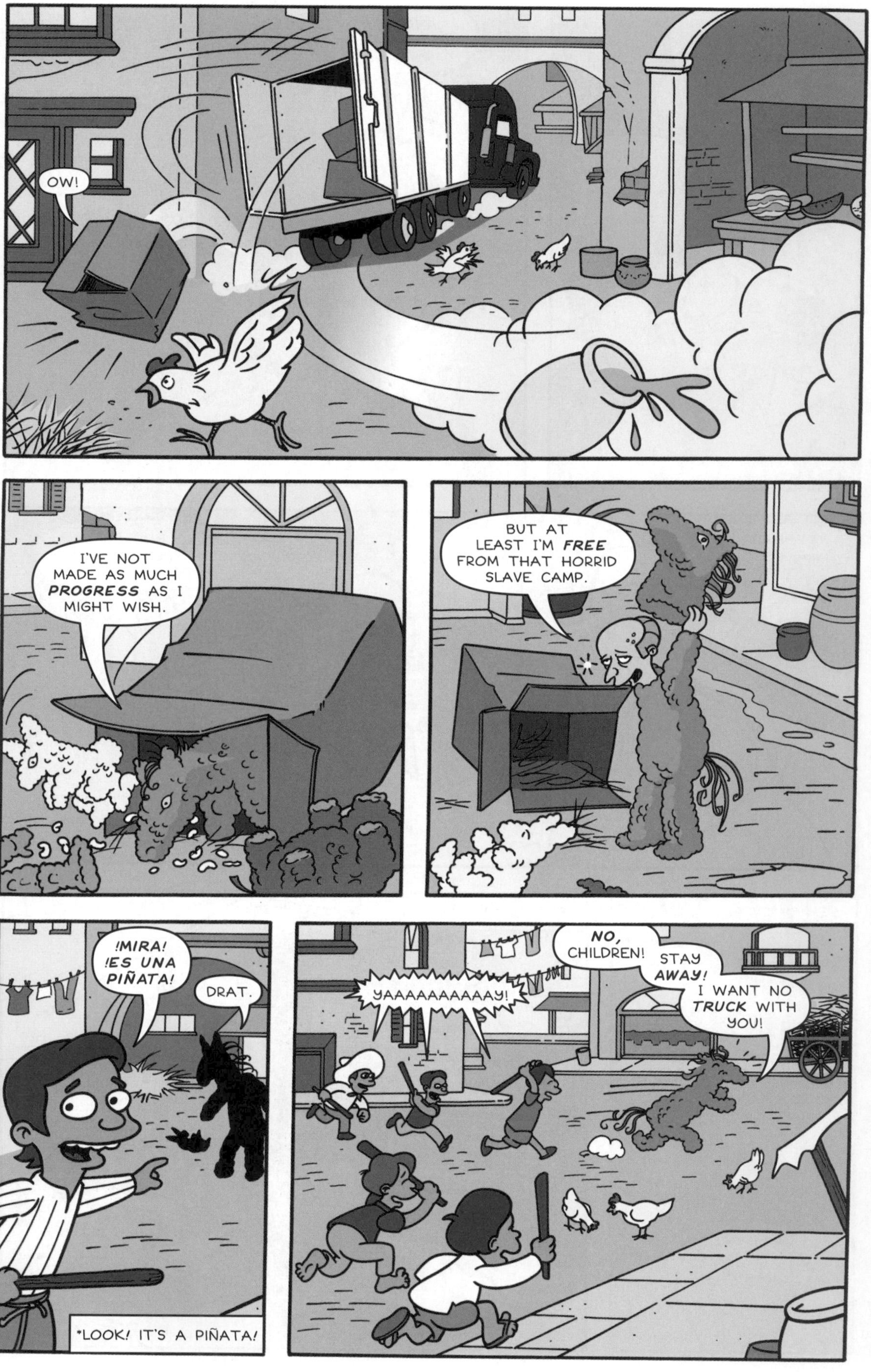

OW!
I'VE NOT MADE AS MUCH PROGRESS AS I MIGHT WISH.
BUT AT LEAST I'M FREE FROM THAT HORRID SLAVE CAMP.
¡MIRA! ¡ES UNA PIÑATA!
DRAT.
*LOOK! IT'S A PIÑATA!
YAAAAAAAAAAY!
NO, CHILDREN!
STAY AWAY!
I WANT NO TRUCK WITH YOU!

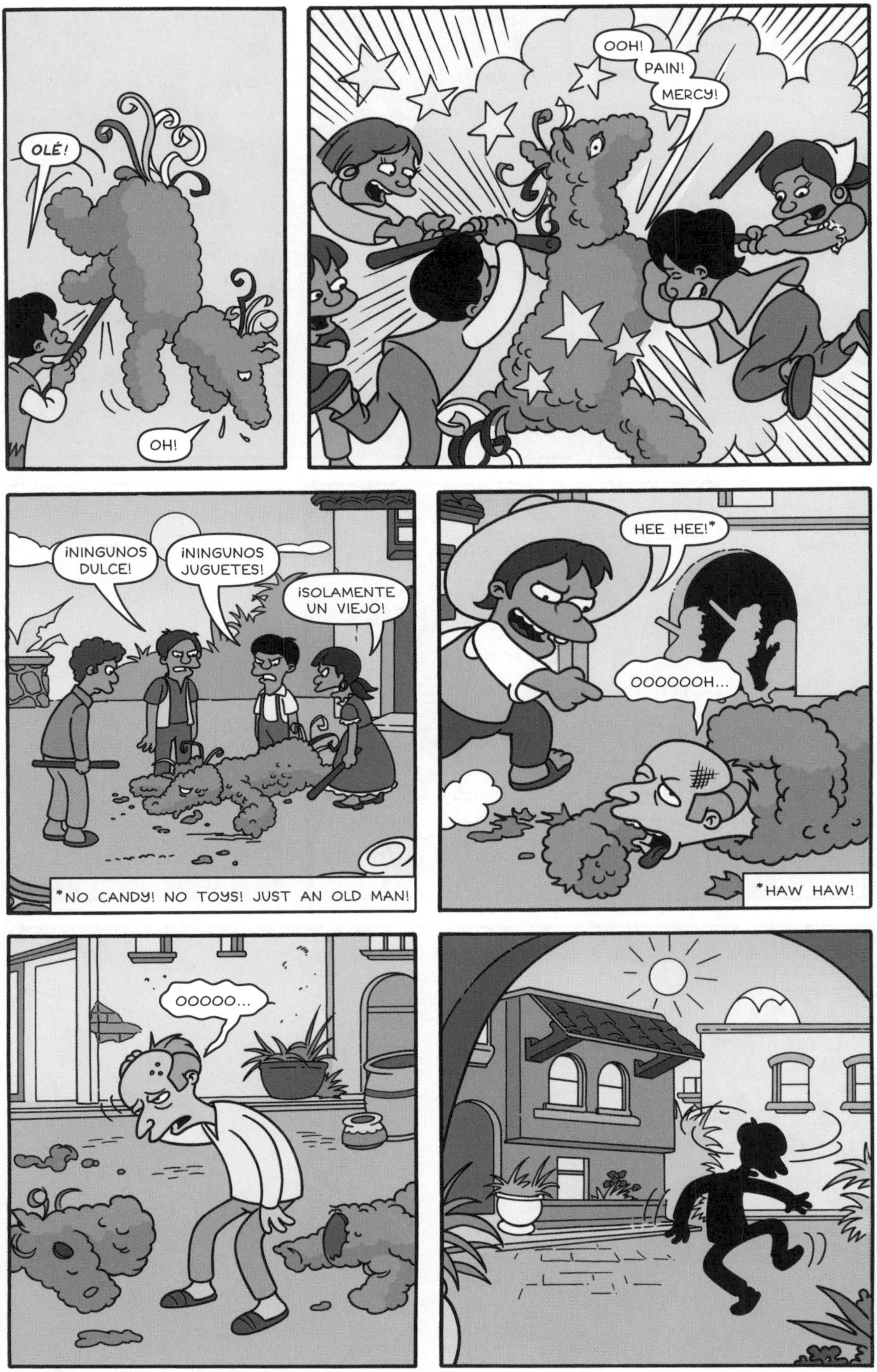
OLÉ!
OH!
OOH!
PAIN!
MERCY!
¡NINGUNOS DULCE!
¡NINGUNOS JUGUETES!
¡SOLAMENTE UN VIEJO!
*NO CANDY! NO TOYS! JUST AN OLD MAN!
HEE HEE!*
OOOOOOH...
*HAW HAW!
OOOOO...

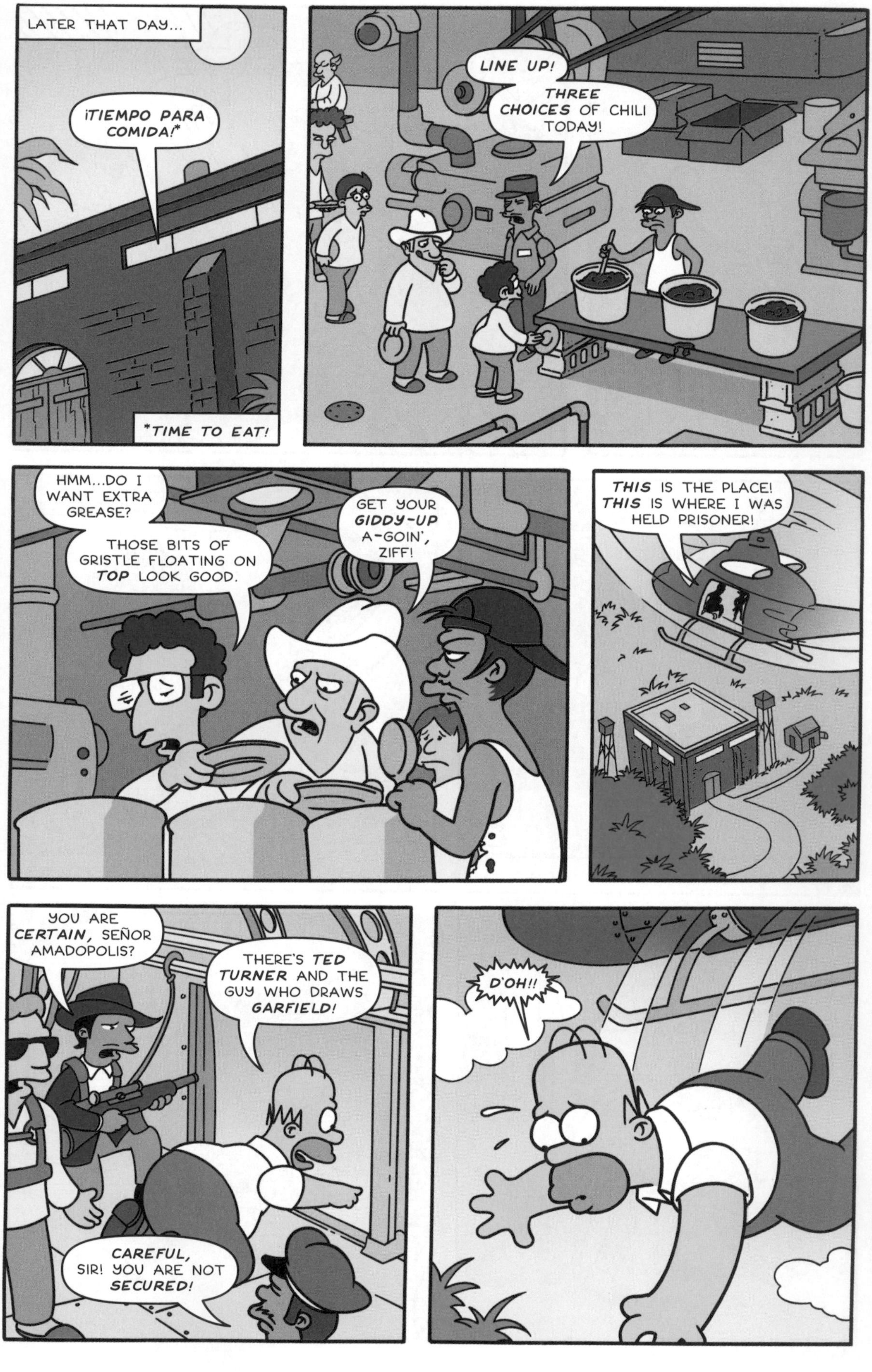
LATER THAT DAY...
¡TIEMPO PARA COMIDA!*
*TIME TO EAT!
LINE UP!
THREE CHOICES OF CHILI TODAY!
HMM...DO I WANT EXTRA GREASE?
THOSE BITS OF GRISTLE FLOATING ON TOP LOOK GOOD.
GET YOUR GIDDY-UP A-GOIN', ZIFF!
THIS IS THE PLACE! THIS IS WHERE I WAS HELD PRISONER!
YOU ARE CERTAIN, SEÑOR AMADOPOLIS?
THERE'S TED TURNER AND THE GUY WHO DRAWS GARFIELD!
CAREFUL, SIR! YOU ARE NOT SECURED!
D'OH!!

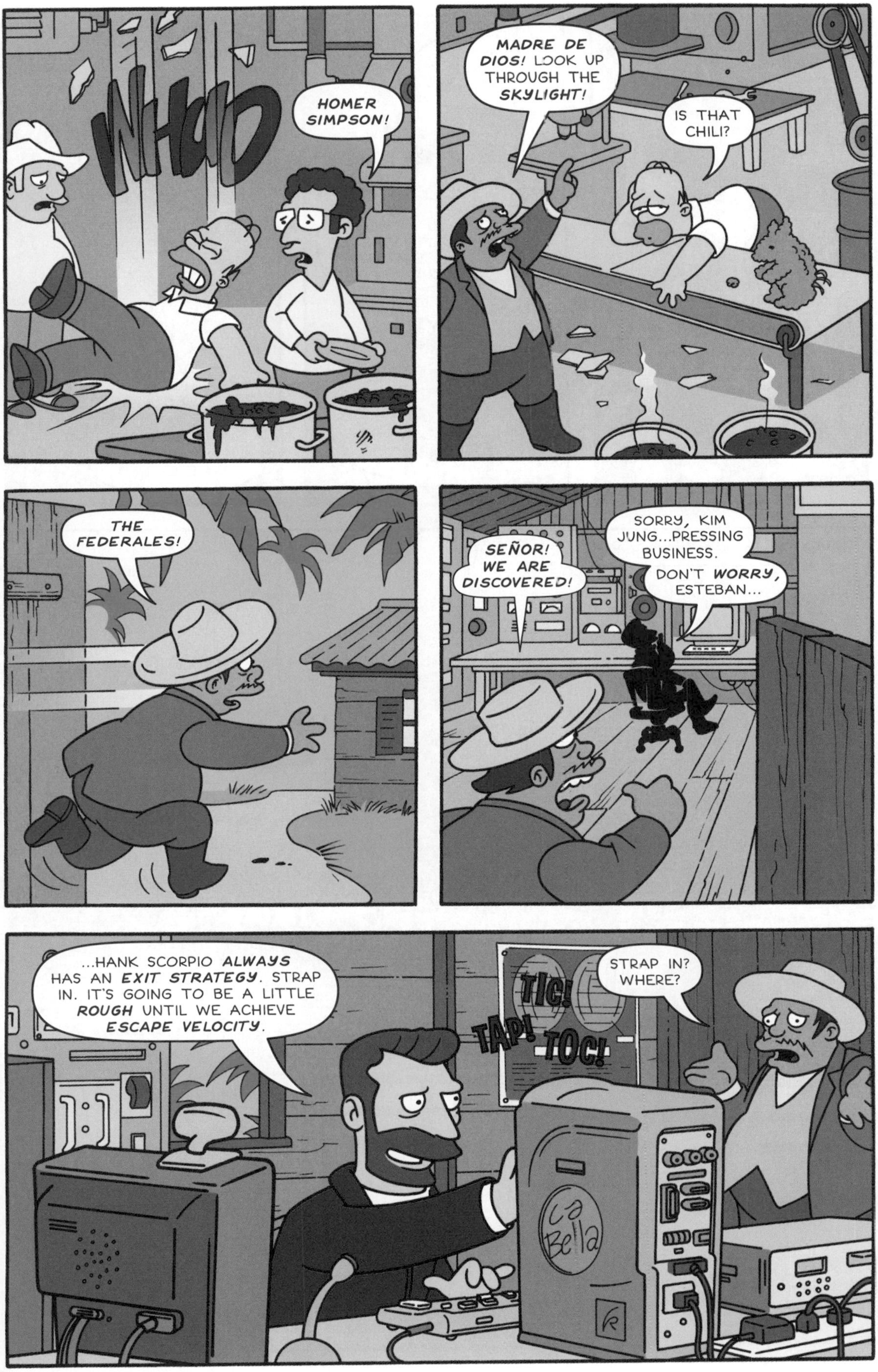
WHOD
HOMER SIMPSON!
MADRE DE DIOS! LOOK UP THROUGH THE SKYLIGHT!
IS THAT CHILI?
THE FEDERALES!
SEÑOR! WE ARE DISCOVERED!
SORRY, KIM JUNG...PRESSING BUSINESS.
DON'T WORRY, ESTEBAN...
...HANK SCORPIO ALWAYS HAS AN EXIT STRATEGY. STRAP IN. IT'S GOING TO BE A LITTLE ROUGH UNTIL WE ACHIEVE ESCAPE VELOCITY.
TIC!
TAP!
TOC!
STRAP IN? WHERE?
La Bella

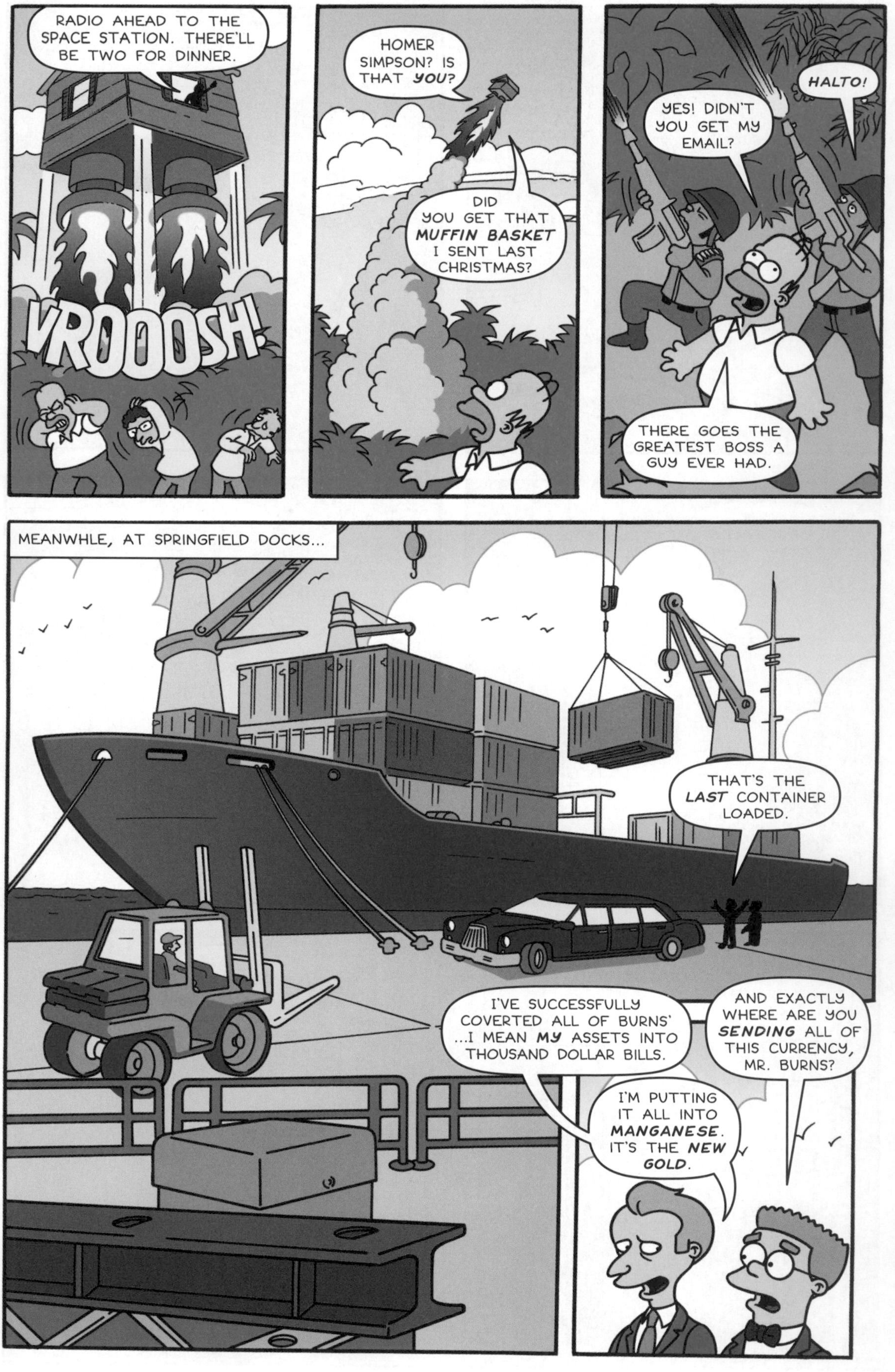
RADIO AHEAD TO THE SPACE STATION. THERE'LL BE TWO FOR DINNER.
VROOOSH!
HOMER SIMPSON? IS THAT *YOU*?
DID YOU GET THAT ***MUFFIN BASKET*** I SENT LAST CHRISTMAS?
YES! DIDN'T YOU GET MY EMAIL?
HALTO!
THERE GOES THE GREATEST BOSS A GUY EVER HAD.
MEANWHLE, AT SPRINGFIELD DOCKS...
THAT'S THE ***LAST*** CONTAINER LOADED.
I'VE SUCCESSFULLY COVERTED ALL OF BURNS' ...I MEAN ***MY*** ASSETS INTO THOUSAND DOLLAR BILLS.
AND EXACTLY WHERE ARE YOU ***SENDING*** ALL OF THIS CURRENCY, MR. BURNS?
I'M PUTTING IT ALL INTO ***MANGANESE***. IT'S THE ***NEW GOLD***.

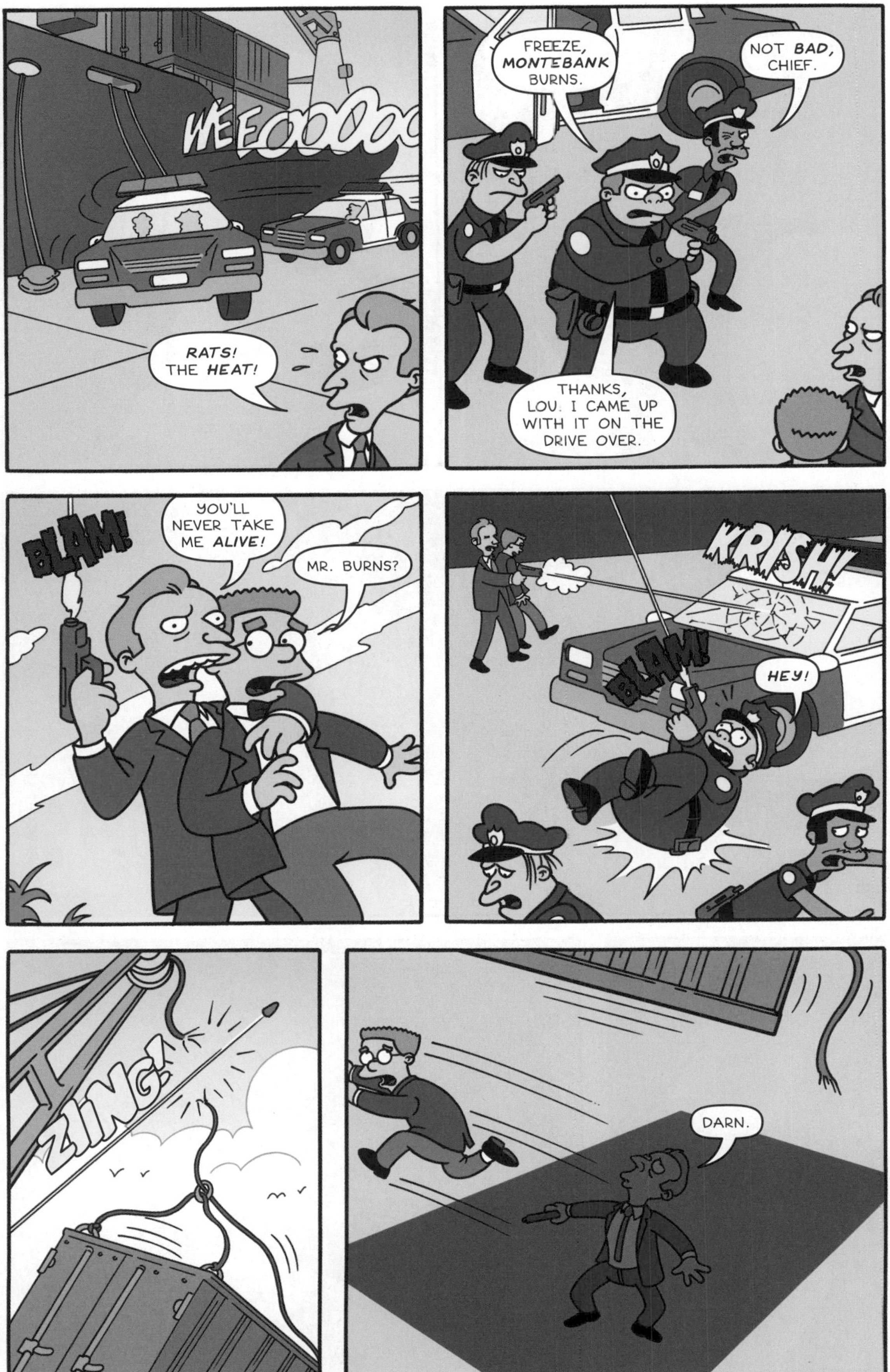
WEEOOOOO
RATS! THE HEAT!
FREEZE, MONTEBANK BURNS.
NOT BAD, CHIEF.
THANKS, LOU. I CAME UP WITH IT ON THE DRIVE OVER.
BLAM!
YOU'LL NEVER TAKE ME ALIVE!
MR. BURNS?
KRISH!
BLAM!
HEY!
ZING!
DARN.

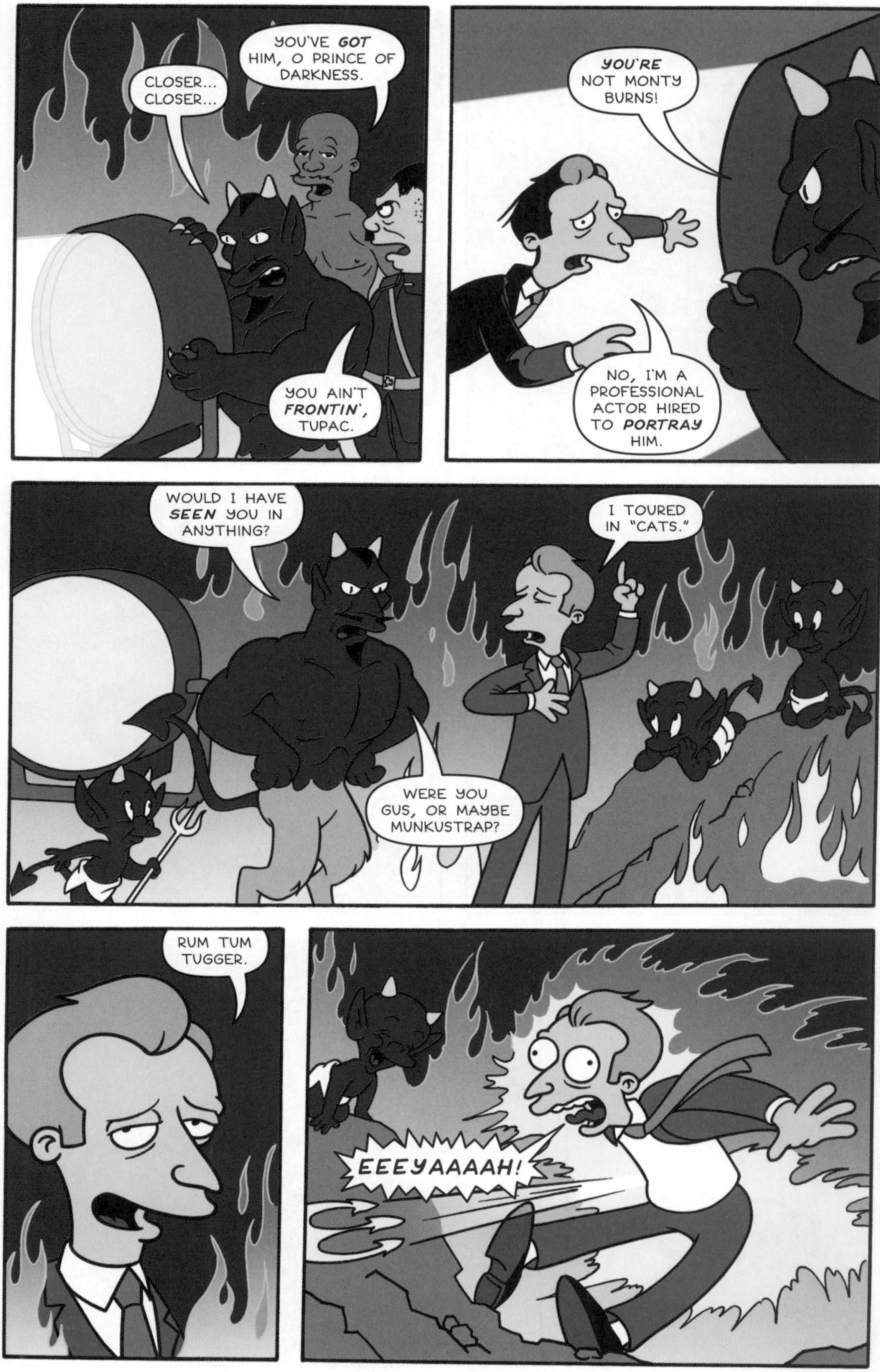
CLOSER... CLOSER...
YOU'VE **GOT** HIM, O PRINCE OF DARKNESS.
YOU AIN'T **FRONTIN'**, TUPAC.
YOU'RE NOT MONTY BURNS!
NO, I'M A PROFESSIONAL ACTOR HIRED TO **PORTRAY** HIM.
WOULD I HAVE **SEEN** YOU IN ANYTHING?
I TOURED IN "CATS."
WERE YOU GUS, OR MAYBE MUNKUSTRAP?
RUM TUM TUGGER.
EEEYAAAAH!

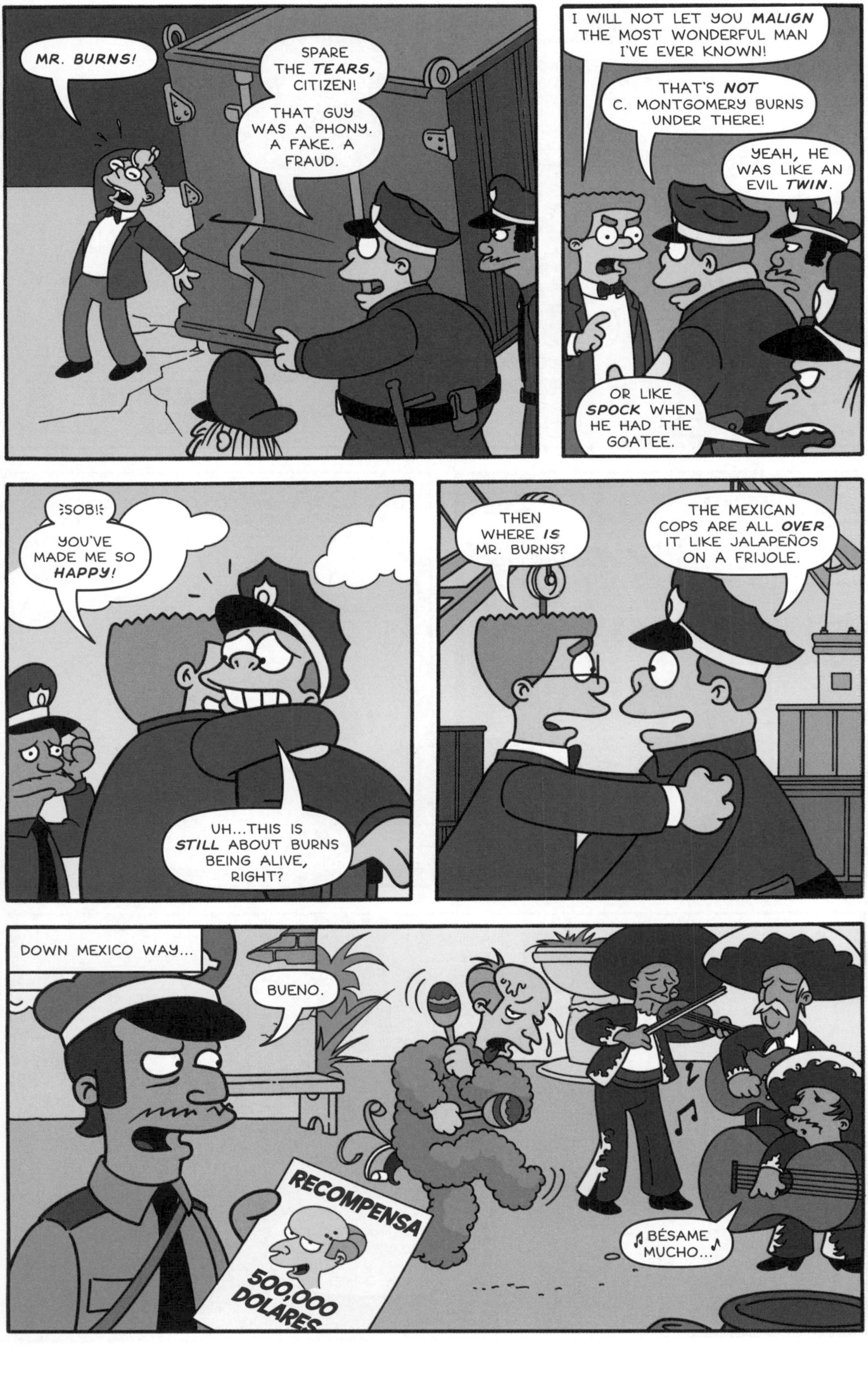
MR. BURNS!
SPARE THE TEARS, CITIZEN!
THAT GUY WAS A PHONY. A FAKE. A FRAUD.
I WILL NOT LET YOU MALIGN THE MOST WONDERFUL MAN I'VE EVER KNOWN!
THAT'S NOT C. MONTGOMERY BURNS UNDER THERE!
YEAH, HE WAS LIKE AN EVIL TWIN.
OR LIKE SPOCK WHEN HE HAD THE GOATEE.
SOB!
YOU'VE MADE ME SO HAPPY!
UH...THIS IS STILL ABOUT BURNS BEING ALIVE, RIGHT?
THEN WHERE IS MR. BURNS?
THE MEXICAN COPS ARE ALL OVER IT LIKE JALAPEÑOS ON A FRIJOLE.
DOWN MEXICO WAY...
BUENO.
RECOMPENSA
500,000 DOLARES
BÉSAME MUCHO...

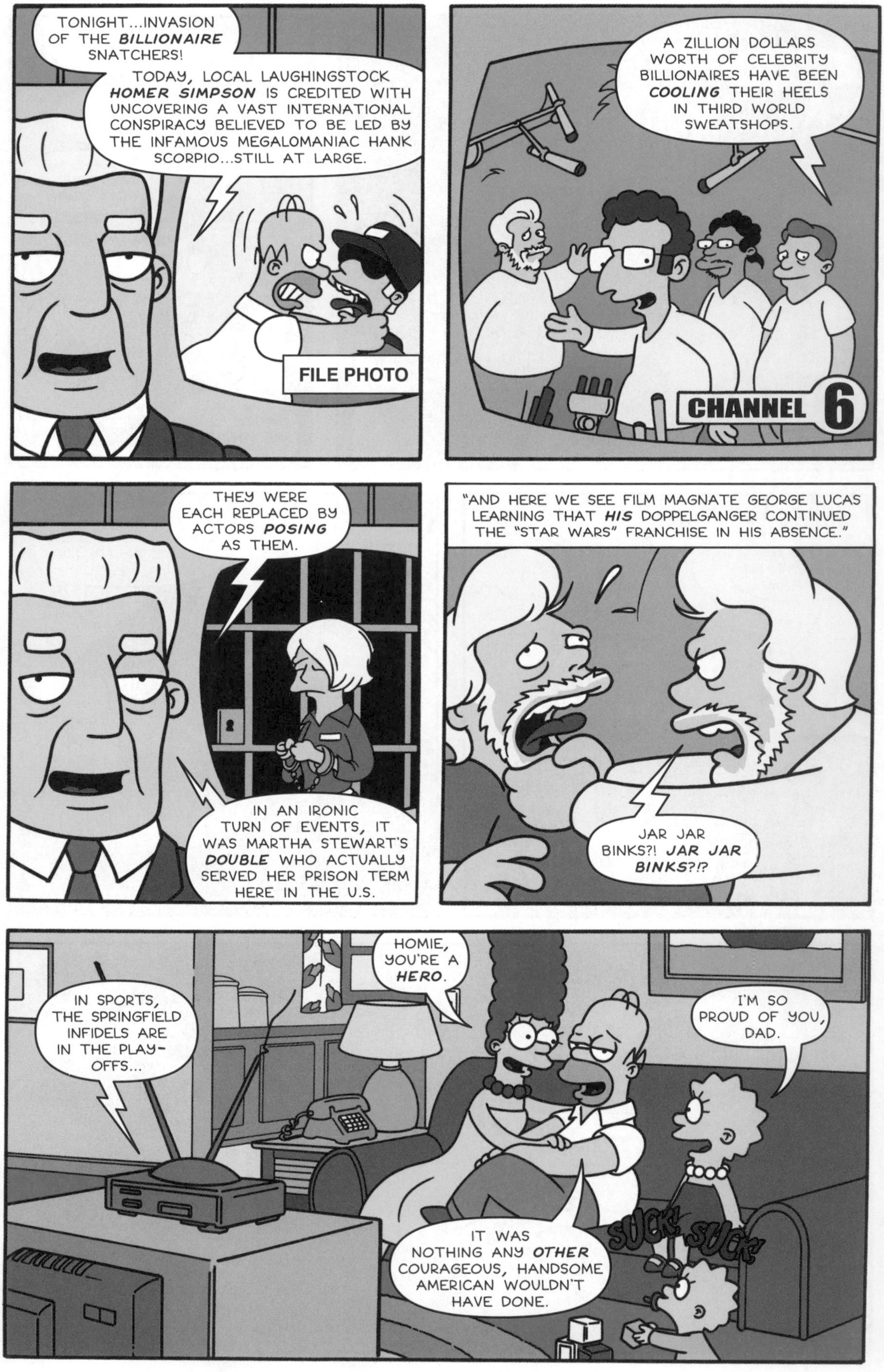

TONIGHT...INVASION OF THE BILLIONAIRE SNATCHERS!
TODAY, LOCAL LAUGHINGSTOCK HOMER SIMPSON IS CREDITED WITH UNCOVERING A VAST INTERNATIONAL CONSPIRACY BELIEVED TO BE LED BY THE INFAMOUS MEGALOMANIAC HANK SCORPIO...STILL AT LARGE.
FILE PHOTO
A ZILLION DOLLARS WORTH OF CELEBRITY BILLIONAIRES HAVE BEEN COOLING THEIR HEELS IN THIRD WORLD SWEATSHOPS.
CHANNEL 6
THEY WERE EACH REPLACED BY ACTORS POSING AS THEM.
IN AN IRONIC TURN OF EVENTS, IT WAS MARTHA STEWART'S DOUBLE WHO ACTUALLY SERVED HER PRISON TERM HERE IN THE U.S.
"AND HERE WE SEE FILM MAGNATE GEORGE LUCAS LEARNING THAT HIS DOPPELGANGER CONTINUED THE "STAR WARS" FRANCHISE IN HIS ABSENCE."
JAR JAR BINKS?! JAR JAR BINKS?!?
IN SPORTS, THE SPRINGFIELD INFIDELS ARE IN THE PLAY-OFFS...
HOMIE, YOU'RE A HERO.
I'M SO PROUD OF YOU, DAD.
IT WAS NOTHING ANY OTHER COURAGEOUS, HANDSOME AMERICAN WOULDN'T HAVE DONE.
SUCK! SUCK!

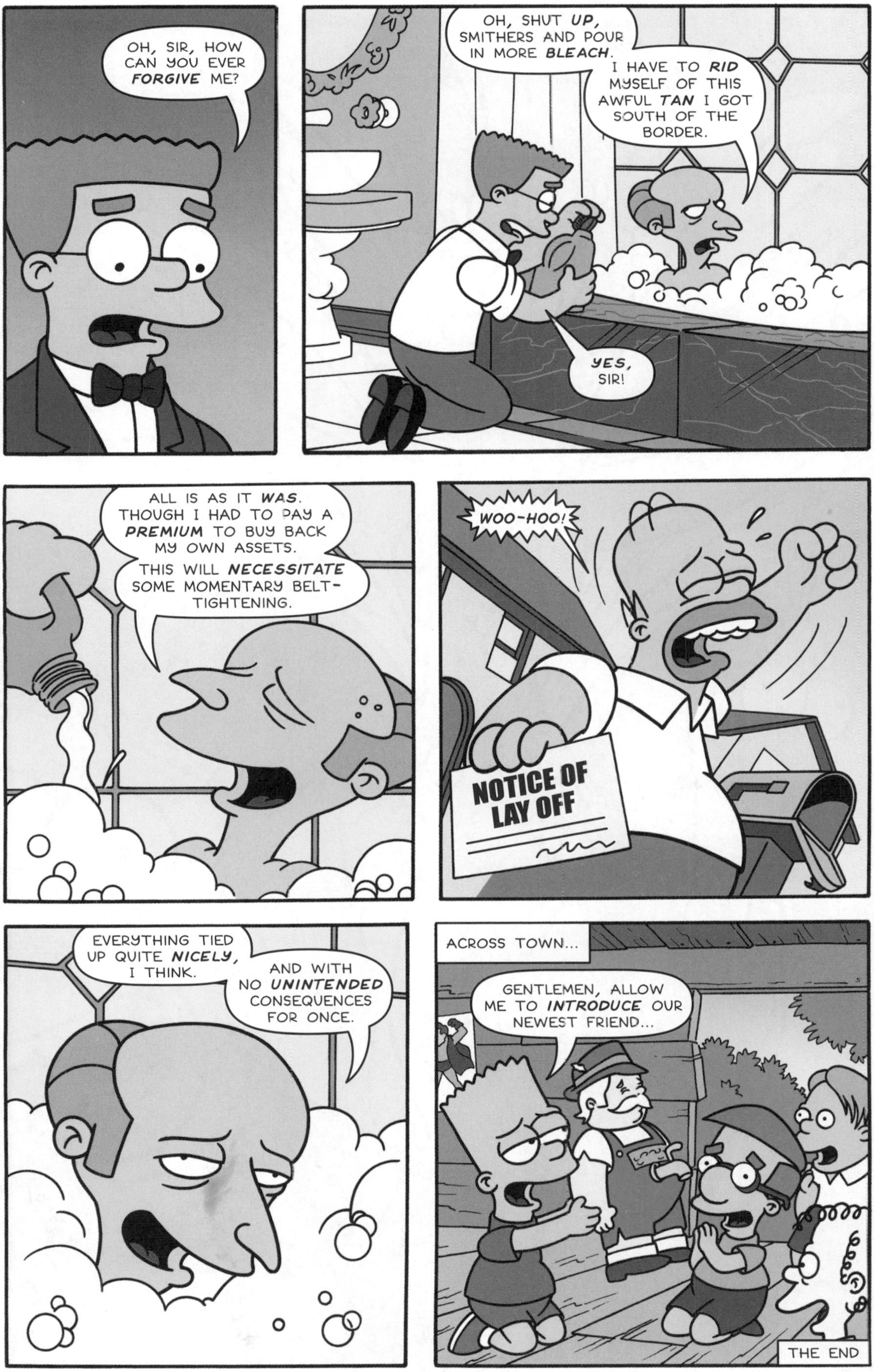

OH, SIR, HOW CAN YOU EVER *FORGIVE* ME?
OH, SHUT *UP*, SMITHERS AND POUR IN MORE *BLEACH*.
I HAVE TO *RID* MYSELF OF THIS AWFUL *TAN* I GOT SOUTH OF THE BORDER.
YES, SIR!
ALL IS AS IT *WAS*. THOUGH I HAD TO PAY A *PREMIUM* TO BUY BACK MY OWN ASSETS.
THIS WILL *NECESSITATE* SOME MOMENTARY BELT-TIGHTENING.
WOO-HOO!
NOTICE OF LAY OFF
EVERYTHING TIED UP QUITE *NICELY*, I THINK.
AND WITH NO *UNINTENDED* CONSEQUENCES FOR ONCE.
ACROSS TOWN...
GENTLEMEN, ALLOW ME TO *INTRODUCE* OUR NEWEST FRIEND...
THE END

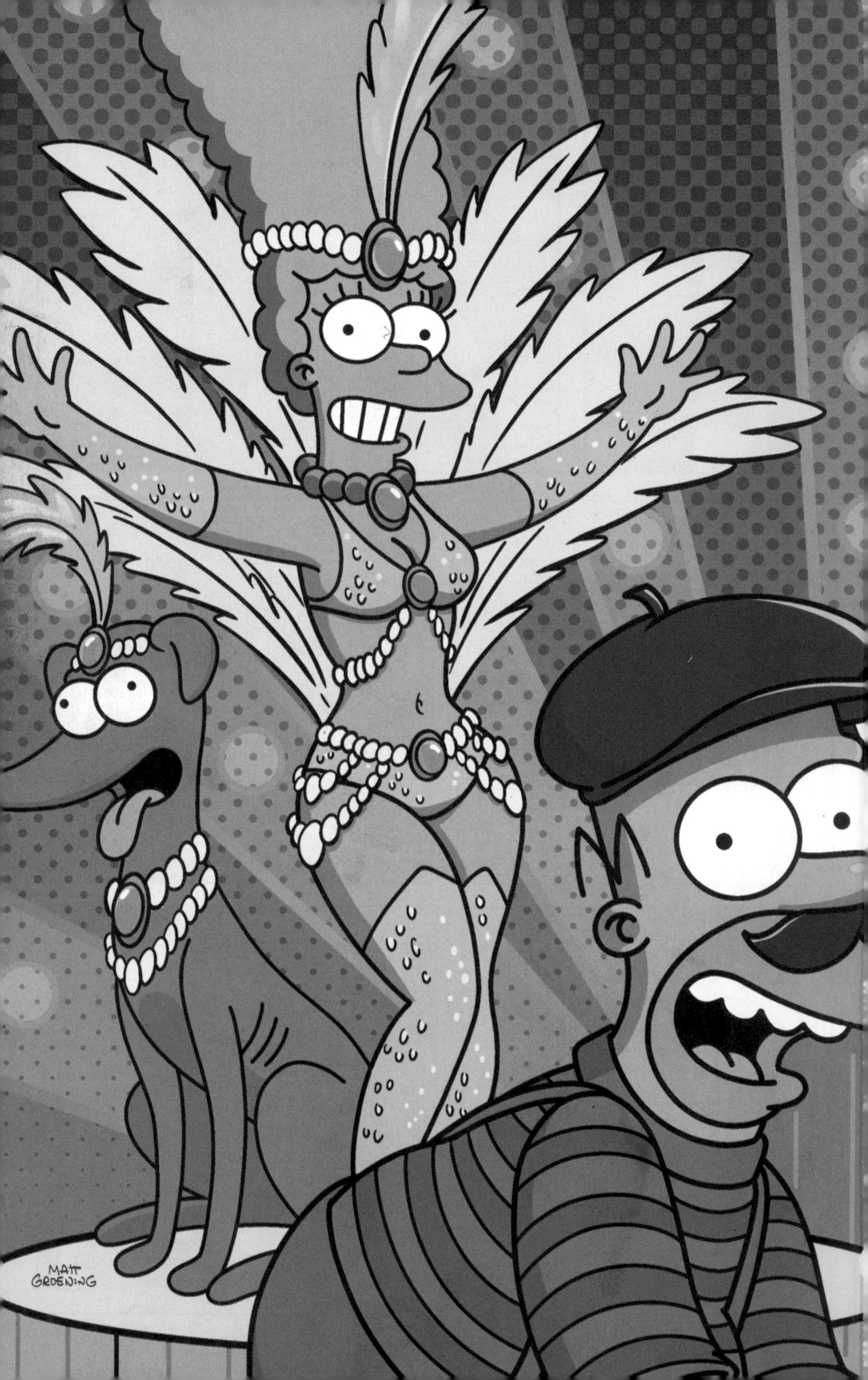
MATT
GROENING